THIS VICIOUS DREAM

STACIA STARK

Copyright © 2025 by Bingeable Books LLC

All rights reserved.

No part of this book may be reproduced in any form or by any electronic or mechanical means, including information storage and retrieval systems, without written permission from the author, except for the use of brief quotations in a book review.

Map by Sarah Waites of The Illustrated Page Design

Cover by Story Wrappers

Interior design by Champagne Book Design

To the women who faced the cold and darkness alone—
And became the fire they needed.
Keep burning.

VALKARYN

ALBERCIA

AMBRELIS

FERELITH

ORANTHIR
AELSTOW FOREST
NYRRIDOR
BLIGHTMERE SWAMP
KOLEGRIFT
LANGSHIRE
TELANTHRIL
WYRDALE RIVER
ELUNTHAR
SYLVARINZ
LIGAN MOUNTAINS

WRESTINOR
EVETHIA

AGHALON

DRACMIRE

VERENIR

THIS VICIOUS DREAM

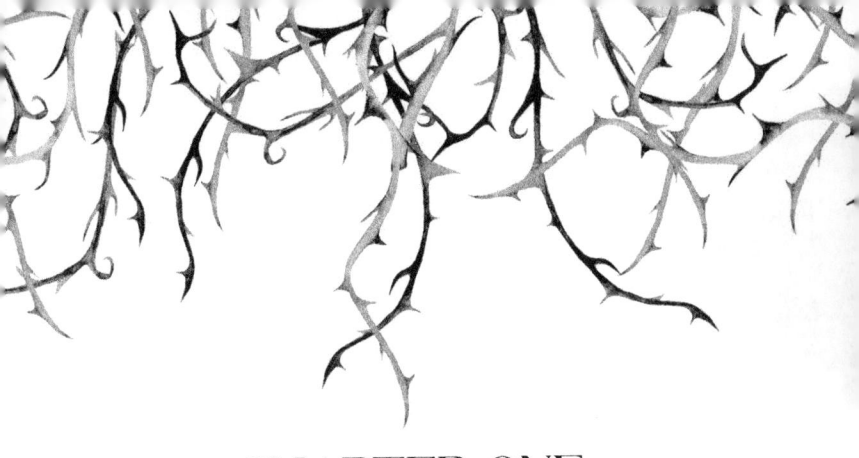

CHAPTER ONE

Madinia

There are few things I hate more than the rain.

Being hunted by my enemies is at the top of my list.

And being hunted by my enemies *in* the rain? Intolerable.

Wet drops splatter against my face, and I tilt my head to the side, narrowing my eyes in an attempt to peer through the deluge.

There.

The approaching ship looms in the distance, massive and dark as it rides the wave like it's part of the storm itself.

The creak of wood and the snap of wet sails as our ship rolls across the waves almost cover the sound of our crew's panicked cries.

Almost.

Daharak makes her way toward me, her steps sure, even as the ship bends and twists across the waves. "You know better than this. You need to get below deck."

And leave everyone else to fight for all of our lives? I level her with a hard stare. "You know *me* better than that."

It's not bravery. It's a very particular kind of cowardice. It's the refusal to be abandoned, even through death.

My insistence on my own space, on seeing the world on my own terms, is tainted with hypocrisy.

Leave me alone, but be available when I need you.

Daharak's jaw tightens, but she doesn't bother arguing as she turns and stalks away. Her stride is long for someone of her height. She's small and slight, but anyone who glanced at her would have no doubt about exactly what she is.

In charge.

Just months ago, she lost both ships and people as we fought for our lives and the freedom of a continent. The loss of her ships was infuriating. The loss of her people was a devastation so great, she's still recovering.

Their ship continues its approach, until it's close enough for me to see my enemies' faces. On our ship, pirates sprint for weapons, calling out to each other as they prepare for battle.

My jaw aches and I force myself to unclench my teeth. They don't shout or announce themselves. They fire no warning shots. They avoid any flashy display of cannon fire. After all, they can't risk killing me.

This isn't a raid. It's a hunt.

Our ship lets loose with cannon fire of its own, the deck shuddering beneath me. The air around the enemy ship seems to glow, and when the smoke clears, it's even closer, no damage to its hull.

Warded.

Just weeks ago, our ammunition could have burrowed through those wards. But over the past few weeks, this hunt has been relentless, giving us little opportunity to refill our stores—of both weapons and food.

A flash of lightning cuts through the dim light, revealing the pale faces of the crew. The pirates know me. Despite my best efforts, some of them even like me.

And if I don't do something, they will die for me.

The rumble of thunder is so loud it seems to rattle my bones. Even Daharak wouldn't have chosen to risk this storm. But we had no choice.

The ship draws closer. Queen Vicana's men are brutal and well-trained. And none are more brutal than Kyldare—her right hand and Queen's Justice—a nicely ironic title.

Justice is a foreign concept to Vicana.

Kyldare stands near the helm of the ship, and our eyes meet for one moment. The thrill of the hunt is written across his face as his ship pulls alongside us, the hull scraping against ours with a chilling groan.

Cold rage slithers through me. And something inside me—something I've managed to keep carefully hidden—opens one eye, purring in approval.

My heart kicks in my chest, and the sudden fear slams a barrier between me and that…*thing*.

My hands scramble for the railing, tightening on the smooth wood.

I don't bother using my power. Not while they're so heavily warded.

Grappling hooks fly through the air, and our crew immediately begin slicing through ropes with both blades and power.

The distant splashes tell me some of them succeeded. But Kyldare brought more than enough soldiers with him. They swing through the air, descending like spiders on a web, boots hitting the deck.

More splashing as bodies hit the water. But not enough. A hook latches onto the railing just footspans from me and I pull my sword, slicing through the rope attached to it.

No splash. They were testing me.

Three more hooks.

I slice two of them. One splash.

Boots on wood.

My flames roar toward my attacker and the wind steals his scream.

Burning is a terrible way to die. So I push the soldier overboard as my flames engulf him.

"You're welcome."

The rain thickens into a relentless downpour. Thunder cracks in the distance, while the wind tears at our sails, straining the rigging to its limit. Icy droplets sting my skin, drenching me to the bone. My breath comes in ragged bursts, the cold air mixing with the heat simmering deep inside me, begging to be unleashed.

Kyldare couldn't have chosen a better time to attack. My power churns in my chest like a caged beast, and I let it free as another soldier swings his body over the railing. But the water-logged air seems to smother every flicker of flame I bring to the surface.

My power is little more than a distraction to the next soldier, but he's forced to dance in place as my fire slices toward his legs.

The distraction is enough.

I swing my sword, slicing through his neck. His head rolls free.

I gag.

More boots hit the deck. More soldiers fall to my sword. One of them manages to slice across my bicep, deep enough that I let out a hiss.

"Alive!" A voice roars, and the solider flinches.

I bury my blade deep in his gut.

Thank you for the distraction, Kyldare.

I take the opportunity to dart down the steps to the main deck. A soldier lunges for me, sword raised. He's dead before he gets two steps, a blade through his back.

Lonn nods at me, pulls his sword free, and whirls, rejoining the fray. I catch a single glimpse of Daharak just a few footspans away. She fights like she's possessed, blade a blur, footwork impeccable as she dashes across the slippery deck.

A hand clamps down on my shoulder. I turn into it, shoving my blade deep into the soldier's thigh.

He curses, stumbling backward, and I clamp my hand tighter around the hilt of my sword. When I rip it free, blood spurts. I hit the artery.

He's dead. Realization dawns on his face and I step away.

Blades clash. The howl of the wind melds with the screams of the dying, the clash of blades, the rumble of thunder. And still, the rain pounds us relentlessly.

The ship tilts beneath my feet and I slip, shifting to meet the next sword. Kyldare may have ordered his soldiers not to kill me, but this man is consumed by bloodlust, face twisted, teeth bared.

I'm off-balance, and I lash out desperately with my power. The warmth spreads, defying the rain, but it's sluggish, like trying to ignite soaked tinder. I grind my teeth, pulling harder, and flames coil and dance toward my attacker. He curses. And then he lashes out with power of his own.

The invisible blow hits me in the side of the head.

I'm not sure what kind of power this is, but it's effective. My legs fold beneath me, my knees slamming into the deck.

Grinding my teeth, I wrap my flames around me until I can stand once more.

Another hit, this time to the other side of my head.

I can't fight what I can't see.

Rage burns through me, and that's all my power needs, despite the river of water soaking us. I blink several times, aiming at the soldier.

His screams are music to my ears.

My head throbs like an open wound as another solider lunges at me with a vicious snarl.

My arm aches under the weight of my sword, but I swing

again and again, the rain blurring my vision. I use my power when I can, but it's almost useless in the downpour.

When the ship tilts once more, the weight of bodies—living and dead—sliding to the right, I risk a single glance around me in an attempt to count who's left. A flash of lightning illuminates the carnage for the barest moment.

We're...losing.

No. After this many months staying one step ahead of Kyldare and his men...it's not possible.

But it is.

I feel the truth like a weight in my gut.

Kyldare chose the perfect time to attack. In two days, we were due to reach land, where we would restock weapons. Where the crew would rest, and enjoy fresh food and catch up on sleep.

A scream pierces the air. To my left, Carix goes down, blood pooling beneath him. My breath stutters.

This isn't just a battle. It's the slow, inevitable slaughter of the people who took me in. The people who gently teased me when I woke screaming after the war. The people who insisted on training with me each morning so I wouldn't get rusty.

Gods, I wish Prisca was here. Her power would make all the difference.

"Madinia Farrow," a voice cuts through the cacophony and I whirl.

Kyldare stands behind me, looking amused and self-assured. For a moment, the sound of the battle retreats, as if we're in our own cocoon.

"You can make this all stop."

Daharak's voice cuts through the sound of battle. "Don't you dare!"

Cold blue eyes glance over my shoulder. Kyldare's lips curve, and a heavy ball of dread takes up residence in my gut.

The sudden screams cut deep into my ears. They're young,

terrified. The cook's daughter Carosa. A child of only eight winters. One of Kyldare's men has his beefy arm wrapped around her waist, his knife at her throat.

"You sick bastard."

A muscle jumps in Kyldare's jaw. But he waves his hand, and his solider drags Carosa toward us. In the distance, I hear her mother's shrieks for mercy.

They were supposed to be safe below deck.

"I'll make this easy for you," Kyldare says. "Your life for hers."

I drag my gaze from his face, meeting wide gray eyes. Carosa's lower lip trembles, and she firms it in an attempt to be brave.

I meet Kyldare's eyes once more. "Done."

"Madinia!" Daharak roars.

"Tell your soldiers to leave," I continue.

Kyldare's eyes light with triumph before narrowing—likely at my easy compliance. "You try anything, and she's dead. Her mother is dead. Everyone on this ship is dead."

I narrow my eyes and scan him from his face to his gleaming boots. It's a look I perfected while growing up at court. The kind of look that makes a man feel small. Irrelevant. Humiliated.

Kyldare is no exception. His cheeks flush.

"They leave now, or I'm not going anywhere."

He sneers at me. "You don't have a choice."

When he glances at the soldier holding Carosa, I know what he's planning.

Men are predictable. And when bad men are embarrassed, they have a tendency to lash out. It's a compulsion they're unable to ignore.

Carosa screams. She knows what's coming.

I raise my blade, positioning it at my own throat. Kyldare goes still, holding up a hand.

No one moves.

"You wouldn't," he breathes.

"I wouldn't decline *your* company?" I sneer at him. "Easiest choice of my life."

He takes a single step forward, and I wedge the blade closer to the thick artery at the side of my neck.

There are worse deaths. And I would gladly die rather than allow his power-hungry queen to get her hands on—

"Fine." Kyldare's eyes burn with retribution, but this time he nods at the soldier. The brute frees Carosa, who darts across the deck, scampering up the nearest rope and climbing high above us, away from the soldiers.

Clever girl.

Slowly, one by one, Kyldare's soldiers remove themselves from Daharak's ship.

Her face is bloodless as she walks toward me. "If you go with him, this was all for nothing. Their deaths mean nothing."

I barely suppress a flinch. Daharak knows me too well. She knows exactly where to strike.

Lightning pierces the sky, followed immediately by thunder.

"I need you to trust me," I say.

She shakes her head, reaching out to grab my hand. When she squeezes tight, the lump in my throat becomes a throbbing ache. I should have known. The moments of happiness I had with these people were too intense for the joy to last.

"Look after them," I whisper.

"Don't let him break you," she whispers back. "I'll find you. Somehow, I'll find you."

The last soldier steps off the ship, and the true destruction becomes evident. They don't bother taking their comrades' bodies, and I watch as the pirates begin heaving them overboard.

The sharks will dine well tonight.

Kyldare holds out his hand. "Well?"

Ignoring his hand, I stride past him toward his ship. The

sea has calmed enough that his soldiers have thrown a plank between our ships, and I take my first step onto the slippery wood.

I'm not sure I have it in me to throw myself at the non-existent mercy of the sharks.

Kyldare clamps his hand over my elbow, stepping up behind me.

"I wouldn't want you to *fall*."

I ignore him again, refusing to look back at the people I'm leaving behind. I know Daharak, and she'll come for me. Not just because of our friendship, but because she knows what will happen if the wrong people get their hands on the grimoire.

A soldier grabs my arm at the other end, and I suppress a wince as his hand tightens close to the deep cut along my bicep.

"Now then," Kyldare purrs as he drops to the deck behind me, grabbing my chin. He holds tight enough to bring traitorous tears to my eyes.

"Where. Is. It? I know it's not on the ship. So where did you put it?"

I give him a hateful little smirk. "I suppose I must have misplaced it."

His hand lashes out, and everything goes black.

CHAPTER TWO

Madinia
Three years later.

THE TOWER CREAKS WHEN IT IS WINDY.

I hear everything. The tree branches tapping against my tower. The howl of the wind sweeping past. The hoot of an owl in the distance.

But the loudest sounds are the incessant whispers from the *thing* I never let myself think about, calling me, urging me to find it.

I strain, attempting the mere flex of a finger, the twitch of an eye. But it's useless. My body remains still, my eyes closed, trapped.

Panic flutters in my chest, but after so many years, I manage to ruthlessly clamp it down, channeling it into cold fury.

It's not time.

Not yet. But almost.

Still, someone dares approach my tower. My *prison*.

Not the one I'm waiting for. But another.

Reaching out with my borrowed power, I let the tendrils

of it sweep from my body, down, down, down through stone and steel, to the damp grass below.

I push the power out further, until the tendrils slide deep into the thicket of thorns surrounding my tower.

Once, the thorns were a garden of roses. But that was before so many saw me as *prey*.

Fury roars through me, and the power allows me to see the one who approaches in my mind's eye. Human. He swings his axe, slashing through the first few branches, and if I could writhe in pain I would.

After so many years of connection to my thorns, it feels as if he is cutting through my own skin and bones.

I don't need to guess his intentions. He's no soldier—not one of Kyldare's men. But the rope slung over his shoulder, the axe in his hand, and the wicked knife on his belt leave no doubt.

My reputation has spread far and wide. And men will always attempt to brutalize the women they cannot control.

For a long moment, I consider letting him go through with his dark plan.

At least then…at least then it would all be over.

But no. There are reasons I can't. Reasons that escape me now. But they feel legitimate enough, and I cling to them.

The man doesn't see the thorned vine that slithers toward him like a viper. He's still slicing through my private garden.

With a slash of that vine, his throat yawns open.

He gapes, clawing at his skin, attempting to hold it closed. But my thorns are sharp as blades.

His blood feeds my creation, and the thorns grow stronger, the branches hauling his body high to join the others.

Sixty men and four women have tried their luck. I occasionally wonder at the smaller number of women. I like to think it's because women are less likely to prey on one of their own, trapped and defenseless. But perhaps I'm merely romanticizing my situation.

The world twists, colors blurring and darkening, and I let my mind take me away. Away to another place, where I'm not trapped. Where I have a purpose. A *life*.

The faces have blurred now, and my mind attempts to provide context where there is none. I see a woman with an hourglass on a chain around her neck. Friend or foe? I have no idea. But she turns to look at me, and her eyes hold something like disappointment.

"You were supposed to protect it."

I pull against my invisible bonds.

"I am," I want to tell her. I've submitted to years of torture for those nameless, occasionally faceless people in my past.

Some small, vulnerable part of me thought they would have searched. Thought they would have found me.

Strangely, it's *that* thought that does the most damage. It sends me spiraling through darkness, until my mind clears once more—perhaps hours later, perhaps days.

I'm all alone.

Calysian

Humans are strange creatures.

I'm unsure if my fascination stems from the fact that I've seen so many of their actions over the past centuries, and so many of those were inexplicable.

Perhaps it's because I'm not human. Although it seems to be a uniquely human trait to be fascinated with the *other*.

I ride through the town without truly seeing it. After several years of searching this kingdom, one human town looks much like another.

And it *is* this kingdom I need to search. I know that much, even as I know little else.

My horse plods along the dirt road, ignoring the deep ruts in the mud created from the wheels of thousands of carts.

The humans here wear clothes that are little more than rags, ripped and mended again and again. But their cheeks are rounded, arms strong and defined. Their health is likely due to their proximity to the forest just a few miles from this town and the animals they hunt within.

A child darts in front of my horse. Fox pauses, lowers his head, and blows air through his nostrils. The child's father appears, scooping the child into his arms and muttering apologies, even as the boy giggles, kicking his legs.

I nudge Fox back into motion.

Never have I had a thought of my own childhood. No memories rise up and greet me, no dreams throw me back to younger days.

I woke centuries ago, naked and alone in a forest on a strange continent filled with people who wielded varying degrees of magic.

I *should* have been as blank as an un-molded piece of clay. Instead, I woke filled with a deep, vicious rage burning within me.

I may not have known much, but I knew something was missing. Something so important, a shock of grief battled with my rage. Someone had taken something from me. Something I desperately needed.

And whoever had cursed me this way was going to be very, very sorry.

Centuries later, I still search for that revenge.

I stop at a nameless inn, allowing the stablehands to take Fox. He snaps at one of them, his teeth coming within inches of the boy's face.

With a sigh, I step between them, giving Fox a look. "Food and rest for both of us. Be good and don't kill anyone."

Both stablehands turn pale. Fox snorts, but finally allows

their approach, plodding slowly toward the stable. One of the boys comes close to his backend, and Fox tenses, lifting one leg, his sharp hoof gleaming.

I clear my throat. Fox lowers the leg.

Shaking my head, I pay the innkeeper for a meal, my mood darkening as I force down lukewarm stew, the meat tough and chewy. I make my way up to the best room this town has to offer, taking in the dusty floors and threadbare sheets.

This should not be my life. The certainty buries deep within my gut. I should not be here. I'm—

The missing memories are like an itch in my brain. Like a word on the tip of my tongue that I can never find.

I use the facilities and lay on the bed, cursing the mattress, the sheets, my own useless mind…

"You're truly choosing to sleep *here*, and not in the forest?"

I sigh, throwing one arm over my eyes. It doesn't help. Eamonn has found me. Again.

"I must say, I thought you were better than this. If you knew what I could scent on those sheets…"

I angle my arm, opening one eye. Eamonn sits in his canine form—a favorite of his.

"If the innkeeper thinks I brought a dog up here—"

He lets out a tiny growl and jumps up on the bed, angling his head. "Scratch my ears. I have an itch."

His damp fur fills the room with an unpleasant odor, and I ignore him, closing my eye once more. I can hear raucous laughter from the tavern below.

Eamonn shoves his furry head beneath my hand. With a sigh, I find the spot behind his ears and give him a scratch.

"I don't like this place," he mumbles.

I've gotten used to hearing his voice inexplicably float from whatever animal he has shifted into. I found him after the Eprothan war, when I returned to this continent. Or perhaps he found me. For whatever reason, he took an interest in my task, and has been following me ever since.

"Fox needed proper rest."

He snorts. "That horse will likely outlive *you*."

Despite his disdain for my accommodations, he falls asleep within moments. I toss and turn, forced to admit that perhaps Eamonn was right. Maybe I would have slept better in the forest. I doze until I can no longer ignore the urge to move.

When I shove my feet into my boots, Eamonn is gone. He'll return at some point. Likely at the most inconvenient time possible.

For now, my heart pounds in my chest. My hands almost…tremble. And a strange feeling overtakes me. A strange knowledge.

I'm close. So close to my destiny. So close to *revenge*.

MADINIA

I'm woken by my thorns screaming a warning.

I reach out with my borrowed power. The power I should never have touched.

The thought is snatched from me, and I shift my focus to the approaching men.

My heart pounds like a drum.

Finally.

Kyldare lounges on his horse, tugging carelessly on the reins as he holds up one hand, ordering the others to stop. His mouth tightens as he looks at the graveyard I've left for him.

Sixty-four bodies, wrapped in thorns, positioned at the entrance to my tower. A few blood-red roses peek out from amongst the bodies.

Sometimes, I think those thorns have a mind of their own.

There can be no other reason for the occasionally whimsical arrangements of heads and limbs.

Welcome, Kyldare. I have a spot waiting for you.

"The bitch is using the grimoire's power somehow," the soldier next to Kyldare mutters. "Are you sure she doesn't have it?"

Kyldare slowly turns his head, dragging his gaze away from the bodies. When that gaze finds the solider, the man visibly wilts.

"I had her stripped naked and searched. I then left her trapped here for three years. The first two years I visited monthly to interrogate her. And yet you believe she somehow hid it from me?"

I'm unsure what *it* is. All I know is it's connected to the dark power I'm borrowing. The power I should never have touched.

But his words dig deep into my memories. Memories of being wrapped in the chains in this circular tower, pinned to the wall as his men leered at my body.

Perhaps I'll leave you here for a while, until you're finally ready to cooperate. Perhaps I'll leave you paralyzed, aware as I fuck you. Perhaps I'll breed you, watch as your body grows my baby and delivers it, all while you scream soundlessly.

I should be thankful to Kyldare. It was those words that broke something within me. Those words that allowed me to reach blindly for the connection to the dark power that had whispered to me for so long.

My sanity was a small sacrifice to pay for the power I'm sinking into my thorns.

Anticipation twists through me. I've waited patiently for this moment. My traps are ready.

My limbs strain against Kyldare's witch's power.

No. Not yet. Wait.

The waiting is the greatest torture. I've waited for Kyldare to return for a year. And from the hard glint in his eyes, his queen has commanded him to do whatever it takes to get the information he needs.

Come a little closer, Kyldare. Let's chat.

The men dismount, leaving their horses tied to a tree at least a hundred footspans from my tower.

Slowly, they approach. Kyldare's presence is like a slow-moving poison. It slithers through the cracks in the tower walls, heavy and suffocating as I fight to use my useless limbs.

I stifle the familiar panic. I've prepared for this moment for so long now, it feels like just another dream.

For now, my muscles won't respond. For now, my body will remain useless, a prisoner within stone, just as I'm a prisoner in my own flesh.

And then I will strike.

But something else moves at the edge of my consciousness. Something dark. Something I've been feeding for months, lending my pain and sorrow, allowing it to grow like the thorns outside my tower.

Kyldare jerks his head, and the soldiers separate into two groups. One group moves around the back of the tower, attempting to approach unseen through the path to the servants' entrance.

As if I can't feel them stepping over my land, their boots sinking into the earth I've claimed. I know every inch of the twisted bramble below. Every stone in this tower is *mine.*

Carefully, gently, I let the smallest flicker of my borrowed power surge out.

I'm excruciatingly aware that this power is limited. Limited, because some part of me knows that if I took more, I would become a monster greater than anything this world has seen for centuries.

Perhaps these people would deserve that.

Faces appear in my mind's eye. Familiar faces. Faces that

I can't place, but that I know once meant something to me. I reach for those faces, but my thorns shiver, already responding.

They move slowly at first, twisting in the undergrowth as the soldiers make their way closer. One of them laughs, arrogant, likely believing it's just the wind stirring the leaves. The others look spooked. As they should.

The first vine curls upward, sharp and black as a dark shadow, wrapping itself around the first soldier's ankle. He curses, stumbling in an attempt to shake it off.

A thorn spears through his thigh.

His scream is brief as he's pulled deep into the mass of knotted, thorny vines.

The other soldiers pause. One of them is smart enough to take a few steps backward, shaking his head.

"Keep moving," a gruff, older soldier barks. "Or what these thorns will do to you will seem merciful compared to Kyldare's punishment."

Idiots.

I leave the soldiers to the thorns. Distantly, I wonder if I should be concerned that my thorns have enough awareness to be hungry for blood. To strike at those who consider me to be prey.

But I return my attention to Kyldare. He stands, hands on hips, eyes hard.

Four soldiers surround him, all frozen in place.

They must have heard the screams.

"Cease this behavior, Madinia Farrow," he calls. "You're only making it worse for yourself."

If I could smile, I would.

They begin walking once more. More screams cut through the night, but I pay them no attention. Kyldare's mouth becomes a thin line, and he picks up his pace.

"Spread out," he orders. "I don't want any tricks."

The soldiers are trembling. I might feel sorry for them, if

several of them hadn't held me down while Kyldare placed those chains around my wrists. He could have done such a thing while my body was still lifeless, but he enjoyed seeing me fight. Loved watching me realize there was no help coming.

I'm looking forward to seeing the same realization in his eyes.

My thorns slither toward the soldiers, and I pull my power tight. For this to work, I need Kyldare closer.

I cast my mind to the other side of the tower. Another solider is crying out as the thorns tighten, ripping him apart. This man once grabbed my breast and twisted, laughing as I screamed.

His blood feeds the thorns. Feeds the dark power. Feeds *me*.

For the first time, the bonds of paralysis begins to weaken, and I take a long, deep breath.

Triumph roars through me, and I open my eyes. My trap is ready. All I need is for Kyldare to step through the front door at the bottom of my tower, and he'll be caught in the same spell his witch cast on me. It will be his turn to live through every moment of my torture.

The soldiers surrounding Kyldare are spooked. With a jerk of his head, he sends them toward my tower.

Coward.

One of them briefly closes his eyes, praying aloud to some goddess I've never heard of. This is his first time here. He has never personally done me harm. Perhaps I will be merciful.

The others forge forward, stomping toward the tower. I ignore my instincts to kill. They need to enter so Kyldare will follow.

Behind the tower, more blood sinks deep into the ground, and the invisible ties encircling my limbs disappear. For the first time in a year, I sit up.

My muscles should be wasted. But that wouldn't have

suited Kyldare's purposes. I'm weak, woozy, and my limbs feel as if they're attached to someone else's body. But I can walk. I have to.

I swing one leg over the side of the bed. And then the other.

My first attempt to stand ends with me falling back onto the bed. I plan to burn this bed. But not yet.

Kyldare takes another step forward.

And I make it to my feet.

Stumbling to the chains in the corner of the room, I lift them, my knees weakening beneath their weight.

The soldiers begin their climb up the stairs. Kyldare rolls his shoulders and stalks toward the tower entrance.

My heart thuds faster, my spine straightening. Almost there.

My thorns scream a warning and I close my eyes, focusing on the ground far below me.

A dark presence approaches. A presence that is somehow familiar but entirely unwelcome.

The man ties his horse a few trees over from the soldiers' horses, sparing them a single glance.

His horse snaps his teeth in their direction, and the man murmurs something too low for me to hear. He places his hands on his hips, and I can't help but pay attention to the roll of muscles beneath his black shirt, the width of his shoulders.

My instincts roar at me. This man is dangerous.

When he glances at my collection of bodies, one dark eyebrow shoots up. I'm not sure if it's appreciation or horror that makes his mouth twitch.

He turns his attention to Kyldare, and it's as if the other man feels his gaze. Kyldare stops walking and glances over his shoulder.

No. No, no, *no!*

"Don't come any closer," Kyldare orders. "We're here on the queen's business."

The other man smiles, revealing straight, white teeth, and a single dimple on the right side of his mouth. It's a compelling smile. But no one who saw it would believe he's pleased.

"I suppose it's a good thing I don't serve your queen."

Kyldare turns, stalking toward him.

No!

He's walking *the wrong way.*

My limbs begin to tremble. One of my thorns slices toward him, but it's slow, sluggish.

What is happening to me?

It's as if my control over the dark power has been dampened, until I can only access the smallest trickle. Each day, I have painstakingly collected this power. And suddenly, I'm almost defenseless once more.

Footsteps sound as Kyldare's soldiers charge up the stairs toward me.

Acid boils in my gut and my entire body trembles with fresh rage. I will *not* be victimized again.

The rage helps, and I launch into action. One of the soldiers left his overcoat here last time they *visited*, and I use it as a make-shift satchel, hauling the chains into the dusty material and wrapping it around my shoulders. If I can't give Kyldare a taste of his own medicine, I can at least make sure he'll never use these chains on anyone again.

My door bursts open, wood slamming into stone. The first solider steps into my room, panting as he draws his sword.

The entire tower shudders. He glances around, eyes widening as he takes in the empty bed. With a roll of his shoulders, he advances on me, and I don't hesitate.

I launch myself toward the window and into the air.

"She's gone," one of the soldier's roars behind me.

My heart leaps into my throat. Fear punches into my gut as I fall.

My thorns catch me. I sense… despair as they slice into my skin, even as they try their best not to hurt me. I send gratitude and tenderness to them as they place me on the ground behind the tower next to one of the soldier's bodies.

I lean over, almost losing my balance. But I manage to grab the soldier's sword and sheath, along with his coin purse. This will at least help me get to the next town.

Thorns lash through the air, rearing up and slicing into my tower. Strangled screams ring out as the soldiers are yanked through the window, impaled on vines as thick as my arm. One gurgles on his own blood while the other convulses in his death throes.

My power has drained to little more than the barest trickle. I can no longer sense Kyldare and the stranger. My thorns open a path for me, and I creep through them, around the side of the tower. The full moon provides just enough light for me to watch as Kyldare stares up at the ruin of the tower and his dead soldiers. His mouth thins, and he sprints from the tower, out of the path of my thorns.

No.

The stranger watches Kyldare mount his horse. With a sigh, he turns, taking in the tower. From here, I can see his profile—brutal lines, a wide jaw, and the kind of sensual beauty that must have women begging for a night in his bed.

His gaze lingers once more on the bodies.

"I know you're here," he says, and I freeze.

"Interesting design choice." He calls, waving his hands at a collection of skulls high in the thicket of thorns. His eyes linger on one of my roses, nestled next to a long femur. "I like what you've done with the place."

For some inexplicable reason, I feel my cheeks heat.

"Still hiding?" he muses. "For someone who has just been rescued, you're not being very polite."

My thorns part so swiftly, the man jolts back. Dark, unfathomable eyes meet mine, and something flickers across his face. Something that looks almost like…recognition.

"*Rescued?*" I hiss. "You think you *rescued* me?"

CHAPTER THREE

CALYSIAN

THIS WOMAN.

Long, wine-red hair curls around her delicate face. Her features seem to have been arranged by the gods themselves—high cheekbones, a sharp chin, flawless skin, and those eyes…

As bright as sapphires, and currently burning with rage.

I *know* her.

Madinia Farrow.

The last time I saw her, she was boarding a ship, and I had the strangest urge to sprint after her.

I'd given into that urge, desperate for *something*.

And I'd been too late.

Fury surges through me, until I'm shuddering with it, hands fisted. Did she do this to me? Is she the reason I am… deficient?

No. That can't be right. She doesn't *feel* ageless.

I stare at her some more, forcing myself to focus on logic.

Not a glimmer of recognition lights her eyes, even though we met several times on another continent, just a few years ago when she was readying for war.

So how did she end up *here*?

I take a step forward and she narrows those startlingly blue eyes.

"Don't come any closer."

"Well now, beautiful woman, what kind of welcome is that? And after I saved you from the attentions of that soldier too."

Her head barely reaches my chest, yet she somehow still manages to stare down her nose at me. If I were a lesser male, that look would make me feel about three inches tall.

"What do you want?" Her voice is flat, and she's already turning away, toward the soldiers' horses. Her gaze moves past the strange tangle of bones and decomposing bodies as if she doesn't even see them.

"Why are you here?" I ask.

She pauses, brow crinkling. Her brows are slightly darker than the wealth of dark red hair tumbling over her shoulders.

"Kyldare kept me here. For *years*. I was about to make him pay, and then you showed up."

My gut clenches. I should have killed him.

It's not that I'm particularly altruistic. But caging a woman like Madinia Farrow isn't just wrong—it's unnatural.

"Why?"

I take another step closer, and her whole body tenses. Something dark stares back at me from behind her eyes. Something dark and familiar.

But those eyes are immediately turning glassy.

Confusion. Confusion and fear.

"He wanted something," she murmurs aloud, her expression distant as she retreats into her mind. For a long moment, it's as if she's not even there.

"What did he want?" I press.

She's silent for a long moment. And I watch as she rebuilds her shields. Her shoulders straighten, and she gives me that look again.

My mouth twitches. Even at her weakest, this woman holds her ground, masking her vulnerability with defiance, head held high, eyes flashing.

"I don't know. It's irrelevant. Now, if you'll excuse me." She gives me a regal nod, as if we're standing in a grand ballroom and she's politely declining a dance.

"And where are you planning to go?" I ask.

She turns, walking along the path, and I follow her. She stiffens, and a thorn-covered vine slithers toward me. I pause, staring at the thorns, the tower.

Perhaps what I need is *inside* the tower.

But...

Madinia Farrow. I remember her name, even if she doesn't remember mine. And my instincts roar at me, telling me she can lead me to what I seek. She can lead me to—

I stumble as a memory slams into me. My hands clench around an object, and it's so realistic I can feel the spine, the pages...

A book. I'm looking for a book.

Elation sweeps through me. Finally. An answer. For the first time, I know what I'm looking for. What I *need*.

And this woman is going to help me find it.

Madinia

"Where, exactly, are you going?" The man calls from behind me.

I'm going to the nearest town, that's where I'm going.

Kyldare's witch may have created a spell that ensured basic hygiene—for Kyldare's benefit I'm sure—but the fact remains that I haven't bathed in *three years*. My stomach is rumbling with newly awakened hunger. And...

I need to be alone. I may not remember much of my past,

but I remember making the decision to forget, so Kyldare couldn't get the information he wanted from me.

Unfortunately, it's not just the location of whatever Kyldare is looking for that I've forgotten. It's everything before Daharak—

Daharak. *"Don't let them break you. I'll find you. Somehow, I'll find you."*

My head begins to throb viciously. Remembering hurts.

But if I can get to Daharak, she'll tell me what I need to know.

The man's stallion snorts at me, and I give it a wide berth as I unsaddle all of the soldier's horses but one, setting them free.

I'd like to sell them, but a woman traveling alone with so many horses in excellent condition would draw far too much attention.

Mounting the horse, I nudge the mare into motion, ignoring the man's eyes on me.

"You're going the wrong way."

The rumble of his deep voice itches at my mind with a sense of familiarity, but when I search the wasteland of my memory, his face is nowhere to be found.

"You don't know where I'm going," I say between my teeth.

"You're heading deeper within the forest. Without any supplies."

He lifts his huge body into his saddle, stroking one hand along his stallion's neck. The horse turns his head and snaps his teeth at him, and the man laughs.

"I'm going to the nearest town," he returns his attention to me. "Travel with me, and I'll keep you safe."

"And why would you do that? Why are you even here?"

He shrugs one shoulder, his horse shifting toward mine, and the moonlight caresses his face.

"Consider it a good deed."

I can feel my mind unraveling at the edges, and I need to leave this place before Kyldare returns with more soldiers.

"If you attempt to harm me, I'll burn you alive." I may not be able to reach for the dark power, but my flames come naturally to me. As does the urge to *burn*.

He bares his teeth in a wicked smile. "Agreed."

"What is your name?"

"Calysian."

"My name is Madinia."

He gives me a grave nod. I keep a careful eye on him as we move toward the only road from the tower. When he doesn't speak again, I focus on the steady beat of our horse's hooves along packed dirt, forcing myself to keep my hands soft on the mare's mouth, even as I grip the reins tight, my knuckles turning white.

Calysian rides a few feet ahead, his back straight, his hands loose on his own reins. His horse is entirely too big, just like the man himself. I don't know him, I'm not stupid enough to trust him, but for now I'll allow him to lead me closer to safety.

I grind my teeth until my jaw protests.

Minutes turn to hours, and I stay vigilant, continually sweeping my gaze over our surroundings in case Kyldare returns. Part of me is convinced he will be waiting for me in the nearest town, but it's much more likely that he fled south, deeper into the forest where his queen keeps a regiment stationed.

At his heart, he is a coward. And he'll need to regroup.

I shift in the saddle, the aches in my muscles a dull reminder of how long I spent without moving. The witch's spell may have allowed me the ability to wake and walk, but each step the horse takes sends a faint throb through my legs and spine.

I just have to focus on the town. On freedom. But my mind won't settle. It keeps circling back, over and over, attempting to remember…

Occasionally, I see flashes, bits of memory that float up to the surface for a moment before they're snatched away. A face, a voice, laughter. But the more I attempt to focus on them, the faster they disappear.

Panic beats at me. What if...what if my memories never return? What if my mind is forever damaged?

I reach for that dark power, seeking nothing more than the reassurance that it's *there*, but its presence is so faint, my heart trips in my chest.

I shift in the saddle again, whispering an apology to the mare.

"Almost there," Calysian says, proving he's been paying closer attention to me than I would have liked.

The town is little more than a cluster of dark shadows as we approach. But the welcoming scent of woodsmoke drifts toward us. The buildings are small, thatched roofs sagging in places. A few lanterns hang from hooks by doors on the main street, casting a yellow glow.

The dirt road beneath us is uneven, dotted with occasional puddles of mud. A sharp, rhythmic metal clang reaches my ears—likely a blacksmith working late into the night.

Calysian scans the town, his gaze lingering on the few people spilling out of taverns and stumbling down the street.

"There," he says, nodding toward the end of the street.

The inn is larger than the surrounding buildings. Light spills from cracks in the shutters in the upper floors, and the sound of voices carries through the night. A woman sings with a surprisingly pleasing voice, and a few people join in, while a group of men laugh raucously.

My stomach tightens as the scent of something savory wafts toward us. We pull our horses to a stop outside the inn, and a couple of stablehands appear. One of them murmurs to Calysian, and he hands him a couple of coins, dismounting and rounding his horse. He grabs the reins, holding his horse's head still as he levels him with a look.

"Be good."

The horse stomps one foot, and Calysian sighs, handing the reins to one of the stablehands. "Be careful. He bites, kicks, and generally becomes a nuisance. Keep at least a stall between him and the other horses on each side."

The stablehand nods, but the color drains from his face as he tentatively leads the stallion away.

I dismount, ensuring I have my sword, along with the chains still wrapped in the soldier's jacket. My own sweet mare nuzzles my hand as I stroke her head. When she's led away, I feel suddenly...lonely.

Calysian jerks his head at the entrance to the inn. "You'll feel better after you get some rest."

A couple of drunks stumble out, almost slamming into us, and Calysian drops his arm over my shoulders, steering me away from them. His scent envelops me—amber and leather and *male*. As soon as we're through the entrance I wiggle away, and he shoots me an amused look.

"Two rooms," he instructs the innkeeper, who nods, stepping away to murmur to one of the barmaids.

Someone lets out a cackle and I flinch. Glass shatters, and I spin, but it's merely a barmaid blushing over a dropped tray.

Each sudden laugh, each shout and cheer, the singer crooning about lost love...it makes my head ring. The noise is a relentless wave, crashing over me again and again, until I want to clamp my hands over my ears. I bury my hands into my own shirt in an attempt to anchor myself, but the air is too thick, the scent of food, smoke, sweat...

I can't breathe.

My heart slams into my ribs.

I stumble toward the door.

A huge hand wraps around the back of my neck, holding me in place.

THIS VICIOUS DREAM

Dark eyes meet mine, glimmering with what might be concern. Calysian curses. "I should have known."

His face melds into another, and then another. The walls are closing in, the warmth from the fire making me break out in a sweat.

Before I can protest, his heavy arm is wrapped around my shoulders once more and he's hauling me away. Distantly, I'm aware of a brief conversation between Calysian and the innkeeper, and then he's practically carrying me upstairs.

I blink, and I'm suddenly standing in a room, alone with him. A room that is almost entirely silent. How many floors did we climb?

"I've ordered food to be brought to us," he says gruffly. "My room is next door. The innkeeper said she'll also arrange a bath. If you need anything, let me know."

He disappears, leaving me staring at the closed door.

I don't know why he's helping me. I still refuse to trust him. But…I suppose I owe him now. The thought sets my teeth on edge, and the fury pushes away the remnants of useless fear as the innkeeper brings up stew and ale, before pointing at the knobs above the tub, murmuring instructions.

The stew is warm and filling, the bath hot and soothing. I relish both, savoring the simple pleasures I once took for granted.

I pull my leggings and shirt on, unwilling to sleep naked.

Someone pounds on the door and I freeze.

"Open," Calysian orders.

I crack the door open and he nods at me. "Switch rooms." His voice is low, and I frown.

"Why?"

"Because you draw attention." His eyes linger on my face. "Several people were listening to the innkeeper's chatter, which means they know you're alone in this room. If I were Kyldare, I'd send soldiers after you tonight, before you can get too far.

Switch rooms and if anyone tries to break in, they'll get a nasty surprise." He flashes his teeth.

His reasoning is sound. In fact...he seems determined to protect me. Wariness wars with gratitude. Wariness wins.

"Why do you care?"

He rolls his eyes. "I didn't rescue you only to watch you be dragged away kicking and screaming."

I let out a hiss. "Once again, you *did not* rescue me."

He gives me a patronizing look that makes me want to hit him. "Move," he says. "I'm tired."

Leaning down, I scoop up the soldier's jacket. The chains clank, and Calysian raises one eyebrow. I ignore him.

His room is a twin to mine, and within a few minutes, I'm curled in the bed. He must have briefly laid down, because the pillow holds his scent. It's strangely comforting, and I let my eyes drift closed.

It's my first night of freedom in three years.

My chest aches, my eyes burn, and yet I don't cry. I *can't*.

"No one is coming for you." Kyldare's voice is a soft croon, attempting to lull me into compliance. "The pirates you traveled with? We went back and killed them all."

No. No, we had a deal.

Kyldare angles his head. "You didn't think we would allow such filth to live? Our queen does not allow piracy in her waters."

Despair swamps me. His words have the opposite effect he intended. I block him out, focusing only on Daharak, on Carosa, on Edorn. I no longer hear Kyldare's voice. Instead, I hear Addie, muttering to herself as she stirs something in a big pot. I hear Lonn's belly laugh as he scrapes coins across the table with a smug grin, pointing to his cards. I hear Neil's grunts as he trains me in hand-to-hand.

"This is useless." I catch Kyldare's disgusted words. He leans over me, and I instinctively struggle, heavy chains clanking around my wrists. "Perhaps you need some time alone to contemplate your life choices."

A woman begins chanting, her voice making the hair stand up on the back of my neck. I thrash desperately, but my limbs are turning heavy. Leaden.

Kyldare pulls me into his arms, and I'm suddenly limp. Horror engulfs me as he smiles. "I'll see you soon, Madinia Farrow."

He places me gently on the bed. The chains fall from my wrists and Kyldare lets out a low hum. "We don't need these anymore, do we?" My eyes drift shut, but I don't dream. I'm trapped in my own body, unable to even open my eyes.

Oh gods, oh gods, oh gods.

I attempt to thrash, but I can't even tense my muscles. How long will he leave me here?

I was supposed to die with a sword in my hand and a smirk on my face. Not alone and trapped, forgotten and abandoned.

Kyldare's words repeat on a loop. "I'll see you soon, Madinia Farrow."

Madinia Farrow.

I fought in a war. I saved a continent. I will not break here.

I will protect it with my life.

Gasping, I sit up, my entire body shuddering. My teeth chatter, my hands clamped to my chest as my heart thrashes against my ribs.

I can move. I'm free.

A war. There was a war. I refuse to believe Kyldare's words. Daharak and her people are alive. They have to be.

But what is it that I'm protecting?

A thud sounds, followed by a loud bang. I jolt, staring at the wall. Did Calysian fall out of bed?

A scuffle, followed by a grunt.

Calysian was right to make us switch rooms. Those men are here for me.

I'm on my feet in an instant, grabbing the soldier's jacket and wrapping it around my shoulders, ensuring the heavy chains won't fall. I strap the sword onto my back over the jacket. With a deep breath, I open the window.

My head swims. Three floors. I might not die in my attempt to get to the roof, but if I broke an ankle, I'd be defenseless.

A shout sounds, followed by a clash of metal.

I hesitate. Should I...help? I may not trust the man, but he did escort me here.

A feeling of doom slides over me, turning my palms slick. I didn't suffer for three years just to hand back my first taste of freedom.

I have to run. Have to protect. Have to move *now*.

Wiping my damp palms on my leggings, I haul myself onto the narrow windowsill. I have moments. Moments before whoever sold us out tells Kyldare's men to check this room.

I stretch one hand up, my fingers sliding against rough stone. My fingertips find a crack, a brick jutting out just enough for my purposes.

My muscles are weak, and I have a sudden vision of my body falling backward, my head cracking like an egg on the stone below.

A man screams. Not Calysian. But the sound is enough to drive me into action and I pull myself up, my arms immediately trembling from the strain.

Rough stone scrapes my fingertips, and my boots slide as I struggle to find a grip. I dangle for one terrifying moment, my whole weight hanging by my fingertips. My right foot finds a narrow ledge and I push.

My relieved breath sounds like a sob.

Go. Go now.

The roof is just a footspan above my head. I reach for the ledge, pulling myself up. My chest scrapes against the edge as I hoist myself onto the roof and collapse, my mouth dry.

Don't stop.

I stick to the side of the roof, not daring to step onto the thatched center. The stables are on the west side of the inn, attached to the main building, but the roof slopes sharply downward. One wrong step and I'll tumble from the edge.

I have to get to my horse.

Crouching, I shuffle along the side of the roof. My foot slips, sending my heart lurching into my throat. But I throw myself to the side, wobbling uneasily.

The stable roof is much lower, and I peer down into the darkness. The sound of horses lures me closer—a soft nicker, the scrape of a hoof, a loud sigh. I turn my back, crouching at the edge, and lean onto the roof, sliding until I'm hanging above the stables.

I drop. My feet slam into the stable roof, and I stumble, dropping to my knees as pain explodes through my legs.

Gingerly, I test my limbs. Nothing broken.

Still, I crawl across the roof until I reach the edge.

The ground below is a manageable drop, and I swing my legs over the side once more. The impact is jarring, but I'm instantly moving, sliding past a sleeping stablehand.

My horse is waiting in the closest stall to the entrance, and I don't waste any time, grabbing the saddle and reins. She shuffles on her feet, likely as unhappy to be fleeing in the middle of the night as I am.

"I know, girl. I'm sorry."

The scent of hay and leather engulfs me as I tack her as quickly as possible. It's been too long since I've ridden bareback, and I don't have the muscle strength to stay on her back at a gallop. Still, my heart pounds in my ears at the sound of more shouting from the inn.

A shadow slips into the stables and I wrestle my sword from my sheath.

Calysian steps toward me. He angles his head, lifting one eyebrow. "Leaving me for dead?" he drawls. "Ice cold."

CHAPTER FOUR

CALYSIAN

Madinia mounts her horse with a sniff. "I had a feeling you'd be just fine. And clearly I was right."

This woman.

I haul my saddle onto my horse. Fox snaps his teeth at me, displeased at having his rest interrupted. "Yeah, yeah, me too," I mutter. I need much less sleep than most creatures, but I spent the last two nights traveling in order to get to the cold-hearted woman currently trotting out of the stables.

Moments later, I'm trotting after her, Fox throwing his head to ensure I'm aware of his irritation.

Madinia glances over her shoulder at me, her hair spilling down her back. "How did they find us?" She's a little out of breath, her face flushed, and the combination makes me shift in the saddle. She'd be flushed and panting just like that in my bed.

I push that thought away. "This is the closest town to your tower. I'd hoped the search wouldn't start until morning, but clearly Kyldare is motivated. What exactly is it that they want from you?"

She opens her mouth, but her face closes down and she turns to face forward. Either she hasn't remembered the book, or she's refusing to tell me its location. I study her tense shoulders. *Was* this woman the one who stole it from me?

My mood turns dark, and the temperature surrounding us drops suddenly. Madinia shivers, eyes wide, clearly spooked. Fox's longer stride brings him up next to her mare.

No. Madinia doesn't *feel* centuries old. And her ingrained haughtiness is little more than a desperate attempt to hide the fact that her mind is cracked.

And still, some part of me remains irritated.

"Where are we going?" she asks.

"How about you tell me? Are your instincts steering you in a particular direction?" Her head whips toward me and I keep my expression carefully blank. She may not have taken my book, but she's connected to it somehow. Even if she's unaware of such a thing.

This is why my own instincts pushed me toward her. This is why I suddenly feel more myself than I ever have, with a strange clarity of mind. Madinia Farrow just became priceless, her safety more important than anything else.

"And if I told you they are?" she asks carefully.

"Then I'd tell you it's likely fate that is steering you in that direction, and you should always listen to fate."

Her eyes narrow and I almost smile. At her core, this woman is sharp, distrustful. But she knows she needs me.

We're both silent for several minutes. When she sends a narrow-eyed look my way, I raise one eyebrow. "What is it?"

"Why are you helping me?"

I shrug. "I'm an honorable man. How could I leave you to die?"

The jab hits, and she stiffens before sending me another dismissive look. "I hadn't realized you would need to be rescued. Now that I know, I'll be sure to help you in the future."

I can't help but laugh. "You do that."

Some part of me wishes she remembered me, even as I'm

sure it wouldn't help my case. If anything, I should be hoping for the opposite. Once she does shake off whatever has been done to her mind, she'll become even more of a handful.

We travel all night, riding along the dirt road, away from the forest. I might be imagining the warmth growing in my chest as I follow her lead. *Or*, it's my book, calling me to it. Twice, she dismounts, walking slightly off the dirt path and shoving something into her pocket. When I ask what she's collecting, she ignores me, peering at her nails.

It sets my teeth on edge. Women have never ignored me.

I focus on the book instead, mulling over its existence as we ride. Why would this book be so important to me? And is it the reason I woke in that forest, fully formed as an adult, but without a childhood, a family, a *life*?

Rolling my shoulders, I slide a glance at the woman currently swaying in her saddle, clearly fatigued. We'll have to stop soon, somewhere away from the main road and her enemies.

Frustration slices through me, but I force myself to jerk my head, gesturing for her to follow me off the trail. This may be the closest I've come to vengeance, but my own instincts urge me to be careful. If I'm going to find my book—and take my revenge—I'll have to cater to the needs of the woman being hunted by Vicana's soldiers.

At least until she tells me where my book is.

Madinia

Calysian's eyes are the last thing I see before I go to sleep in our small camp off the side of the road. They're dark and shadowed.

Perhaps that's why I dream of him.

A man stands next to a woman with long, curly blonde hair.

THIS VICIOUS DREAM

They're surrounded by bodies, limbs strewn carelessly across the clearing. He clamps one hand on her shoulder, and I nudge my horse.

"Let her go," I demand.

The woman whirls. "Are you seeing what I'm seeing?"

"Oh yes," the man purrs. "I see her too."

I raise my hand, allowing a few orange sparks to jump from my fingers. The woman gapes at me. "How...? What?"

I toss my hair over one shoulder. "I'm here to help you escape." I make a show of wrinkling my nose at the bodies. "If you didn't do that, then we need to be on our way before they return."

The man stares at me, and his eyes heat. "Well, well, well."

I look down my nose at him and meet the woman's eyes. "Are you well enough to sit on a horse?"

"Yes."

"Then let's go."

"What about your life debt?" the man asks.

The woman shrugs. "Madinia just saved my life. Give your debt to her."

I don't have time for this. I gesture for the woman to move.

"You'd leave me here?" The man asks. There's something unsettling about his dark gaze. Something that sends a shiver up my spine.

I open my mouth, but he sends me a wicked grin. "Forget it. I have some unfinished business to take care of. But I'll see you again. In the meantime, good luck to you both."

I jolt awake.

I knew Calysian was familiar. But who was the woman with him? We spoke as if we were...friends.

It hurts—discovering memories I carefully hid away like precious jewels.

Sitting up, I run a hand down my face. Calysian lounges next to the fire. Sudden fury engulfs me, and I itch to pour my power into those flames, sending them straight into his lying face.

"Why didn't you tell me we knew each other?"

He raises one eyebrow. "Would you have believed me? I figured you'd come to that conclusion in your own time. What did you remember?"

"Bodies. A woman with blonde hair. You told her you owed her a life debt."

He gives me a wry look. "Tonight wasn't the first time you left me for dead." There's a hint of affront in his voice.

I roll my eyes. "Clearly you survived. Who was the woman?"

"Her name is Prisca. And she's the queen of the hybrid kingdom."

Prisca. I mouth the name. "How did I know her?"

"I'm not entirely sure. You were with her when I met her, already unlikely friends."

"Unlikely?"

He angles his head. "I don't know Prisca well, but I know enough about her to know she *likes* people. And people tend to like her."

His tone is pointed, and I curl my lip at him, ignoring the way his words slice into me.

Since neither of us are going to get any more sleep, I roll to my feet, stalking to the small stream to splash water on my face. I can feel Calysian's eyes on me.

The strange power calls to me, rocking through my body and leaving my head ringing until I'm dizzy.

Calysian is suddenly standing in front of me. "What was that?"

I give him a withering look, and he clamps his huge hands on my shoulders. "Answer me."

He tenses, and I know he can feel my blade at his balls. "Ask nicely," I purr, shifting my knife closer. I found it in my mare's saddlebag, along with a few rations and a change of clothes.

A glint of something I don't recognize enters Calysian's eyes. "Ah," he says. "So you are in there after all, Madinia Farrow."

THIS VICIOUS DREAM

His words remind me of the way he has kept silent about my past. About having met me before.

He leans close, ignoring my knife. His eyes burn into mine, and another memory explodes in my mind's eye.

I open my eyes and jolt. A man has taken the empty seat in front of me, and I hadn't even noticed. My hands warm, and the man grins at me. This is the man who'd escaped Regner's dungeon with Prisca. Calysian.

He's shaved his beard, and his eyes glint with wicked humor. He's a handsome bastard, that's for sure. Handsome and far too large. What exactly is he doing here?

"Tired?" he asks.

"What do you want?"

"I did a little research about you, Madinia Farrow," he says.

"Did you? Then you know I could turn your insides to kindling."

Calysian laughs. "Relax, beautiful woman. I'm here to help you."

I force a bored expression onto my face. "And why would you do that?"

"I owe your friend a life debt. Since she didn't seem inclined to let me pay it before we went our separate ways, and she told me to give it to you, it's yours."

"I don't need a life debt."

"Too bad. Where I come from, a man's honor rests on his word. Who do you need killed? Or perhaps you have someone who wants to kill you? Name the time and the place, and I'll be there to protect you."

His expression is serious, his words solemn. But I don't trust strange men.

"I can protect myself."

"Something else, then."

My hands cool, and I lean forward slightly. "What is it you think you could help me with?"

"You'd be surprised what I can help you with," he says. I roll my eyes, and he laughs at me, folding his arms. "I know this city. I know the people in it, and I'm relatively confident I know what you're planning."

I tense and he waves an elegant hand. "I want you to succeed. So I can go home."

"Home?"

One side of his mouth curves. "I'm from...elsewhere. When Regner's little barrier went up, it trapped me on this continent."

Of course. Of course there were people here who became stuck, unable to get home. Curiosity slides through me despite myself. If I'd known this man, I might've asked him to tell me of his homeland. And any other places he'd seen.

"Why were you in Regner's dungeon?"

Calysian just shakes his head. "Irrelevant. Just tell me what you want."

What if he could help me? I'd be an idiot to turn him away.

"What kinds of people did you say you know?"

"All kinds of people."

"Get me a meeting with Caddaril the Cleaver."

Surprise flashes across his face. "You continue to surprise me."

I shrugged. "Can you do it?"

"Yes. You're sure this is what you want to use your life debt for?"

"I'm sure."

"In that case, I'll find you when I've arranged the meeting."

He gets to his feet, towering over me. "Be careful."

I keep my expression cool, blank. He angles his head, curiosity glinting in his eyes.

"Prickly. I like that."

"Come closer," I say. "And you'll see just how prickly."

He lets out a laugh. "I'll see you soon, Madinia Farrow."

I wave my hand, a clear demand for him to leave.

"What did you see?" Calysian is tense, his fingers digging

into my upper arms. When I glance pointedly down at them, he loosens them. But he doesn't release me.

"A meeting. You were going to get me a meeting with someone called Caddaril the Cleaver." I pause, attempting to understand everything I've just remembered. "Who is Regner?"

Calysian angles his head. "I'll answer your question if you answer one of mine."

"Fine."

He releases me, stalking away to stare at the bubbling water. "Have you seen it?"

"Have I seen what?"

"Have you seen what it is that your instincts are pulling you towards?"

Sudden realization hits me like a splash of water to the face.

Calysian knows what it is. And despite his insistence that he's an *honorable* man, he's not here to keep me alive. He's here because he wants it.

Betrayal. The feeling is intimately familiar. And yet I'm somehow always surprised by it.

"No."

His shoulders slump. Likely in relief. He believes I'll be easier to manipulate if I don't know he wants whatever it is I'm supposed to protect. My teeth clench.

"Who is Regner?"

He sighs. "A king. He enslaved a continent and used religion to manipulate humans into giving up their power in a war against the fae. He told them they were sacrificing their magic to the gods in exchange for protection from fae invaders—all while hoarding that power for himself. Hybrids like you couldn't be stripped of your power. So they were branded as *corrupt* and hunted and killed. But your people rallied behind the hybrid queen."

Prisca. The hybrid queen is Prisca. And her face flickers

in my mind once more, this time with a crown on her head. A crown I helped put there.

My heart thuds against my ribs. It's coming back. But…

If I helped her, why did she never help me? Why did she leave me in that tower, trapped and alone?

Because no one can be trusted. If you want to survive, you'll have to do it alone.

The thought is depressing, even as it rings with truth.

Whatever it is that I'm protecting, I gave three years of my life to keep it safe. I voluntarily went with Kyldare and refused to give him its location—even through his worst torture. I trust my past self enough to know that I wouldn't have suffered Kyldare's attentions if it wasn't critically important.

So no. I will not be leading Calysian directly to whatever it is he wants.

In fact, I believe it's time to head in the opposite direction.

CHAPTER FIVE

MADINIA

TIME TURNS SLOW AND SLUGGISH.

The weather becomes slightly warmer as we travel east toward Langshire—the coastal city that was our destination before Kyldare took me. Memories of Daharak and the others have slipped into my mind as we rode, although I still can't recall much before the days leading up to Kyldare's appearance.

Still, it's something. As soon as we get to Langshire, I'll quietly begin asking the locals if anyone remembers Daharak's ship docking.

Three years ago.

Hopelessness swamps me, but I refuse to give into it.

I refuse to believe they're dead.

Calysian has begun brooding. When he's not sulking in his saddle, he's sending suspicious looks my way. Today while we picked up supplies at a small village, he shadowed me relentlessly, ensuring I was never more than two footspans from his hulking body.

His suspicion means it's time to strike.

I pretend not to notice his dark mood as we set up camp.

When he disappears toward the river to bathe, I take the soldier's jacket and place it behind the tree next to Calysian's sleeping mat. And then I hurry back toward the road where I spotted the moonshade weed.

It's my turn to cook. The activity doesn't come naturally to me, but by the time Calysian returns, I've poured the stew into the small wooden bowls we bought when we stopped for supplies.

Calysian is silent as we eat. It's not until we're finished that he leans against the tree.

"We're traveling in the wrong direction. Aren't we?"

My eyes fly to his. They're heavy lidded and just a little blurred.

Kyldare's witch inadvertently taught me everything I needed to know about poisons.

I shuffle over to him. He watches me distrustfully, but when I throw one leg over his thighs, his eyes turn hot and wild. His hands clamp down on my ass, drawing me closer.

Men. They're so easy.

"Uh-uh," I smile. "I'm in charge here."

Humor flickers through his eyes. Humor and arrogance—as if he truly believes he's the one controlling this situation. Irritation roars through me at the thought, and his lips curl in a smirk.

He knows what I'm thinking. It's even more irritating, knowing he has somehow got me figured out already.

At least he thinks he does.

I smirk back, and we have one perfect moment of understanding. Neither of us will let the other win. It's not how we were made.

"Why are you leading me in the wrong direction?" He asks, pulling me even closer, until he's pressed against me, hard and thick. I barely suppress the urge to grind down.

It has been a long, long time since…

"Wrong direction? You told me to follow my instincts. And my instincts say I can't trust you."

"You can't trust me? *You* lied to *me*. That means you're the one who can't be trusted." He gives me a dark, sullen look and I almost laugh at the audacity.

"You said you would keep me safe."

"I *am*," he growls, tightening his hands on my ass. His blinks are becoming longer, and I suppress another smile.

"No. You're traveling with me because you want what I'm protecting."

"You've remembered?" his expression turns blank.

I think about lying, but Calysian's voice turns cold, even as he begins to slur his words. "You haven't, have you? You know what I think? I think you don't *want* to remember. You're blocking it yourself, because remembering will be painful. You'll find yourself wondering how you ended up here alone, and where your so-called friends are."

Pain stabs into me, and I drown it in rage. Leaning forward, I lower my head until my lips brush the shell of his ear. With a shudder, he pulls me even closer, until my breasts are pressed against his chest.

Reaching behind me, I clamp my hands onto his wrists, pulling his arms above his head. His eyes turn feral, but he allows it. Or perhaps his head is swimming. Those blinks are becoming slower and slower.

"What did you do to me?" he slurs.

"Nothing you wouldn't have done to me the second I brought you close to your goal."

CLICK.

Calysian's eyes fly open, but it's too late. I'm already snapping the other cuff around his wrist.

"You fucking—"

"Shhh," I press my finger to his lips and climb off him, raking him with an amused look I know will chafe. "We've had such a nice time together. Don't ruin it by saying something you'll regret."

He gives me a killing look, but I'm already turning to walk away.

"Don't..." he mumbles. "Protect...you."

I glance over my shoulder. His eyes are slitted as he fights against the moonshade weed I slipped in his stew.

"You think I need you to protect me? Someone who has been lying to me the entire time? Someone who has been using me for their own purposes?" My voice cracks. From *rage*, not *hurt*.

At least that's what I tell myself.

Leaning down, I pick up his heavy woolen cloak, wrapping it around myself.

"I may not remember much, but I remember this: I'm Madinia Farrow. I don't need a hulking brute to keep me safe. And I don't need a liar trying to fool me at every turn." Harnessing my temper, I blow him a kiss. "Thanks for the cloak."

CALYSIAN

"Well, well, well. This is embarrassing."

I open my eyes. My head swims and I lean to the side, retching.

Eamonn jumps onto my thighs, his tail wagging as he ponders the cuffs clamped onto my wrist, the chain between them.

"How did this happen?"

My mind provides me with an image of Madinia.

Her lips were red and pouty and she smelled like hot, wild woman, and she was leaning so close...

"I don't want to talk about it."

Eamonn nudges me with his nose, his ears flopping. I sigh. "Just help me get out of the chains."

"And how exactly did she get hold of these?"

"She's been carrying them since we left the tower. I didn't take them from her because I thought she was planning to use them on *Kyldare*." I grind out.

"Nasty things."

That's an understatement. Fae iron may weaken the fae, but it drains hybrids and humans too. And the moment the cuffs closed around my wrists, I couldn't feel even a drop of my own power. Combined with whatever Madinia used to drug me, I'm lucky there were no bandits traveling this road last night, or my throat would likely have been slit.

"Break them," I order.

Eamonn lets out a bark. "It's a little difficult in this form."

I drop my head against the trunk of the tree. I don't know much about Eamonn, except that centuries ago, he was cursed to never be able to use his human form. When I ask about it, he grows quiet or disappears for days.

Just as he disappeared recently.

"Where have you been?"

"I can't have adventures of my own?"

"Not when I end up like this."

"How could I have expected this outcome? You certainly didn't."

I snarl, and he leaps off my thighs. "Do you have anything to pick the locks?"

"In my rucksack."

A blink, and Eamonn is suddenly a small monkey. He scampers over to my rucksack, finds the small kit and leaps up my body to get to work on the chains.

It feels as if an icepick is relentlessly slamming into my head. When Eamonn finally frees me, my power returns in a dizzying rush.

"Thank you."

The monkey lets out a shriek—likely in an attempt to hide Eamonn's chuckle. "Anytime."

I pack the chains into my own rucksack. If Madinia wants to play the game this way, I'm more than happy to oblige.

My mind throws me back to the feel of her settled on top of my thighs, her plush red lips curved in a smile as she leaned close.

Luring me in.

A trick I'll make sure she regrets.

Madinia

My head swims with fatigue, but I force myself to keep moving north, drawn toward the dark pull. At first, I thought about disappearing, ensuring no one can use me to find it. But the pull is overwhelming, and if I reach it first, I can hide it.

The cloak I stole from Calysian keeps the worst of the chill at bay, but it's still cold, and, my poor mare's steps are getting slower and slower as she plods along.

More of my memories have come to me as I've ridden through the night—mostly of my time traveling with the pirates, along with my decision to board Daharak's ship in the first place.

"What is it you want when all this is done?" she asks.

I shrug. The pirate queen can't be trusted. Still, she interests me. Her life interests me. She could go anywhere. See anything. I stare out at the water, wondering what that must be like. "Why would you care?"

"I see a lot of myself in you."

I turn, giving her a look of disdain. She laughs.

"I want to be left alone," I say. "When this is done, I want to go somewhere no one knows my name. I want to start a new life. Alone."

"You don't really want that." She shakes her head. *"But by the time you learn that, you'll be half an ocean away."* She taps her temple. *"I like to believe I have a hint of my mother's sight."*

I grind my teeth at her patronizing tone, and her eyes light with humor. "I believe I'll help you with your plans anyway. If we bring down this barrier, find me after the war, and I'll take you with me."

My entire body tenses. I can practically taste freedom. "Why would you do that?"

"For the same reason I do everything, of course. My own amusement."

Bitterness wars with dark irony and I let out a humorless laugh. I got what I wanted. I'm entirely alone. The only people who know my name either want to capture me or wish to use me for their own purposes.

I wish I could turn back time. Could go back and shake the woman who so badly wanted to leave everything behind.

Along with the memories of my life, I remember more about this kingdom too. Hours of poring over maps on that ship have given me a basic understanding of my route, and my first stop will be the city of Kolegrift—the closest city on my path north. There, I can stable my mare, eat, and rest.

Hopefully, Calysian is still chained to that tree.

I chew on my lip, a hint of guilt stabbing through me. I probably should have chosen a tree further from the road. Leaving him unconscious and chained, his weapons and clothes displaying signs of subtle wealth…

I practically left a sign next to him stating *Unconscious victim. Bandits and thieves, do your worst.*

I let out a sigh, directing my horse toward the river so she can drink. I left the horse feed with Calysian, which means I'll need to buy more.

"I think you don't want *to remember. You're blocking it yourself, because remembering will be painful. You'll find yourself*

wondering how you ended up here alone, and where those so-called friends are."

Is that what I'm doing?

I can't afford to let fear drive my decisions. Without my memories, I'm weak, uncertain. If I don't remember, I'm dead.

I did this to myself. As a protective measure. To prevent Kyldare from getting his hands on...something.

And if I did it to myself, surely I can *undo* it.

Dismounting, I let my horse drink deeply, then tie her lead rope to a tree branch, leaving her grazing. I feel stupid, but I sit on an overturned log and close my eyes. I have to try.

Remember.

Curly blonde hair. Calysian said her name was Prisca.

My head immediately aches, but I push through it. I'm not afraid. I *refuse* to be afraid of my own memories.

A branch cracks and I launch myself from the log, stumbling backwards.

"Well, what do we have here?" A tall, thin man leers at me, another moving up beside him. "You look remarkably similar to a woman with a bounty on her head, doesn't she Ostir?"

The other man grins, revealing gaps where teeth should be. "She sure does. All that red hair. Come with us and we won't hurt you," he calls to me.

I rake them with a disparaging look. As expected, both men stiffen, striding toward me.

And straight into my flames.

I drop to my knees as memories slam into me. This isn't the first time I've burned men alive.

Solider after soldier have succumbed to my flames. I lived through all of it, the reek of burned flesh crawling up my nose and into my mouth.

The soldiers disappear, and I'm suddenly sitting in a plush room, staring at a boy with sad eyes.

"The dark god knew his siblings were going to strip him of his

incredible power. His memories. They were tired of the favoritism his father showed him, and they didn't approve of his plans for this world. Before they could attack him, he learned of their plan. He poured much of his knowledge, power, and self into three grimoires, casting them out into this world. He knew they would be used, and when they were, that knowledge would call to him."

I tense. If Regner ever found the other two grimoires, we were doomed. I couldn't let him become that powerful. He didn't get to win. After everything he'd taken from all of us... The life I could've had...

More memories.

The swing of a sword, my father's head rolling free. War. So much death.

Leaning over, I vomit, then give into dry sobs, my entire body trembling.

When I return to myself, I'm covered in a cold sweat. I don't know how long I've been here, but the bodies on the ground are no longer smoking.

I grew up without a mother and I watched as my father was beheaded by a tyrant king's soldier. I lived at court as one of Regner's queen's ladies, forced to fawn over that queen daily.

There are still holes. But I know I met Prisca and Asinia. I escaped certain death. I fought in a war.

Most importantly, I know what I'm protecting.

A grimoire. One of three. A grimoire filled with incredible, unspeakable power.

Calysian wants it. Kyldare wants it. The Sylvarin Queen wants it.

That one book held enough power for a king to enslave a continent and hold a magical barrier around that continent for hundreds of years.

Prisca gave me the grimoire after I...used it. I used it to undo Regner's magic and return the power he had stolen to the humans in Eprotha.

Is that why I can sense it? Is that why I could borrow some of its power in the tower, striking out with my thorns?

I stare down at my shaking hands. Was I using the grimoire…or was the grimoire using me? No matter how much I strain, I can no longer access that power.

Considering who it belongs to, that's probably a good thing.

As much as I want to kill Vicana, I can't give in to the urge to find the grimoire. I have to get off this continent, which means I need to get to a ship before I'm captured again. Before those who hunt for the grimoire use my strange connection to it to take its dark power.

Calysian's words echo in my head and I force my mind to return to the moment I saw him at the tower. Surprise had flashed across his face. He hadn't expected to see me. Hadn't known I was the one there.

Someone must have told him the woman in the tower could lead him to the grimoire.

My mind races. Stumbling to my feet, I roll my shoulders, making my way past the bodies, to where the men left two horses tied near the road. The men were likely following me for some time. I don't regret their deaths.

I search their saddlebags, finding a coin pouch, a map, and some horse feed.

Unrolling the map, I crouch near the horses as I use a couple of rocks to pin the map in place. I crossed the Wyrdale River with Calysian less than a day ago, so the city of Kolegrift should be just a few hours from here.

A warm bed, a hot meal, a stall for the mare.

I reach up to stroke her nose. "I'm going to call you Hope. I know, it's whimsical—and I'm not exactly the whimsical type—but for the first time in a long time, I feel a tiny spark of optimism." I pause, meeting her eyes. "Don't worry, it's unlikely to last."

THIS VICIOUS DREAM

Just days ago, I was trapped in that tower, unable to move. Now I'm alone, with money, horses, and most importantly... freedom. I know who I am, I know where I've come from, and I know what I'm protecting.

I untack one of the men's horses, setting it free, before untying Hope's lead rope and mounting the larger of the two horses—a dappled gray which seems placid enough.

I don't let myself think about Calysian, likely still chained to the tree. If a tiny pang of guilt slices through my newfound positivity, well...that's no one's business but mine.

Perhaps this will teach him a lesson. Cross me at your own peril.

I take the quiet road north toward one of the main trade roads to Kolegrift. The sun begins to rise, and the early morning light flickers through trees, casting long shadows. Slowly, the landscape begins to change—trees thinning out, giving way to rolling fields dotted with livestock and the occasional small farmhouse. The air grows cooler, and the faint silhouette of Kolegrift comes into view as I take a left onto a trade road.

This road is much wider, filled with travelers on both foot and horseback. Merchants roll by with carts, farmers head toward the market, and Vicana's guards patrol the path. I pull the hood of Calysian's cloak over my head, my heart thumping, mouth turning dry as I pass a group of guards stationed near the city gates.

The gates themselves loom high enough that only the very stupid would attempt to climb them.

Four bodies hang from the stone walls on either side, swaying gentle in the breeze, their faces covered with dark hoods. A wooden placard swings from the neck of the nearest corpse, words scrawled in dark ink:

Traitor to the Crown.

Vicana. Likely, they were spies. Perhaps they were brave enough to speak out against her.

I dismount, leading both horses as I take my place at the back of the line forming ahead of me. A few merchants are waiting for inspection, a family with two children in a cart packed with turnips, and a couple of fae wait patiently, well-dressed and at ease even while surrounded by hybrids and humans.

The parents don't bother covering their children's eyes. They've probably passed through these gates a hundred times before—and seen bodies hanging from these walls more often than not.

In front of me, a few merchants nod at each other. One of them looks exhausted, his face tight with temper.

"What's wrong with you?" a bearded man asks.

"Fucking troll," the merchant says, rubbing at his eyes. "20 miles from the eastern entrance. I had to come all the way south to avoid it. Took me an extra day of travel."

The other man winces. "Territorial beasts. Too much magic, not enough sense. Hopefully the Queen will send someone to dispatch it."

The guards' eyes scan me briefly as I pass through, but they don't linger. I know Kyldare well enough to know it's unlikely he's told Vicana I escaped. He may have set bounty hunters and mercenaries after me, but he'll still be hoping to find me before Vicana learns her hope of finding the grimoire is gone.

I've never been sure exactly what Kyldare is. If he's a hybrid, he must have some strong fae blood in his lineage, because I've seen him use his power in dark ways with the help of his witch. Of course, there are many strange, powerful creatures on this continent that I'd never heard of before I stepped foot on this land. And I'm sure there are many more I will never encounter.

I mount my horse once more, riding down cobblestoned streets lined with taverns and market stalls. Faces blur as my blinks turn long and slow, fatigue swamping me.

Row houses stand tightly packed next to each other, each

four stories high, but less than twenty footspans wide. Tall and narrow, the buildings are tiled, painted in bright, clashing colors—red, orange, yellow, even a strange shade of pink—seemingly chosen precisely to clash as much as possible with their neighbors. The intricate patterns on each tile save the row of houses from being garish, transforming it instead into something unexpectedly beautiful.

Despite my current situation, I pause, blinking away the fatigue.

I've been on this continent for three years. And yet I've seen so little of it. This city is so different, so delightfully *foreign*, it makes warmth spread through my chest.

People bustle by, many of them wearing loose robes in bright colors as they laugh and gossip, wandering in groups or striding past with a clear direction in mind. Several women walk into a tavern, arms linked, and one of them throws her head back with a laugh.

The sun is warm on my face, the brightness stinging my eyes. *That's* why I blink several times, turning away from the women and their friendship.

I choose another inn—one next door to a tavern. My mind provides me with the feel of Calysian's arm wrapped around my shoulder at the last inn, his brows lowered as he gazed at me in concern.

Now I know that concern wasn't for me. It was for himself. It would, after all, be more difficult for him to use me to find the grimoire if my mind broke.

I give both horses to the stablehands and stumble into the inn, my entire body aching from so long in the saddle.

The innkeeper is a short, curvy woman with a baby on her hip. The child blinks at me owlishly as the woman takes the coins I hand her. "Your stay includes two meals in the tavern next door," she says, bouncing the baby when she begins to fuss.

The tavern is quiet around this time of the morning. It's

still on the early side for lunch, but I order anyway, barely tasting the chicken and root vegetables.

I almost sleepwalk next door and up the stairs, where I wedge the lone chair beneath the doorknob, bathe, and fall face down onto the bed.

A tiny grave, next to a river. A woman, hugely pregnant, curled onto that grave.

"I promised him I would keep him safe. It was my job to keep him safe."

The forest melts into a new place. A lush room filled with color and warmth.

Prisca, beaming at me.

My words slashing into her like knives. "I never asked to be part of your little group. I'm here to win this war and leave. So stop trying to make me care about you. All of you."

Her smile slowly falling.

Asinia's eyes hardening, her expression filled with both fury and pity.

Tears sting my eyes, and I attempt to wake.

Three of us, dressed for a day of joy, staring into a mirror. I'm wearing a crown of flowers, and I look strangely...soft.

Asinia is grinning at me, while Prisca's eyes are filled with happiness once more. "I'm not sorry that you care, Madinia. Because when someone like you takes an interest...worlds change."

I force my eyes open, staring up at the ceiling as I swallow around the burning lump in my throat.

Perhaps...perhaps the loss of my memories is a gift.

But I can't ignore that tiny grave. Or the knowledge that if I don't protect the grimoire, thousands of mothers will feel that same agony.

Already, Vicana has been encroaching into other kingdoms, grasping for more land to feed her ambitions. My years at court—and at war—taught me that great leaders don't take what isn't theirs. Not through conquest. Not through quiet theft. The rulers worth following build, protect, and strengthen. Vicana only devours.

Just as Regner did.

I roll to my feet, dress, and push the curtains open. The sun is high in the sky—I must have slept for a few hours, although it feels like only minutes.

My best option will be to try to find a seer here. They're revered on this continent—seen as a direct link to the gods.

And yet, even the most powerful seer will admit that a single choice can have a ripple effect that will change the future entirely. It's one of the reasons seers so often turn mad.

Still, I'm hoping a seer can tell me how to hide from Calysian. Perhaps they'll even be able to give me some information about Daharak and the others.

I just...I just need *something*.

It's not difficult to find a seer. The difficult part is handing over my few remaining coins in exchange for an hour with her.

The seer lives in a bright purple row house, and a woman with pale skin and bright orange hair opens the door, her eyes hard.

"Today is not a good day," she tells me. "Come back tomorrow."

"Let her in," a voice calls. "I have been waiting for her."

My stomach roils with unease. It's never a good sign when a seer has previous knowledge of your existence.

The woman gives me an unfriendly look but opens the door further. The inside of the house is dark, the curtains drawn closed. I follow the woman through the entrance and into a small, cramped sitting room.

The seer sits on a sofa, a cup clutched in her hands. When she gazes at me, her eyes are filled with a strange knowledge. A knowledge that makes the hair stand up on the back of my neck.

"Finally," she says. "You took your time."

"I'm sorry, was my torture and imprisonment inconvenient for you?"

She stares at me, and then her mouth curves in a surprisingly infectious grin.

When she waves one hand toward the sofa in front of her, I sit, the warmth from the fire making my eyelids heavy.

"One would think you'd had enough sleep to last a lifetime." She leans back, crossing her legs.

Ah. She clearly enjoys poking at people. "I wasn't sleeping. As you likely know." I let my gaze flick over her tight leggings, bejeweled tunic and carefully coiffed hair. "You don't look like a seer."

"What are seers supposed to look like?"

Crazy.

I don't say the word, but she smirks at me.

"What's your name?" I ask.

"Shaena. And you are Madinia Farrow. A woman who was caught within a vicious dream. One that wasn't truly a dream at all. For three years."

I grit my teeth. Three years of my life. Stolen. I'll never get those years back.

"I know why you're here, Madinia Farrow."

"Then you know I'm searching for my friends."

"What do you know of the grimoires?"

I sigh, pinching my nose. My scant hours of sleep didn't help. If anything, I feel even more exhausted.

"I came to you with questions of my own."

"This is important. Focus." Her voice is hard, and I lift my head to find her looking at me with renewed urgency.

"The gods were fighting amongst themselves. They decided one of them had too much power. The Dark God."

She nods. "His name was Calpharos, and he was clever, but forever bored. He and his twin grew tired of their siblings and their petty arguments as they shaped our world. His father had always had a soft spot for his youngest sons and had created one of the twins to be a little stronger than the others. And oh, how their siblings hated him for it."

A strange sensation sweeps over me, making my skin crawl.

Shaena continues. "Tronin, the god of strength, fought Calpharos for years, becoming more and more frustrated as his brother bested him. So he conspired with Faric—the god of knowledge—and together, they went to their sister Creas, the goddess of memory."

"They took his memories."

She smiles. "They tried. But Calpharos was both betrayed and forewarned by another. He poured everything he was into those grimoires—his memories, his power, pieces of his soul. Then, he cast them out, intending to find them later, when it was safe. Those grimoires call to him, across continents, urging him to reclaim them. Urging him to become whole. And when he does, his fury will lay waste to this world."

Tiny dots appear in front of my eyes.

Cal. Calpharos. Calysian.

"We have a problem," I say, and my voice somehow stays steady.

The seer narrows her eyes and I force myself to continue.

"The dark god has already found me. And he's looking for the grimoire I brought to this continent."

CHAPTER SIX

Madinia

Shaena's eyes roll up, and she slumps in her chair. "You must go before the queen's men find you in this city. I can see you refuse to go with them, can see you choose death instead. But your death would lead to destruction on an unimaginable scale." Her voice is hoarse as she relays her vision. With a sharp breath, she falls from her chair to the ground, her body seizing.

I launch to my feet.

"Mama!"

A young girl leaps into the room, falling to her knees as she attempts to cradle the seer. But her mother is thrashing, and the girl is forced to watch, trembling almost as much herself.

Prisca told me about this once. Her mother was a seer, and after her worst visions, she would be bed-bound for days.

The orange-haired woman rushes in, gently pushing the young girl away. "Go on, Fliora."

The girl looks like a miniature version of her mother, with the same large, blue eyes and wide mouth.

"The man who hunts you…"

I go still. The woman tuts, taking Fliora's hand, but Fliora gives her a stubborn look and I step closer.

"Which man? There are a two of them." No one should be able to free themselves from those chains, but something tells me Calysian will manage to do it.

"The Queen's man." Fliora shakes off the woman's hold. "He has left a group of soldiers north of here, in the Aelstow Forest."

I don't doubt her. She was likely present during her mother's visions. "How big is the group?"

"Fifty men or more."

Kyldare. He figured I would go north—of course he may have ordered some of his men to wait for me at the southern border as well—keeping me trapped.

My pulse triples, suddenly pounding in my ears, and I fight to keep my expression neutral.

If I head west, I'll come close to the Lacana Mountains. When we first docked on this continent, the pirates spoke of those mountains—and the creatures within them—with hushed voices.

I push the thought away. That decision can be made later, once I've made sure Calysian is no longer on my trail.

Shaena has stopped thrashing. Now she lies trembling on the ground, her face pale and drawn.

Pity churns in my stomach, mixing with guilt.

"Is there anything I can do for her?"

"No." The orange-haired woman's mouth is a thin line. "You've done quite enough."

Shaena opens her mouth and lets out a low moan. But she's reaching for something.

Fliora takes the coin purse her mother is pulling from her pocket and reaches for the gold coins I gave them.

"Go," Shaena gasps as Fliora hands me the coins. "Now."

Calysian

It's not difficult to predict where Madinia will go next. She'll need supplies, but she may even be hoping to temporarily hide herself amongst the seething mass of humanity within the city of Kolegrift.

When I stop to let Fox drink at a river, the scent of death caresses my senses, as enticing as a lover. Following my instincts, I find two bodies, burned until they're unrecognizable.

Madinia Farrow is vicious when cornered, but she doesn't kill without cause. If she killed these men, they likely attempted to take her.

They deserve every moment of pain they suffered.

You're attempting to do the same to her.

No. These men would have returned her to Kyldare. I merely want what is mine.

And still, the knowledge that Madinia sees me as just another man attempting to steal her freedom…it eats at me.

Steeling myself against the guilt, I ride through the southern gates, keeping my eyes peeled for a flame-haired vixen.

It's a huge city, but my instincts are never wrong. And the innkeeper clutching a wailing baby to her chest gives me a long look when I describe Madinia.

"No," she says. "I've never seen her before."

She's lying, and if she was lying to anyone but me, I would appreciate her attempt to keep Madinia safe.

I'm not enough of a bastard to threaten a woman with a child in her arms. But I don't need to. The stablehand doesn't hesitate to tell me which way she went.

"She headed that way," he points north. "She was moving quickly too. Seemed scared."

"And yet you just told someone who is clearly hunting her which way she went."

His mouth drops open and I lean close. "Spread the word. If anyone else comes looking for her, and any cowards such as yourself think to tell them which way she went, I will return. And I will kill you all."

The stablehand nods, his eyes wide. Mounting Fox, I head in the direction he pointed, allowing my instincts to steer me.

It's half an hour before I find her at the market, handing over a few scant coins for horse feed and a few apples.

She looks spooked, her eyes constantly darting. She knows she's being hunted, and yet had to stop to refill her stores.

Dark circles linger beneath her eyes, and she looks like she needs a good meal. Guilt eats at me once more.

Our eyes lock.

Her mouth drops open, her face flushing with fury. Leaving the food behind, she sprints toward her horse, tied at the edge of the market.

Guilt turns to rage.

Fox attempts to break into a trot, but a crowd of women stroll between us, and Madinia makes it onto her horse, spinning her mare around and taking off.

I ride past the stall, holding out my hand. "Give me that."

The man gives me the horse feed and apples, and I take a moment to secure them to Fox. He throws his head, clearly impatient. He feels the thrill of the hunt as much as I do.

"Relax," I tell him. "I know exactly where she's going."

Madinia is clever, and she rides down alleys and hidden side streets. I catch sight of her occasionally as she moves toward the southern gate, breaking into a canter as soon as she makes it past the disinterested guards.

Good. The sooner she is away from anyone who might keep her from me, the better.

"Ready, Fox?"

I don't need to nudge him. I simply lean forward slightly, and he breaks into a gallop.

Madinia casts a look over her shoulder, eyes wide. Her mare is plucky, but the horse doesn't have a chance at outrunning my stallion.

I don't say a word as I ride up beside her. Madinia frees her foot from the stirrup and kicks out at me. Her mare jolts, almost unseating her.

A jolt of fear slices through the thrill. If the mare stumbles and throws her, she could die.

And then I'll never get my grimoire.

That's what I'm concerned about. Not the thought of her head cracking open, her face frozen in death.

Madinia kicks out again, her face tight.

Fresh rage floods my body. "Give up," I yell. "I'm not going anywhere."

She ignores me. Her mare is tiring, and the horse bucks as Fox gets too close. Madinia bounces in the saddle, fear flashing through her eyes.

After three years without riding, her body no longer has the muscle she needs to stay on the horse in these circumstances, and she knows it.

Enough of this.

"Now," I tell Fox.

He lunges toward the mare, and the horse darts to the side. Madinia begins to fall.

I yank her into my arms, scooping her from the horse.

Fox slows, and I haul Madinia from him as her mare stops dead in the center of the road, chest heaving.

Annoyance burns through me as the hellion lashes out with feet and fists.

I grip her arms tightly, keeping her from reaching for the sword strapped to her back. She fights longer than I'd expected—and

THIS VICIOUS DREAM

dirtier—lashing out with her flames. But I'm prepared. I raise a personal ward between us, shielding myself from her fire.

She's powerful, I'll give her that. The little minx's flames eat at my ward, but I'm furious enough that I lean close, growling into her ear.

"You're just tickling me, sweetheart."

She stiffens and then fights with renewed rage.

I heave a sigh. I knew this wasn't going to be easy.

Taking her to the ground, I place my knee on her lower back, holding her in place while I reach for the chains. The metal clinks together and she goes wild, bucking, slamming her head backward, and kicking out with her little foot. I grind my teeth, taking both her wrists in one of mine.

"No, don't," she says, still writhing in an attempt to slip from my grasp. "Please." She twists, turning her head, and when her eyes meet mine, they're wide, stark with fear.

A hint of remorse stabs into my gut. I stand by my first thought when I recognized Madinia Farrow. *No one* should steal her freedom.

And the only time she should beg is when she is lost in pleasure.

But I harden myself to her pleading eyes. This woman would have run to the edge of this continent before allowing me to find my grimoire. The time for reasoning with her is over.

I'm…tired. Tired of the blank space before my life began in that forest. Tired of searching for my vengeance.

"Just…cooperate," I grit out. "I won't mistreat you. You should *know* that, woman."

We stare at each other for a long moment. I'm not sure what she's thinking.

I squeeze my hand.

The click of the cuff around her first wrist seems to echo through the clearing. Madinia bucks, but I have all the leverage here. The next cuff goes on, and the blood drains from her face in a rush.

When I roll her onto her back, she winces as her weight falls onto her arms, and I instantly pull her into a seated position. A lock of her thick hair falls in front of her eyes, and she tosses her head, since she can't even lift her hands to brush it away. I should have cuffed her hands in front of her.

When I tuck the lock of hair behind her ear, she *flinches*.

Something twists in my chest.

Madinia seems to gather herself, rolling her shoulders and lifting her chin. Her eyes meet mine, and they're no longer filled with fear and despair. No, they're filled with a fury so dark and deep, I know better than to attempt to unchain her hands and rechain them in front of her.

This woman would slit my throat if she could. And then she would gleefully burn my body to ash. There must be something wrong with me, because that look in her eye makes me want to crush my mouth to hers.

Instead, I pull her to her feet. "You may not believe me, but I didn't want it to be this way."

"You're not the first man to chain me," she says, and the disdain in her voice carves into me. "At least Kyldare didn't *pretend* to be decent."

Frustration slices through my self-control. She's deliberately provoking me. And yet I can't help but respond. "You compare me to him?"

"Why wouldn't I? Both of you have chained me so you can find a *book*," she says. "The only difference is you don't seem to have a tower to lock me in."

"Because I don't need one," I grind out. "You're going to take me to the grimoire."

"Or?" She asks her tone bored.

I lean close, ignoring the urge to sink my teeth into her

THIS VICIOUS DREAM

throat and prove which of us is in charge here. Even chained, she's still getting under my skin.

"I don't need an *or*. You will do this, because I will *make* you."

She snorts, her eyes firing with grim amusement.

And I can't blame her. The queen's right hand attempted to make her locate the grimoire for three years, going as far as to keep her entombed in her own body within that tower. And still, Kyldare couldn't make her cooperate.

But this is different. That grimoire is *mine*. I'm only trying to take what belongs to me. And this woman is actively attempting to keep it from me.

She is the one in the wrong here. *She* is the villain in this situation. *She* needs to stop looking at me with hurt and rage and betrayal in her eyes before I do something criminally stupid like unchain her.

"Let's go."

Madinia gives me a *you must be stupid* look. I haul her over my shoulder, ignoring her struggles. When I lift her onto my horse, Fox's lips lift back from his teeth.

"I know," I mutter to him. "But the vixen can't be trusted."

I lean over to grab the reins, and Madinia slams her head back into my nose. I curse, my hand flying up, and she attempts to wiggle off Fox's back. He chooses that moment to rear, and she slides back toward me.

"I should have let him dump you on the ground," I mutter, pulling her close. "Keep trying your tricks, witch, and you'll see what happens to those who defy me."

She turns quiet. Some part of me misses the sound of her voice. But only because it might give me a hint as to what she's planning.

My nose aches, and I turn Fox toward Madinia's horse. A sense of disquiet fills me as I catch a glimpse of Madinia's cold expression.

Even now, she is plotting against me.

CHAPTER SEVEN

Madinia

I may not care about much, but even I don't want to watch the dark god destroy this world. So I lead Calysian south from the entrance I used to the city, before heading east and then north.

Neither of us speak. I bury my rage beneath grim determination.

And only one of us is surprised when we stumble upon the troll.

It crashes through the trees, its hulking form towering over us, swiping massive, club-like arms through the air. Just one hit with one of those boat-sized hands, and we're dead.

At least I am. Calysian is likely very difficult to kill. I shoot him a filthy look, which he ignores.

The horses jolt backward, Hope lets out a shriek.

The troll roars, deep and guttural, displaying a row of blunt teeth as it lumbers toward us. Its gray, mottled face is thick with patches of rough fur, and its eyes—small, dull, and deeply set in its oversized head—gleam with territorial fury.

Calysian freezes for half a second, clearly surprised.

I hold up my arms. "Free me so I can defend myself."

THIS VICIOUS DREAM

He gives me a patronizing look. "I'll defend you."

I barely suppress a smile as he jumps from the horse. I slide down, sidling away. Calysian gives me a warning look, but I'm not stupid enough to run.

I have other plans in place.

He ponders the troll, which takes another step, the ground shuddering beneath us.

The troll angles his head, clearly confused when Calysian doesn't retreat. Its beady eyes narrow, and it takes another step, out of the forest.

I slam my eyes shut.

The troll is a male. And it's naked.

It lets out another roar, and I trip backward, falling on my ass. Calysian holds his ground, raising his hands. A strange crackle fills the air, as if lightning is about to strike. The hair stands up on the back of my neck, and I wiggle to my knees, cursing the chains holding my arms behind me.

Calysian turns slightly, and his face is grim, feral. For the first time, he looks truly dangerous. Heat rolls off him. Heat, and something darker.

My stomach churns. He really is a god. To the gods, even the fae are expendable. And hybrids? Our lives would be the equivalent of an ant, carelessly crushed beneath their feet.

And still, even knowing how dangerous he is, how he could ruin this world, ruin *me*...I can't take my eyes off his wide shoulders. I can't stop watching the way he carelessly swings his sword, warming up his wrist.

Clearly, the moment I free myself, I'll need to find a man so I can release some of this tension.

He watches the troll with idle resignation, as if this is a training exercise he wasn't planning to complete today...and now he needs to get it out of the way so he can do something more interesting.

I awkwardly get to my feet, my wrists aching.

"Two lumbering oafs," I muse. "I know which one I'd rather spend my time with."

Calysian sends me a quelling look and I scowl back at him.

The troll lumbers forward once more, and a silver ward appears between them.

Ignoring the memories that itch at the corner of my mind, I keep my gaze on the ward Calysian creates between him and the troll. Even *he* can't hold that kind of ward forever.

The troll leaps, hitting the ward with its face. The sound it makes is somewhere between a howl and a scream so loud, I wish I could slam my hands over my ears.

Calysian keeps the ward in place, and the troll hits it again and again. Calysian winces, the ward flickering, and I smirk.

It's a smart choice, letting the troll wear itself out. It doesn't understand why it can't get to Calysian, and the ward enrages it, distracting it from Calysian as he waits.

The ward flickers once more, until Calysian is forced to drop it. The troll stumbles forward.

Calysian *moves*.

Lunging toward the troll, he thrusts his sword into its thigh. The troll lets out another howl, lashing out with his fist, but Calysian has already leapt back, raising his ward into place once more.

I blink. The entire thing happened within moments, his movements blazingly fast.

I almost feel sorry for the troll as Calysian repeats his technique over and over. By the time the troll slumps to his knees, it's bleeding from both thighs.

"Leave it," I order. The words are out before I can stifle them, and Calysian spares me a single glance.

"You know I can't."

Because the next people who stumble across the troll might be a young family.

I glance away as Calysian takes the troll's head. He stalks

toward me, pausing to wipe his blade on some long grass, and I step backward.

His shirt is painted red, drenched in enough blood that it squelches as he moves. I wrinkle my nose, and he glances down with a sigh.

"Come on then."

With no other choice, I follow him to a nearby stream, attempting to ignore him as he removes his shirt, swirling it through the water before using it to wipe at the blood covering his torso.

Corded muscle. Smooth skin. A light scattering of hair. Several scars, that only serve to highlight his beauty.

Even the way he moves is saturated in predatory confidence. When his eyes lock with mine, I glower at him, careful not to allow him to catch my gaze drifting down.

His mouth twitches, and I turn away.

"Are you thirsty?"

"No."

"Are you sure? I can't have my captive suffering."

"If you cared about my suffering, you'd remove these chains."

"I would if you could be trusted, Madinia." His voice is almost…gentle.

I ignore him, stalking back toward the horses. "I want to ride my own horse."

"No."

I grind my teeth as Calysian follows me, taking my waist and easily hauling me onto his shoulder. With my arms clamped behind my back, I can't even slap at him.

I'm entirely helpless.

The demon horse snaps his teeth at us as we approach, and Calysian tuts at him.

"Why force me to ride with you?" I grind out.

"We both know that riding with your hands tied behind

you would require more abdominal and thigh strength than you currently have. And if your horse spooks, you'll get hurt."

His hands find my waist once more and he transfers me onto the saddle.

My teeth clench at the easy way he maneuvers my body. "Then release me."

"Enough." Calysian's voice hardens and he swings himself up into the saddle behind me.

When he leans forward to take the reins, he smells cool and fresh.

"I hate you."

"Well, sweetheart, I'm currently not too fond of you either."

My eyes burn at the injustice. If I had a sword in my hand, I'd gut him.

Calysian sighs, his warm breath caressing my ear as he turns the horse, leaning over to take Hope's lead rope. "It won't be forever, Madinia. Eventually you'll decide it's not worth the fight."

I snort. Despite our few moments of shared history, it's clear he doesn't understand me at all.

But he will.

And so I lead him toward the Aelstow Forest. I gave him a choice. He chose poorly.

Fifty men. That's what Fliora said. After watching the troll slam into Calysian's ward over and over again, I'm sure he's tired. I'm also sure his drugged sleep against the tree couldn't have been too restful.

Poor baby.

And yet I also know the dark god can kill fifty men without blinking—or at least he could if he'd found his grimoires. Not only will those men provide me the distraction I need to escape, but Calysian will take care of the soldiers in that part of the forest, allowing me to travel north.

Alone.

THIS VICIOUS DREAM

I don't say a word for the next several hours. Calysian attempts to engage me, and I ignore him. At one point, he holds a canteen of water to my mouth.

"Drink," he says warningly. "Or I'll pinch your nose."

Any hint of guilt about potentially leading the man to his death disappears.

If the dark god dies, at least this world will be safe from the threat he presents.

"We'll camp in the forest," he murmurs as we approach, two hours later. My arms ache, and my hands have gone numb. When I don't reply, I can practically hear him brooding behind me.

"The book is mine," he says. "By now, I'm sure you know that. Why would you keep me from something that's *mine*?"

"You must sense the kind of power it holds. Why are *you* searching for it?"

He's quiet for a long moment. Then he shifts in the saddle, his muscular thighs pressing against mine. "I've gone my whole life with this...hole inside me. Can you imagine what it's like to live for centuries, knowing you're missing a part of yourself?"

My heart races. He still has no true concept of what he's searching for. He doesn't know he's looking for three grimoires, or that he's a god.

A hint of pity stirs within me at the lost note in his voice, and I ruthlessly stamp on it. For him to get everything he wants, this world would suffer.

"No reply?" I feel him shake his head. "I knew you were cold, Madinia Farrow, but I didn't think you were cruel."

His words have their intended effect. My chest twists.

But I've lost too much in my life already.

I *am* cold and cruel. But those traits aren't weaknesses. They're strengths. Because they'll prevent the dark god from raging through this world.

We ride in silence some more. Calysian has given up

attempting to speak with me, and when I glance over my shoulder, he's staring into the forest, his eyes narrowed.

Weak sunlight makes it through the canopy above us, dancing across his face. His eyes are cool when he looks at me, and I turn to face forward. The trail narrows until we're surrounded by forest, and I feel the moment Calysian realizes something is wrong. His instincts are sharp, and he pulls both horses to a stop.

But it's too late.

Kyldare's men surround us on three sides. One of them lets an arrow loose, and it thunks against Calysian's ward.

"Idiot!" One of them shouts. "Don't kill the woman."

Calysian is quiet. I can practically feel him sizing up each soldier. He hauls me off the horse and several footspans from the trail, standing in front of me as more arrows slam into his ward.

"You need to free me," I say.

"You know I'll protect you."

I stare at him.

After our encounter with the troll, he has little power left. He may be a god, but without his grimoires, he's only slightly more powerful than the fae.

His ward was flickering when he finally dealt with the beast. And it would take one stray arrow from these men to kill me.

Already, his ward is flickering again. I can't even lift my hands to defend myself.

"Be. Serious."

"No," he growls, turning to face me.

I gaze past him, letting my eyes fill with tears. When my eyes meet his again, his expression turns tortured.

Triumph floods through me.

When I truly cry, tears ravage me. My nose and eyes turn as red as my hair.

But I know what I look like when I *make* myself cry. I learned the technique at court when I was just a girl.

THIS VICIOUS DREAM

My eyes turn wide and liquid. I look young. Innocent.

These tears are a tool. And they've served me well throughout my life. I let my lower lip tremble, biting down on it as if attempting to still the motion. "Calysian. Please. You know what they'll do to me if they take me."

With a sigh, he takes a small leather case from his pocket. Within seconds, he has picked the locks, and I'm free.

I almost grin.

Men.

My power fills my veins in a rush. Unlike the last time these chains came off, I'm not immediately forced into an almost-sleep. This time, the fae iron has allowed my power to build beneath the surface, waiting for my use.

By chaining me, Calysian did me a favor. Of course, he's unlikely to see it that way.

CALYSIAN

Madinia stretches, rolling her shoulders and peering down at her wrists. They're chafed and bruised.

Regret gnaws at me. When this is done, I'll wrap her wrists in a soft cloth before I chain her again. I'll even chain her hands in front of her.

Perhaps then, she'll stop giving me those looks filled with frustration and rage.

The soldiers continue to send their arrows into my ward. When a few of them use their power, the silver shield begins flickering once more.

I hand Madinia her sword and take my own. She's being suspiciously quiet.

Likely because she's terrified.

"I won't let them hurt you," I tell her.

She raises her eyebrow at me, turning to face the soldiers. Several footspans behind us, a massive oak stands, its trunk twice the width of a man.

"Go stand behind that tree," I tell her. "You'll be safe when my ward falls."

Surprisingly, Madinia turns and walks away. Finally, she's being compliant. Perhaps she's seeing things my way.

I slap Fox on the rump. "You know what to do. Take the mare with you."

He doesn't hesitate, barreling into the mare until the horse trots away from us. He'll lead her back later.

My ward flickers, and the soldiers move closer. Madinia steps backward.

"Stay where you are," I snap. "They might circle behind us."

She ignores me, moving even further away.

I glance at her cold, calculating face, and realization slams into me.

She led me here.

She knew these soldiers would be in this location—and that they would be powerful. She knew after our encounter with the troll, my ward would be weakened until I got some rest. She knew I'd have to free her.

We weren't just traveling in circles. Madinia had a clear destination in mind. A clear path. She led us to the monster, knowing it would take most of my power for me to kill it. Which is why she brought us into this territory directly after.

If I'd watched her trick anyone else this way, I might have applauded.

My ward falls, and I swing my sword, beheading the first soldier who rushes toward me. But I can't help but glance at Madinia. She hesitates, as if wondering if I'll truly survive.

Nice of her to show some concern, however unwarranted.

"You truly risked your life to escape me?"

Her eyes turn to flint. "And I'll do it over and over again.

Here's a hint. If you want my cooperation, maybe don't hold me prisoner with Kyldare's chains."

"You used those chains on me first." I glower at her, slamming my fist into another soldier's face. "Be careful, sweetheart, your hypocrisy is showing."

Madinia takes a step backward, flames engulfing the first soldier who launches himself at her. I know this woman, and she's about to flee.

"Don't you dare," I snarl, driving my sword into a soldier's gut and then kicking him off the blade. "If you run, I will find you."

It's a dark promise, but the little witch *winks* before glancing over my shoulder at the soldiers pouring toward us. Her flames shoot high into the air, so hot that no soldiers dare brave the fire. And still I can hear her voice.

"Sounds like a date," she purrs. "But something tells me you're going to miss it."

She disappears into the forest. The soldiers immediately shift their attention from me, most of them sprinting after her.

Cursing, I cut down the soldiers, one after the other. I know I can find Madinia again, but if Kyldare's men get to her first…

I form smaller wards, then use the wards to punch into them, carving holes in their backs as they turn to chase Madinia. I'm well aware that this isn't a normal ability, but I've never been normal.

I slice out again and again, attempting to burn through the worst of my fury. But I'm mostly enraged at myself.

Unchaining Madinia was the stupidest thing I could do. And yet…she might *not* have survived if I'd left her in those chains, unable to use her power. All it would take is one arrow. One soldier to sneak up and steal her away.

But *she* did this. It's humiliating—how easily she

manipulated me. All it took was the despair in her eyes as they flooded, turning as dark as the depths of the ocean.

Eventually, the soldiers thin, turning to run—and no longer following Madinia. Their general is dead, and can no longer roar at them to stay and fight for Kyldare.

So they don't.

Fox wanders close, the mare nowhere to be seen. "You lost her horse, too?"

He ducks his head. If I didn't know better, I'd think he was ashamed.

A flap of wings, and Eamonn lands on a branch above us. He angles his head, and for a moment, there's something so familiar about him, all I can do is stare.

He makes a show of exploring our surroundings. "Where is she?"

"Gone."

"I thought you learned this lesson last time."

I wipe the blade of my sword on one of the dead soldier's shirts. "Clearly I didn't. She's…clever. Wily."

Eamonn makes a strange choking sound and I turn to face him. "Are you…laughing?"

"You have to admit it's kind of…" his voice trails off and he adjusts his wings. "Uh, not at all funny. Not even a little bit. I have to go now."

"Eamonn!"

Too late. He's arrowing into the sky. And the cry he lets loose sounds a lot like a howl of laughter.

CHAPTER EIGHT

Madinia

I TRAVEL FOR ALMOST AN HOUR, GALLOPING THROUGH the forest, careful to stick to the trail. Hope wasn't difficult to find once I escaped Calysian, and I used some shameless bribery to separate her from Fox.

Still, Calysian has likely found Fox by now, and the demon horse is much faster than my mare, which means I need to find somewhere to hide.

But memories are slamming into me. Memories of fighting with him in another forest.

Calysian tuts as he lifts his hand, reinforcing his ward against a sudden barrage of dark power and fae-iron-tipped arrows.

I send more power toward those arrows, and several of them drop straight to the ground. "Feel free to help whenever you get tired of watching."

"There's that sharp little tongue. Do you ever get tired of wielding it?"

I ignore him.

"Ah, silence. Adorable. Tell me, just how did you end up here, Madinia Farrow?"

Grinding my teeth, I ignore him some more. A life-or-death situation, and he wants to chat. Idiot.

The memory fades, and I urge my mare on. Calysian was fighting at my side.

Attempting to protect me.

Even worse?

I tried to protect *him*.

Another memory rises, even as I try to ignore it.

An arrow streaks toward Calysian's unarmed back.

I slash at it with the last of my power—just enough to send it off course.

He turns, one eyebrow arching as the arrow clatters harmlessly to the ground. His lips curl back, baring his teeth in a snarl, irritation sparking in his eyes. "That's another life debt."

"You would have saved yourself anyway," I snap, breathless.

"It doesn't matter. Intention matters," he growls. "Make me owe you again, and I'll kill you myself."

I bare my teeth at him in return. "Try."

His gaze sharpens, narrowing on my face. For a moment, irritation flashes hotter, but then it cools, slipping into that lazy, maddening amusement that makes my skin prickle. I look away, my chest heaving, the effort of staying upright draining what little strength I have left.

"That one was free," I pant, leaning heavily against the tree at my back. The world tilts and spins, my vision darkening at the edges. I can barely feel my fingers, let alone call a spark to them. "You don't owe me anything."

He shakes his head, his tone flat but not unkind. "Wait here."

For once, I don't argue. My legs give out and I slump to the ground, the rough bark of the tree digging into my shoulders. A single muffled yell cuts through the silence, and when I glance up, Calysian is already striding back toward me, wiping blood off his blade as if it's nothing more than spilled wine.

I guide my horse around a fallen tree branch, my heart

slamming into my ribs. Calysian had said he owed me, but then...

"Madinia," he croons, his voice low and smooth. "Look at me."

I draw a long, steadying breath and turn, ignoring the way his tone makes my lungs squeeze, like they're being wound too tight. This man is a predator through and through.

His dark eyes lock on mine, filled with a ruthless calculation that sends a prickle of unease skittering down my spine. He stares at me like I'm nothing more than a pawn on his game board, a piece he's considering putting into play.

"The fates have seen fit to push us together more than once," he says, his voice calm, confident. "One day, when I need you, you will help me with my own goals."

The entitlement dripping from his words makes my stomach churn, anger sparking like a flame catching dry wood. I say nothing, but my silence feels like its own kind of defiance. Still, he seems content, as though he's already decided I'll fall in line with his demands.

He truly is an idiot.

My breath catches as the memory fades. *I* was the one who was an idiot. I'd known he was dangerous and yet I never took him seriously.

Still, how could I have known he was the dark god?

His true nature helps to explain why he's so convinced I will help him. Not just because I know where his grimoire is, but because he believes in *fate*.

I snort, petting Hope's neck as she echoes the noise. I wonder if Calysian will still believe in fate when he learns just who he is and how much was taken from him.

My distraction costs me, and it takes me too long to realize someone's following me. I pull Hope to a stop, both of us panting.

"Come out," I say, my hand a ball of flame.

Calysian wouldn't bother hiding, which means it's likely a soldier—

Huge eyes stare at me, wet with tears. The girl is covered in blood, and she sways dizzily on her horse.

"They're both dead," she says, her voice empty. "Dead."

"Fliora." My lips are numb as I stare at her, and she stares back at me. Devastated. Heartbroken.

She must only have seen ten or eleven winters, and she looks even smaller than when I first met her earlier today, as if some of the life has been sucked from her bones.

Slowly, her head turns, as if she can hear something I can't. Her gray eyes lighten until they're almost white. "He's coming," she says. "I can show you where to hide."

I follow her off the trail to a small clearing. The forest is dense but not impassable, and I dismount, guiding my horse into the undergrowth and willing her to stay still.

"How did you find me? How did you avoid the soldiers?"

"I know this forest well. I used to live near here. With Mama…" her lip trembles, and she gazes up at me.

I wrap one arm around her shoulder and she leans into me. When she stiffens, I release her, and she turns, pointing.

"He's coming."

We're only a few footspans from the trail, close enough that I can still see glimpses of the path through the trees. The sound of a galloping horse cuts through the forest—it has to be Calysian. Blood roars in my ears, but I crouch next to Fliora, steadying my breath.

If he dismounts and searches, he'll find us instantly. But he won't.

Calysian expects me to be fleeing, putting as much distance between myself and this forest as possible. And if not for Fliora, I would be.

The undergrowth around us is thick enough to break up our shapes, to blur the outlines of us and our horses into shadow and brush. Not enough to be impenetrable—but enough that, at full speed, Calysian's gaze will be fixed ahead.

At least I hope it will.

Hooves thunder past, the sound fading into the distance as he rides past us. I let out a long breath and survey the girl in front of me. She's covered in blood, her face white. Now that she's found me, I can see the realization of what happened slowly seeping into her.

"We'll stay here tonight," I say gently. "I stole plenty of food from Calysian."

His horse tried to bite me, but I gave him an apple and he settled down.

I continue talking, telling her about the horse, about the troll, about anything I can think of. My words seem to give her something to focus on as we set up camp. We're close to a small stream, and I hand Fliora soap and one of my spare tunics. "You need to wash. But I'm not sure if it's safe to build a fire."

"It is." Her eyes are dazed. "The soldiers have gone, and the dark god travels north."

I go still. "You know who he is?"

"Mama told me," she whispers. She turns away to wash, and I finish setting up camp. When she returns, she takes a seat next to me on a fallen log.

"Here." I hand her some bread and soft cheese.

"Thank you."

I push more of my power into the fire, adding another branch. "Do you want to tell me what happened?"

Fliora's eyes fill with tears, but she sniffs, holding them back. "They came after you left. Mama was still unwell, and Laysa was helping her to bed. They burst through the door and up the stairs." Her gaze turns stark. "Laysa pushed me into the closet and slammed the door shut. But I could hear."

My chest aches for her. She must have been so scared.

My fault. It's my fault.

"They wanted to know where you went, and Mama wouldn't tell them, so they…they killed Laysa first."

I close my eyes. There's no apology to give, nothing that can ever make up for what she has lost.

"They said they would find you anyway. And then they cut Mama in the stomach. When they left, I ran from the closet." She hangs her head. "I should have come out earlier. I could have helped her." Tears roll down her cheeks and I wrap my arm around her shoulders.

"No." My voice is hoarse. "If you had left the closet, you would have died. Do you understand that? Your mama would have been so upset with you if you didn't stay hidden."

She's quiet for a long time. Eventually, her hunger must begin gnawing at her, because she takes a bite of bread. "Mama said I was to find you."

"What do you mean?"

"Before she died." She places the bread in her lap, gazing into the fire. "She told me to find you."

They left her alive. A sword to the gut is a terrible death. And the bastards left her alive to bleed out in front of her daughter.

Likely I should be telling Fliora that her mother is in a better place, or maybe that her mother didn't suffer. But all I can give her is the same promise I would have wanted. "I'll make them pay."

She nods, and more tears trickle from her eyes. My throat aches, and I suck in a slow breath. Why would her mother have sent her to me? I'm being hunted by hundreds of ruthless men.

What were you thinking, Shaena?

"Do you have other family?"

She nods. "My aunt lives in Ferelith. Where we used to live."

It's on my way, just a few miles from here. "I'll take you to her."

"Mama said I was supposed to stay with you."

"Fliora…the dark god. He's hunting me. He won't hurt

you if he finds you with me, but he's still dangerous. And the soldiers…you know what they'll do to you."

"I can hide you from the dark god. It won't last for long, but it will cloak you from his senses."

I stare at her. "You can do that?"

A tiny smile. "My grandmother could do it too. She protected women from bad men who wanted to find them." Her smile drops. "She died too."

I wince. "I'm sorry. Uh, are you doing it now?"

"Of course." She blinks at me with those huge blue eyes. "Otherwise he would have found you already."

CALYSIAN

I search for Madinia for hours, before I'm finally forced to set up camp in the forest. Fox is tired, and I won't risk him breaking a leg in the dark.

By the time the sun rises, I'm searching once more.

Hours later, I have to admit I have no idea where she is. That strange *knowing* that has pushed me in her direction is gone, my instincts useless.

A deep sense of unease lingers beneath my frustration. The soldiers who escaped will have told their superiors what happened in this forest. Which means more of them will be coming.

Even with her impressive power, Madinia is only one woman. They could take her, could *hide* her, and I'd never find her again.

Or my book. Most importantly, my book.

I've begun dreaming about it. Each time I close my eyes, I can feel it in my hands. I remember enough to know that the last time I touched it, my hands shook with despair. Despair and fury.

I travel through the forest, heading north. It was, after all, the direction we were moving in originally, and I can't imagine Madinia turning back toward the city and the risks waiting for her there.

Although, perhaps that's exactly what she would do.

I grind my teeth, and Fox snorts, likely sensing my frustration. Attempting to understand Madinia is like trying to decode a puzzle without a key.

And yet…

For once, I'm fully engaged with the world. I'm not watching it from afar, shifting pieces into place in an effort to get what I want. I may be *reactive* instead of proactive, but I'm fully alive for the first time in centuries.

It must be because I'm so close to my book.

CHAPTER NINE

Madinia

I'm not surprised Shaena moved her daughter away from Ferelith. The town is small and isolated, tucked away from the bustling trade roads. To reach it, you must first travel through the Aelstow Forest.

Uneven cobblestone streets link weathered stone cottages, which are dotted around the town square. The square itself is little more than a slight widening of the main road with a small market. A lone tavern is positioned next to an inn at the edge of the square.

And yet, the market is filled with laughter and haggling, the people dressed simply as they greet their neighbors.

The people in Kolegrift reminded me of butterflies. In comparison, the people in Ferelith remind me of ducks on a pond, drifting across the water's surface, their robes mostly muted versions of the bright colors I saw in the city.

"I know where my aunt lives," Fliora says. This morning, she warned me that her power was drained, and Calysian will now be able to find us.

But her gift gave us a head start.

She didn't want to come here, insisting that she needed to

stay with me. I managed to convince her that at the very least, we needed to tell her aunt what had happened to her sister. And now I'm hoping the woman will take over from here.

Our horses' hooves clop along the cobblestones as Fliora leads me to a cottage at the edge of town. We tie the horses to a weathered post outside the cottage, and by the time we're finished, a woman has appeared in the doorway.

"Fliora!" Her gaze darts from me to the girl, then lingers on her niece as if checking for damage. "What happened?"

Fliora bursts into tears. I don't blame her. I gently encouraged her to cry if she needed to while we were traveling, but she mostly sniffled, keeping her pain to herself. She's overdue for this.

Her aunt darts out of the house, her movements faster than I would have expected for such a short, curvy woman. But when she throws her arms around Fliora, I catch sight of several sheathed daggers.

Someone has trained her.

I step backward, giving them privacy as Fliora tells her what happened.

The color drains from her face so quickly, I leap forward, ready to catch her if necessary. Her eyes fire as she meets my gaze. "You."

"Uh—"

"You had better come in. The horses will be fine there for a few minutes. We'll untack them after this conversation. My name is Yalanda."

"I'm Madinia."

I follow her into the house, even as my skin prickles with warning. Without Fliora's power hiding me, it's likely Calysian is on his way. And yet, I can't just leave Fliora here without ensuring she will be safe. Not after the way I got her mother killed.

"Sit," Yalanda bustles around the tiny kitchen, gesturing for both of us to sit at the small table near the window, its surface blistered and worn but glistening faintly with fresh oil. A bright woolen cloth lies draped across the center of the table, a glass jar of wildflowers brightening the space.

The room may be sparse, but it's still filled with small personal touches—a crooked shelf of books, a string of dried herbs hanging above the table, a collection of handmade pottery in soothing blues and grays.

But it's the small table in the far corner I'm most interested in. Kyldare's witch owned many of those same tools, would pour her dark tonics into vials that looked just like those sitting out in the open in this small, cheerful kitchen.

My attention lingers on the tiny white petals sitting in a neat pile next to those vials. Breathtakingly rare and shockingly expensive, blightflower petals are lethal in large doses. In small doses and when brewed with several other ingredients to make a tonic, they allow the drinker to see their past lives.

"I'll make tea," Yalanda says. She wipes her eyes as she moves to the cupboard, and I don't have it in me to decline, even as I keep my gaze on the blightflower petals, the candles, the ritual knives, the vials.

Yalanda places cups in front of both of us, adding a third for herself before pressing a kiss to Fliora's forehead and taking a seat next to me.

She follows my gaze. "Our grandmother was a witch. She passed some of her secrets down to us." Her eyes meet mine once more. "He's not here yet. The one who searches for you."

"How do you know about him?"

Yalanda sighs. "Shaena was not the only seer in the family. Her gift...it is...*was* much greater than mine. Which has allowed me to have a mostly normal life. But both of us had visions of this time. And—" her voice cuts off and she flicks a glance at Fliora, who is staring at her wide-eyed. "Perhaps this is a discussion for another time."

"No," Fliora's chin sticks out.

Yalanda studies her for a long moment, and then sighs again. "Very well. Shaena had a vision when she was younger, not long after Fliora was born. She learned about the grimoires, the dark god, and Vicana's plans to use any grimoires she could find. My sister knew you would find her, and that it would lead to her death."

I force myself to look at Fliora. She's staring down at the table, her shoulders shaking. I open my mouth, but nothing comes out.

Yalanda follows my gaze, her eyes sparkling with her own tears. When she turns back to me, her mouth trembles, but she wipes at her eyes.

"While you were trapped, the queen had her people hunting for any mention of you, your friends, and your ship. She knows your exact path to this continent, and each place the ship docked. Her men have bribed and tortured for three years to learn where and when you left the ship, and they are close to finding the first grimoire. Even now, they are on the way to its location."

Fucking Vicana. Why is it that people in power are never content with what they have? They're like leeches, growing fat and swollen and still needing *more*.

"The dark god placed one grimoire on each continent," she says.

I know what she's implying. That I should be the one to protect *all* of the grimoires. Slowly, I get to my feet. "Thank you for your time."

Her hands tighten around her cup. "What would your friends say if they knew you were choosing to ignore such a threat?"

Hundreds of men have withered at the look I give her, and yet she merely raises an eyebrow.

I clench my teeth. "My *friends* are safely on another continent, enjoying their lives."

The words come out evenly, without inflection. But I feel part of my soul crack, my blood turning to ice.

I was foolish to imagine they would come for me. Foolish to hope. Whatever friendship we had, it ended the moment I left that continent. Or perhaps it was never a true friendship, merely an alliance formed only due to impending war.

She gives me an impatient look. "And so you would let this continent fall?"

No. And not just because I won't watch the people here suffer. But because Vicana took three years of my life. I won't let her get her hands on the grimoire. And I won't rest until she's dead.

She nods at whatever she sees on my face. "There you go. Find the grimoires. Protect them. Just don't let them *in* or you will become a worse threat than the dark god."

I know what she's saying. I miss the dark power, miss the way it made me feel.

Powerful. Like I'd been wrapped in vengeance.

Yalanda slowly turns her head, her eyes darkening. "He's here."

MADINIA

Calysian strides toward the house, his long legs devouring the ground, his expression oddly resigned. When I step out to meet him, surprise flickers in his dark eyes.

He was expecting me to run.

We stare at each other in silence for a moment that seems to stretch on for years.

"You left me to die again."

I give him a humorless smile. "And yet you're still here."

"I won't leave you alone," he vows, and I can hear the truth in his words. "I'll continue to follow you for years, if that's what it takes."

"I'll kill you."

Calysian gives me a patronizing smirk and I grind my teeth, stalking toward my horse. He steps in front of me.

"Enough. I've been watching you closely. I've watched the way you bite down on the words you almost say. The way you open your mouth and then slam it closed. The way your eyes search me as if looking for something. You know who I am, Madinia Farrow. It's why you continue to run. Why you won't work with me. You will tell me."

"Or what?"

He frowns. "Or what?"

"Threats need an *or what*. That's why they're threats."

Frustration flickers across his face. "You understand what it is like to lose memories. To lose parts of yourself. And yet you are already finding yourself again. I have been this way for centuries, continually scheming and searching to find *something*. Now I know it's a book. A book you have knowledge of. I know you weren't the one who stole it from me. You're far too young. Did someone in your family take it? An ancestor?"

I heave a sigh. At some point, Calysian is going to learn who he is. It seems inevitable at this point.

"Madinia?"

"I'm thinking."

His dimple appears. "Then by all means, continue."

It's difficult for me to imagine this man turning truly evil. But I can't ignore the life I've lived, and the men I've known.

When given a chance to conquer and enslave, most men will take it and indulge their vices.

But...I knew other men on another continent who fought for peace. Men who protected their women with everything they had, refusing to betray them.

I study the man—the *god*—in front of me. His humanity

is a skin he has been forced to wear, but the reality of him is evident in the occasional dark glint in his eyes. He covers it with easy smiles and warm humor, but if he gets the first grimoire, he will crave the other two.

I turn and pace. Calysian watches me, his eyes turning hard.

Vicana has sent Kyldare after the grimoire. I'd like to think I can get there before him, take it, and run, but…

I blow out a breath, gazing down at my body. Three years without training has eaten away at my muscle. I have little stamina, and even with my power, I can't take out an entire regiment alone.

But Calysian can. As he recently proved.

Sometimes in life, there are no good choices. Sometimes, it's about making the choice with the least pain *now* and dealing with the consequences later.

I won't let Vicana bring the same dark fate to this continent that Regner brought to ours.

"Fine," I say, and Calysian's eyes darken with triumph. I glance behind me at the cottage. "But not here."

CALYSIAN

The dark god.

According to Madinia, I'm the dark god.

If not for the way the color has drained from her face, and the way she studies me from beneath her lashes—as if waiting for me to suddenly lash out—I might believe she was playing some kind of trick.

And yet, she's not.

Beneath my shock, there's a strange kind of certainty. That certainty is tinged with an ancient rage.

Hundreds of years spent wandering this world. The ones who did this to me will *pay*.

Madinia gives me a wary look and I open the door to the tavern. The building leans slightly to the right, as if even the foundation has given up.

"Three grimoires," I say.

She nods, scanning the tavern. A lone man with a long gray beard sways in his seat near the fire, several empty glasses in front of him.

Striding across scuffed, worn planks, Madinia chooses a table next to the wall. Her eyes are shadowed, her fiery hair tangled, and she looks like she hasn't slept properly for days.

Because she was busy running from me.

After she tricked me.

I scowl at her, lowering myself into the rickety chair. "And you're suddenly going to help me. Why?"

The disheveled man gets too close as he walks past, leaning down to whisper some filth in Madinia's ear. She pulls her knife, but I'm already moving. I slam my fist into his face with a satisfying thud, the sting in my knuckles a welcome distraction.

The man stumbles away, falling onto an empty table.

"Garit," a voice calls. "You know better than that. Out."

The man staggers toward the door.

I take my seat, and Madinia gives me a cool look, tucking her knife away. "A year before I landed on this continent, Vicana ordered an entire village slaughtered—men, women, and children—because some of them had given aid to Telanthris citizens fleeing Vicana's invasions. They did nothing but offer food and water to innocent people, and Vicana killed them for it."

My hand fists on the table between us. Madinia glances at it before meeting my eyes once more. "Someone who can commit that kind of brutality against her own people without the grimoire would become even more of a monster with it.

THIS VICIOUS DREAM

According to the seer I spoke to, Vicana now knows where the grimoire is. Which means we have to beat Kyldare to it."

"Because you'd rather risk giving the grimoire to me than to Vicana."

A sharp nod, even as she glances away. Madinia has made her choice, but she's not happy about it.

Because she's convinced I will destroy this world.

I grind my teeth. "Did it ever occur to you that perhaps I'm *not* evil?"

She looks down her nose at me. "You forget, I've felt the power in that grimoire. I've *used* the power in that grimoire. And even from a distance, I could feel it…changing me."

Yet she has no choice. Either I take back my own power, or she watches Vicana destroy this continent.

I lean back in my seat. "This is no longer your problem. Tell me where the grimoire is, and you can go about your life."

She examines her nails. "I don't think so."

I clench my teeth until my jaw aches. Mules could take lessons in stubbornness from this woman. "Why?"

"Because I have a feeling you'll begin to change as you get closer to the grimoire. As it calls to you. And if I sense you're about to become a true threat, I'll allow Kyldare to take it instead."

I gape at her. "You'll *what*?"

She shrugs one shoulder. "I can steal it back from Vicana. Even if it takes years, I'll find a way to take the grimoire and hide it again. But if you take it, there's a chance you would destroy the world, Calpharos."

My fists clench. "Don't call me that."

A hint of resigned amusement flickers through her eyes, but it's quickly gone.

Waving down a serving girl, I order for both of us. Madinia allows it, her gaze on the fire, eyes empty.

"We've stabled the horses," I mutter. "We may as well spend the night at the inn next door."

She shakes her head. "We can't risk it. We should continue to move."

"Why don't you tell me which direction we're traveling, and I'll determine that?"

Taking a map from my pocket, I unfold it, placing it on the table between us. She gives me that stubborn look again. The one that makes my gaze drop to her lips.

"You know we need to work together," I remind her.

With a sigh, she brushes one finger over the map. "We're traveling west."

There are only a few places she could have hidden the grimoire that could have ensured no one would find it for so many years. I study the map, and she leans back in her chair, crossing her arms.

"And you wonder why I won't tell you where it is. Already you're attempting to find it without me."

"It's *mine*," I grind out.

"And it has already cost countless lives. Because Regner found one of *your* grimoires and used it to fuel his madness."

She's placing the blame at my feet, and I want to kick it away. But...I can't.

I have no memory of the man I was—the man who poured everything into three grimoires and let them loose on this world. Knowing what I *do* know of myself, I would have planned to find them immediately.

But I didn't. Instead, a tyrant king found one. And that's just the first grimoire. Madinia knows nothing of the second or third. Have they also caused the same pain and suffering on other continents? Centuries from now, will humans and hybrids and fae curse my name?

It's...confronting, learning that *I* am the threat, even if I have no memory of such a life. I do remember the war, though.

THIS VICIOUS DREAM

I remember this woman, fleeing with villagers through a forest, ready to sacrifice her own life in order to buy innocents just a few more seconds. She lost people to Regner's evil. People she cared about. Because of me.

Her face is pale as she pokes at her food, and my stomach churns as I push my own plate away.

I know nothing of her family—she has never spoken of them in my presence. But this is a woman who has known great loss. Most recently, she lost three years of her life, trapped in her body. Because of *my* grimoire.

Who might Madinia Farrow have been if not for *me*? What kind of life might she have enjoyed?

After everything she has lived through, most people would have saved themselves. Would have handed the grimoire to Kyldare, boarded a ship, and found a quiet life somewhere far from this place.

But she didn't. She fought for people who will never know how much she sacrificed for them. And now she's still fighting.

"Madinia."

Her eyes meet mine, and they're chillingly blank. This woman is such a force of nature, it's almost easy for me to forget how fragile she was just days ago.

I reach for her hand, and she allows it, a hint of life returning to her eyes. "I am no longer that man. I've had centuries walking through this world, living as a mortal. I need you to trust that I will not destroy it."

She studies my face. After a long moment, she nods.

"Fine. We'll work together."

"Fine."

I ignore the voice whispering in my head. The one urging me to become whole once more. The one whispering that if Madinia stands between me and my full recovery, she will be the first to die.

CHAPTER TEN

Madinia

I HAVE LITTLE TIME TO CONSIDER WHETHER TELLING Calysian the truth about the grimoire—and his past—was the smartest decision. We're up with the sun, Calysian waiting while I say goodbye to Fliora. Her thin arms circle my waist and squeeze tight, even as I fight not to drop to my knees and beg her forgiveness for everything I've cost her.

"He's very handsome," she whispers, and Calysian pretends not to hear, although I catch his smile.

"Looks aren't everything," I mutter.

"But they don't hurt," Yalanda appears, placing a hand on her niece's shoulder. She gives Calysian an appraising look that tells me she knows who he is. And something dark and malevolent flickers through her eyes—so quickly, I wonder if I imagined it.

"When all this is done, I hope you find a handsome man of your own," she tells me. "One who will give you a quiet life with laughter and joy."

The undertone is clear but unnecessary. She's warning me away from the dark god. As if I would be that stupid.

THIS VICIOUS DREAM

I give her a nod. "I don't need a man for that life," I say aloud.

She smiles at me. "No. You don't." She hands me a canvas bag. "Some clothes and other supplies."

"Thank you."

Fliora hugs me again. When she finally pulls away, tears are rolling down her cheeks. "Will you visit?"

"You want me to?"

She nods, and my chest tightens. "Yes. When all of this is done, I'll visit."

Her eyes suddenly lighten, her head tilting unnaturally. "You need to take the horses."

I stare at her. "We are."

"Not now. Later. When you think you shouldn't take them, you're wrong. They have to go too." Her eyes clear, and she frowns.

"A hint of your mother's sight," Yalanda murmurs. "A gift."

My eyes are hot as Calysian and I leave Ferelith behind, and neither of us talk, so it takes me a couple of hours to realize he's in a dark mood. When I finally glance at him, he's practically seething, his jaw tight.

"What's wrong with you?"

His knuckles turn white as he tightens his grip on his reins, but he still doesn't look at me. The air around me turns cold, and I shiver. "A quiet life with laughter and joy? That's what she wished for you? With an imaginary handsome man to provide it for you?"

"Uh—"

"You would want such a life?"

"A joy-filled life?" I stare at him. "It sounds a lot better than the life I've lived so far."

He nudges Fox into a trot. "Forget it. We need to move faster."

Hope picks up her pace without me needing to cue her,

and I scowl at Calysian. "Is this the grimoire? Is it already changing you?"

His brows slam down. "No."

The path narrows, and I roll my eyes, falling behind him. I know enough from studying the map to tell we'll soon be leaving Sylvarin and reaching disputed territory.

To many people, the territory west of the Lacana Mountains isn't disputed at all—the mountains providing a clear border between the kingdoms of Sylvarin and Telanthris. But to Vicana, the territory is, and always has been, part of Sylvarin.

What little I know about the territory is thanks to Lonn. He would read aloud from history books occasionally while we ate lunch on the ship. Together, we'd spoken of the places we wanted to go. The things we wanted to see.

And if I choose to believe Kyldare, Lonn is dead.

Grief carves a hole in my chest, and for a moment I can't breathe. Lonn, with his infrequent yet wide smile. Lonn with his sly teasing and love for the early morning hours. Lonn, who insisted I learn to fight with knives when he noticed my overreliance on my sword.

My bones ache. If Daharak and her pirates are truly dead, I'm responsible. Not to mention, I already cost Fliora two people she loves—one of them her mother.

I'd witnessed how much she adored her mother when she dropped to her knees beside her, concern etched on her face.

"Madinia." Calysian's voice is rough. The path widened at some point, and he has slowed, drawing up beside me. His brow creases and I blink away the hot tears that have filled my eyes.

"I'm fine."

"What is it?"

"Nothing."

He scowls at me. "I may be able to help you."

I let out a bitter laugh. "I went to the seer to find out how

THIS VICIOUS DREAM

to hide from you and everyone else looking for the grimoire. And by doing so, I cost Fliora's mother her life."

"That wasn't your fault. Surely you can understand that."

I clamp my mouth shut. I'm not talking about this with him.

With a sigh, he turns his attention back to the trail and begins a steady climb toward the pass that will lead us into Telanthris. Beneath us, packed dirt gives way to loose stone, while the air grows thinner. Within hours, the rocky path begins winding through jagged cliffs dusted with snow.

The path narrows, winding through huge rock formations. I pull the hood of Calysian's cloak over my head, hunching my shoulders against the biting wind. By the time we crest the ride, my body aches from leaning slightly forward in the saddle in an effort to help Hope navigate the incline.

Calysian nudges Fox forward, and we round a bend. The air rushes out of my lungs in a whoosh.

From here, the kingdom of Telanthris stretches before us, edges blurred by the cloudy haze clinging to the valley. To the south, the jagged peaks of mountains loom, flanks streaked with veins of snow.

Closer to the mountain, the soil darkens, pockmarked with rocky outcrops and winding crevices. Telanthris unfurls beyond that, distant treetops glinting in the afternoon sun, a river winding through sprawling plains and dense forest.

Below us, the disputed territory is a patchwork of muted browns and greens. It's easy to see the effect Vicana has had here.

The soil is churned and raw. Fields that might have once blossomed are barren, the earth bruised and pitted with makeshift fortifications and abandoned trenches. Across the land, small villages sit in clumps, smoke rising in thin columns, while a few broken fences mark where livestock once grazed. Now, only scattered tracks remain.

Calysian gestures at the trail in front of us. "We're about to enter the disputed territory."

"What do I need to know?"

He studies my face, and I'm not sure what those dark eyes see, but he doesn't attempt any more empty platitudes. "I last visited a few years ago after I returned to this continent. Even then, it was dangerous. And it has only gotten worse. Vicana wants the land, and she refuses to give it up."

"Why does she want it so badly?"

"She insists it was once part of Sylvarin. Apparently, an ancient text has been handed down within Sylvarin for centuries, laying claim to the territory."

"You think she's lying."

A languid shrug. "Centuries ago, I wandered this continent, before I traveled to yours. And I know the land here is rich in natural resources. As much as Vicana insists it is her divine mandate to claim the land, I find it too coincidental that it's also fertile farmland—which Vicana is in desperate need of to sustain her population. She is also finding it difficult to provide her army with weapons, since Dracmire won't trade with her."

"Dracmire?"

"Her neighbor to the south."

Understanding hits me. "Because they're worried she will try to invade."

He nods. "The disputed territory is also home to veins of iron ore that Vicana can't access from her side of the mountain range."

"Does she have access to risplite?"

Another sharp nod, and my stomach churns. Risplite is a mineral that turns iron into fae iron. The chains Kyldare used to drain my power—which Calysian is likely still carrying now—were infused with fae iron.

Calysian flicks a glance my way. "One of Vicana's scouts

THIS VICIOUS DREAM

discovered the iron a few decades ago, which—coincidentally—was when the ancient text was found."

I roll my eyes. "The text claiming the territory was always Sylvarin's."

"Yes. Telanthris would have ignored the iron. They have everything they need. But as Sylvarin began to push into their kingdom, they began using the iron—and their own stores of risplite to make weapons to defend themselves."

Calysian scans the territory, but it's as if he doesn't truly see it. And I'm sure his mind is on the grimoire. Even as he spoke of Vicana's evil, his voice was empty, as if he was recounting something of little meaning.

My stomach clenches. It's a tiny glimpse of who he will be when he gets his grimoires.

He urges his horse on, and we travel down into the scrub, our horses carefully picking their way through loose rocks and stones. At one point, we both dismount, leading them down the narrow trail. The wind bites at my face, sharp and cold. I pull Calysian's cloak even tighter around my shoulders, and he smirks at me. Earlier, I offered him the cloak back, but he merely chucked me under the chin and told me I needed it more than him.

An hour later, Fox throws a shoe. Calysian's expression is dark as he wraps Fox's hoof in leather. The ground is rough and rocky, and if we keep riding, the stallion risks becoming lame. "We need a farrier."

The sun will go down in a few hours. Which means we don't have time to make it through the disputed territory. "We'll have to stop at one of the villages."

Except the first few villages are nothing but charred remains. What were once homes are now razed and abandoned.

The next villages are flying Vicana's flag.

"Invaders," Calysian says when I ask. "Which means

soldiers. Soldiers who have likely been given your description. Cover that distinctive hair of yours."

I do as he says, tucking my hair out of sight. The next village we come to is heavily guarded by Vicana's soldiers. They've rebuilt the village, but the signs of occupation remain—charred beams in half-mended homes, a market square too quiet for this time of day. A few villagers move with downcast eyes, while a hunched old man presses a basket of apples into a soldier's waiting hands with a forced smile, his fingers trembling.

A muscle ticks in Calysian's jaw as he glances between me and the few buildings scattered before us, his gaze lingering on the lone tavern at the edge of the village.

"You can wait at the tavern," he says, nodding toward the squat, lopsided structure. "Rest, and I'll go to the farrier."

I sweep my gaze over the farrier's shop at the other end of the village. It's one of the sturdier buildings, wide doors flung open to let the heat escape. A soldier leans against the entrance, talking idly with the blacksmith—his helmet stamped with Vicana's seal. Another soldier examines a row of horses in the small paddock next door.

Vicana's people have taken control of the farrier, just as they've taken everything else.

"No." My voice is thready, and Calysian pauses. Whatever he sees on my face makes his brows lower.

Fury mingles with a kind of dull grief in my chest. "I won't stay here. Not for one minute."

"Madinia."

"I won't give them a single copper."

He studies me like I'm a puzzle he's trying to solve. I don't blame him. I just traveled through Vicana's kingdom, spending what little coin I had. And yet, the thought of voluntarily interacting with the same people who destroyed the villages we just passed...

I can't do it.

"The hybrid kingdom." Calysian's voice turns gentle. "This isn't the same."

"No. It's worse. We lost the connection to our kingdom. Many of us didn't even know it existed before the war. But these people have watched their own homes be taken from them. The next village." My voice is hoarse. "Please."

The next village isn't just home to soldiers—it's worse. Sylvarins have moved in, claiming the Telanthris people's homes as their own.

The sight makes my blood hot, and I lock my gaze on Calysian's broad shoulders as we ride past. Which is why I see the moment he stiffens.

I duck.

An arrow slices through the air, narrowly missing my head.

Calysian is already moving, wrenching Fox around and closing the ground between us. I scan our surroundings, my pulse hammering. Where did the arrow come from? How many of them are there?

We could be surrounded.

"Dismount," Calysian orders, letting Fox free.

I know it's the smart move—we're easy targets on horseback. And yet I feel even more exposed on foot.

Calysian is at my side an instant later, yanking me to the right, his ward forming between us. The next arrow drops harmlessly to the ground.

"We've been recognized," he snarls.

A flicker of movement. A soldier, half-hidden behind a thin tree. Our eyes lock, and he bolts left. I track him as he ducks behind the ruins of what was once someone's home.

"One of Kyldare's men." I grind my teeth. "We can't let him report back."

Calysian crouches next to me. "I thought Kyldare wanted you alive."

I gesture at the solider as he peers around the crumbling wall. "I guess he didn't get the message."

I let my flames free. They roar toward him—licking hungrily at the rotten wood to his left. But the soldier bares his teeth, holding up his hand.

The wind shifts. My fire recoils, leaping back toward me. My heart jolts and I smother the flames. But the soldier is already fleeing.

To my left, Calysian pulls the chains from his saddlebag. He lunges after the fae—then hesitates.

I let out an impatient hiss. "Go!"

"There could be more of them."

"Go!" I demand again.

His jaw tightens, but he vanishes into the scrubland. I wait, my muscles coiled, but no more arrows slice through the air. No one else attacks.

I don't know how long the soldier has been tracking us, but when Calysian finally returns, my fists are clenched so tight, my nails bite into my palms.

"He was definitely fae," he says grimly and I wince.

While hybrids have only power, fae possess one dominant ability—along with many other powers.

Calysian must be following my thoughts, because he gives me a nod. "The wind wasn't his only power. He somehow managed to disappear. It's likely why he was able to hide his presence from us."

We collect the horses in silence, and Calysian shoves the chains back into his saddlebag.

I don't point out that he shouldn't have hesitated.

He doesn't point out that he was trying to keep me safe.

The next village we come to is still in Telanthris hands. The sun has already set, and Calysian cuts his eyes to me. "I'll find a farrier and stables. You find somewhere for us to spend the night."

Nodding, I leave my horse with him, then walk through the tiny village square. Unsurprisingly, there is only one inn—a tiny cottage with only three rooms to rent.

"I've only got one room free," the innkeeper says.

Sighing, I hand over a few coins. "We'll take it."

"Leave your clothes outside your door, and I'll ensure they're cleaned."

"Thank you."

There's no hot water, but at least the water is clean, and I crouch in the bath, splashing it over myself as I shiver. Each time I close my eyes, I see the Telanthris villages—little more than rubble. And I see the others—taken by the Sylvarins. If it came down to it, I would rather see my home destroyed than see my enemies living in it, taking my things for themselves, letting their children play on the graves of my neighbors.

By the time Calysian returns, I'm standing in the middle of the room, wrapped in a towel as I search my canvas bag for my last clean tunic.

He shuts the door behind him with more force than necessary and I glower over my shoulder at him. "Turn around."

"What happened to you?" His gaze is stuck to the swathe of bare skin my towel doesn't cover.

I can feel my cheeks heat, and I glance away. "I don't want to talk about it."

"I don't care," he declares with that arrogance I loathe. "You will tell me."

My gut roils. I haven't seen the ruin of my back. But I've felt the roughened skin. And Kyldare made sure to describe just how ugly it is. There's not an inch left unscarred.

He enjoyed using his whip.

"Madinia."

"Why?"

"So I can kill whoever hurt you."

I open my mouth, his words stealing whatever I was about

to say. It has been a long, long time since anyone cared about my pain.

"Thank you for the offer. But this debt is mine to collect."

His eyes fire, and I turn, taking a step closer. His gaze doesn't drift down to the towel I'm clutching, but his fists clench. "Tell me."

He's not going to let this go. I sigh. "Did you think the tower was Kyldare's first option? He needed to torture me enough to cause unthinkable agony but not enough to break my mind. A delicate balance."

Calysian suddenly looks as if he is the one who was tortured. "And you would have killed him that day. If I hadn't arrived. You were planning to make him pay."

"Yes."

A muscle twitches in his jaw. "I'm sorry."

The words are stark, unexpected. I stare at him, too shocked to revel in them.

"I'll kill him for you," he says.

I shrug. "Why would you care? You chained me. You'd chain me again if you thought I was planning to leave."

He rears back as if I've hit him. "I would never have hurt you. And if you don't know that by now, you don't know me at all." Turning, he storms out of the room.

My gut twists, and I instantly block out his words. I don't have time for his hysterics, but at least he left his bag. I find one of his shirts and pull it on, braiding my hair while I wait for our meal.

Calysian returns with the food, which is simple but hearty—some kind of pastry with shredded meat and vegetables. "The farrier has a stable, and he said he'll take care of Fox's shoe first thing in the morning."

I nod, taking another huge bite.

We eat in silence and when we're done, Calysian leaves the tray outside, along with his own clothes. He narrows his eyes when he notices I've helped myself to his shirt, but doesn't say a word.

There's no fireplace, and I curl into a ball, shivering while Calysian bathes. When he slides into the bed, my eyes pop open.

"What are you doing?"

"Sleeping. You should try it."

The brute sprawls over most of the bed, forcing me to lay far too close to him or risk rolling off the edge of the mattress.

Fine. He may as well be good for something. I wiggle my toes between his calves.

He jolts. Curses. "You believe those blocks of ice will force me from this bed? You must be jesting."

The man radiates heat like a furnace, and he thinks to deprive me of it? I don't think so.

Smirking, I wedge my toes in even further and close my eyes. "Goodnight."

CHAPTER ELEVEN

Madinia

I'm warm. So, so warm. And comfortable. It's been a long time since I've been this comfortable, and I nestle closer to the heat, surrounding myself with it.

Warm, hard heat.

That heat spreads to my core, a slow blooming that makes me sigh. My nipples harden, and I shift to relieve the ache.

Someone groans, low and rough.

For the first time in years, I feel…safe. Relaxed.

I shift once more, nestling my face against warm skin.

"Beautiful woman, you need to wake up."

I let out a sigh, my eyes heavy.

And then I'm on my back, my eyelids flying open as Calysian glowers down at me.

He's leaning over my body, his mouth inches from mine. When he shifts, I feel him, hard and thick and hot between my thighs.

"What—"

"Playing with me, Madinia?" he purrs. "Using your wiles on me again?"

I blink up at him. "Again?"

THIS VICIOUS DREAM

"You know exactly what you did in that forest, you little witch."

It takes me a moment to understand what he's talking about.

Oh.

Convincing him to unchain me. Not to mention, I chained him first.

I smirk. "You made it too easy."

A growl, and then his mouth is even closer.

"Don't you dare," I snap.

He smiles. "Are you sure, sweetheart? You're giving me mixed messages."

I freeze, stilling the roll of my hips and unclenching my fingers from where they've buried themselves in his hair.

Gods, I was grinding against him.

"I'm sure." My voice is hoarse, and he gives me a knowing look as he rolls away.

I don't mourn the loss of that huge body above me. Not at all.

It has been a long, long time since I was last with a man in that way. *That* man was rough with his hands and uninterested in my pleasure. He left with me an ache between my thighs and a heavy sense of disappointment.

If I'm honest, the disappointment wasn't unexpected. Not once has a man ever lived up to my expectations.

But Calysian…

I've seen the looks women give him. They scan him from head to toe, taking in the predatory look in his eyes, the roll of his muscles as he moves. When women look at him, they think of sex. Hot, dangerous sex.

He might not just live up to my expectations. He might exceed them.

"I'm going to the farrier. I'll meet you when I'm done."

113

Calysian shoves his shirt over his head, pushes his feet into his boots, and stalks out the door.

I shake my head. I'm not sure why he's suddenly so emotional. Perhaps he's worried about Fox.

The innkeeper brings our clothes upstairs and I shove them into our bags, tucking Calysian's shirt into my own satchel. *Not* because it smells like him. He simply has more clothes than I do, and I need something to sleep in.

When I'm finished, I haul the bags downstairs, taking a seat in the tiny dining room where the innkeeper is serving breakfast.

Her face is pale and drawn, and her hand trembles when she pours my water.

"What's wrong?"

She swallows. "All is well. You'll be wanting to get on your way soon though."

"Why?"

"Our spies say Vicana's soldiers are on their way."

I go still. "What do you mean?"

She gives me a trembling smile. "They came just a few months ago, and we fought them off. They killed three children and vowed to return. I'm sure they will bring more men with them this time."

"Why does your king not help you?"

"I believe he considers this territory a lost cause. He sent soldiers, but only to protect the mines. He has suggested we *leave*. So the soldiers can focus on keeping the iron out of Vicana's hands."

Fury begins to burn in my gut, and she gives me a stiff nod.

"Four centuries we've lived here, farming the land." She points out the window to a small, weathered house. "I was born in that house behind you, as was my mother and her mother before her. We're simple people. We don't matter to the king."

I study the house. There are clear signs that Vicana's soldiers were determined to cause as much destruction as possible during their last visit. The roof has collapsed, letting in the elements. And it's evident from the scorch marks that the collapse wasn't natural.

The innkeeper turns back to face me, and her eyes are wet. Lifting a hand, she wipes at them impatiently. A child toddles into the room, and the innkeeper transforms in front of my eyes, the way I've seen mothers tuck away their grief and pain countless times across four kingdoms. The deep line between her eyebrows smooths, and she wipes the last tear, pasting a smile onto her face.

"Good morning my darling," she says as a child runs to her, wrapping his arms around her leg. She hoists him up, balancing him on one hip, and he wraps his arms around her neck, nuzzling into the gap between head and shoulder. "The children are scared," she says grimly, beginning to sway slowly from side to side, her hand stroking down the boy's tiny back. "Who could blame them?"

Calysian strides into the room, and the innkeeper turns to murmur to the boy.

"Fox is ready." Calysian follows my gaze to the houses outside, but it's as if he's merely collecting information, and not as if he actually sees it. When I don't move, he raises one eyebrow. "Madinia."

"Vicana's men are going to ride through here today and kill anyone who hasn't left."

He frowns. "Then these people need to leave."

"This is their home." He stares at me and I throw my hands in the air. "Clearly, I'm talking to the wrong person. I'll ride back into Sylvarin and hire some mercenaries."

Calysian gives me an affronted look. "You will not. Why should I care about these kinds of problems?"

Once, he did. Once, he fought with me to keep hybrids safe. The closer he gets to the grimoire, the more it dulls his humanity. I saw it in the way he spoke about Vicana's activities in the disputed territory, and in the cool, remote way his eyes drifted past the destruction as if he didn't truly see it. And yet I'm supposed to believe it won't make him a monster?

I level him with a hard stare. "You want me to trust you enough to lead you to the grimoire?"

His voice turns cold. "You know I do, and you agreed to do exactly that."

I continue as if he hasn't spoken. "Then I need you to care about *these kinds of problems*."

"Why?"

"Because only one of us can be emotionally stunted, cynical, and detached. And I've got that covered." I give him a humorless smile.

He ponders me. "That's remarkably self-aware of you."

"Are you going to help them or not? And remember, you have to actually *care*."

Calysian gives me an indulgent smirk—the one that makes it clear he finds me adorable. It's the kind of look he knows will irritate me.

It works. I barely suppress a snarl, and Calysian's smirk widens. He's pleased with himself.

Across the room, the innkeeper watches us, hope splashed across her face.

Calysian glances at her, and then back to me. With a roll of his eyes, he saunters out of the inn. I watch as he stands, feet spread, his hand shading his eyes from the sun as he scans the tiny village.

I let out a long breath.

The future is fluid. I refuse to believe Calysian is destined to burn down this world during his revenge. Maybe…maybe I can make him care about this world and the people in it. Maybe that will be enough to keep this world safe from his inevitable rage.

Or maybe I'm being remarkably naïve.

THIS VICIOUS DREAM

At the very least, we can help these people and make Vicana's soldiers think twice before they attempt to take the next village.

For now, that has to be enough.

CALYSIAN

I kill every soldier who approaches the village.

Madinia doesn't lift a finger. She merely watches with those sapphire eyes that see far too much. At one point when I glance in her direction, I catch her sharpening her nails.

When the soldiers are dead, and the villagers are collecting the bodies to bury, I stalk over to her, finding her speaking to the innkeeper. The woman beams at me, then hands Madinia a young boy to hold while she steps away to speak to a group of villagers.

Madinia and the boy stare at each other. Slowly, she holds out her arms in an attempt to hand him to me.

I step back, gesturing at the blood soaked into my shirt. "I need to bathe. You're on your own, sweetheart."

The boy reaches out and grabs a lock of Madinia's hair, pulling viciously. She winces, narrowing her eyes at me.

I smirk. The few hours we were delayed were worth it just to watch Madinia attempt to wrestle her hair back from him, a hint of panic in her eyes. She mouths a dark curse at me, and I make my way back into the inn, where one of the innkeepers' daughters brings me water, along with an offer to help me wash.

I accept the former, decline the offer of help, and by the time I make my way downstairs, Madinia is murmuring quietly with the innkeeper once more. The woman presses a sack of food into my hands. "Thank you."

The gratitude discomforts me. Perhaps because I know if

not for the flame-haired woman watching me so closely, I would have left these people to die.

We leave the villagers to their grim task of burying the dead, winding our way west through scrubland.

"You know the soldiers will return," I say quietly.

Madinia's mouth thins, but she gives me a stiff nod. "We're no saviors. We bought them a little time, that's all. Maybe not much, but enough."

And yet she seems strangely content. My instincts fire. "Tell me you're not planning what I think you're planning."

Her gaze darts away, even as her chin juts up. "I already helped kill one tyrant monarch. Vicana is no different."

"Several factions and thousands of soldiers allowed you and your friends to get close enough to kill Regner," I grind out. "How exactly do you think you'll kill Vicana?"

She sends me a cool look before turning her attention forward. "What business is it of yours? You'll have your little book, and my activities will be no business of yours."

Your little book.

This woman. She knows exactly how to get under my skin.

A strange kind of panic takes up residence in my chest. I know Madinia Farrow. I've seen her at her most devastated, sprinting through the forest with a group of survivors. I've also seen her at her most unhinged, decorating her tower garden with various body parts, and using her thorns to kill anyone who dared approach.

Not once, since the moment I met her, has she ever backed down. If left to her own devices, she will be consumed by vengeance. She'll stop at nothing to make Kyldare pay for each of the scars on her back, for each day she spent trapped within her own body.

And she'll consider the loss of her own life worth it if she takes Vicana with her.

In the distance, scrubland thickens into forest. Within a

THIS VICIOUS DREAM

few hours, the dry, rocky earth softens, the dusty wind replaced by the crisp scent of damp earth and greenery.

As I watch, Madinia dismounts her horse, collecting something from the dirt once more. She shoves it into her pocket before I can see what it is.

So many secrets. They intrigue me even as they make me crazy.

"You've certainly been busy," a familiar male voice says. A hawk swoops down, landing lightly on my shoulder. Its sharp talons dig into my skin, and it tilts its head, watching Madinia with a keen, unsettling intelligence.

She's already back on her horse, a throwing knife in her hand.

"Relax," I sigh. "This is Eamonn."

"Pleasure," he says, ruffling his feathers and stretching one wing out lazily. Beneath me, Fox plods on, used to Eamonn's antics in any form.

I've never seen Madinia speechless before. Her eyes are wide, stunned, and she casts Eamonn a look that's drenched in suspicion. "The bird can talk?"

"He takes many forms."

"What *is* he?"

"I don't know," I admit, brushing a stray feather off my shoulder as Eamonn shifts his weight. "We met a few years ago when I returned to this continent."

Madinia seems to accept this, but she drops back, allowing me to take the lead once more, clearly unwilling to have Eamonn at her back.

"Suspicious little thing," Eamonn mutters.

"You have no idea."

"I can hear you." Madinia's voice is haughty, and Eamonn fluffs his feathers once more.

I can't help but glance over my shoulder. Her long hair is pulled back into a braid, the sun dancing across the strands.

She's still regaining her stamina after so long in that tower, her face still pale, eyes dark with fatigue.

And even without my memories, I know she is the most beautiful woman I have ever seen.

The thought hits me out of nowhere, and I shift in my saddle. Madinia frowns at me. "What is it?"

I clear my throat, turning to face forward once more. "Nothing."

"I saw the bodies you left at that village," Eammon says. "Do you really think it makes any difference?"

No. But Madinia does. And I played right into her hands when she told me she would hire mercenaries to help.

"It only cost us a few hours," I say. "We've been making good time so far."

"And where is it you're heading?"

I clamp my teeth together, unwilling to admit that the vixen listening oh-so-quietly behind us has refused to tell me. "West."

She snorts, and Eammon takes to the air. "I'll go scout your surroundings."

He's gone in the next moment, and I find Madinia pondering the bird as he takes to the sky.

"He's remarkably helpful," she says. "Is he the reason you were able to free yourself from those chains?"

There's a hint of amusement in her voice and I clench my teeth. I was forced to sleep against a tree until Eammon helped me, while Madinia merely had to *ask* me to free her, and I complied.

When I don't reply, she lets out a laugh. It's the first true laugh I've heard from her, and the sound makes the world seem brighter, sharper. It's a warm caress that leaves me wanting more.

Scowling, I nudge Fox into a faster pace.

THIS VICIOUS DREAM

Madinia

"Multiple regiments." Eammon calls, circling in tight, uneasy loops above us. "One of them must have traveled through the southern pass."

Calysian slowly turns his head, meeting my eyes. "Is this a problem for us?"

"Yes."

We're heading southwest, through the disputed territory and across Telanthris. A grim reality settles into my bones. Vicana's soldiers could beat us to the grimoire. A muscle twitches in Calysian's jaw, and he glances up at Eamonn.

"Suggestions?"

"Slow them down." Eamonn says, as if the answer is obvious. "But that won't matter if you can't survive the smaller regiment waiting to take you by surprise. You'll reach *that* regiment within the hour."

Calysian goes quiet. He doesn't look at me, but I know what he's thinking. By the time he finished killing the soldiers attacking the village this morning, his ward was flickering once more.

And that means his ward is likely to fall at some point against Vicana's regiment of soldiers—who will wield both their own power…and fae iron.

Unease flickers through me. "The soldier who attacked us made it back to his superior. He told them we were coming this way."

Calysian reaches into a saddlebag and withdraws his map. When he dismounts, Fox stomps a hoof, but the horse allows him to spread the map on his saddle.

"Show me," Calysian says, and Eamonn lands next to the map. I guide Hope next to Fox, and one of his ears twitch.

"Don't even think about it," I tell the horse, turning my attention to the map. The regiment is perfectly positioned, waiting for us at the northern tip of the lake. If we attempt to avoid it, we'll be forced to backtrack east along the shoreline, searching for a place to cross the wide river flowing down from the Lacana Mountains.

It would cost us so much time, the regiment that Vicana sent through the mountain pass would easily beat us to the grimoire.

"We have no choice but to face them," Calysian says, swinging himself into the saddle. "Let's go."

Scattered brush has given way to tall, thin trees, branches mushrooming from the top of pale gray trunks. Sunlight filters through the canopy above our heads, shadows stretch long across the ground, and the muffled roar of rushing water grows louder and louder, until all I can hear is a steady crash where river meets lake.

We follow the shoreline, leaving the horses tied loosely so they can escape if needed. Calysian prowls toward the edge of the forest, silent as death, and I follow closely behind, my hand wrapped tightly around the hilt of my sword.

When he stops, I crouch behind him, peering around his shoulder. We're positioned on a rocky overhang, about five footspans above the lake. The water glitters in the sunlight, and I shuffle back further from the edge. From here, we have a clear view, down the shoreline to the rocky outcrop jutting out along the water.

Kyldare has stationed his regiment behind a boulder cluster. My pulse thunders in my ears, my vision dimming until his face is all I can see.

Calysian goes still. "Why is he here? He's the Queen's right hand. He should be with the regiment closest to my grimoire."

My mouth turns dry as Kyldare stalks back and forth, snarling something to one of his men. The solider glances over his shoulder, and Kyldare buries his hand in the soldier's leather tunic, pulling him close as he continues his tirade. The soldier stammers something, his gaze darting nervously toward the tree line.

Calysian nudges my shoulder with his. "What aren't you telling me?"

"I escaped him." My voice is flat, my face oddly numb. "Kyldare wants the grimoire, but he *needs* to make me pay. He's been trying to break me for three years, and now I'm walking free."

Something feral enters Calysian's eyes, and his face turns cold.

Below us, the sound of the water clashes with the dark power pulsing through me. Now that I'm no longer trapped in my own body, the power is terrifying. And yet, if it builds within me enough—if I can access it again—I can finally make Kyldare pay for everything he has done to me.

A tall, beautiful blonde woman stands next to Kyldare, the hint of a smirk on her face. My heart leaps into my throat, even as my blood heats with rage. Slowly, Calysian turns to look at me. I lower my head. But it's too late. He catches my chin, holding tight.

"Flames dance in your eyes." He cuts his eyes to the woman next to Kyldare. "Who is she?"

"Kyldare's witch. Her name is Bridin."

His eyes sharpen. "She frightens you. Even more than Kyldare."

"She should frighten you too," I snap. "She can do things that defy the laws of power." Things like trapping me in my own body and somehow keeping me alive without food or water for three years.

"Tell me what I need to know." His voice is even, expression intent as he evaluates the threat.

"I...I'd never met a witch on my continent. I'm not sure

if that's because Regner's barrier kept them out, or if they were able to hide their presence from him."

My mind turns fuzzy as I'm assaulted by memories of Bridin following Kyldare's commands. Fae, hybrids, humans… all of us are born with our power. But witches take their power through sacrifice to their god. White witches sacrifice from themselves, while black witches sacrifice others.

"Madinia." Calysian's voice is soft, and I blink, shoving the memories away. "Bridin is a black witch. She sacrifices animals often, humans occasionally, but she especially enjoys children."

His eyes darken, and I nod. "She's evil. And she can sense power. It's one of the reasons why Kyldare began working with her in the first place. He thought she would be able to locate the grimoire. But she has never been able to find it, no matter how many people she sacrifices to her god." I force myself to channel Calysian's calm, focused evaluation of the situation. "The moment you use your ward, she'll know we're here."

Calysian shrugs. "I've tussled with witches before."

"She's not just any witch. She's a monster."

Calysian turns away to study the regiment. I study Kyldare, basking in the feel of the grimoire as it slides tendrils of power toward me. The feel of that dark power is seductive, comforting and… terrifying.

I haven't felt it since it helped me escape the tower. The fact that it's now calling to me is as unnerving as it is comforting. It's as if even the grimoire wants to watch Kyldare die.

A faint shimmer catches the light, a subtle distortion in the air near Bridin and Kyldare. It ripples, almost like steam rising from a pot, and Calysian stiffens, titling his head, eyes narrowing.

"What is it?"

"A trap. The witch has found a way to replicate my power, turning it against me. She may not know where the grimoire is, but she understands exactly how to use an unclaimed link to its power. You should go."

"What?"

"You heard me. Leave. I'll take care of this and find you when it's done."

Dread sinks into my gut like a stone and slowly expands, pushing against my lungs.

He pins me with a hard stare. "Go."

"You heard him," Eamonn says, and I jolt. He's sitting in a branch above our heads, watching Kyldare.

"I don't take orders from birds. Or gods." I match Calysian's glower with one of my own.

He heaves a sigh. "Is there anyone you *do* take orders from?"

"No."

He shakes his head, but his eyes drop to my lips and linger. My heart thuds, my breath catches, and his eyes meet mine. They glitter with lust. And something that looks almost like…longing.

I open my mouth, but Calysian freezes, tension thrumming through his body.

A moment later I feel it too. The sudden pulse of power is invisible yet suffocating, as if the world itself is recoiling from Bridin's evil. There's no visible sign of anything wrong—no explosion or even a flash of light—and yet the dark power within me snarls, desperate for release.

They know we're here.

Calysian whirls, his lip curled as he watches the soldiers. From within the ranks of Kyldare's regiment, a bolt flies toward us, unnaturally fast, its path bending ever so slightly, as if guided by an unseen force. Calysian raises his hand and his ward appears, a glimmering silver wall.

The bolt travels directly through the ward. As if it's not there.

Calysian shoves me down, moving with unnatural grace as his body shifts left.

I hit the ground, and the bolt slices into his neck, grazing his skin but not penetrating deeply. He lets out a low growl, seemingly unbothered, his body taut with readiness. And then his eyes roll up, his legs buckle, and he crumples backward, falling like a stone into the water below us with a heavy splash.

Eamonn lets out a shriek.

My eyes meet Kyldare's. Even from here I can see his teeth bared in a grin as he points toward us. His soldiers charge up the coastline.

Ripping my gaze away, I wait for Calysian to surface. But he's slipping deeper, the rippling surface of the lake closing over him. My heart thunders in my chest.

"What happened?" I demand.

"I don't know," Eamonn shrieks. "But he's sinking."

It doesn't make sense. Calysian isn't just strong—he's frighteningly difficult to kill. It would take a lot more than a scratch with an iron arrow to bring him down. And yet he's being dragged into the depths as though the lake itself has claimed him.

It can't have him.

Eamonn swoops close to the surface of the water. "He's drowning!"

I kick off my boots. "Perhaps if you squawk some more, you'll annoy him into regaining consciousness."

Outraged silence.

With a sigh, I jump from the overhang and plunge into the freezing water.

CHAPTER TWELVE

Madinia

The sudden shock of frigid water hits me like a slap, the cold slicing into my skin like shards of ice. I let my body sink and then twist, arrowing down into the depths of the lake.

The sunlight fades as I dive, kicking my legs as my heartbeat pounds in my ears, frantic and insistent.

How long can Calysian last without air? My own lungs are already screaming at me, but I push deeper, scanning the murky gloom.

There.

Calysian's hulking form is a dark shadow, drifting below me. His limbs hang limp, his head tilted back as though in surrender. Panic claws at my chest. He's too still.

I kick harder, straining to reach him. When my hands find his shoulder, the solid feel of his muscle is almost startling.

I grab at the front of his tunic, my fingers numb and clumsy as I shake him.

He doesn't move.

I tighten my grip, my nails digging into the fabric as I pull him toward me, twisting my body to face the surface. The effort is brutal. His weight drags at me, pulling me down, even as I kick with everything I have.

The cold seeps deeper, turning my limbs sluggish. My lungs are on fire, each second stretching unbearably as I clamp down on the urge to inhale. The surface is footspans away, impossibly far, unreachable.

Grinding my teeth, I kick harder.

The light grows brighter, fracturing into ribbons as I stretch toward the surface. My face breaks through and I gasp, my chest heaving as sweet, cool air floods my lungs. Hauling Calysian up, I turn him onto his back as his head lolls against my shoulder, his face pale and slack, his lips tinged blue.

"Wake up," I choke out.

"There!" A voice calls, and cold terror shudders through me. Kyldare's soldiers are on their way.

"Calysian!" I swallow lake water, my arms screaming, every muscle in my body trembling as I half-drag, half-push his massive body toward the shoreline. The overhang looms above our heads, and I let the current carry us sideways toward a narrow stretch of muddy ground. My knees hit mud, and I stagger to my feet, pulling Calysian onto the shore.

Dropping to my knees, I press my lips to his, pushing air into his lungs. I can feel Kyldare's eyes on me, can sense his soldiers clambering over the rocks between us.

I could have escaped. And instead, I attempted to save this unconscious brute.

This *stubborn, infuriating* man who won't *wake up*.

A dark flame lights in the center of Calysian's chest, spreading throughout his body until he's surrounded by a shadow. The shadow curls toward me invitingly, and I jolt backwards. It freezes, and I get the strangest feeling that I've rejected something important.

Eammon lands next to me. "His chest."

"I know. Something is happening with his power."

THIS VICIOUS DREAM

"No. His chest is *rising*. He's breathing."

Relief shudders through me, until I'm light headed. But the soldiers are almost here. I need to get Calysian on his horse.

No. There's no time.

Already, I can hear the first soldier's boots pounding as they charge up the bank.

"He wouldn't have wanted you to jump in after him," Eamonn says.

"He's used to me denying him the things he wants."

Calysian's eyes slowly open, dazed and filled with pain. But his gaze drops to my mouth. "She speaks the truth."

He shifts his attention to my hands. I've begun trembling. The cold. That's all it is. My clothes are heavy, sodden with frigid lake water.

"I need you to get up." Panic leeches into my voice and Calysian's eyes immediately sharpen. When he sits, his face turns gray, his huge body swaying.

"Your eyes," he murmurs. "They're glowing again."

"You need to focus."

He studies me, and I can practically see him creating a plan. "I know what to do. But I need you to trust me."

I hesitate, my skin prickling, and one side of his mouth kicks up. "I know. You'll have to suppress all of your instincts. But it's our only chance."

"Fine."

With sheer force of will, Calysian manages to make it to his feet. The soldiers are less than fifty footspans away.

"Hand over the woman, and we'll let you live." Kyldare's voice is silky, his tone oh-so-reasonable as his words curl around our heads. It's as if he's standing a footspan from us. Another trick from his witch.

They don't know who Calysian is. They can't. If they knew the dark god was standing in front of them, they wouldn't be attempting to bargain with him.

129

Not when he is all that truly stands between Vicana and the grimoire.

"You've been up to no good, Madinia," Kyldare smiles at me, and I barely hide a flinch.

Calysian glances between me and the soldiers.

He could give me to them right now. I'm sure if he keeps traveling west, he'll eventually sense the grimoire.

The world turns fuzzy at the edges, my heart slamming into my ribs. But I won't let any of these men see my terror.

"You want her?" Calysian asks, and my stomach sinks. "Come and take her from me."

Wait, what?

He casts me a disappointed look. "Do you really think I'll hand you over? Just moments ago, you agreed to trust me."

"We'll talk about this later."

"You bet your pert little arse we will."

Kyldare snaps something, and the regiment attacks.

My heart jumps into my throat, but I don't have time to linger on my terror. Because Calysian grabs my hand and *pulls*.

I instinctively pull back, but it's not my body he's pulling. It's the dark power within me. The power that has been rising to the surface over the past two days.

I gasp, attempting to free my hand, but Calysian holds tighter. His eyes darken, turning black, his expression suddenly remote.

Another yank at the power within me, and my own power jumps to my other hand, reacting to the threat. Calysian steps forward, pulling me with him. His lips curl in a humorless smile as he strides toward Kyldare's men, and a chill ripples through me. Power lashes from him, and black smoke pours down the throats of the closest soldiers, until they're clawing at their necks, choking and seizing. They slump to their knees, and I flick my own power toward them.

My flame is so hot, it's *blue*. When I pull my power back, the soldiers are gone. Only ashes remain.

Calysian laughs.

With a wave of his hand, he sweeps out with more of that black smoke. Several arrows slice through the air toward us, and Calysian's ward surrounds us.

It's no longer silver.

No, now it's obsidian, speckled with silver filaments.

My heart kicks in my chest as more bolts hit the ward.

I *feel* the fae iron, but there's also something new. Something dangerous. Something that slices into me. Still, they don't break through Calysian's ward. This time, it protects us, the bolts dropping harmlessly to the ground.

Several soldiers turn and run, but Kyldare cuts them down before turning his attention back to us.

"This might hurt," Calysian muses absently. His voice is distant, and he doesn't look at me. For the first time, I'm truly afraid. Of him.

He's himself…but not. His head tilts in a way that's not even remotely human, his blackened eyes are narrowed as if considering whether he will squash the bugs moving toward us. He's cold, predatory…amused.

It does hurt.

He pulls more power. Dizziness swamps me and I use my other hand to claw at his forearm. Still, he ignores my struggles. Dark smoke pours from him, a haze that fills my vision until it's all I can see.

Screams. Terrible, agonizing screams.

My limbs tremble, my knees buckling, and I tug harder, but his grip is unyielding.

"Calysian!"

I shove my own power at him, and this time, my flames dance up his arm, burning his tunic. It's a warning, and he slowly turns his head, his eyes pinning me in place.

"Don't make me hurt you," I rasp.

My heart stutters once. Twice.

Calysian's brow furrows, as if he hears the missed beats. Horror flickers over his face, and he releases my hand. The smoke disappears.

The soldiers are gone. Nothing but weapons remaining.

Occasional piles of ash mark the places where a few of them once stood.

Kyldare watches us from behind his witch's ward.

Bridin has turned gray, her face lined, as if holding her own ward against Calysian's power has drained the life from her.

Good.

Kyldare's eyes meet mine, and there's something I don't recognize within them. His hateful voice crawls over my skin.

"Ah. So Calpharos walks this world once more. Whoring yourself to the dark god won't save you, Madinia Farrow. I'll take you back. And when I do, you'll *wish* for the days when you were left alone in your tower."

Calysian snarls. Fear flashes across Kyldare's face, and he gestures to his witch. Her ward remains high, and they disappear into the forest.

My head spins, my body breaking out into chills.

"Coward," Calysian hisses, before dropping to his knees in front of me. "Are you hurt?"

Kyldare's words echo through my head, over and over again. *"I'll take you back. And when I do, you'll wish for the days when you were left alone in your tower."*

"Madinia."

A flap of wings. "What did you do?" Eamonn demands. "I could barely see through all your smoke."

I'm shuddering, vision narrowing as my entire body breaks out in chills. "I won't be taken back." My lips are numb, but the words come out anyway, repeating on a loop. "I'll *never* go back."

My heart pounds like a drum, echoing in my ears until it's all I can hear. Calysian's lips move, but there's...nothing.

Just as there was nothing for three years.

Sometimes...sometimes I would almost look forward to Kyldare's visits. Because I could feel my mind cracking. And despite his viciousness, despite his torture, at least for the short time when he was there, I was allowed to move. To talk.

"I'll slit my own throat before I go back," I choke out.

Calysian's hands move to my shoulders, and he gives me a gentle shake.

Our eyes meet.

"He will never take you," he vows. "If ever such a thing was to happen, I would come for you. And I would kill him."

I let out a shuddery breath. "Why?" My voice is hoarse.

"Because this universe has laws. I know this in my bones. And one of those laws is that Madinia Farrow is no one's captive. She is no one's victim. You know this, despite your terror telling you otherwise."

Shoving his hands away, I stumble to my feet. "*You* tried to make me a captive."

He sighs. "A *temporary* captive. One I would have left with unspeakable wealth."

I curl my lip at him, and amusement flickers across his face. "There you are." His hand cups my face, and amusement turns to a strange kind of tenderness.

Slowly, he leans down. I can see his intention in his eyes. I have more than enough time to push him away. To turn my head.

But I don't.

His mouth is a gentle, warm caress. He teases my lips open, stroking with his tongue, and I sigh against him.

No.

I don't want gentle from this man.

I nip at his lower lip, and he stiffens. One of his huge hands is suddenly buried in my hair, holding me steady for him as his tongue strokes mine, exploring every inch of my mouth. His hard body crowds mine, walking me backward until my back meets the unyielding trunk of a tree.

My core clenches, demanding more. Demanding *everything*.

Calysian's hand slides to my waist, one thumb brushing my ribs in a gentle caress. I shiver, the tenderness so at odds with the way he's plundering my mouth.

Just that thought is enough to seep into my awareness, and I let out a yelp, the sound muffled against his mouth. I slam my hands against his chest, wrenching my face away. "This isn't happening."

Calysian raises his head, giving me a slow smile filled with dark promise. "Oh, it's happening."

The satisfaction in his eyes sets my teeth on edge and I shove at him again.

His smile widens and he steps back, allowing me to pass. "You never should have let me taste you. Now I'll stop at nothing to make you mine."

I let out a low groan. What was I thinking?

Turning toward where we left the horses, I stumble. Calysian is immediately there, his hand gripping my elbow as he steadies me.

"You're dizzy." The heat in his eyes is gone, along with the teasing note in his voice. If not for the way his gaze lingers on my lips, I'd think it had never happened.

"I'm…drained. Exhausted. What did you do when you…"

When he took my hand. When he turned into someone I didn't recognize.

His expression tightens and he releases me. "You have access to the grimoire's power. Don't you?"

I hesitate, but there's no point lying about it when he can see the evidence. "Yes."

"How?"

THIS VICIOUS DREAM

"I don't know. It might be because I used it once before. It might be because I spent so much time with the grimoire pressed against me as I hid it in my cloak while traveling to this continent."

His eyes gleam with something that might be realization.

"The last time I saw you, I felt a sudden urge to chase you. It was an instinct I couldn't ignore."

I frown. "When?"

"You were boarding a ship in the hybrid kingdom. You had my grimoire then, didn't you?"

My stomach churns. I never saw him.

"Yes."

"So you took the grimoire, hid it, and then you somehow used that power—*my power*—to kill any who attempted to enter your tower. And to escape."

I nod, my mouth dry. "At first…at first I couldn't use it. There was just…nothing. And then one day after Kyldare visited, I was filled with such burning rage, I could feel the power calling to me. In my madness, I didn't understand what it was. Didn't understand it was the grimoire until later. In that moment, I just knew I could use it to find freedom."

Calysian studies me. And I get the feeling he sees more than I would like him to.

"For some reason, I cannot access that power myself," he says. "But I could sense it within you. So I used you as a conduit to the grimoire."

And he'd nearly killed me. I can see the knowledge in his eyes. The horror had flickered across his face when my flames startled him back into himself.

"You told me to trust you, but you didn't trust me enough to let me know what you were doing."

He takes a step back, gazing at me thoughtfully. "You're right." He turns away, and then almost immediately whirls to face me once more. "You saved my life. Why?"

I stalk toward the shore. "You likely would have lived."

He catches up to me easily, his long stride worth two of mine. "Not if they'd cut off my head while I was unconscious. The power that makes me invulnerable to mortals is still out of my reach."

I flick a glance to Eamonn, who lingers in a branch above us, pretending to mind his own business.

"Your pet bird wouldn't stop squawking."

Eamonn swoops to the ground at our feet, and in the blink of an eye, I'm staring at a jaguar. When it lets out a low snarl, I go still.

Calysian eyes him. "Where was that form when the soldiers were attacking, hmm?"

Eamonn merely yawns, revealing a mouthful of sharp teeth.

But Calysian turns his attention back to me. "You should have left me. If such a thing happens again, you will run."

I sneer at him, and he takes a step closer, his face carved into hard lines. "You will do as I say."

Clearly, he's feeling the leftover traces of the power he drained from me. There can be no other explanation for why he would think he can intimidate me into falling in line.

When I don't deign to reply, he throws up his hands. "Who do I think I'm talking to? You reject any plans *you* haven't chosen. You probably wonder to yourself 'what would Calysian prefer for me to do,' and then you do the exact opposite."

I raise one eyebrow, because there's something so fucking reassuring about seeing him hot-blooded and furious after the way he just became something so *other*.

"Bold of you to assume I consider you at all while making my decisions. Will these hysterics last long? We need to leave this place."

He snarls.

More relief shudders through me. In this moment he

couldn't be further from the cruel, emotionless god I caught a glimpse of during Kyldare's attack.

"Children." Eamonn steps between us, his furry body pressed against my leg. "We have more important things to discuss. Such as how that bolt could take Calysian down."

It's a good question, the answer important enough that we spend precious minutes searching for it. It's Calysian who eventually finds it buried low in the trunk of a tree.

"Perhaps you shouldn't touch it," I murmur.

Ripping his tunic from his body, he wraps it around his hand and pulls the bolt free, making the motion look easy. I carefully avoid looking at his wide shoulders. At the way his muscles shift along his back. At the expanse of smooth skin covering those muscles.

"Madinia?"

"Hmm?" He raises one eyebrow and I ignore the amused knowledge in those eyes. "What is that black oil sticking to the iron?"

Calysian holds my gaze for one more long moment, his lips curving.

"Smells like a dead body," Eamonn says, prowling between us.

He's right. Calysian raises the bolt between us, and I don't need to lean forward to scent the cloying reek of rot.

"What is it?"

He shrugs, and I raise a hand, pressing against his cheek to angle his face away from me. He goes still, allowing my touch, and I force myself to focus on the scrape across his neck and *not* the prickle of scruff beneath my fingers or the hard line of his jaw.

"Your wound is still bleeding. It's as if your body managed to cleanse the wound with your own blood, rejecting this oily substance."

I remove my hand, and Eamonn nudges closer to Calysian. "Show me."

Calysian sighs but lowers himself to his knees, and Eamonn sniffs at the wound, his ears twitching.

"Madinia is right. The wound is clean, but the surrounding skin is covered with that same black poison. Vicana must have created something powerful enough to kill a god."

It makes sense. Kyldare hadn't been prepared to come across Calpharos. But his witch was more than prepared. Whatever filth she created, the bolt had struck true. Which means we can't rely on his wards to protect us.

And now that Kyldare knows who—and what—he's dealing with. He'll only be more dangerous.

Calysian shrugs one shoulder, wrapping the arrow entirely in his tunic as he moves toward the horses.

"We'll see if they can still weaken me with this once I have my grimoire."

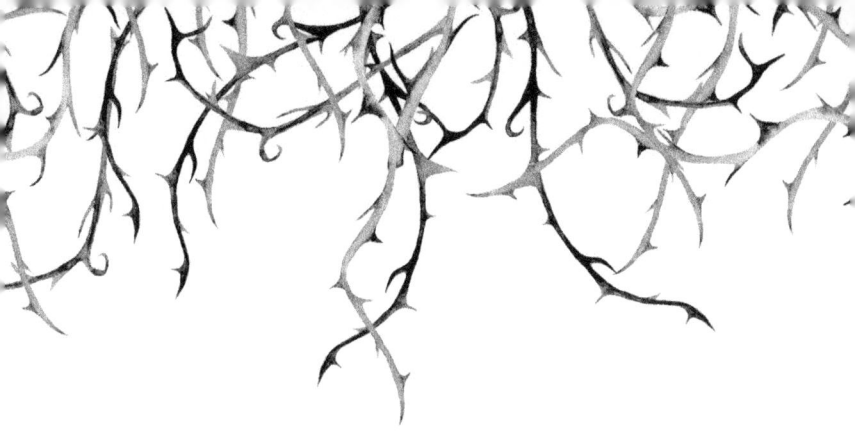

CHAPTER THIRTEEN

Madinia

WE TRAVEL THROUGH THE DISPUTED TERRITORY for three days. The evidence of death and pain is everywhere—from the destroyed, abandoned villages, to the children who stare at us as we ride by, eyes hollow, limbs thin.

We grab a few hours of sleep each night, both of us committed to closing the distance between us and Kyldare's soldiers.

"I want to renegotiate," I say on the third day, after we've passed through a village where only the dead remain, corpses picked clean by the animals. Eamonn disappeared yesterday, but Calysian doesn't seem at all worried. Apparently, he comes and goes as he pleases.

Calysian shifts in the saddle. "And what is it you want, beautiful woman?"

Something about his tone sparks a memory. My mind twists.

Calysian leads me through the slums, his expression relaxed, even as his eyes scan the streets relentlessly.

By the time we arrive at the abandoned building, smoke is curling from my hands. Calysian sends me an amused look. "Scared?"

I ignore him, but he nods anyway. "That's good. Only an idiot wouldn't be scared. You're smarter than you've demonstrated so far."

"What is that supposed to mean?"

"You shouldn't have come here alone. I could have killed you nine times already."

My hands fire. "Try."

His eyes glitter. "You'd like that, wouldn't you? To be able to kill something? Or for someone to finally kill you and put you out of your misery?"

My spine tingles with fury. "You don't know me."

"I've seen everything I need to know."

It doesn't sound like a compliment.

"You believe you're invulnerable," *Calysian murmurs, his breath warm against my ear.* "So, go on. Wander into that building alone."

I shrug, stalking toward the dilapidated excuse for a door. My heart may be thundering in my chest, but I'll never allow this bastard to see it.

It's a test—only I'm not sure if he wants to see if I'm a coward or to prove I'm reckless. Either way, I'm going into that building. Hesitating will simply make this take longer or confirm to whoever is watching me from inside that I'm afraid.

Only idiots allow predators to see their terror.

Calysian lets out a choked laugh behind me. "Gods, woman. Do you have no fear?"

I glance over my shoulder. "Yes. I fear that you'll continue to draw this interaction out even longer. Leave."

His expression turns flat. "The debt has not been satisfied."

"It has."

"Weren't you listening? I decide. One day, I will find you, Madinia Farrow. When you're ready to be the woman I think you are."

Cold fury slides through my veins. "If I see you again, you'll regret it."

THIS VICIOUS DREAM

He chuckles "Likely, I will. But I'll still find you." Turning, he strolls away.

"Madinia." My horse pulls to a stop, and I slowly meet his gaze. He's holding my reins, his expression tight. "What is it?"

I hiss out a breath. "You know, I can now remember almost everything about my past. And yet I'm still remembering my interactions with you. Why do you think that is?"

"Perhaps because you're actively trying not to remember me. Why do you think you'd do something like that, hmmm?"

I know what he's implying. That I *want* him, but don't want to want him, so I'm doing everything I can to suppress any thought of him.

Overconfident bastard.

"Or perhaps my subconscious knows you're a threat," I mutter, and he gives me a slow smile as he runs his gaze deliberately down my body.

"A threat," he murmurs. "Hmm." He releases my reins, and I take the lead, ignoring his low laugh.

"You want to renegotiate?" His voice is still filled with amusement.

"Yes. It just occurred to me that I'm helping you find something you've spent centuries searching for."

"And preventing the grimoire from falling into Vicana's hands isn't enough?"

"No."

"Let me guess. You want me to kill her." Calysian rides up next to me. Hope throws her head, and Fox nudges at her with his nose, the movement oddly...playful.

"Yes." I vowed to do so myself, but even I can admit that Calysian is more likely to succeed at such a task.

He ponders me for a long time. Long enough that I focus on the forest in the distance.

"This territory...it seems to enrage you almost as much as the mention of Kyldare."

I shrug, but Calysian continues. "I can feel your rage increasing with each village we pass through."

"I know what it's like to have your kingdom stolen from you. When the Hybrid Kingdom was invaded, hundreds of thousands of our people died. Those who survived were forced to flee, spending their lives in hiding, until their descendants believed they were corrupt." My stomach roils at the memory of keeping the dark secret that would have led to my death if I was discovered. My generation….none of us knew who we were or where we were from. All of us grew up hunted, without a home."

"You could have stayed," he says. "After the war." There's no blame in his voice, simply curiosity.

I swallow around the burning lump in my throat. "I spent my entire adult life away from my kingdom. Even now, I would die to protect it."

"But?"

"But… it doesn't feel familiar. I have no memories tying me to the land. I have no grandmother or great grandmother there to tell me our stories. Regner stole that from me. And when I was in Regner's castle, gossiping about courtiers for hours with the queen, I used to dream I would escape. I fantasized about exploring this world." I take a deep, shuddering breath. "Still, if the hybrid kingdom had felt like home, I would have stayed. At least for a while."

"And you wouldn't have been trapped in that tower."

I shrug that off. "Vicana is doing that to these people. She's ripping their land from them. Their home. She's stealing their connection to their ancestors. She's killing the neighbors they celebrated with, mourned with, survived with."

My eyes burn, and I stroke Hope's neck.

"We may have won the war, but the hybrids that returned…they were forced to rely on the kindness of those who had been lucky to remain. They were forced to integrate into a kingdom they should have always known but now felt foreign."

THIS VICIOUS DREAM

Calysian doesn't speak again. But each time we come across a devastated village, his eyes linger on the destruction. On the death.

Finally, the disputed territory begins to fall away behind us, the fractured earth swallowed by the dense embrace of ancient oaks. The air changes as we move deeper into the forest, the dry scent of dust gradually replaced with the heavy scent of damp greenery. Calysian's body is tense, and a hard, furious light glints in his eyes.

"I will do this," he tells me, on our fifth day of traveling. We've stopped to allow the horses to drink, and I'm stretching out my cramped legs. Just a few hours ago, we found recent signs of Kyldare's soliders—a fire that hadn't been properly put out. We're catching up to them.

"You will do what?"

"I will kill Vicana. You are right—everything you said. I know what it's like to have something precious stolen from me. Something that leaves your life in ruins. It's not the same, and yet in some ways it is. I can see how some people would consider their homes, their land to be as important as the grimoires I seek. It's a part of them, just as my grimoires are a part of me."

My heart trips in my chest. The closer we get to the grimoire, the more Calysian changes. They're small changes—the tilt of his head when he looks at something he doesn't understand. The way he occasionally speaks, as if the common tongue is foreign to him. The slight pause before he reacts to something I say.

Yesterday, while we were setting up camp, I asked him to pass me a water skin, and he stared at me for a long moment, as if he couldn't understand what I was saying.

This morning before the sun rose, he was sleep talking in a strange language that sent a chill down my spine.

And then there are his eyes. Even now, they've darkened, until they're almost black.

Something in my chest wrenches. Calysian's vow to kill Vicana is exactly what I want, and the fact that he feels for these people is exactly what I was hoping for.

And yet...

"You won't even care about this world when you get your grimoires," I snap. "Everything I've heard about Calpharos has made it clear you will burn this world as you take your revenge."

I'm not sure why I'm lashing out. He can't help who he is.

Perhaps it's the arrogant gleam in his eye when he declares what he will do. Perhaps it's because I barely recognize this man as the same man who glowered at me when he realized I'd tricked him, or the man who vowed he would stop at nothing to make me his. The *mortal* man.

Confusion darts across Calysian's face, and he looks suddenly *lost*. "In that case, why are you helping me with this task?"

"I don't know. I suppose I hold a glimmer of hope that you will take your revenge without destroying everything in your path. And because if it does seem like you'll turn this world to ash, I'll do everything I can to kill you."

We both turn quiet, saying little over the next few hours. Gnarled trunks claw upward, roots knotting together beneath the horses' hooves.

Our conversation has one effect. He's no longer watching the world through cold, distant eyes. And those eyes have lightened slightly.

Finally, he pins me with a look. "Will you tell me where we're going now?"

"Blightmere."

"Blightmere?" The word is incredulous, and Calysian stares at me, nostrils flaring.

"Yes."

"You hid my grimoire in the swamp?"

I sniff. "Yes. And thanks to my foresight, it has stayed safe all this time. You're welcome."

THIS VICIOUS DREAM

He gapes at me, and I continue riding.

When he catches up with me, he rides too close, and Hope snaps her teeth at Fox. I stroke her neck. "Good girl."

Calysian lets out a low growl. "If I'd known we were traveling through the swamp, I would have stopped for supplies."

"The innkeeper from the village you defended...she has an aunt who traveled to Blightmere. She told me there's a small village that borders the swamp along the route we need to take. It's not ideal, but it will have to do."

We ride in strained silence. At least, it's strained on Calysian's side. I won't apologize for not giving him the information he would need to leave me and go after the grimoire himself.

Finally, the swamp begins to creep into the forest. Vines choke the life from trees, pulling down branches weakened by their attentions. The closer we get to Blightmere, the heavier and stickier the air becomes. When I visited the swamp that day so long ago, I'd returned to Daharak's ship covered in mud and insect bites. But beneath the irritation I'd felt a strong sense of satisfaction. The knowledge that I'd done my part to protect this continent.

Now, my stomach is churning with anxiety, my palms slick with sweat.

Within a few hours, we've reached the outskirts of the swamp. We haven't seen any signs of Vicana's soldiers, which means they're likely already traveling within the swamp.

We'll need to move quickly.

I pull the hood of Calysian's cloak up to cover my hair. If Vicana's soldiers have come through, it's likely they've questioned the villagers, and my hair is memorable. The road turns into a narrow track, the mud sucking at the horse's hooves as the village comes into view, and voices sound in the distance, raised in either barter or argument.

It's impossible to know if this place has clawed its way out of the swamp, or if the swamp itself has encroached on the village. Wooden buildings are streaked black, slick with moss, while roofs sag beneath the weight of rot and neglect. A few crooked chimneys release a trickle of smoke, curling up into the murky sky and mixing with the already heavy reek of wet earth and mildew.

A cart rolls past, its wheels fighting the thick mud. When I peer into it, I find it filled with some kind of tiny fish.

The closest building appears to be an inn, a wooden sign swinging above the doorway, its paint too faded to be legible.

We urge the horses forward, stopping near a cluster of stalls. A short, slight woman stands at the first stall, her hands moving quickly as she ties bundles of dried herbs with thin twine. She sweeps her gaze over us, looking entirely unimpressed.

"What do you want?"

"Food," Calysian says, swinging himself down from his horse. "And supplies."

"You're going into the swamp."

"Yes. We'll also need to stable our horses."

She spares him another glance, her eyes flicking to me before returning to her work. "You'll find bread and salted meat a few stalls down. If you're looking for better, you've come to the wrong place."

"How did you know we're going into the swamp?" I ask.

She raises one brow, tying off her current bundle and placing it in a pile with the others. "You're not covered in mud, so you can't be traveling *out* of the swamp. And we've seen a steady stream of visitors passing through for the past several days."

My skin prickles. Just as I'd anticipated, the soldiers have made it here first.

"What kind of visitors?"

When her lips thin, Calysian places a gold coin on her stall. It's more money than she has likely seen in her life, but she merely slips it into her pocket with a nod.

"I have a feeling you know what kind of visitors. The kinds

of visitors who have removed their uniforms and traveled into our kingdom, hunting for something within our swamp."

Calysian's eyes meet mine.

"We heard screams last night," the woman continues, a slight smile playing around her face. "Our swamp does not take kindly to those who seek to destroy it in order to get what they want."

I swallow, my mouth suddenly dry. "You speak of it as if it's almost...alive."

"That swamp was ancient long before the fae were ever created," she says. "It does not take kindly to those who would attempt to burn their way through it."

I shiver. "Thank you for the warning."

"I'll give you another one. Beware the Blightmere Serpent."

Unease ripples through me. The last time I visited this swamp, I approached from the west, traveling just deep enough to find a suitable hiding spot. This time, we're approaching from the northeast, which means we'll need to spend much more time traveling within the swamp itself—directly through the heart of Blightmere.

I wish we could travel around the outskirts, but we'd lose too much time. Precious time we need to catch up to Vicana's soldiers.

Calysian gives the woman a grave nod. "Thank you for your help."

We move toward the stalls she pointed out, loading up on food and water. By the time we're ready to leave, the sun is high in the sky.

Calysian glowers at the stable, and Fox tosses his head as if instantly rejecting the thought. But we can't take the horses with us. Unstable ground, sinkholes, mud, twisted roots, insects...

Fliora's voice echoes through my head.

"You need to take the horses."

"We are."

"Not now. Later. When you think you shouldn't take them, you're wrong."

I heave a sigh. "We have to take them."

Calysian snorts. When I don't dismount, he glowers at me. "You're serious."

"Do you remember Fliora?"

"The baby seer?" He raises one eyebrow, but I can tell he remembers every word she said.

I wait him out. After the way Fliora's mother helped me, I'm choosing to believe her daughter.

Calysian eyes the horses. "We don't have enough fresh water for them."

"There's an aquifer beneath the swamp. I learned about it last time—I needed to know I'd survive if I got lost. It releases water into springs dotted throughout the swamp."

Calysian lets out a low growl. "This is going to be a nightmare."

CALYSIAN

Moments after we leave the village, the trees close in around us, stifling the sounds of the market at our back.

The wet slaps of boots on mud, the creak of carts, the haggling voices—all of them fade quickly as we take the road leading toward the swamp.

Calling it a road is an exaggeration. My instincts insisted Madinia ride at my side, but there's barely enough room for both horses. Madinia's mare hesitates, ears flicking back and forth as twisted branches sway in the wind, brushing against tree trunks slick with swamp moss.

Eventually, the road narrows into a trail, and I'm forced to ride ahead of Madinia.

The forest smells alive here—not in the vibrant way of fresh grass or blooming flowers. But in the way of rot—teeming with things that feed on death.

The ground grows softer, and Fox's front hoof sinks into slick mud. He jerks backward, pulling it free with a squelch. The mud is a dark, putrid black, thick with the scent of something foul.

When the path splits, I don't need to ask Madinia which way to turn. I can feel the insistent pull of my grimoire calling to me.

The swamp clings to us, exhausting the horses, and we'll need to stop to rest even earlier than I'd anticipated. Within an hour, we're forced to dismount, leading the horses through water that rises above Madinia's thighs. She's tense, her eyes continually scanning for threats. Clearly, she feels it too.

I feel a strange burst of unfamiliar power, and the hair on the back of my neck stands up. The swamp has encroached on the path, and we need to make it the fifty or so footspans to firmer ground. But Hope suddenly balks, tossing her head and side-stepping into Madinia, who stumbles, unbalanced. She catches herself, murmuring to the horse. But the mare is staring at something, refusing to go any further.

Horses are prey animals.

I follow her gaze to the water to our right, where ripples spread out from a shadow. A shadow that wasn't there before.

The surface glimmers, and a dark shape glides beneath it. A smooth, serpentine shape.

A shape that radiates a strange, unfamiliar power.

"Move," I order. "Now."

I tug on Fox's reins, leading him toward the higher ground, but Hope throws her head in a move that almost wrenches the reins from Madinia's hand.

"Leave the horse," I snarl. But she won't. I know it before the words are even out of my mouth.

Releasing Fox, I slap him on the ass. He's smart enough to bolt for safety as I whirl toward Madinia.

Snatching the reins from her, I resist the urge to slap her on the arse the same way I just slapped Fox. She would likely disembowel me.

"Go!"

She stumbles through the water, and I yank at the reins, forcing Hope to meet my eyes. Her eyes roll, but I reach for that power so close to me, staring her down.

She calms.

Fox whinnies, and Hope finally begins moving toward him.

"Calysian!" Madinia's voice is filled with terror. I spin, but...

It's terror for *me*.

A hint of warmth flashes through my chest, but there's no time to bask in the smug certainty that this woman cares for my safety. Not when the dark shadow is almost on me.

I pull my sword, bracing for impact.

CHAPTER FOURTEEN

MADINIA

M Y KNEES QUAKE, TERROR SHREDDING MY INSIDES.
Calysian is going to die.
Wings explode into my vision. Wings so massive, they stir the air. A deafening *screech* pierces the swamp, the sound so sharp, the serpent darts away, its body coiling down, disappearing into the depths of the water.

I stumble back, slamming into Fox.

Talons rake through the water, throwing up a spray of mud and reeds. The wings are larger than any I've ever seen, each feather sharp-edged and glinting like a poised blade.

Its hooked beak snaps at the air, and it lets out one more victorious screech.

"You have the most interesting timing," Calysian says.

The mammoth bird lands next to me. "That's a strange way of saying thank you."

Eamonn.

A heavy weight lifts from my chest and I crouch down, looking him in the eye. "Thank you."

Calysian keeps a wary gaze on the water as he makes his way to firmer ground. "I appreciate the help."

"I can't hold this form for long." A blink of the eye, and Eamonn is a tiny gray bird. "The larger the form, the more energy it takes." He darts into the air, wings beating as he flies away.

Calysian begins checking Fox for injuries, and I do the same, gently running my hands down each of Hope's legs. But my mind remains on Eamonn.

"You don't think it's strange that he keeps showing up to help you?"

"He has done so since I crossed into this continent after leaving Eprotha."

"Why?"

Calysian is quiet for a long moment. "Eamonn never talks about his past. All I can determine is that he was cursed to never use a human form."

Just as Calysian was cursed to roam without his power. Without his memories.

I suppose it makes sense that the two would become friends.

"We need to find somewhere to camp." Untying Fox's lead rope, Calysian begins walking him along the narrow path, pants sticking to his legs, water pouring from his boots.

I keep a careful eye on the water surrounding us as I follow with Hope. And all I can see is the grim resignation on Calysian's face as he reached for his sword just minutes ago.

"I thought you were going to die." The words are out before I can clamp down on them.

Calysian stops, ignoring Fox's displeased snort as he turns to face me. "I'm hard to kill."

"Something tells me that serpent could have done it." I'm suddenly so tired, my limbs heavy with exhaustion. And the thought of him dead... "Stay alive, Calysian."

His expression turns almost tender. "Would you mourn me, sweetheart?"

I level him with a hard stare. "No. If you left me alone in this place, I would curse your name and spit on your corpse."

He bursts out laughing. The sound is warm and open, and it curls around me, caressing all kinds of hidden places.

"Ah, beautiful woman, I'd expect nothing less."

I swallow thickly. Despite my best efforts, I haven't forgotten his promise. *"You never should have let me taste you. Now I'll stop at nothing to make you mine."*

Calysian hasn't forgotten that promise either. I see his commitment to that promise each time his gaze lingers on my mouth, his eyes hot, lips curved in a sensual smile.

And yet he's waiting for me to go to him. It's not what I would have expected from him. But Calysian excels at doing the unexpected.

When he continues walking, I have to catch my breath.

He's the dark god. According to anyone who knows of him, he's morally destitute.

And yet…men have been trying to *take* from me since before I grew breasts. Despite his vow that I'll be *his*, Calysian has been achingly careful. He wants *me* to take from *him*.

This man chained you and would have kept you that way until he got what he wanted.

There is that.

But…some small part of me—the part that allowed me to survive in that tower—respects Calysian for besting me. Unlike Kyldare, he didn't cheat. Didn't threaten innocents.

He didn't need to.

And when he realized I might truly be in danger…

He let me go.

The mud sucks at my boot, and I stumble. Calysian's eyes cut to me and I wave my hand, gesturing for him to keep moving.

The deeper we travel into the swamp, the darker the water becomes, until I find myself staring into the depths, lungs tight as I wait for whatever lurks within to show itself. The ground shifts unpredictably between patches of firmer earth and stretches of sucking mud. The horses are slow, cautious, as we guide them through shallow pools of water in places where the track disappears.

Somewhere to our left, something splashes, and I jolt. Hope lets out a snort, and I tighten my grip on her lead rope.

I *hate* this place.

Hours later, I spot something I can't ignore, close enough to the water to make my mouth go dry.

Inching toward the edge of the path, I watch the water carefully. When nothing lurches from the depths, I snatch the tiny trinket, shoving it into my pocket.

"What are you doing?"

Calysian's gaze is hungry as he watches me. No one has ever looked at me like that before—as if they're desperate to learn everything about me.

I shift uncomfortably, and he narrows his eyes. "I've watched you do this since the tower. Just give me this. Please."

It's the first time he's ever said *please*, and my eyebrows shoot up. His lips curve in a crooked grin, his dimple flashing.

It's the dimple that does it, although I'd never tell him that.

I pull the small handful of rocks from my pocket, each carefully chosen for its uniqueness. One is a strange shade of purple, while another is covered in tiny swirls. My favorite is a pebble so smooth it feels like glass in my hand.

"Daharak…." My throat closes as grief threatens to swamp me, and I take a shaky breath. Strangely, it's Calysian's eyes that help tether me to the here and now.

"She collected…*collects* stones. Not just any stones. She loves the unusual. Sometimes, she wouldn't even bother leaving the ship when we docked—she was always so impatient to get back to sea. But when she did, she would inevitably find some stone that delighted her." I let out a hoarse laugh. "The wild pirate queen had a secret collection of pretty rocks."

"And now you're collecting them for her."

I shrug, feeling my cheeks heat. "She likes them. They make me think of her."

And each time I choose a stone I think she'll like, I'm reaffirming the fact that she's not dead. One day, I'll give them to her.

"Were you lovers?" Calysian's voice is low.

"No. It wasn't like that with us. It was…she was a friend. And I don't have any friends."

"You did. Once."

He's talking about Prisca and Asinia.

Asinia grinning at me, a ridiculous crown on her head. A crown made of flowers. Despite myself, I feel my lips curve, and her grin widens.

Prisca watching me with those strange eyes. "Stay." Her voice is tight. "Stay with us, Madinia. We need you."

They *had* needed me, and I'd left anyway. Was that why they had never come for me? Why they'd left me to the consequences of my actions?

"You said when I regained my memories, I'd find myself wondering how I ended up here alone, and where my so-called friends are."

Calysian winces. "I shouldn't have said that."

Shoving the rocks back into my cloak pocket, I get to my feet. "We should find somewhere to camp."

"Madinia."

I swallow around the lump in my throat. I don't want to talk about this. Can't he see that?

"Look at me."

I meet his eyes. His expression is gentle. There's no sign of the arrogant coolness I associate with the other part of him. With Calpharos.

"You fought a war together. You saved each other's lives. Friendship like that doesn't just fade away. You'll see them again.

And Daharak...we'll search for news of her people. After I get the grimoire, I'll go with you to Nyrridor."

The city closest to where I hid the grimoire. It's the third largest city in Telanthris, and we'll need to stop to buy supplies. It was also the second place Daharak docked so long ago—just days after we restocked in the small town of Elunthar.

My heart aches as memories slam into me, one after the other.

Daharak's satisfied smile, the pirates jostling, ready to disembark and enjoy everything the city had to offer. It was before I knew Kyldare was hunting me, and I slipped off the ship, returning without the grimoire. I'd been so certain I had done my part, and that time in my life was over.

"Madinia." Calysian's voice is firm and I meet his eyes once more. They're serious. Intent. "We will learn what happened to them. I promise."

I nod, glancing away. I'll take the offer for the kindness that it is. But the chances that Calpharos will want to help me with anything are...low.

And yet...if Calysian is making promises to me, he's the one in charge, and not the dark god. Calpharos wouldn't bother explaining himself or promising anything. He would coldly inform me of our plans.

They're the same man, you fool. And you're about to ensure this part of him disappears forever.

My breath hitches, and I focus on Daharak and the others. Logically, I know a few days won't make any difference in my search. Not after three years. And still, my bones ache to *do* something.

Calysian continues to scan our surroundings, looking for the best place to camp, and I follow his instincts, so tired I'm almost stumbling. When he lets out a pleased hum, I have to force myself to lift my head.

"What is it?" The track has widened just enough for the horses to fit side-by-side, and I follow his gaze.

The plants are brighter here, the green even more vivid against the drab browns and yellows of the surrounding swamp. Broad leaves spread out like fans, water pooling around the roots.

Calysian kneels to inspect the ground. He runs his fingers over the mud, before surveying a series of tracks.

Relief sweeps through me in a rush that leaves me lightheaded. This kind of vegetation, plus animal tracks…

Fresh water. Somewhere close.

The tracks lead us along the edge of a shallow pool, the water green and stagnant. But the tracks continue, disappearing into a dense patch of undergrowth. Calysian breaks off a large tree branch, allowing us to carefully lead the horses deeper.

And then I hear it.

The sound is faint, barely more than a trickle. We break through the undergrowth, and my breath stutters from my lungs.

The swamp opens into a small clearing—a glimpse of joy carved out of the endless muck. A shallow stream winds through the clearing, the water clear as it flows over smooth stones. The horses don't wait, moving toward the water and lowering their heads to drink.

Calysian crouches by the stream, cupping his hand and inhaling deep before taking a cautious sip.

"It's fresh. Cool too."

The stream is flanked by raised patches of grass, soft and bright green. It feels like a different world after slogging through the muddy, dark mire surrounding us.

"There's more," Calysian points upstream to a small pool, where the stream widens and slows. It's edged by moss-covered rocks. "I'll check it."

He turns and makes his way toward the pool while I kneel next to the stream, gulping at the water until my thirst is quenched. We've been conserving our own supply, aware that it could take us some time to find a fresh source.

"It's deep enough to wash both the horses and ourselves without stirring up the drinking water downstream," Calysian announces.

As we untack the horses, checking them again for injuries, tendrils of dark power sweep toward me, luring me toward the grimoire. Grinding my teeth, I ignore the urge to turn and sprint toward its hiding place.

Calysian catches my wrist as I go to pull Hope's saddle from her back. "Go bathe. I'll finish here."

I open my mouth, but he has that steely glint in his eyes that tells me he'll be stubborn about this. Besides, I'm desperate to soak away the dirt that clings to every inch of my body.

Poking around in my saddlebag, I pull out clean clothes and a bar of soap, then leave Calysian to his task.

The water is cool enough to make me shiver, and I dunk my entire body, sloughing away sweat and mud. I keep one eye on Calysian, but he's ruthlessly angling his gaze away from me, his jaw a hard line.

I watch him as I lather soap across my skin.

As much as I've attempted to ignore reality, he won't be traveling with me to find Daharak and the others after he gets the grimoire.

I've felt the lure of that dark power. I can feel it even now. And Calysian won't be able to help himself. He'll need to find the other grimoires.

These are the last days I'll spend with him. And then we will separate.

And if he truly does appear to be a threat to this world—and anyone I've ever cared about—my only chance will be to kill him before he gets the other two grimoires.

Can I do that? Can I thrust my sword through his back?

Nausea sweeps through me, and my chest turns strangely hollow.

He wouldn't be the same man. I have to remember that. Killing him would save this world.

My lip trembles and I bite down until it aches. No. I refuse to accept such a thing. I won't accept it until I'm staring into Calpharos's eyes and I know for sure that there is no other way.

Pushing the thought from my mind, I sweep the soap down my arms, basking in the feeling of finally being clean.

Calysian murmurs something to Fox, as he checks Hope's hooves. His gaze is still carefully turned from my body as he begins to set up our camp.

This is a man who is used to taking what he wants. And yet in this, he's waiting for my invitation.

He freezes, and I can see the stiffness of his muscles. He knows I'm naked, my eyes on him. And it's taking everything in him not to turn and face me.

The thought of all that passion and fury unleashed…

I shiver.

"If you're done, I'd like to bathe before the sun sets," Calysian's voice is tight.

I'm vindictive enough to splash my way out of the water, my blood turning hot, my fists clenching.

I don't want to obsess about the way his damp clothes cling to his hard body, caressing every ridge and plane. I don't want to bask in the caged need in his eyes when he looks at me. I don't want to fantasize about the raw power of him unleashed, devouring me whole.

But I do. It's a tension that thrums beneath my skin, refusing to be ignored.

And it's utterly infuriating.

The humid air caresses my skin as I pull on the shirt I stole from him. When I'm finished, Calysian stalks toward the water, as if I've suddenly turned invisible.

I sit on an overturned log next to the blankets he piled on the ground—our bed for the night. He may have given me privacy, but unless he asks me to return the favor, I'm going to enjoy the view.

Calysian knows I'm watching. I can tell in the way he rolls his shoulders, his chin jutting arrogantly. When he turns, I suck in a sharp breath.

Gods.

Every part of him is…large. He's tall, thick, built like he was born to swing a sword. To lead armies. His broad shoulders only serve to highlight the slab of muscle he calls a chest, while his ridged abdomen makes my fingers twitch with the need to touch and explore. His thighs are thick and muscular, but my gaze is already moving just a little higher…

I swallow, my mouth suddenly dry.

"Your gaze burns like a brand," he growls, and I shiver.

"Would you prefer if I looked away?"

"No. Look your fill, sweetheart. I'll see *you* soon enough."

My body is suddenly hot, needy.

His eyes meet mine across the distance. "You need relief. Ask me to give it to you."

"Calysian…"

"I'll make you feel good, Madinia. I want you. You want me back. That's all that matters. Tell me you want me."

I take a shuddering breath. When I don't reply, he shakes his head, turning away.

"Calysian."

"I want the words. Say them."

"I want you." The words are out before I can pull them back.

The look Calysian gives me is half baffled surprise, half sensual promise. And then he's out of the pool and prowling toward me, water dripping from his naked body.

CHAPTER FIFTEEN

Madinia

CALYSIAN MOVES UNNATURALLY FAST, AND I HAVE A single moment to wonder if the grimoire is already affecting him before he's standing in front of me, unapologetically naked. He catches the tip of his tongue between his teeth and gives me a smile so filthy, I'm momentarily speechless.

"This is a one-time occurrence." I lay the rule down in the scant inches between our bodies, and he steps forward until we're pressed together, those rules crushed.

"I'll allow your delusions."

"I'm serious. If I have to kill you, I will."

"Of that, I have no doubt." He drops his head slowly. So slowly, I catch my breath. Despite his possessive words, he's still giving me the chance to refuse him.

Fisting his hair, I pull his head to me.

He doesn't hesitate. His kiss is a slow, deep taunt, designed to make me crave more. I shiver against him and he lets out a feral sound, pulling me even closer.

My breasts swell, my core turning liquid, and his other

hand wraps around my waist, pulling me as close as he possibly can, as if determined to imprint my body with his.

The world spins, and he lays me on the soft blankets. He stares down at me, and there's a possessive glint in his eyes that makes me tense.

He lowers his head, pressing kisses along my jaw. "It should be impossible for you to be this beautiful." When his teeth nip a spot beneath my ear, I jolt, my thighs clenching. With a low laugh, he nips again. And again.

"Calysian."

"Now that's a pretty sound. Say my name like that again, and I'll reward you, beautiful woman."

My cheeks flame, and he laughs again, but the sound is strangely…tender.

"No one would believe you have this shy, sweet side of you. It pleases me that I'm the one to see it."

I narrow my eyes at him, but he's already pulling his shirt over my head. He says something in a language I don't recognize. A language that burns my ears.

My nipples tighten until they ache, and Calysian stares unapologetically. I suck in an unsteady breath, shifting restlessly.

Calysian stares at my breasts some more. "Putting on a show for me?"

I glower at him and he laughs, his mouth capturing mine. When I bite down on his lower lip, he lets out a low growl, his hand sliding up to cup my face, holding me steady as he dominates our kiss with lips and tongue and teeth.

He kisses me until I'm dizzy, and then slowly lifts his head, lips curving at whatever he sees. I get the strange feeling he's attempting to…tame me.

I tense, and he laughs, crushing his mouth to mine once more. This time, I bury my hand in his hair, holding him where *I* want him. He lets out a rough sound that sends warmth straight to my core.

THIS VICIOUS DREAM

He gentles our kiss until it turns intimate. We breathe into each other's mouths, and he presses his body close, so warm and hard against mine.

When he lifts his head, he immediately returns his attention to my breasts, one calloused finger teasingly stroking around and around my nipple.

I break out in violent goosebumps, my nipples aching, desperate for…

That.

Calysian's mouth is warm, his tongue flicking against my nipple, and the sudden jolt of sensation makes me shudder. He gently bites down, and I gasp as he soothes the tiny pain with his lips.

"More."

The word is a low, hoarse demand, and he chuckles, the vibration a delicious sensation against my skin.

I'm aching deep inside, in a way I've never ached before. It's…unexpected, thrilling, and…terrifying.

"Shh," Calysian murmurs, turning his attention to my other nipple. "You said you'd let me make you feel good."

I did. And yet, I didn't know what that meant.

Never has a man wanted to *give* to me. My entire life, they've only ever wanted to take.

Tomorrow, Calysian will no longer be the man who sends me lust-filled looks with those dark eyes. He won't be the man who risks his life for mine, or the man who is so obsessed with my pleasure. This might be my only chance to experience this.

He lifts his head, watching me. "Still thinking. Clearly I'm not distracting you enough." His teeth graze my nipple and I hiss a breath, closing my eyes as I revel in the sensation. When he flicks his tongue against me, I let out a low, throaty moan.

Mortification flashes through me and my eyes fly open.

Calysian gives me a smug grin. "Now that's the kind of sound I like to hear from that pretty mouth."

I scowl at him and his grin widens. And then he's shifting his body down, the muscles in his shoulders taut as he leans over me.

I can't help it. I sweep my hands over those muscles, feeling them jump beneath my palms. Calysian shudders, and when his eyes meet mine, they're so dark, my breath catches in my throat.

We stare at each other for one long moment.

And then he's moving lower once more, pressing my thighs apart as he ponders me. "You're even beautiful here."

His strong hands lift my legs, until they're splayed, resting on each of his shoulders.

"C-Calysian."

"Do you trust me?"

"Uh…"

He shakes his head in mock disapproval. And then he lightly sweeps one finger over the heat of me, his eyes darkening. "So wet. For me."

A strange light enters his eye and I tense, but he's already kissing my inner thighs, paying special attention to the places that make me twitch. I lift my hips and he lets out a low laugh.

"I'm the one in control here, sweetheart. I suggest you lie back and enjoy it."

I curl my lip at his patronizing tone, but he's already turning his attention to my core, his finger gently drifting over me once more.

My abdominal muscle tense, and Calysian lowers his head, stroking his tongue across me in one long sweep.

My skin breaks out in a sweat and I lift my hips, desperate for more. He lets out a rough groan, his hands tightening on my thighs as he laves me with his tongue again and again, until he finally switches to deep, dirty kisses. He leaves no place untouched, exploring every inch of me before returning to those that make me gasp and moan.

When he finds my clit, I jolt. He simply holds me tighter and *feasts*.

His mouth is demanding, and I claw at him, burying my fingers in his hair and pressing myself closer. I grind against him, my desperation outweighing any hint of self-consciousness. When he circles my clit with his tongue, I cry out.

"Calysian!"

"Hmmm," he murmurs. "Say my name again."

"You—I—"

He laughs, and I arch, needing his mouth on me once more.

"Calysian." The word is more of a growl than a plea, but he rewards me by circling my clit again. Every muscle in my body tenses, my thighs tremble, and I let out a strangled moan.

I'm so close—

"You know I've been thinking." Calysian lifts his head, his mouth curving.

I let out a strangled stream of curses, the words leaving me in a rush.

He throws his head back with a roar of laughter. "Ah, beauty, I don't dare risk your wrath."

This time he doesn't relent. When he slips his finger inside me, my breath shudders from my lungs. By the time he begins moving that finger, his tongue still caressing my clit, all I can do is pant and writhe. I'm embarrassingly close to *begging*.

My entire body tightens, and Calysian adds another finger, sucking on my clit with a low growl.

I cry out, my climax crashing through me in wave after wave. The dizzying pleasure engulfs me, and I ride it out, Calysian continuing to kiss and lick and *nip* until I push him away, suddenly sensitive.

I reach for him, and he catches my hands. I can feel his cock throbbing between us but he slowly shakes his head.

I expect him to rise over me, to thrust inside me, but instead he lays next to me, pulling me in to his arms.

"What—"

He gives me an indulgent look. "I know how your conniving mind works, Madinia Farrow. You were hoping to take as much pleasure as you could tonight and then never think of me again."

I tense, but he doesn't sound angry or irritated. No, he sounds *amused*. And that's worse.

"And what is it you think will happen instead?" My tone is icy, and he lets out a low, pleased laugh.

"I think you'll come to me when you no longer want to fight this thing between us. And tonight will be just a shadow of the pleasure I'll give you."

CHAPTER SIXTEEN

Madinia

I wake to the feel of Calysian's arm clamped around me. I tense, and he merely pulls me closer, then loosens his arm just enough for me to twist to face him.

Pushing against his chest, I look up into amused dark eyes. Tiny flecks of gold shimmer within them, and I go still, momentarily entranced.

"Good morning." His voice is rough, intimate.

Too intimate.

When I look at him, I can feel the remnants of lust burning within me even now. I can feel the ghost of the desperation that made me come so close to begging.

"Release me." The words are cold, my tone even colder. Calysian's eyes turn flat, and he gives me an empty, lifeless smile.

Something in my chest wrenches. I instantly want to take the words back. But his hands have already loosened. And the gold has disappeared from his eyes.

Pulling one of the blankets free, I wrap it around me, ignoring his considering expression as he watches me. Within moments, I've gathered my clothes and disappeared behind a clump of warped trees where I dress.

"That was poorly done," a male voice says, and I jolt, cursing as Eamonn lands on the branch closest to my head.

I slap my tunic to my bare breasts. "Go away."

The bird lets out a strange sound. "Please. I've seen better. I've *touched* better."

Turning my back, I shove the tunic over my head. "Is that so? And how long ago was that?"

Silence.

I regret the words as soon as I've said them.

"Does it help?" Eamonn asks, his voice carefully neutral.

"Does what help?"

"Pushing away anyone you might grow to care about. Does it help you feel less pain when they *do* leave?"

Pain scours my chest, and I yank my leggings up over my thighs. "I suppose I'll let you know when Calysian gets his grimoire."

My voice is empty, and Eamonn doesn't say another word. A flap of wings, and he's gone.

I give myself a few moments to wallow, but I can't indulge myself for long. My skin prickles with the haunting feel of dark power, so close, so *familiar*, it makes my head spin.

My boots are still damp, and I cringe as I pull them on, before making my way back to the small clearing. Calysian has already packed up our camp, and I open my mouth to thank him, but he's stalking toward me.

"You can feel the grimoire," I say. It's evident in the restless way he moves, the way he sweeps his gaze over the tree line, as if he's listening to something only he can hear.

"Yes. You can feel it, can't you?" His voice is low, edged with something dark. "The power."

I don't bother lying. "Yes. Yes, I feel it too."

He nods slowly, but his head is angled in that strange way that warns me of his true nature.

"You won't attempt to take my grimoire from me, will you, sweetheart?"

My heart kicks in my chest, and I give him my most sincere smile, looking up at him from beneath my lashes.

"Of course not."

His own smile is a dark threat. He doesn't believe me. "Men would kill to possess you," he murmurs. "Who could resist that face? That...mouth?" His eyes heat, and my breath shudders from my lungs.

I just stare back at him. If it seems Calysian will become a threat to this world, I'll take his grimoire without a second thought.

When he turns to lead Fox back toward the main trail, I make my way to Hope, checking her girth myself as I force my racing heart to slow.

Eamonn lands on Calysian's shoulder, pointedly angling his body away from me. Calysian glances between us and I shake my head.

"Any signs of Vicana's soldiers?" he asks.

"Yes." Eamonn's voice is low.

"And?"

"You'll see." He shoots up into the sky, flying toward the murky swamp.

We backtrack to the trail we traveled yesterday, neither of us speaking. Calysian's expression is oddly distant, as if he can also hear the grimoire calling to him.

By the time we make it back to the trail, I'm already cursing the mud squelching over my boots.

"I'm sorry. I swear I'll never bring you back to this place," I mutter to Hope, stroking her nose when she nudges at me.

Calysian stops walking, and I almost run into Fox. I peer around him, and it takes a moment for my mind to comprehend what I'm looking at.

Unlike us, Vicana's soldiers were unable to find fresh water.

Instead, they camped just footspans from the trail, directly next to the swamp.

Now, all that remains are…bones. They're stacked together in neat piles, dotted across the camp. Strewn amongst them are weapons, food, and clothes. But the bones are bleached white, as if they've been sucked clean.

I force myself to walk closer, surveying the piles. "This should be impossible."

It's as if something has eaten these men and left no trace behind. It's impossible to know how many of them were here, but from the sheer number of bones, I'm guessing at least twenty.

Calysian steps up next to me, the solid warmth of his body a comfort. When he moves forward, crouching next to a pile of bones, I have to fight the urge to yank him away.

Slowly, he reaches out a hand, touching what might be a rib.

It crumbles into dust.

I'm instantly next to Calysian, pulling him away from the bones. He allows it, stepping backwards as I place myself between him and the bones.

"Madinia." His voice is gentle as he leans close, murmuring into my ear. "I was in no danger."

"I don't like it."

I can feel him studying me, and I don't meet his gaze, too perturbed by my own strange reaction.

"What could have killed them?" I murmur. There's no sign of any predators, no tracks. It's as if their muscle and flesh and blood melted away into nothing, leaving nothing but bone behind.

"Whatever it is, it's still out there," Eamonn says from above our heads. "I suggest you stay alert."

He flaps away, and Calysian leans over, pressing a soft kiss to my neck. "You were worried about me." There's no smug satisfaction in his voice. Just a strange tenderness.

I *was* worried about him. And that's unacceptable.

Shrugging him off, I stalk toward the horses. "I'm guessing this isn't the only regiment Vicana sent into this swamp. We need to move."

Up until now, the insects have mostly been an annoyance. But as we travel deeper into the swamp, they become worse and worse. I grit my teeth, slapping at mosquitoes and flies, waving them away from Hope the best I can.

They avoid Calysian as if his blood is poisonous. When I glower at him, he gives me the slow, smug grin he knows irritates me the most.

"God blood, sweetheart. Some of us are simply built differently." I curl my lip at him and his eyes darken. "Now you're just giving me an invitation."

A few hours later, the ground is solid enough for us to mount our horses and trot—hopefully making up some lost time. Bright red flowers catch my eye, their waxy petals as wide as one of Calysian's arms. They line this part of the swamp, bold and unnatural against the tangled undergrowth. The air is thick with their sickly-sweet perfume, the cloying scent laced with something sharp that burns at the edges of my lungs. With each breath I'm desperate for fresh air, but there's none to be found.

A strange, loud buzzing fills my ears, and I angle my head slapping out with my palm.

That insect was unnaturally large. Larger than anything I've ever seen, with bright blue wings.

Calysian waves his hand. "Hate this place," he grumbles, and I have to hide a smile at his sulky tone.

More buzzing fills my ears and I slam my hand into another insect, shuddering at the feel of it against my skin.

Eamonn circles above our heads. "I know what they are!" His voice is filled with panic, and I freeze. "They're Sorrowflies."

"Sorrowflies?" Calysian turns Fox to face me.

Eamonn lands on his shoulder. "They—"

I slap a hand to my neck with a hiss. Calysian's eyebrows lower, just as a huge fly wings toward him, biting his hand.

He stares at it incredulously.

The fly that bit him drops out of the air. Dead.

God blood indeed.

The fly that bit *me* comes back for more.

I lash out at it, and almost topple from the saddle, swaying dizzily.

My entire face turns oddly numb, and my hands fall from the reins, my body listing to the side.

"Madinia!"

Calysian nudges Fox, aiming for me, but his huge body is wavering in the saddle.

He falls to the ground with a thump.

CALYSIAN

"You dare take from me?"

Her face...it's breathtakingly beautiful, each feature seemingly designed to draw attention to the next. Her lips are a blood red, curved in the mockery of a smile, her eyes a light green, fringed by dark lashes.

I despise her with everything in me.

The woman chokes, as I tighten the smoke wrapped round her neck like a noose. She gasps a breath.

"You stole my future from me. So I took yours from you." Her words are a low taunt. "You didn't think I'd allow you to live in happiness, did you, lover?"

The temple begins to collapse. Columns near the altar crash to the ground, and fear flashes across her face.

The pain threatens to engulf me. Threatens to make me tear the very fabric of this world apart. My power begins to build, and a hint of fear enters her eyes.

She should be afraid.

"They're coming for you," she gasps out. "I'm giving you a warning so you can fight."

My laugh is cold, and ice forms on her skin. But if I am to do what needs to be done, I don't have time to kill her. Not now.

But I will.

"Calysian!" I blink my eyes open, staring at pale blue streaked with white.

"Where am I?"

A bird appears, azure wings blocking out the sky.

"They're attracted to fear and misery!" Eamonn flaps his wings close enough to my face to force me to focus. "They'll trap you here and feed until you die unless you do something!"

Another bite. I stare at my arm, uncomprehending.

I gaze down at the books in my hands, stomach roiling. How can I do this? How can I sacrifice any chance to—

No. This is the only way. Either I do this, or my vicious siblings take these memories, and I'll never find—

"They'll kill her," Eamonn slashes at me with his beak. "That one has seen more terror and despair in her short life than most would see over centuries. The flies will glut themselves on her pain, Calysian."

"Who?"

"Madinia."

"No." The word is hoarse, and I stumble to my feet, moving toward her crumpled body. The mare nudges at her, clearly unaffected by the flies.

They feed on fear and misery?

Then I'll focus on the woman at my feet.

Madinia, who came to me last night with her soft hands and her eager mouth. Madinia, who allowed me to lose myself in her body, even as she lost herself in mine. Madinia, who looks at me with that befuddling mixture of innocence and wickedness.

The woman infuriates me until I want to wrap my hands around her pretty little neck. And she fascinates me until I want to force her to tell me all of her thoughts and secrets.

"Calysian?" Her voice trembles, and I haul her into my arms.

"Focus on something *good*, sweetheart. They can't hurt you if you focus on the good."

Her eyes fill with tears, and another fly bites her. She lets out a choked sob, lost in the agony of her worst moments.

And she has had *so many* bad moments.

I slap at the fly that bites my neck, falling to my knees with a roar. Seeing this woman in pain gives true meaning to the word *despair*.

I hit my knees, tightening my grip around her as I clench my teeth.

"Everything you love is gone. We took it. Perhaps now you'll show some respect."

"Tronin…" another voice says. *"There are no memories here. He's already done away with them. And his power."*

A vicious roar.

"You think you can find those memories again? Then you can wander the mortal lands until you do. But don't worry, brother. We won't make you wander alone."

Another slash of claws, blood running down my cheek. But it's enough to bring me back to myself, and I stumble to my feet.

"Fox," I grind out, and the horse follows, Madinia's mare trailing after us.

I study her face, forcing myself to block out the sight of her tears. Her real tears.

The buzz of a sorrowfly whines near my ear, and I slap it away.

A pink blush traveling to her cheeks when I asked why she

saved my life. The feel of her hand in my hair as she pulled me closer, unapologetic in her need.

If this woman ever learns that it's thoughts of *her* I use to block out my own despair, she will laugh and laugh.

My mouth twitches, and I stumble down the track.

"You're almost there," Eamonn says, circling low above me. "The flies spawn near those red flowers, and once you cross that small bridge, the flowers—and the flies—disappear."

"They'll follow us."

"They can only travel so far from their nest. They're already dropping away."

I scowl, but I don't have time to argue. Instead, I focus on the warmth of the woman in my arms.

When she opens her eyes, I press my lips to hers.

MADINIA

I sigh against Calysian's mouth, attempting to wiggle closer. But I'm in his arms and he's…moving?

"Shh," he murmurs. "Just focus on me. Focus on what I'm making you feel."

His arms tighten around me, and I relax, even as he stumbles across the path.

I laugh against his mouth, and he grins.

"They're gone," Eamonn says, and Calysian raises his head, gently placing me on my feet.

"Are you hurt?"

I frown at him, and it floods into me. The flies, biting at me continuously, the memories I relived one after the other.

I flinch.

Calysian pulls me close once more. "They're gone. If we

come across them again, you need to think of anything that brings you joy."

I nod numbly, but I have so few things that bring me joy.

This man has been searching for his memories for centuries, and he was able to get *both* of us free.

The dark god has more joy in his life than I do.

It would be amusing if it wasn't so sad.

I wipe at my damp face. "Thank you for helping me." The words sound oddly formal, and Calysian tenses against me, slowly taking a step back.

"You don't need to thank me for that."

Silence stretches between us, and I turn my attention to our surroundings.

"We're in the heart of the swamp."

Calysian gives me a stiff nod, turning to check on the horses. Something has shifted between us, gone wrong somehow. Just as it did this morning when I ordered him to release me.

You promised yourself it was one night. And you wouldn't get attached.

Blowing out a breath, I survey the ground. It's little more than patches of earth floating on the water's surface, islands of tangled roots and grass that we'll need to somehow navigate with the horses.

Already, I'm questioning Fliora's advice.

Calysian takes Fox's lead rope. His back is straight, his shoulders tense, his jaw tight. "We should continue moving."

"Fine."

I follow after him, keeping a wary eye on the gnarled trees that rise from the water, their trunks split and broken. The buzzing of insects makes me shudder, but the fly that swoops past is a plain black color, not the silver and blue of the Sorrowflies.

We walk for hours, Calysian turning unerringly toward the grimoire at each fork in the trail. The air is thick and suffocating,

THIS VICIOUS DREAM

soaking our clothes and making each breath an effort. Hope stumbles as the ground shifts beneath us, and I murmur soft words that do little to calm her.

Calysian points ahead, where the path narrows into a raised strip of land, no wider than a horse's body. Trees crowd too close on either side, roots tangled into the mud below. If we step wrong here, we'll fall straight into the water.

And I'm exceedingly aware of the serpent that lies in wait somewhere in this swamp.

Eventually, we have no choice but to lead the horses through hip-deep water. "Come on girl," I say, and Hope throws her head, but continues walking as the water ripples around her legs.

Calysian guides Fox ahead, the water rising to the horse's chest, his dark coat slick and gleaming. The water is colder than I expected when I move deeper, seeping into my boots and clinging to my legs. The hum of insects fades, replaced by silence.

It's an anticipatory silence. A silence that makes the hair on the back of my neck stand up.

The water ripples to my left, a slow deliberate movement that makes my teeth clench as sparks fly from my hands. But my power is useless here.

This water-logged path is endless. And already, I can feel that same, primal power from the last time we were hunted in this swamp. The serpent has found us.

Hope snorts, jerking backwards and tearing her lead rope from my hand. She thrashes, her hooves sending waves rippling outward, and I lunge for the rope, holding it tight.

"I'll take her." Calysian is at my side before I realize he's moved. "Take Fox."

I'm prepared for a kick or a bite, but surprisingly, Calysian's horse doesn't play any of his usual games. He cooperates, surging forward as a different power slices toward us. Not the primal power of the serpent. This is something else. Something familiar. I brace myself, but it isn't aimed at me.

It flows into Calysian.

And his eyes turn black.

The grimoire.

When the water ripples once more, he waves one hand, sending something dark and vicious toward the serpent.

The long, sinewy shape thrashes, then disappears into the depths of the water.

A muscle jumps in Calysian's jaw. Clearly, it's not dead.

"It's hunting us," I say, keeping a careful eye on the man at my side. He's connected to his grimoire—enough that it allowed him to attack the serpent.

"Yes."

We make it across the water to the comforting stability of a muddy path. Calysian's eyes are still black, and he slowly turns his head, as if he can feel my gaze on him.

"Are you scared of me now?"

I swallow, my throat dry. "No."

He shakes his head at me. "You know who I am. You've always known."

It's *Calysian's* voice, *Calysian's* glower, and yet I still shiver. I did everything I could to protect the grimoire, and now here I am, about to hand that grimoire over to the dark god himself.

By the time the sun is high in the sky, we've made it through the center of the swamp.

Screams sound in the distance and Calysian angles his head, satisfaction flickering in his dark eyes. "Another regiment we won't need to worry about."

"Kyldare is here somewhere. Bridin will have ensured he's the closest to the grimoire." And if he's that close, I can kill him before he gets to it.

The ground hardens, but we continue to lead the horses.

THIS VICIOUS DREAM

A strange sense of grim anticipation gnaws at me, but when Calysian nods at a tiny pool of fresh water, we stop briefly to rest.

"You must have faced men like Kyldare before," Calysian says. "In Regner's court."

"Yes. But I grew up in that court, and my father was favored enough that it gave me a certain level of protection."

"And you hid your power." Calysian's tone is neutral, politely interested. But he's studying me, his expression inscrutable.

"Yes."

He's silent for a long moment, as if waiting for me to continue. Hope lowers her head to drink, and I stretch my aching legs.

"That must have been...exhausting."

"It was," I murmur, wading through memories of court politics and power struggles, forever tinged with the dark, terrible fear of discovery. "You can only keep so much of yourself buried before it starts to burn you alive. Ironically, that's almost what happened."

"Tell me."

I glance at him. He's several footspans closer, his eyes intent.

"Why?"

"I want to know you. In exchange, I'll tell you something about me."

I wish I could say I wasn't interested in his past. But in truth I'm fascinated at the thought of him wandering this world for so long.

Calysian gives me a slow smile. He knows he has me.

"Fine," I sigh. "My father was one of Regner's patriarchs. A powerful man who knew the truth of the *corrupt*. He knew the so-called corrupt were hybrids—solely a threat because Regner couldn't steal our power the way he could steal others. I was counting down the days until I would turn twenty-five winters and would be discovered. I knew of the dungeon far below my own feet, knew I would be burned with the others when I was caught."

"I can't imagine living with that fear."

"It made me cold and mean. I hated *everyone*."

"It made you a survivor."

I swallow around the lump in my throat. "The day Prisca learned what I was…my father was ranting about the corrupt. He blamed them for my mother's death and I could no longer control my power. Flames formed in my hands, and I knew my life was over."

Hope nudges at me with her nose, and I stroke her silky cheek.

"You tried to take your own life."

I jolt, and Hope sidesteps. "Shhh, it's fine." I murmur to her before turning my attention back to Calysian. "How did you know?"

"I know how you think. You wanted to die on your own terms. You never would have given Regner the satisfaction of watching you be hauled away. And you never would have allowed your death to be a spectacle."

I stare at him. It's strange how well he knows me, considering how few interactions we had before we met on this continent. "Yes. I touched my burning hand to my dress. And that's when Prisca appeared. She used her own power, dumped water on my dress and told me the truth of the so-called corrupt. That's when I learned that my father knew the gods had never demanded our power. And that Regner had been taking that power for himself."

"I'm sorry."

My eyes burn, and I blink away the dampness that clings to my lashes. Even after all this time, the betrayal cuts like a blade. "My father knew. He knew that the corrupt were just hybrids, living their lives. But he enjoyed being so close to the throne, would never give it up. When he learned I was a hybrid—and that my mother must have been one too...he looked at me as if *I* had betrayed *him*."

Calysian cups my face, tilting my head until his dark eyes meet mine. "You're allowed to hate him. And to love him. You're allowed to choose not to forgive him."

"He's dead. Regner killed him." My lungs burn and I fight to take my next breath. "I watched his h-head—"

"Shh." Calysian pulls me close. And for some reason, I don't push him away. Instead, I allow him to press my head to his chest, the steady thump of his heart a warm comfort.

"I may not understand family," he rumbles. "But I understand betrayal. I know the mark it leaves on you, the bitter taste that clings to the back of your throat."

I tilt my head back to find him staring into the distance, his brows drawn.

"I know the myth of Calpharos," I murmur. "They say it was your siblings who did this to you."

He stiffens, and his eyes meet mine. Something dark paces behind them, waiting to be freed.

And then he blinks, and he's Calysian once more. "I have heard this too. I learned of it just a few years ago. This kind of betrayal cuts deep. The centuries I have wandered, the feeling of that aching hole inside me where my memories and power should be...it seems it was all because I was a threat to *their* power."

"Do you remember them?"

He shakes his head. "When I think of them, I feel a deep sense of dread. A knowledge that this is not all they took from me. When the Sorrowflies bit me, I remembered a woman who betrayed me to them. And I remembered the moment I made the decision to place pieces of my soul into the grimoires." With a sigh, he shakes his head. "We need to continue moving."

Hours later, we find the remains of Vicana's regiment.

CHAPTER SEVENTEEN

CALYSIAN

REMAINS ARE SCATTERED THROUGHOUT THE SMALL clearing, organs and viscera strewn next to boots and cooking supplies.

"Whatever did this...it's not the same predator that attacked the last regiment."

"No." That predator left only bones. "I can sense the grimoire close by."

Madinia gives me a stiff nod. "We should leave the horses. They'll make too much noise. But...not here."

We find a clearing near another small pool of water, and I gratefully refill my flask, watching as Madinia does the same before urging her mare to drink. She's unhappy at the thought of leaving the horses—truthfully, I am too. But bringing them close to Kyldare would be much more dangerous. He strikes me as the kind of man who would gleefully cut down both of our horses.

Besides, I can't believe the baby seer would have told us to bring the horses if they were going to end up dead in this place. I felt no sense of malice from her.

No, that malice had come from her aunt.

Madinia nuzzles her mare's face, her hand shaking as she gives her a final stroke.

It's a tiny flicker of vulnerability, and I ruthlessly suppress the urge to pull her into my arms. I'm ignoring all of my instincts with this woman, forcing myself to allow her to come to me, time after time, as if she's a wild animal I'm trying not to spook.

Leaving the horses, we make our way toward the grimoire. I can sense Madinia's wariness, and she glances at me continually, as if waiting for me to suddenly strike her down.

Clenching my teeth, I allow it. For now.

Just minutes later, the insects fall quiet once more—a sharp, unnatural stillness coiling around us. Like a warning. Voices drift through the humid air, low and tense. I meet Madinia's eyes, and she gives me a grim nod. Kyldare and his soldiers are lying in wait just around the bend.

My grimoire is so close, urging me to approach.

Madinia brushes by me, and I catch her arm. "I want you to wait here."

She gives me that haughty look that makes me crazed.

I can't help it. I take her mouth, swallowing her gasp.

"I don't want anything to happen to you," I mutter. "There's no need for you to come."

"There is. I can't tell you why, but I know I have to go with you."

I can tell by the stubborn jut of her jaw and the hard glint in her eyes that she won't be dissuaded from this. And truthfully, I'm torn between warring impulses. As much as I want to leave her behind, I also want her where I can see her.

"Fine. But you do exactly as I say."

Her mouth curves.

Shaking my head, I release her. "You make me insane, woman."

Jerking my head, I gesture for her to follow me away from the bend and into a thicket of trees. The mud swallows our boots, making each step a long, exhausting process. But finally, we're able to crouch behind a twisted tree as we survey the clearing.

I can feel my grimoire, lodged within a tree so impossibly vast, nothing natural could have caused such a growth. When I glance at Madinia, she winces.

"I hid the grimoire in the trunk of that tree. Parts of it had rotted away. But...the tree didn't look like this. I...I didn't realize the grimoire would...alter it."

There's no sign of rot now. The power in the grimoire has leached into the tree, and it stands huge and healthy, looming high above our heads. Twisted roots are sprawled across the waterlogged ground, some of them as thick as a man's thigh.

Kyldare stands in the mud, flanked by his men as the swamp water laps at their boots. Even from here, his satisfied smirk is evident.

I count ten soldiers around him, weapons ready, but their faces are twisted with unease, and they continually glance over their shoulders, clearly spooked. They've felt the oppressive weight of the swamp as they've traveled this far. And they can't have missed the remains of the other regiments.

Madinia's breaths are shallow, her eyes locked on Kyldare and his soldiers. Her face is pale, but her eyes glitter with blue fire.

The witch steps close to the tree, hovering her hand near the bark. A vivid green light surrounds her hand, her power saturating the air between them and us.

Oh, she's powerful.

But her shoulders sag, and she wipes sweat from her brow, stepping back to survey the tree.

"Do not stop," Kyldare barks. "Break it."

Madinia leans close. "You need to get to the grimoire." Her voice is a bare whisper, and the feel of her warm breath on my neck makes me heavy lidded.

I reach for her, and she gives me an icy look. "Focus."

My lips curve, and her eyes darken. Ah. I'm not the only one remembering the feel of her thighs on my shoulders.

She casts me a wary look but returns her attention to the scene in front of us.

Kyldare's witch paces in front of the tree, hands twisting as she attempts her magic. Deep lines are etched in her face, her blonde hair now gray in places.

Satisfaction burns through me. Holding the ward against my power required years of her life. Years she will be hoping to reclaim with my grimoire.

But she won't.

"We'll split them," Madinia murmurs. "I'll draw their attention to the left, toward the water. You circle behind, get close to the tree. Use the distraction to take out the witch."

Let this woman play bait? "No." My refusal is instant, and Madinia's expression tightens. With a wave of her hand, she waits for me to expand. To provide reasoning.

I remain silent. If I choose not to allow her to do such a thing, she will comply. I am a god.

Slowly, Madinia leans close, her voice colder than I've ever heard it. "If you think temporary access to my body means you now have the right to determine my actions, you are so very, very wrong," she whispers. "I will incapacitate you and *leave* you here before I'll allow you to give me orders."

My hands tighten on her shoulders, and I lean close. Madinia shifts, and some of the fury drains from her expression.

"The grimoire is calling you."

"Yes." I grit out.

"Then *think*," she hisses. "If you can come up with a better plan, I'm willing to hear it."

I...can't. Madinia can't kill the witch. Not alone.

And without access to more of my power, I can't kill both the soldiers and the witch in one blow.

"You have a plan to get to the grimoire."

She nods.

"Fine. I will allow this."

Angling her head, she gives me a long, cool look. I know her well enough to know what that look means.

Fiercely independent Madinia is mentally barring me from her bed. She has decided I'm too much of a threat to the freedom she holds closer than any lover.

I nip at her ear. "Keep thinking such thoughts. I'll merely fuck them out of you."

She stiffens, but I'm already moving. "Go."

Madinia

Calysian melts away to my left, his body moving seamlessly, silently through the mud and muck. The canopy above our head lets in only fractured, dim light, while the haze of humidity and thick tangle of roots and trees should help us stay hidden.

Since I'm nowhere near as graceful as Calysian I'm forced to move much slower.

My lungs strain for each breath, my mouth so dry I'm almost tempted to rinse it with swamp water. My sweat has turned ice-cold, and despite the suffocating humidity, I'm shivering as I slowly inch toward the swamp.

No, I didn't tell Calysian about this part of my plan. Because the brute would have found a way to stop me.

Kyldare is still standing at the edge of the swamp with most of his men, his gaze locked on Bridin as she works desperately to get to the grimoire.

Today, Kyldare looks like he has climbed from the depths of the swamp himself. His face is unnaturally flushed, his eyes glittering as he stares possessively at the tree.

THIS VICIOUS DREAM

It's the same look he would give me each time I was chained to the walls of that tower.

My stomach roils. I know Kyldare. And Vicana made a mistake sending him after the grimoire. He's weak—not physically, but inside, where it counts. Weak men always believe they can hide their weakness by accumulating power. They can't help themselves.

Sucking in a deep, steadying breath, I remove my boots, leaving them next to the trunk of a warped tree, along with my sword. Slowly, I slip into the swamp, the water curling around my ankles, my thighs, my waist.

I pull the knife at my hip, my hand aching as I clench the hilt. The swamp swallows everything—sound, light—even natural instinct. Thick roots and mangroves obscure my path. They help hide me, but they make it almost impossible for me to map out a clear path toward the soldiers.

I sink deeper, the water rising to my ribs. I ruthlessly suppress the urge to slide right out of the swamp and back onto land.

Kyldare's men shift uneasily, casting sidelong glances at the water, the tree, the thick branches above our heads. I crouch lower, letting the reeds close around me like a shield. My breaths are shallow, my heart slamming into my ribs. I have two options: Circle through the deeper water to my right, or duck under the cover of the low hanging branches closer to the soldiers.

The sickly green light is still spilling across the clearing. Bridin paces, her hands twitching. The glow flares brighter, and my heart stops. Her laugh rings out, sharp and triumphant.

Her laugh turns to a choked scream, and she drops to her knees, clutching at her chest.

Calysian.

"They're here!" Kyldare roars.

The soldiers instinctively recoil from Calysian. Likely, they've heard what he can do. They back toward the swamp, and the water laps hungrily at their boots.

Still, I wait.

And wait.

My muscles scream from the strain, my chest aching for more air.

There.

The long, sinewy form has just rounded the bend, entering this part of the swamp. It's far enough way that my plan has a chance of working—but it will be breathtakingly close. Already, the serpent is slicing through the water, shockingly fast. It moves like a shadow, so fast it's almost a blur, its sleek, muscular body undulating beneath the surface.

As expected, the creature couldn't resist.

Not after hunting me and Calysian for days.

Now I just have to time this perfectly.

Breathless and trembling, I count down in my head, ruthlessly suppressing the need to move.

Now.

Ducking my head, I dive into the water, beneath the tree branch. Cold weight presses against my skin, and panic claws at me.

I can't see anything. Not my hands, not the roots beneath me, not even the faintest shimmer of light.

I'm going to die, here in this swamp.

No. I know where the shore is.

Yes, you know where it is. Now fucking swim.

I strike out, my movements clumsy, desperate. The swamp churns around me, and I make it six strokes before I feel it. That same cold, primal magic.

The serpent has turned. And it's aiming directly for me.

I veer to the side, kicking hard, my lungs burning. The creature closes in.

Go, go, go.

Lifting my head, I gasp for air, and an arrow slices toward me, so close I can feel the tiny breeze it creates.

"Don't kill her!" Kyldare roars.

My blood burns hot, and I channel my rage, diving again. Even if he gets the grimoire, Kyldare will never let me go. No, he'll make me pay for escaping him. And he'll enjoy it.

Murky water rushes over my head as I kick blindly for the shore, a sob clawing up my throat at the feel of solid ground. Surging forward, I claw my way onto the bank. Mud clings to my skin, reeds tangle around my legs, but I crawl forward.

Don't stop.

I need to put as much distance between myself and the water as possible.

A deep ripple surges behind me, and the serpent breaks the surface of the water, just footspans from my previous position, right next to the shore. My heart slams into my ribs and I scramble for firmer ground.

The creature is easily thirty footspans long, its sinewy body covered in dark, glistening scales. Its blunt, wide head is framed by a ridge of bony, spiked protrusions that curve backward, almost like a crown.

Scanning the chaos with eerie intelligence, the serpent blinks, and I choke on the horror of it.

Slitted pupils are surrounded by a pale glow that fixes on the nearest soldier. The idiot is standing too close to the shore.

The soldier turns to run, but the serpent opens its maw, revealing a single row of jagged teeth. It strikes, plucking him off the shore and dragging him under in an explosion of water and foam.

The screams begin.

Even Kyldare stumbles back, his face twisting in disbelief as the serpent lashes out, its tail whipping through the air and catching another soldier, slamming him into the water.

I cast a single, desperate glance toward the tree where Calysian stands. His eyes burn with pure, unrelenting rage.

Rage, and terror.

"Move!" he roars.

I stagger to my feet, mud slick beneath me. My lungs heave, and I reach deep for my power, aiming at the soldier furthest from the swamp.

The waterlogged air makes my power sluggish. But my fire startles him, and he stumbles towards the others, who bolt from the flames.

Toward the swamp. And the serpent.

Even Kyldare is forced to run as the serpent's body coils, striking out at the soldier closest to him.

The chaos is exactly what we needed, and yet—even with the knowledge of what those soldiers would do to me—I can't help but shudder at the thought of their watery demise. All I can hear is the sound of splashing water and panicked screams.

I sprint for the tree, and Calysian glowers at me, reaching out to slam his hand into the trunk.

"You're welcome," I snap.

"Don't push me." His voice is mild, but fury lingers in his eyes.

I'd thought the tree would fight him as it fought Bridin. But the trunk peels back, the tree sacrificing itself as it strips layer after layer of bark, until the grimoire is exposed.

So much trouble for such a small, ordinary-looking book.

Calysian sucks in a breath, and it's as if the grimoire is all that exists in the world as he reaches for it, his entire body tense.

"No!" Kyldare screams, but it's too late.

The moment Calysian touches the cover, the grimoire disappears. Along with the sun.

BOOM

Power explodes from Calysian, and I drop to my knees, dizzy. The sun reappears, and when he turns, he looks larger, his eyes distant and cold once more. His lips twist into a cruel smile.

I suck in a breath as he surveys the soldiers.

Calysian is gone.

This is Calpharos.

My lungs turn to stone. I swore I wouldn't let this happen. I promised myself I would keep him here.

"Calysian," I say.

He ignores me, his eyes narrowing on the witch at his feet. He kicks her onto her back, and her eyes flutter open.

"You thought to take from me," he purrs. "Now I'll take from you."

"Calysian!"

"Silence," he hisses, and when he finally looks at me, I freeze, my instincts warning me to be small and quiet. To slowly slink away and hope the predator in front of me ceases to notice my existence.

But it's too late for that. "You were the one who hid this from me." His voice is a low croon, and I shudder beneath the weight of it. "You thought to deny me what is mine."

"You swore you wouldn't do this," I snap.

A hint of surprise flashes across his face. "You dare speak to me in such a tone?"

Something wrenches in my chest. Something that feels almost like...betrayal.

And yet I'm the one in the wrong here. This *god* is only revealing who he truly is. I'm the one who somehow thought I could control him. I'm the one who thought he would stay human.

For me.

Stupid. Gods, I'm so stupid.

Bridin writhes, attempting to make it to her stomach. Calpharos takes a step closer to her.

An arrow slices through the air, aimed at the dark god's head, and he merely raises a hand, his obsidian shield jumping into place around his body. The arrow drops to the ground, immediately followed by three more.

Two soldiers remain, far enough from the swamp that the

serpent can't reach them. Kyldare is half hidden behind a tree, and yet I can hear his hateful voice ordering them to fire.

Calpharos ignores them as each arrow they aim at him continues to fall uselessly to the ground. His head tilts, his eyes turning blurred, unfocused. It's as if he's frozen—lost somewhere I can't reach.

More arrows hit his shield, and he smiles, his eyes sharpening. "Try harder," he purrs. Slowly, he turns his head, focusing on Bridin.

The witch freezes, her eyes meeting mine. They're the pale, faded eyes of an elderly woman who has lived for decades more than she truly will. "Please," she croaks.

A flash of triumph rushes through me. "Remember that time you trapped me within my own body?"

Calpharos ignores us, but his hand is suddenly wreathed in dark smoke and he looms over Bridin. There's nothing human in his eyes. Nothing remotely close to the man I took to bed.

I'm going to have to try to kill him. And he'll probably kill me.

Agony erupts in my chest, hot and horrifying. It blazes through my body, until the only sound I can make is a choked moan. I stare uncomprehendingly at the arrow lodged in my chest.

Kyldare's voice winds through the space between us.

"If I can't have your life, I'll gladly take your death. Think of me as you die choking on your own blood."

CHAPTER EIGHTEEN

CALYSIAN

THE WOMAN WITH THE DARK RED HAIR LETS OUT A choked sound.

It's an irritating sound that slices through my nerves. When she slumps to her knees, I remove my attention from the witch at my feet.

I'm instantly engulfed in deep, sickening horror. It's as if I've been plunged into a pool of ice-cold water, the shock of it freezing my lungs.

Madinia.

My mind rebels against the sight in front of me. The sight I know to be true.

No.

My two selves merge, memories of *before* knitting seamlessly with those from the past several centuries.

It's agonizing.

Among the memories, this woman stands out like a flame in the darkness—vivid and unyielding. It's as if the rest of my memories are painted in black and white, while those involving her alone blaze with color: her sharp tongue and unexpectedly soft heart. Her withering expressions and her breathtaking face.

Absently, I strike out at the witch, ignoring her as she chokes and writhes. Madinia slumps to her back, eyes wild as she stares up at the sky. Stumbling to her, I drop to my knees at her side, momentarily frozen.

Movement to my left.

Kyldare's soldiers are dead or dying, and yet he has remained, likely unable to resist watching Madinia take her last breath.

"She's going to die." He looks suddenly lost. But within moments his eyes turn crazed and he gives me a slow smile. "I've taken her from you, *Calpharos*."

I slash out with my smoke, but he's already diving into the swamp, risking the serpent. I ache to chase him, to make him pay.

Madinia lets out a sound that makes cold sweat drip down my back.

Sickness claws at me.

I didn't shield her. If my ward had covered her, she would not be dying at this moment.

Instead, I lost myself to my memories. To my power. And those few moments of inattention were enough.

Fox approaches the clearing, Madinia's mare trailing him. We tied them loosely enough that they could easily escape if necessary. Instead, they came here.

As gently as I can, I sweep Madinia into my arms.

"Don't." The word is a guttural moan, a plea I never could have imagined her making.

"I'm getting you to help."

"Too... late."

Fox kneels, allowing me to mount with Madinia still held carefully in my arms. When he rises to his feet, she lets out a whimper.

"It's not too late. This is why the baby seer told us to bring the horses. Rest, beautiful woman. I'm going to find a healer."

She's not listening. No, she has already lost consciousness, her face shockingly white, her body far too fragile in my arms.

MADINIA

Pain.

I thought I knew what it was. What it meant.

I had no idea.

Agony blazes through my body, sharp and hot. It spreads outward from my chest, each of my shallow breaths an unspeakable torment.

Calysian's eyes are more gold than black. They're wild as they meet mine, his expression terrible. "You're awake. Good. Stay that way."

His arms are wrapped tightly around me, protecting me from the natural jostling from his horse. One of his hands is pressed against my lung, next to the arrow. An effort to slow the bleeding. But I know my chances of survival with a punctured lung in the middle of a swamp.

And they're not high.

I cannot believe Kyldare was the one to kill me.

That thought allows me to stay conscious for several minutes, the rage sharpening my mind.

But my head begins to swim, and when I cough, black dots dance across my vision. I know what that wet cough means.

Blood.

Calysian's eyes meet mine once more, and they're suddenly black. Cold. He looks inhuman, the way he did in those moments after he took his grimoire.

I tense, suddenly certain he's about to dump me off his horse so he can turn his attention to the other two grimoires.

Instead, he lowers his head. "I have not given you permission to die."

The words are saturated with his usual arrogance, but I

can hear a strange underlying thread of something within them. Something that sounds almost like…fear.

I cough, more blood spilling from my lips.

Can't…breathe.

Unconsciousness is a relief. Distantly, I hear Calysian's curse, but I welcome the incoming numbness with everything in me.

"Madinia."

When I next crack open my eyes, the sun is setting. The air smells sweeter, fresher. We're no longer in the swamp.

Calysian's arms tense around me. "You're smiling."

"Didn't…want…to die…there."

Speaking is exhausting, and the sweet relief of unconsciousness beckons once more. The pain has lessened, which even I know is not a good sign.

"You're not dying." His voice is strained…shaken. He's ignoring the facts, turning to delusion instead.

Gods. Clearly they're not all that different from us.

The world wobbles around me, and I stare up at the sky. It's as if some other god has been finger painting swirls of lavender tinged with gold. The breeze lifts my hair, carrying the scent of flowers and greenery.

I should have focused more on these moments over the past days. Regret is a heavy weight to bear. And yet I'm so, so grateful to have escaped that tower. Even my worst moments were still moments of freedom.

"We're less than an hour from Nyrridor." Calysian's voice is tight, and when I manage to tilt my head, his gaze is fixed, focused forward.

Nyrridor. It was a smart choice. We're closer to the western coast. And the healers are likely to be much better than anything on offer in the village we visited before plunging into the swamp.

"Need you…to do…something for me."

Calysian glances down, and there's nothing soft in his expression, nothing warm in his eyes.

"I am the *dark* god. I don't complete last wishes or answer deathbed pleas. If you want something done, you'll have to live and see to it yourself."

"Hate...you."

A muscle feathers in his jaw, and when he rips his gaze from my face, I suddenly feel colder.

He knew what I was going to ask of him. Find Daharak and the others.

When he glances down at me once more, his eyes are like burning coals. "Madinia Farrow, felled by an arrow," he muses. "It sounds like a song. Or a rhyme. Maybe even a *joke*. Few will believe it. Although those who have wished you dead—and with your attitude I'm sure there are many—will laugh and laugh."

I know what he's doing, and still, I glower at him. Even as I cough up more blood, my chest burning like the hottest flames.

Unsurprisingly, he seems pleased by my glare. But he drops his gaze to my lips, and his face drains of color.

I don't have to ask what he sees. I've seen enough people die this way.

My lips will be turning blue. Already, I feel chilled, with the disconcerting feeling that I'm floating somewhere above my body.

I return my attention to the sky. The lavender is darkening now. Will I live to see a few stars appear above my head?

This is not a good death. It's not one I would have chosen for myself. And still, it's better than wasting away in that tower. I may be dying, but I'm dying while wrapped in the arms of someone who would prefer for me to live. Just days ago, such a thing was unimaginable.

I'm living again. Even as I'm dying. The irony isn't lost on me.

But I want to *keep* living. Useless frustration flashes through me, melding with the pain that burns relentlessly through me.

"Just...just hold on." Calysian's voice is a low growl. I can't see his face. Panic floods me as my vision darkens once more. I'm not ready. Not—

Calysian

I've allowed Fox to slow while Madinia was conscious, aware that the jostling of his faster gait will be agonizing. When Madinia's eyes roll back into her head, I urge Fox into a gallop.

A cold, endless rage burns through me.

Eamonn lands on my shoulder, and I almost kill him for his impertinence.

"Where were you?" My voice is frigid, and he shifts his wings.

"I saw her go down and scouted ahead. I found a healer at the edge of the city. They're expecting you."

This appeases the worst of my fury. Wisely, Eamonn holds his silence for the next few minutes while I wrestle with my temper.

"How much do you remember?" His voice is quiet, and I turn Fox at the next fork, heading west. The mare follows several footspans behind, beginning to lag. Madinia will be pleased that the horse came with us when she recovers.

Because she will recover.

"Calpharos?"

"Do not call me that!"

Madinia lets out a low groan, and I gently stroke her ribs with my thumb, continuing to hold pressure to her chest.

Eamonn flaps his wings, and I fight the urge to shrug him from my shoulder.

Calpharos is the one responsible for this. The one who shielded himself while Madinia was unshielded. Vulnerable.

I don't feel the need to analyze my memories. Don't wish to focus on anything other than getting to the healer.

Already, I had silently promised Kyldare a long death filled with immense suffering. Now, the urge to find him is almost inescapable. What I will do to him will become legend. It will be whispered about for centuries, written into history.

Distantly, I realize this preoccupation is a distraction from my true task. With one grimoire found, I should be turning my attention to the next.

Still, killing the man who did this would make a pleasing reward for Madinia for her loyalty.

In my arms, she has begun to shiver.

My teeth clench until my jaw aches. Madinia agreed to help me. She braved that swamp for my needs. And in return, I allowed *this*.

I may be the dark god, but even I have a conscience. I do not reward loyalty with disregard.

At my side, Eamonn is quiet. If he can sense the struggle between my two *selves*, he does not comment.

I've been funneling every drop of my power into both horses. Fox's hooves pound the ground and he practically flies, galloping faster than I could have imagined, while Hope follows slower, still keeping us within sight. The effort leaves me weakened, but I keep the link between us open, until black dots crawl across the edges of my vision.

Finally, the city appears in the distance. I ignore the guards at the gates, even as one of them steps forward, likely planning to ask about the woman in my arms. But no one dares approach as I ride into Nyrridor, following Eamonn's directions to a small cottage close to the city walls.

The healer is waiting outside. She's a short woman, but she places her hands on her hips, leveling me with a hard stare. Her presence is sharp and commanding, but when her dark eyes lock onto Madinia, a flicker of pity softens her otherwise stern features.

When I dismount, she strides toward me.

"You know this is a fatal wound."

"She will not die."

Her eyes meet mine, and she shakes her head at whatever she

sees on my face. "Bring her inside. Your…bird gave me enough time to prepare."

The cottage door creaks as she opens it, the scent of drying roots, fragrant herbs, and old magic washing over me. Carefully, I carry Madinia to the single bed tucked in the corner of the front room.

When I lay her down, she doesn't so much as stir—her breathing shallow, her skin pale and clammy. My heart begins to pound.

"My name is Heava," the healer murmurs as she bustles around the room, washing her hands and gathering supplies. She sets a bowl of steaming water on the table, along with a collection of metallic tools.

Nudging me out of the way with a boldness few would attempt, she leans over Madinia, studying her wound.

"She's lucky. The arrow created a partial seal, slowing the bleeding." Her eyes meet mine. "But it needs to come out. And it's going to create more damage. I will have mere moments to attempt to save her life, and I don't have time to waste sparing her from pain. You will need to hold her steady."

Madinia

Blinding pain. The pungent scent of herbs and flowers. Dim light dancing on the walls.

Most worryingly, I can feel strong hands, holding me down.

Someone else touches the arrow and I scream.

I know what's coming next.

"Don't." The word is a choked sob. "Please."

"It has to be done, sweetheart." Calysian murmurs, pressing

THIS VICIOUS DREAM

his lips to my ear. "You need to live, which means your new accessory needs to go."

"Don't—"

The pain steals my breath, unbearable agony razing my body as someone wrenches the arrow free.

I devolve into sobs, desperate for it to all just be over.

"Live, Madinia. You have much to stay alive for."

Do I?

"Your friends may still be waiting for you."

My eyes flutter closed. If Daharak and the others are still alive, they're probably better without me. What have I brought them except suffering?

The healer does something particularly nasty, and I moan, fighting against her torturous hands.

"Kyldare escaped," Calysian continues. "If you die, you release him from your vengeance."

Kyldare's hateful voice echoes through my head. *"If I can't have your life, I'll gladly take your death. Think of me as you die choking on your own blood."*

Fury edges out the agony. It lasts only moments, but it's long enough for me to take a full breath. Then the healer does something else to make me cry out.

But the thought of revenge is enough. For now.

Calysian's lips meet my temple. "There you go. It will all be over soon."

My entire body shudders, the pressure in my lung unrelenting. I'm not sure why Calysian is doing this. Why he cares. We may have had one night of pleasure, but I shoved him away like I *always* do, and then he found his precious grimoire.

So why is he still here?

"Infection has already begun," a low, female voice says. "I must burn it out."

That doesn't sound good. In fact, it sounds terrible.

"No burning," I mumble.

"Shhh." Calysian's hand is cool as he strokes my hair back from my forehead. "Rest."

Warmth spreads through my chest. Warmth that becomes blazing heat. I writhe, pushing uselessly at the healer, but Calysian captures my hands in his.

"Finish this." His voice is low, dangerous. I tense, but he's not talking to me.

"You came from the swamp. I must remove all of the infection. To skip this step would mean her death."

"Do *not* speak of her death so casually."

I crack open my eyes. Calysian's face is just inches from mine. "It's almost done," he assures me, his face bone-white. "And then you'll sleep and rest and heal."

The burning finally ends, replaced by an icy sensation that offers relief for approximately one minute before it makes me shudder.

"I have done all I can." The healer sounds weary. I can't see her, but Calysian spares her a glance.

"Will she live?"

"I've done my part. The rest is up to her."

He tenses at that, and I twitch my fingers. His eyes meet mine. "Stop intimidating her. She's trying to help."

His mouth twitches, but he nods. "You must be feeling better if you're giving me orders already."

I'm not. The pain has dulled to an ache, but I feel an exhaustion that goes far beyond normal fatigue, along with the sense that I left most of my blood in that swamp.

"Sleep," Calysian says. "I'll ensure no one dares harm you."

I frown at him, but my eyes are already drifting shut, his savage expression the last sight I see.

CHAPTER NINETEEN

Madinia

Warmth. Comfort.

I drift.

Occasionally, I surface, only to dive deep once more, flashes of dreams and memories flickering through my mind.

It's the voices that wake me. Low, male, familiar.

I attempt to open my eyes, but my eyelids are so heavy, I fall deeper into the hazy place between sleep and waking.

"How long have you known who I am?" Calysian's voice is hard. For a moment, I think he's speaking to me.

"Don't ask me this." Eamonn's tone is more serious than I've ever heard it.

"Tell me."

"Since the moment you were cast into this world."

"We met just a few years ago."

"I knew of you."

"And you allowed me to wander for centuries." Calysian's tone is cool. Remote. My skin suddenly feels too tight, and I attempt to open my eyes once more.

I *loathe* when he speaks like that. When he becomes Calpharos.

Eamonn sighs. "I searched for you the first time you were on this continent and could not find you. It was only when you returned that I could sense you. When I did, I was unable to speak of your true nature."

"Cease your excuses."

I finally manage to open my eyes. The room is lighter. How long have I been asleep?

Turning my head requires too much strength, but from here I can see Calysian sitting by the window, Eamonn laying at his feet in the form of a large, shaggy dog.

"It's not an excuse. I was *physically* unable to speak of it," Eamonn clarifies. "Cursed. Just as you are. Not only to never walk in my true body, but to never tell you the truth of who you are. It was an impossibility. Now that you know, I will share what knowledge I can."

Calysian lets out a cold, hollow laugh. "You expect me to trust you?"

Silence. I get the sense Eamonn is…hurt.

He gets to his feet, his tail low. "For centuries. I looked for you. For years, I came when you needed me. I've saved your life, scouted for your enemies, and hinted as much of your true form to you as I could. And now you no longer trust me?" Turning, Eamonn trots toward the door, using one paw to pull down the handle. The moment the door swings open, he's gone.

Calysian sighs, pinching the bridge of his nose. Getting to his feet, he closes the door behind Eamonn, before wandering back toward the window. Our eyes meet, and he freezes.

Almost instantly, he's at my side, and my heart slams into my ribs at the strange movement. He has always been fast, his grace somewhat unnatural. But this is a reminder of who he is now.

Who he always was.

He angles his head. "Are you afraid of me?"

I open my mouth, but my throat is too dry to speak. Calysian's expression gentles, and he takes a cup from the table, one arm encircling my neck as he leans me up, holding me steady.

The water is the best thing I've ever tasted, and I drain the cup. Calysian refills it, his eyes holding mine as I drink it down again.

He offers one more, but I shake my head, my stomach already sloshing unpleasantly.

My chest aches, things inside feeling strangely...new. But I attempt to sit up, and Calysian wedges several pillows behind my head.

"Where are we?"

"Nyrridor."

He told me we would make it here. And he told me I would live. For a moment, I stare at him, coming to terms with it.

"Thank you."

He shrugs like it was nothing, but his eyes are darting across my face, and I have the feeling he sees more than I would like him to.

"Kyldare almost killed me."

A stiff nod. Rage glitters in Calysian's eyes, and his chest rises with a slow breath. "He ran the moment he shot you. He knows you're a threat to him, even when you're bleeding out."

I shake my head. "He was scared of you."

"He's fixated on you. Some part of you scares him, which is why he needs to break you. He's a coward."

That much is true. Pushing Kyldare from my mind, I crane my neck, surveying my body.

I'm no longer covered in blood—one of his shirts buttoned to the throat. Shakily, I unbutton the first few buttons, preparing myself for the ruin of my chest.

Calysian catches my hands. "What are you doing?"

"I want to see."

His lips twitch. "Don't worry, sweetheart, those breasts are still *perfect*."

I glower at him, ignoring the warmth that attempts to spread through me at the teasing note in his voice.

He thinks my breasts are perfect.

I bite down on my lower lip, still needing to see. When I stretch my fingers, he releases my hands, watching closely as I unbutton the next button.

The evidence of my near-death is little more than a faint line, slicing below my collarbone, along the top of my breast. I'd expected puckered skin, a thick red scar to join those on my back—a reminder for the rest of my life.

Calysian watches me avidly, drinking in my every reaction. "I told you."

At this moment, he looks nothing like the dark god. His eyes are tired, his hair mussed. He looks like a man who has had little sleep.

But I know what I saw. And his ability to tuck away that murderous other side of him is…unsettling.

"The healer is extremely competent," I say.

"Thank you," a feminine voice says dryly. The voice is familiar, and I study the woman who appears from the door at our left.

She's at least a footspan shorter than me, wearing a sleeveless tunic that showcases muscular arms and shoulders. Her eyes are a cool gray, and she takes me in with a clinical gaze, lingering on the scar across my chest.

I offer her a smile. "You saved my life."

"I helped," Calysian mutters sullenly, and then stiffens, as if appalled by his own words. He lets out a low growl, getting to his feet and stalking across the room.

The healer's eyes glitter with amusement. "My name is Heava. You're very lucky. Another few minutes and there would have been nothing I could do."

I shiver. Minutes.

Her hands are cool as she examines the scar, before asking me to raise my arms, checking my movement on each side.

"Any pain?"

"Just a dull ache. When can I—"

"Two days from now. Perhaps three. *If* you actually rest properly."

"She will," Calysian says from his position by the window, his voice tight.

I don't argue. Truthfully, the thought of even standing is intimidating, despite how much my bladder is screaming at me.

Heava gives me a knowing look before glancing at Calysian. "We need privacy."

He snorts, as if the thought is ludicrous. When I pin him with a glare, he holds his hands up and stalks out of the cottage.

"He is in a terrible mood," I mutter.

"The man hasn't slept. You were feverish and ranting, and he stayed by your side, murmuring into your ear for days."

I stare at her, uncomfortable with the thought of what I might have said while in the midst of that fever. "How long have we been here?"

"Five days."

My fingers clutch at the soft sheets. Five days of travel Calysian has lost. And yet he stayed.

Heava moves next to the bed, gesturing for me to get up.

"Lean on me. The outside wound may be healed, but things are still healing inside."

I can feel it too. The tenderness that warns me a single sharp movement could tear something important. Still, with her help, I manage to hobble to the bathing room before slumping back into bed, dizzy from the effort of taking a few steps.

The moment I'm finished, Calysian returns. Heava shakes her head at him but leaves us alone.

"You should drink more." Calysian takes a seat on the

narrow bed next to me, handing me the cup of water. When he angles me up so I can drink, his warm breath caresses my neck.

I shiver, and his lips curve.

"Why did you stay here?" I ask him. "I know you want to find the other two grimoires."

Offense flashes across his face. "You think I would leave you?"

"Most people would."

His eyes turn to slits. "You mean most *men* would. Do not compare me to your previous human lovers."

There aren't many previous human lovers to compare him to, but I would never admit that to him.

"Fine, Calpharos, but if you don't mind, I'd prefer to speak to Calysian at this moment."

My tone is caustic, and surprise flashes across his face, followed by something that might be…uncertainty.

Regret immediately flashes through me. "I shouldn't have said that. I'm sorry." Calysian has been…kind. When I close my eyes, I can still feel his arms around me, can still hear him murmuring in my ear, urging me to stay alive.

"I am the one who is sorry. I allowed you to be hurt. You almost died."

"I think Kyldare is the one to blame for that."

"No. The grimoire…engulfed me," he admits, and something that might be shame flickers through his gaze.

It's disconcerting to see Calysian as anything other than supremely arrogant.

"What was it like?" I can't help but ask.

He sighs. "It was pure power. Even now I can feel the rush of it. I felt the horror and betrayal from the moment I was forced to split myself in such a way. And I knew I could make those responsible suffer. It was…"

"Addictive." I know just how alluring vengeance can be. I

THIS VICIOUS DREAM

also know how the flames of revenge will burn you alive if you let them.

But that won't stop me from hunting Kyldare. And Vicana.

Calysian's brow furrows. "I was so consumed by that power, I couldn't even recognize you. I couldn't protect you."

My instinct is to snap at him that I don't need his protection. But considering I'm still recovering from a hole in my chest, that feels like a lie. And it doesn't improve my mood.

He studies my face. His eyelids are drooping—unsurprising after five days without sleep. That must be a strain, even for a god.

I shift over. "Lay down."

Surprise flashes across his face, and he gives the narrow bed a pointed look.

"Go on," I insist.

He doesn't argue. I shift over to the wall, and he angles his huge body so he's facing me. We're so close, our bodies are almost pressed together, and I have a moment to regret the intimacy I've invited.

"You're going after the next grimoire." My voice is little more than a whisper, but Calysian nods, his eyes blurred with fatigue as they meet mine.

"I have to. The loss of what they took from me is an ache in my soul."

It's a surprising admission of vulnerability, and one that I doubt he would have made if he wasn't already moments from sleep.

"I'm going with you."

Calysian's eyes sharpen. "Why would you do that?"

"Kyldare will hunt for that grimoire too. It's on this continent, isn't it?"

"Yes. What about your friends?"

"I will search for information about them at each town and city we visit. I can achieve two goals at once."

He studies my face, and for a moment I'm sure he sees my true plans. But he must be even more exhausted than I thought, because he gives me a nod, his eyes sliding shut.

I let out a shaky breath. I'm not just hoping to make Kyldare pay for everything he has done to me.

Regret tastes bitter on my tongue as I brush a finger over Calysian's cheek. He's already asleep, but he angles his head, chasing my touch.

His soul aches.

And I'm going to be the one responsible for ensuring it continues to.

Because the glimpse I saw of Calpharos was enough for me to know one thing:

I will never allow the dark god to fully wake.

Calysian

The need to move is a prickle down my spine. It's a tension in my muscles, a tightness in my chest, an unrelenting urge that claws at me night and day.

I now have a new awareness of the other grimoire on this continent. I know exactly which direction we need to travel. But I can also sense others making their way toward it. Others who would take it from me.

Still, I wait for Madinia to heal. And unsurprisingly, she insists she is ready to leave before the healer agrees.

It takes all of my willpower to deny her. Knowing others are searching for what is *mine*… it makes my blood burn. And yet each time I look at Madinia, I see her face, robbed of color, her lips, tinged blue. I see the knowledge in her eyes that she is about to die.

And so I ignore her hissed curses. I grin at the dark looks she shoots me each time I agree with Heava.

Truthfully, I'm small enough to enjoy her irritation.

Finally, three days later, even the healer is forced to agree Madinia can travel. I've secured everything we need for our journey, including new clothes for Madinia, who looks vaguely bewildered when I drop them on her bed.

No one has taken care of this woman before. And that knowledge sets my teeth on edge.

I give Heava more coins than she likely would have earned in a year, and she frowns at me. "This is too much."

"She was dying. You saved her."

The healer shakes her head but pockets the sack of coins. "Her stamina will be low."

"I know. I won't push her."

"I can *hear* you," Madinia snarls, and Heava smirks.

"Then take my advice and don't do anything stupid."

Madinia mounts her horse, giving Heava a nod. "Thank you. For everything."

The healer nods back. "You're welcome. Good luck on your journey."

Within minutes, we're riding toward the dock. It's the opposite direction we need to travel, and yet I promised Madinia this.

She hisses at me to stay several paces behind her, insisting I'll be a distraction, but I keep a careful eye on her as she moves from group to group.

The travel delay is worth it as I watch her transform.

For the swaggering, drunken sailors, she becomes a flirtatious, empty-headed strumpet, all wide eyes and teasing smiles, searching for the handsome rogue who promised her a ring and vanished with the next tide.

For the gruff dock masters, she becomes a hard-nosed, steely-eyed madam, demanding answers about the pirates who slipped away with unpaid debts. Her face is cold, and she's all sharp tones and icy glances as she lies through her teeth.

For the young deckhands, she becomes a frightened sister, wringing her hands as she asks about her brother, her words faltering, her lower lip trembling, until even the most hardened deckhand vows to find her answers.

She wears her personas like borrowed cloaks, slipping in and out of them as effortlessly as breathing. A scowl here, a smile there. A feigned blush. A calculated threat.

By the time she is done, I'm filled with reluctant admiration. And hard as stone.

Finally, Madinia is forced to admit defeat, her shoulders slumped, her expression weary as she walks toward me.

"Nothing," she says.

"You said this was one of the first places you docked."

"Yes."

Her eyes hold such a deep sadness. It makes me feel claustrophobic. Uncomfortable.

It makes me feel like I have failed somehow.

I take her hand. Shockingly, she allows it. "You were taken in Sylvarin waters. I find it unlikely that the pirates would have returned here as they searched for you."

She peers up at me. "You think they searched for me?"

I search her face, but there's no sign of the confident, occasionally arrogant woman I know so well. This is a deep insecurity. A fear that she is somehow not enough.

Fury roars through me with such strength, it leaves me shaken. Fury and powerlessness.

I want to turn back time. I want to find her father and make him *suffer* for creating this insecurity. The insecurity that makes her wonder if those she would do anything for have abandoned her.

And yet…they have.

THIS VICIOUS DREAM

Where *are* her friends from Eprotha? Where are Prisca and Asinia and all the others she fought with?

"Calysian?"

"Of course they would have searched for you. We're traveling south, and we'll continue to ask about their ship each time we stop."

With a nod, she straightens her shoulders and mounts her horse. I lead her toward the southern gates of Nyrridor, following the call of my own power.

Madinia is quiet, but I know her plans. Our minds are surprisingly similar, and I can't deny the satisfaction I feel when I outmaneuver her.

She believes she can beat me to the grimoire and hide it somewhere I will be unable to locate. I'm not sure how she thinks she will achieve this, since I can feel it calling to me even from half a continent away.

But her attempt will be interesting all the same.

CHAPTER TWENTY

Madinia

We leave the dock, traveling in silence as we make our way to the city gates. Calysian sends me the occasional concerned look, but seems content to leave me to my thoughts.

I glance over my shoulder one last time, watching as the city begins to shrink behind us. Twice I've passed through this place—once while on my way to the Blightmere Swamp—the grimoire tucked away in my cloak—and now again, my chest still aching faintly from the arrow that nearly killed me.

One day, I'll return. I'll take the time to lose myself in the maze of tangled streets, to wander through the vibrant markets. Perhaps I'll even paddle my feet in the sea, just as I saw a group of young women doing earlier, their laughing shrieks piercing the salt-soaked air.

The city gates loom ahead, the shadowy expanse of towering oaks and tangled underbrush waiting beyond them. We pass through, the noise of the city fading. Almost immediately, Calysian's shoulders relax. I bite down on the impulse to ask him about Eamonn. He's been very careful not to mention his

THIS VICIOUS DREAM

friend, and I haven't caught sight of Eamonn in any of his forms since I woke to their argument.

We stop after just a few hours. My time searching the dock cost us, but Calysian insists on an early night, seeing to the horses while I set up camp.

He doesn't say a word when I place our blankets several footspans apart, but I feel him watching me as I close my eyes, and again when I open them the next morning.

The moment I'm awake, Calysian gets to his feet, and I can almost feel his desperation to reach the grimoire. The forest thickens as we travel south, trees pressing in closer, while a thick mist clings to the ground until the sun finally rises above the highest branches.

By the third night, the chill has deepened. And it takes all of my self-control to ignore the hot invitation in Calysian's eyes and curl up on my own sleeping mat on the other side of the fire.

I want him. I can admit that much. I'm torn between accepting the inevitability of his naked body pressed against mine and denying that such a thing can ever happen.

On the fourth morning, I wake to find Calysian watching me with a predatory gleam in his eyes. My thighs clench, my toes curl, and I let out a long, shuddering breath, avoiding his gaze until we mount our horses.

Information is currency between us, and we trade memories. I tell him of my time at court, and the women who were once my rivals, enemies, and companions.

He tells me of his time exploring the fae kingdom, describing breathtaking sunrises and fields of wildflowers.

When he turns Fox west at the crossroads—in the direction of Elunthar—warmth spreads through my stomach.

It's unlikely I'll find any information about the pirates in Elunthar. It was the first place we docked so long ago. But still...

"Thank you." My voice is rough, and Calysian's gaze drifts over my face. I've felt him watching me constantly. For a man committed to his grimoires, he still insists we make camp each day hours before the sun goes down, demanding that I rest.

And, when I'm sure Calysian isn't paying attention, I watch him too.

Everywhere we travel, women caress him with their eyes, likely picturing him naked. They watch as he radiates his casual confidence, and it's easy to see why they're so attracted. Calysian has the air of a man who knows what he wants and has no doubt he will get it.

"What are you thinking?"

I clear my throat. "Nothing."

Calysian gives me that indulgent look he so enjoys—the one that tells me he knows I'm lying, and he's choosing to allow it.

I give him the haughty look I've perfected—the one I know irritates him to his core.

He merely grins at me.

I roll my eyes. "Are you going to tell me where we're going yet?"

"South."

"That's all you're telling me?"

He angles his head, as if waiting for me to snarl at him, but I know what he's doing. I did, after all, refuse to tell him anything that would allow him to get to the grimoire before me.

It's a strange feeling—knowing we can trust each other with our lives, but not with information.

I clear my throat. "Are you still…weakened?"

I've seen little of Calysian's power. When I asked him about it yesterday, he admitted he channeled that power into the horses to ensure we would get to the healer in time.

His eyes jump to mine. "Yes. You were worth it." The words are stark, his eyes strangely clear. I suck in a breath, and he gives me a strange smile. It's almost…gentle.

My heart thunders in my chest, and he returns his attention

to the town in the distance. Elunthar is only a tenth of the size of Nyrridor, but that should make my questioning easier.

The sun is high in the sky by the time we make it through the town to the dock. And everywhere I look, I see Daharak.

On one corner, we'd sat outside with drinks in our hands as we took in the oddly slanted roofs patched with mismatched shingles, the buildings painted in bright teals and sunburnt yellows. I'd laughed as I'd watched seagulls swooping low, stealing bites of fried fish from those who grew distracted, failing to guard their plates.

These were the first steps I took on this continent. And it had seemed as if my life was finally beginning.

"What are you thinking?" Calysian's voice is carefully neutral, and I blink away hot moisture.

The lump in my throat aches, but for some reason, I tell him.

I tell him of the night I spent in one of the taverns with the pirates, all of us betting and laughing and eating our way through plates and plates of fresh food. I'd eaten so much fruit I'd felt queasy, but it was worth it when I conquered the craving that had plagued me for weeks on the ship.

Someone had begun playing music, and the whole room had erupted into motion. Tables were shoved aside, old leather boots stomped in rhythm on the polished wooden floor, hands clapped to a tune so lively, it was as if it had been composed by someone who had never known anything but joy.

"You danced in a tavern?" Calysian asks, flashing his dimple.

"I did. If you could call it that." I was raised in ballrooms, and this wasn't *that* kind of dancing. "Mostly, I stumbled around, tripping over my feet while the others laughed at me. But it didn't matter. I was...free, in a way I had never been before." I smile, despite the ache in my chest.

"And weeks later, you were taken. Trapped in your body for three years."

"Yes."

Calysian's eyes turn flat. "I'm going to make them pay for every second of life they stole from you."

My stomach flutters, but he's already angling Fox toward a hitching post, dismounting as he gives his horse a stern warning.

I follow, my mouth dry. It's not the first time Calysian has sworn vengeance for me. But it…does something to me to see his rage.

We leave the horses, and I wander the dock, asking the same questions I asked in Nyrridor. I'm about to give up when a strong hand grabs my arm, whirling me around.

I sense Calysian moving before I see him, his stride long, his expression filled with cold fury as he stalks toward us.

"Madinia." The voice is gruff. My eyes meet pale blue, and the breath rushes from my lungs.

He's older, his shoulders more rounded. He's gained some weight in his gut, and his arms have lost some of their definition—likely because he's no longer hauling ropes and walking back and forth across the deck for hours at a time.

But there's no doubt this is Haldrik. He still has the same kind smile, that same chip in his front tooth.

His hand shakes as he raises it to my face, his smile wobbly. "It *is* you."

Calysian looms at my side, and I grab his hand before he can do anything stupid. "Calysian, this is Haldrik. He was one of Daharak's pirates." I stare at him. "I don't understand. How did you end up here?"

"I wanted a fresh start. After the war…well I don't need to tell *you* what that did to me."

Twice, Haldrik shared a hot drink with me after I screamed myself awake from a nightmare.

He glances around, angling us toward a small tavern close to the dock. Calysian's brows are low, but he allows it, although he plants himself in the seat next to mine.

"I'm still confused," I murmur.

THIS VICIOUS DREAM

"You didn't notice I was gone," Haldrik gives me a gentle smile, but his eyes flicker with something I can't place.

I shift awkwardly in my wooden chair, breathing out a sigh of relief when the barmaid approaches.

No, I hadn't noticed he was gone. Haldrik was a quiet man, and other than those two nights in the galley, I hadn't spent much time with him.

"I asked Kavrik to cover for me," he says. "He agreed to sign in for me before the ship disembarked in Ambrelis. I took some work on a fishing boat and ended up here for a few months. I'm thinking about returning to Eprotha in the spring."

Ambrelis was the last city we docked at before Kyldare found us that last time.

Daharak would have noticed Haldrik was gone. But she'd never said anything. Her pirates were under contract, and yet she hadn't dispatched anyone to look for him.

She could be a hard woman, but she was also a fair one. And clearly she'd decided Haldrik deserved his new life.

"Have you heard anything?"

Haldrik frowns. "What do you mean?"

My stomach swims. How do I tell him what happened? How do I explain that they might all be dead because of me?

Beneath the table, Calysian takes my hand, stroking my wrist soothingly with his thumb. "The ship was attacked by the Sylvarin queen's right hand," he says. "A man named Kyldare. He boarded with his soldiers and took Madinia. We don't know where Daharak and her crew are now."

Haldrik places his elbows on the table, dropping his head into his hand. Silence reigns.

"No one has seen them?" he finally asks, lifting his head.

"I was detained for three years," I say. "Kyldare—the man who took me—told me they were all dead."

Haldrik sucks in a shuddering breath, glancing between Calysian and I. "But you don't believe him."

"He would have said anything if he thought it might break me," I say, my voice flat. "And Daharak...all of them survived so much. I can't believe they were slaughtered by Kyldare's soldiers. I won't."

"So you've been trying to find them."

I nod, and Haldrik sighs. "I haven't seen any sightings of them here, although it's unlikely they would have revisited this town."

The barmaid brings over several bowls of stew, and my stomach rumbles. At some point, Calysian must have ordered dinner.

I lift the spoon to my lips, but the stew is tasteless, my mind providing me with images of Daharak and the others being slaughtered over and over again.

My stomach clenches, and I place my spoon down. Calysian squeezes my hand again. "We'll keep looking."

I nod, and the two men fall into conversation about the town and our route south.

"I'm coming with you," Haldrik announces, his shoulders set, chin jutting out.

"We're traveling inland," Calysian says.

Haldrik's mouth firms and he meets my eyes. "And you never expected to find me here did you? Who's to say where the others might turn up? You know as well as I do that pirates don't just haunt the coast—they trade, they hide, they follow opportunity. Besides, we might meet someone who's heard word of them."

I open my mouth, but he's already shaking his head. "What if Kyldare did attack, and they were forced to scatter? More people searching means a higher chance we'll find them."

He's got a point. When I don't reply, Haldrik nods to the stairs on our left. "This inn is probably the best in town. You should both get some rest, and I'll meet you in the morning."

Calysian doesn't argue, but his gaze lingers on my face. And when he leaves the table to speak to the innkeeper, I know we'll discuss Haldrik further when we're alone.

And I know he's asking the innkeeper for one room.

THIS VICIOUS DREAM

MADINIA

The room is surprisingly spacious, steam already rising from a large tub near the window. Calysian steps to the side for me to enter, and I give him a look.. "This was presumptuous of you."

He drops our bags by the door. "Was it?"

I'm suddenly tired. Tired of depriving myself. "No."

His eyes burn with hunger when he looks at me. But his hands fist at his sides, and I watch him douse his lust, his eyes turning flat and cool.

"We need to talk about Haldrik." He grinds the words out and I almost smile. Haldrik is the *last* thing Calysian wants to talk about, but he's determined to get this conversation over with.

I lean against the door. "I know you don't want him to come with us."

A muscle in his jaw twitches. "I promised you I would help you find your friends. If you think Haldrik can help with that, then he can travel with us."

Warmth spreads through my chest. I know Calysian, and I know the way he thinks. He never would have abandoned Daharak and the others without warning, and the fact that Haldrik did has shaped the way he sees him.

I don't blame him. And yet…

"Haldrik deserves to know the truth. I can't imagine what it's been like for him to learn they've been missing for all this time. We won't tell him about the grimoire if you don't want to."

Calysian narrows his eyes in thought. "We're traveling toward a city on the coast," he says, clearly reluctant to tell me even that much. "Haldrik can travel with us that far. If we haven't heard anything by then, he can head north or south along the coast to search for them on his own."

"Fine." My mind races. A city on the coast. If we're traveling inland first, then it's most likely we'll—

Calysian gives me a slow smile and strips off his shirt, revealing smooth skin poured over thick muscle.

My thoughts scatter. All plans and reasoning vanish.

I glower at him, and his smile widens. But his eyes soften. "You should bathe before the water cools."

I hesitate, and he prowls toward me, the light playing over his bare chest. He didn't douse his lust at all. He merely hid it.

My mouth turns dry. I'll ponder Calysian's travel plans later.

Slowly, gently, he reaches for my tunic, pulling it over my head and immediately removing the band holding my breasts in place. He swallows, looking momentarily stunned before meeting my gaze, his eyes hot. "I've missed these."

My cheeks heat and he gives a low chuckle. "I've missed *that*, too." He nuzzles at my cheek, and the movement is oddly… sweet. But he's already steering me backward, toward the bath, and a sudden thrill jolts through me.

Am I…are *we* really doing this?

"I thought you were waiting for me to come to you."

His eyes darken. "I'm tired of waiting. You nearly died, Madinia." And then his mouth is on mine, and I let out a sound that makes him smile against my lips.

"Shh," he murmurs. "We'll share the bath."

I get the strangest sense he's gentling me—the same way he occasionally croons to my mare when she spooks.

"You have no idea how long I've fantasized about this," Calysian says, already rolling my leggings down. My underwear is gone a moment later, and I blink up at him.

There's something strangely tantalizing about standing naked in front of him while he's still half-clothed. I'm vulnerable but in a way that makes me shift restlessly, makes me reach out in an attempt to pull him closer.

He slowly shakes his head, still running his gaze over me. I attempt to cover myself, and he instantly catches my hands.

"No," he warns. "Don't ever hide yourself from me."

There's a strange note in his voice that sends a prickle of unease up my spine. A sense that this decision will have repercussions I can't yet imagine.

"You're tensing up," he murmurs. "I'll relax you."

He drops teasing kisses across my neck, my shoulders, my breasts. His lips linger in the spots that make me moan—the spots he already has memorized, and new ones that he pays special attention to. I yank at his pants, and he finally indulges me, pushing them down his hips.

I watch, unable to look away. He gives me a wink as his pants fall to the ground.

Long. Thick. Hard. His cock is perfect, just like the rest of him. I shouldn't be surprised. He is, after all, a god. And from the arrogant glint in Calysian's eyes, he's practically waiting for me to break into applause.

I hate that I find his arrogance so strangely endearing.

"Why now?" I murmur. "You've been…different since the swamp."

"You were hurt. And then I was waiting for you. But you're stubborn, and I'm out of patience." He drops a kiss to my forehead. "Get in the bath."

I don't argue, my breath shuddering in a low moan as the warmth sweeps up my legs and through my body as I sink into the tub.

When I glance at Calysian, his eyes are so dark, I suck in a breath.

He catches my hand, pulling me forward so he can sit behind me. "I'm going to ensure you make that sound over and over again tonight."

"One night," I say, my voice hoarse as I lean back against him. "This can only ever be one night."

His huge body tenses, but he doesn't argue, just takes the soap and begins lathering my back, my arms, my breasts. Those huge, calloused hands are breathtakingly gentle, and by the time he finishes washing me, a ball of warmth is spreading through my core, my nipples tight, my breaths uneven.

When he hands me the soap, I turn to face him, water lapping at my breasts.

Reaching out one hand, I stroke his cheek, and his eyes immediately turn heavy-lidded. How is it possible that he's this touch-starved after so many centuries walking this world?

Leaning forward, I press a kiss below his ear. It's a spot that makes *me* shiver, and Calysian goes tense, his body leaning toward mine.

His breaths are shallow, his eyes strangely vulnerable. He's barely holding onto control. Because of *me*.

The thought is heady.

I know what I look like. I have, after all, been weaponizing my face and body since the moment I realized that women must use whatever tools the world begrudgingly grants us.

I've endured the leers of men old enough to be my father, their stares like a layer of filth dripping over my skin. And I learned early that the continual pursuit by men my own age had little to do with me, and everything to do with their need to prove themselves. To turn me into a conquest for their friends to admire.

Beautiful woman. Calysian has called me this since we met, and yet he's never made me feel as if that's all he can see.

He's commanding and arrogant and so supremely sure of himself that he makes my teeth clench with fury.

But he's also kind. When I poke him into caring about something, he *commits*.

I bite down on my lower lip, and Calysian's gaze instantly drops to my mouth. When his eyes meet mine once more, they hold a possessive gleam that makes me shiver.

I run the soap over his chest and arms before placing it

on the small table next to the tub and using my hands to caress his body. His tense muscles remind me of a huge cat, readying itself to leap at its prey.

I let my fingers wander, allow my palms to stroke. I explore the ridges of his muscles, sweeping my hands over his smooth skin and learning every inch of him.

Finally, he reaches for the jugs of clean water next to the bath, using them to rinse the suds from both of us. When he pulls me to my feet, I'm shivering.

But not from the cold. From anticipation.

"Say the words," he murmurs, and I don't need to ask what they are.

I stare up at him, my breath hitching.

I've wanted many things over my lifetime. I wanted Regner dead. I wanted my freedom. I want Vicana and Kyldare to pay for what they've done.

But my craving for Calysian burns inside me with frightening intensity.

"I want you."

His eyes blaze, and he leans close, brushing his lips down my throat, his hand curving around my lower back and holding me in place.

I shudder and feel him smile against my skin. "So responsive."

My teeth clench—as they always do when he speaks with that arrogantly amused tone. Calysian captures my jaw, gently squeezing until my mouth opens. "None of that. You offered yourself to me. And I accept." His voice is husky, and despite the dark promise in his words, I allow him to tilt my head back.

His tongue thrusts deep, swallowing my moan. Heat curls through me, my heart tripping in my chest. Our kiss goes on and on, tongues tangling, until Calysian raises his head, a dark promise in his eyes.

He lifts me out of the tub, the movement easy, careless, as if such an action didn't take an incredible amount of strength.

It seems unnatural—that such a large man can move with such careless grace. The natural grace of a god.

But he doesn't seem like a god now. No, he seems like a man who wants to take a woman to bed.

When he presses the towel to every inch of my body, I feel…cherished.

"Now you," I murmur, and he shakes his head, wiping roughly at his own body before dropping the towel to the floor.

His gaze caresses me, and he steps close, his mouth gentle as he brushes his lips against mine.

If I hadn't spent so much time with this man, I might be intimidated by the span of his shoulders, the muscles that coil beneath my hand as I stroke his chest and back, learning his body the way he has already learned mine. My hands drift over muscle and sinew, and when I poke a finger into one of his ribs, he…shudders.

"You're ticklish?"

"Surprised?" Calysian's lips curve, and he strokes over my own ribs, watching me squirm.

I smirk back. And then I drop my hand, cupping his impressive length.

Hmmm. Perhaps some parts of him are *too* impressive.

"Do you believe I would hurt you?" Calysian's words are a low rumble, and I meet his eyes.

"You're…large."

The look he gives me is very smug and very male. "You will take me and beg for more."

I glower at him and he grins, kissing my snarl away. I know how much he enjoys riling me with his arrogance, and yet I still fall for it every time.

His lips soften, turning coaxing. My head spins as he places me gently on the bed, the sheets cool against my skin. I gasp against his mouth, but he doesn't let up. Calysian kisses me until I'm shifting beneath him, angling my hips to grind against his

THIS VICIOUS DREAM

length. A flush sweeps over my body, my nipples hardening until they ache. He sweeps his thumb over one, swallowing my moan.

Deep, drugging kisses. His fingers plucking and teasing and stroking. Sensation unfurling through my body, until I'm dazed with it, panting and desperate.

I let out a ragged groan, clutching at him in an effort to pull him even closer. When I grind against him again, heat blazes through me, and he hisses out a breath.

"Madinia."

A thrill shoots through me at his rough tone, the way his hands tighten on me as he lifts his head, his eyes dark pools.

He inches lower, but I sink my nails into his shoulder. "I want you."

A wicked smirk. "I know."

"Now."

He hesitates, sending a longing look between my thighs. One finger trails down, sliding against the wet heat of me, and he lets out a shuddery breath. He brushes his finger against my clit and I gasp. So he does it again, his avid gaze on my face.

I let out a rough groan, and Calysian moves that finger lower, slowly pushing inside me. Widening my thighs, I arch my hips, needing more. Another finger joins the first, until I'm panting, lifting my butt to chase the pleasure he offers.

His thumb finds my clit, and my breath catches. I'm on the edge when he removes his hand.

"You—"

But he's pushing my legs wider, settling between them, and I hold my breath as he presses himself against me.

Shaking his head, he pokes a finger into my ribs, and the air whooshes from my lungs.

"Relax," he murmurs. His cheeks are flushed, his eyes glittering with lust and something darker. But he takes his time, slowly entering me. I tense up again—he's too large for me to take him comfortably—but Calysian slips his hand down to play with my clit once more.

Warmth spreads through my core, and just like that, I'm angling my hips for him. He lets out a breathless laugh and slides deeper, his clever fingers caressing until I'm on the edge again.

His hips roll, and he withdraws, then thrusts deeper. This time, he hits something inside me. Something that makes me break out in a light sweat, my body trembling.

"So fucking perfect." The words are a low growl, and I open my eyes. I hadn't realized they'd drifted closed. But Calysian is still watching me, his eyes on my face as he takes in my every reaction.

My smile is fractured by a moan, and Calysian captures the sound with his mouth, driving deeper. Long, deep thrusts, his hips hitting that spot again and again until I'm clawing at his shoulders, panting against his mouth.

"That's it," he murmurs. "Unravel for me, sweetheart."

My thighs tense. My breath catches. Pleasure explodes through my body, my vision blurring, until all I can see is his face as I shudder and moan. It goes on and on, and Calysian continues moving, drawing out my climax until I'm weak, boneless.

With a growl, he presses his lips to my neck and shudders, finding his own pleasure.

CHAPTER TWENTY-ONE

CALYSIAN

This time, when Madinia wakes up, I don't allow her to squirm free. If she thinks she can push me away after such a night, she will stay trapped in my arms until she thinks again.

Yes, I'm aware that such a thought isn't one most women would welcome. Particularly a woman as independent and strong-willed as Madinia.

And still, when I feel her wake, feel her muscles tensing, I merely nuzzle closer, surrounding her with my body.

She sighs. "I seem to have traded one cage for another."

That she can already joke about her imprisonment is surprising. Even more surprising? Her voice isn't cold, and her tone doesn't cut like the lash of a whip.

Madinia wiggles, turning, and I know she can feel my length press against her. When her eyes meet mine, my breath catches.

She's heavy-lidded, her eyes so blue, it's as if they were formed from crushed sapphires. Her hair is tousled, her skin flushed with sleep, and when she leans forward to press a gentle kiss to my chest, I almost claw through my skin, crack open my ribs, and hand her my beating heart.

That thought is enough to make me jolt, and she gives me a questioning look.

I pull her close, careful not to crush her as I roll her to her back, capturing her mouth with mine. She lets out one of those little sounds that makes me hard as stone, and I hiss in a breath.

How is it that I can still need her this much after last night?

BANG. BANG. BANG.

Someone pounds on the door, and Madinia lets out a yelp, pushing at my chest. Reluctantly, I lift my body off hers, my mood darkening.

"I thought we were leaving early?" Haldrik's voice booms from the hall.

"We're coming," Madinia calls, pulling the sheet from the bed and stumbling toward her clothes.

I sigh, hauling myself out of bed.

"Your modesty is unnecessary," I murmur, and Madinia glowers, tightening the sheet.

Warmth rushes through me, and I can't help but grin, stepping toward her. She backs up, tripping on the sheet, and I catch her, steadying her on her feet.

Madinia shoves her hair off her face, hand tightening on the sheet. "Don't even think about it," she hisses. "I'm not going to see Haldrik in a…state."

I shake my head. For a woman who grew up at court, she can be charmingly innocent. "I enjoy this prudish side of you. But I'm going to enjoy destroying it even more."

"One. Night." She grits out, and I shake my head at her. Already, her eyes are dropping to my chest, her teeth sinking into her lower lip. She stiffens, whirling away, and I don't bother to hide my grin, whistling a merry little tune as I find some clean clothes. I'm fully dressed before she has finished rummaging through her bag.

"I'll leave you to collect yourself," I announce, ignoring her low growl as I step into the hall.

Haldrik is nowhere to be seen, but I find him in the tavern below the inn, eyes narrowed as he watches people from his table by the window.

"The horses are being saddled," he says. "I took the liberty of speaking to the stablehands about your horses. Although they seemed strangely frightened of the stallion."

I nod, turning away to speak to the innkeeper. I order far too much food, but this might be our last chance at a decent meal for at least a few days.

Haldrik frowns at me. "I thought we would leave immediately."

"Madinia needs to eat." She didn't eat enough at dinner last night, and the healer made it clear that she wasn't to skip meals.

Haldrik's frown deepens, and I study him, making no effort to hide my perusal. For three years, this man has lived his life, without even attempting to contact his so-called family.

His eyes cool. "I know what you think of me."

"You do?" I keep my tone neutral, but a muscle jumps in his jaw.

"I abandoned my crew. I didn't finish my contract. I left my family. There's nothing you can say that I haven't already said to myself."

Madinia appears, and Haldrik opens his mouth, likely planning to urge her to hurry. I lean over the table, into his space, and his mouth snaps closed.

I won't allow his sudden eagerness to prevent her from eating her fill.

Madinia sinks into the chair, her hair freshly braided, her clothes clean. If I leaned close and pressed my nose against her skin, would I scent myself on her? The thought makes my muscles tense, and she sends me a warning look, which swiftly changes to shock as the barmaids begin placing plates on the table.

"Are we feeding a regiment?"

I pile potatoes and eggs onto her plate. "Eat."

Madinia shakes her head at me but lifts her fork, and satisfaction slides through me.

I nod at Haldrik. "You should eat too. We'll spend hours in the saddle today."

He doesn't protest, loading up his own plate.

I eat distractedly, my mind already sharpening, moving away from the woman sitting across the table and to the grimoire whispering to me.

Soon. Soon it will be in my hands.

Madinia

Traveling with another person is…strange.

Calysian and I had fallen into an easy intimacy, communicating with the barest flick of a glance, intuitively knowing when we would stop to water the horses, stretch our legs, or make camp for the night.

These things now have to be explicitly stated, and—when Haldrik has his own opinions—negotiated.

We're heading southeast, closer to the mountain ranges that cut through the center of this continent.

My skin prickles constantly with the sensation that we're being watched, but if Calysian and Haldrik also sense it, they don't say a word.

Just a few hours after we leave Elunthar, we begin passing stone pillars—crumbling with age, and scattered amongst the forest as if a giant became enraged and slammed some kind of huge structure into the ground.

Eamonn is still nowhere to be seen. And despite Calysian's refusal to talk about him—or their argument—I've seen the way he cranes his head, searching the sky for any sign of his friend. I've caught him peering into the forest, as if expecting Eamonn to prowl through the trees at any moment.

We spend the night in the forest, away from the main trade road. Calysian gives me an indulgent look as I roll out my sleeping mat on the opposite side of the fire, but thankfully, he keeps his thoughts to himself.

And still, I crave the feel of him. Without him wrapped around me, I sleep poorly, my mood turning dark.

Three days later, the forest begins to thin, trees giving way to more broken columns that rear out of the underbrush like bones. Carvings emerge, half-worn faces carved into those columns near a massive archway covered with moss.

Calysian seems to sense my curiosity, because he calls out to Haldrik. The older man nods, gesturing to the small stream running alongside the road. He disappears, likely planning to refill his water skin.

I dismount with a wince that I'm careful to hide from Calysian. My chest is still achy, and I'm still recovering my strength. But Calysian tends to hover when he thinks I'm in pain, and I need to feel like myself again.

I leave Hope tied to a tree and turn my attention to the ruins, reluctantly fascinated. Something about them feels almost familiar, in a way that makes the back of my neck itch. I peer through the forest, spotting more stone carvings amongst the trees. "What is this?"

Calysian swings himself off his horse, rolling his shoulders as he takes in the ruins.

"The southern half of this continent is dotted with the remnants of ancient temples."

"Temples?"

He flashes me a smirk. "Temples devoted to the old gods."

It dawns on me then. My blood turns hot.

He *is* one of the old gods. This man, who—just days ago—was inside me, is an ancient being. He's no more mortal than the stream to our left, or the ground beneath our feet.

Calysian curses in that language he used once before. The one that makes my ears feel like they're going to bleed. "I don't like that look on your face."

I swallow. "What look?"

"Don't play with me." He prowls closer, and the dappled sunlight flickers across the lines of his face. "You've always known what I am."

"Knowing and understanding are two different things."

"And what exactly do you understand?"

"You'll still be alive when I'm dust beneath the earth."

Realization flickers across his face, quickly followed by... grief. "Madinia."

I force a smile. "I know who—and what—you are. I just...I suppose I let myself forget for a little while."

His eyes search my face. "Why do I feel like I've lost something in this moment?"

I don't know what to say. Turning, I mount my horse, nodding at Haldrik when he reappears. "We should get moving."

To our left, I can see the Lacana mountains in the distance, towering above the forest. We'll be skirting around the southern tip of the mountain range, but that's as much as Calysian has told Haldrik and I—another point of contention between them.

Within hours, it's clear we're several days from crossing the foothills at the bottom of the range and moving east into Dracmire. And yet the further south we travel, the more my skin has prickled with an unwelcome awareness.

I wait until Haldrik is far enough ahead of us and then lower my voice, directing Hope close to Fox.

"Do you feel like you're being watched?"

Calysian gives me a sharp nod. "I haven't seen any sign of

Vicana's regiment, but her witch lived. It's likely she sensed the second grimoire and Kyldare sent his soldiers south while you were recovering."

There's no blame in his words, but my stomach still twists. "You didn't kill the witch."

"No." His eyes meet mine. "When I saw you dying, I forgot she existed. I'm sure she crawled away somewhere and Kyldare found her."

I suck in a sharp breath. This kind of stark honesty is new. It's raw and vulnerable, and I don't know what to do with it.

"Thank you."

Haldrik waits for us at the next bend, his eyes darting between our faces as we approach, the ghost of a smile playing at his lips. "I never thought I'd see the day," he marvels. "Madinia Farrow—"

"Quiet," I snap, and Calysian raises one brow.

With a sniff, I nudge Hope into a trot, ignoring the twin male snorts behind me.

The days begin to blur together. Calysian turns strangely moody, switching from gazing at me with that intent, determined expression to ignoring me completely. The shift is subtle at first, so gradual I almost convince myself I'm imagining it. His silences grow longer. Heavier. When he does speak, his words are clipped, delivered with a cool efficiency that scrapes at the edge of my nerves.

The casual intimacy we'd fallen into disappears entirely.

A week after we found Haldrik, we camp in the shadow of a towering oak, its branches creaking in the wind. Haldrik builds the fire and I flick my hand at the branches and logs, my flames instantly engulfing the wood. He sends me an appreciative grin, but I turn my attention to Calysian.

He sits on the other side of the fire, sharpening his dagger with slow, methodical strokes. His eyes are distant, his attention on something far away.

I have a feeling I know what he's thinking about, and I take a deep breath. "Calysian. Are you—"

His gaze snaps to mine, and the air between us seems to shift. His dark eyes gleam with something sharp and predatory, and my words wither on my tongue. Haldrik glances between us, his eyes wide, and I shake my head warningly at him.

The next day, it's worse.

We ride side by side, but there's an invisible wall between us. Calysian's posture has turned straighter, stiffer, and even Fox seems to be restless, his ears twitching back as if reacting to something I can't see.

In the distance, the foothills ripple out from the base of the mountains, the terrain dotted with sharp ridges and outcroppings. Calysian keeps his gaze on the trail, occasionally scanning the forest for threats.

"Do you want to talk?" I murmur. "Is this about Eamonn?"

"No." His voice is empty. Flat. And he doesn't even look at me. Frustration coils in my chest, and I rein Hope in, forcing her to slow until Calysian rides ahead of me with Haldrik. There's something unnervingly detached about his voice. His movements.

We stop in a small town, but of course no one this far inland has seen or heard from Daharak or her people. Calysian stays with the horses while Haldrik and I ask our questions, and the moment he sees us approaching, he mounts Fox, clearly eager to leave.

By the time we stop for the night, the tension is unbearable. His presence feels wrong, like a storm cloud settling over our camp, oppressive and damp. The night turns muted, as if even the insects no longer dare to draw attention to themselves.

I have a feeling I know what is truly happening. The grimoire's power is seductive. Enthralling.

To my left, Haldrik's snores cut through the night. I don't sleep. Instead, I spend hours gazing up at the stars, attempting to understand. The first grimoire didn't do this to him. Yes, I'd seen more glimpses of the dark god, as we approached, but he'd remained in control until the moment he took it.

If the second grimoire is already affecting him like this, I can't even imagine the damage the third grimoire would do.

I roll over, staring into the flames. For the first time since I met Calysian, I feel truly…alone. When I roll again, switching to my other side, Calysian lets out a frustrated growl.

"I don't want to be this way, Madinia." His voice is rough, but I can hear the thread of vulnerability beneath. "I didn't want this to happen."

I don't answer. Because it *is* happening. And it will continue happening until the man I knew as Calysian is gone.

A hot tear slips down my cheek, and I close my eyes.

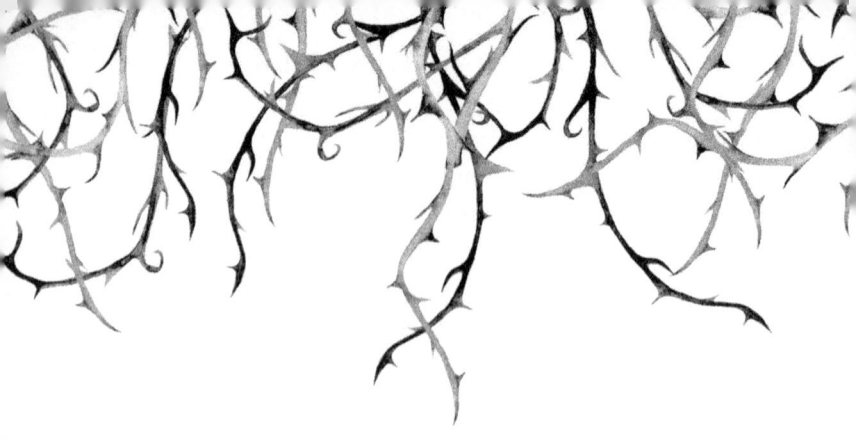

CHAPTER TWENTY-TWO

MADINIA

I'M UP EARLY THE NEXT MORNING, AND I LEAVE THE MEN sleeping as I gather fresh clothes and make my way toward the river.

I've spent my life seamlessly transforming hurt into fury. I learned how to fuel myself with my rage, blocking out any vulnerability that could threaten what little peace I could find.

But my usual techniques are no longer working. As Calysian disappears with each step closer to the grimoire, Calpharos appears in his place.

I strip, placing my clothes on a larger rock as I shiver in the morning air. The water is only waist deep here, and I've picked a sheltered bend where the water is calm.

Slowly, I step into the river. It's shockingly cold, and my teeth immediately begin to chatter. But the frigid temperature is an acceptable distraction, however temporary.

My skin prickles and I force myself to take another step. I scrub my skin with river sand before switching to soap, debating whether to wash my hair.

"Now that's a sight I've missed." I whirl, and Calysian grins at me.

"What are you doing?" My voice is sharp, even as the sight of his dimple makes relief shudder through me.

He scans my naked body, his gaze lingering on my hardened nipples. His eyes turn glazed, and he takes a step closer. "Bathing." His voice is hoarse, his expression tight.

"Does Haldrik know where we went?"

He gives a disinterested shrug, his hands moving to his shirt. I search his face, Calpharos is nowhere to be seen. Something itches at the edges of my mind, but Calysian's shirt hits the ground, and he winks at me.

When his pants follow, I turn back to the river. Perhaps, if I don't look at him, I'll be able to ignore the heat radiating through my body. The water is no longer frigid on my overheated skin, and I move deeper.

"Madinia."

Calysian steps into the river and he lets out a hiss. "Look at me."

His scent drifts over me, and I take another step, unsurprised when he catches my shoulder, turning me to face him.

He gives me a smug, very male look. "You're afraid of your reaction to me. You want me."

I heave a sigh. "I've already *had* you." The words are strangely lewd when I say them aloud, and my cheeks heat.

Calysian merely grins. "And *I've* had you. That doesn't mean we can't have each other again. And again."

"That was one night. We agreed."

"You agreed." He gives me that arrogant look—the one I find both infuriating and frustratingly appealing. "But you knew you were lying even as you said the words." He reaches out, trailing one finger down my arm, and just that simple touch makes me shiver.

He's right.

I *never* should have allowed him to kiss me the first time. That mistake led to my downfall.

Calysian has never lied to me. He's never been cagey about his intentions. He wants to find his grimoires and take revenge against his siblings. He wants to make them pay for what they did to him, and truthfully, I don't blame him.

But there's no room for me in that plan. Calysian has never specifically said I won't be going with him, but he doesn't have to. He's going up against *gods*. He's a god himself.

I was stupid enough to let him in, and truly idiotic to let myself begin to feel something for him.

When he leaves—and he will—it will hurt.

But if I allow him to get any closer, it won't just hurt. It will break me.

These past days are proof of that.

"What are you thinking?" Calysian's voice is soft.

I force my coldest expression onto my face. "I'm thinking you've ignored my existence for days at a time, and now that I'm standing here naked, you've decided to acknowledge me again. I'm thinking I've made many mistakes in my life, but beginning whatever this is with you may have been the biggest one."

His expression turns flat. "I never thought you were a coward, Madinia Farrow."

"And I always suspected you would be a power-hungry bastard." I give him my coldest smile. "I ignored my instincts, but I won't do that again."

I leave the water, pick up my clothes, and find a tree to change behind. I walk back to camp, miserable and shivering.

Haldrik paces next to the remnants of our fire, his eyes hard. "Where's Calysian?"

"Bathing. What's wrong?"

A muscle jumps in his jaw, but he turns away, continuing to pack. "I've saddled your horse—Calysian's stallion wouldn't let me near it. But we should leave soon if we're going to make the most of the daylight."

I study his face, my instincts pricking. Something *is* wrong.

"Haldrik...is everything—"

Glancing over his shoulder, he gives me a tense smile. "I'm fine. I'm just worried for Daharak and the others."

Calysian returns, his eyes hot and furious. But they turn cold as he saddles Fox, and by the time we begin traveling south, he's remote and withdrawn once more. Haldrik keeps close to him, attempting to engage him in conversation, but Calysian offers little more than the occasional grunt.

My stomach turns to knots, my chest tight. If traveling toward the second grimoire is doing this to Calysian, by the time he finds it, he'll be unrecognizable.

If only I could sneak away and find the grimoire myself. But he's been careful not to give me any clues about its location.

I wish Eamonn were here. Even if he couldn't help, he would likely understand.

Eventually, we stop for the day and set up camp.

And when I open my eyes the next morning, Calysian is gone.

I sit up, staring at the spot where he should be sleeping. Somehow, he managed to pack and saddle Fox without waking either of us.

Haldrik gives me a grim look from his own sleeping mat. "I didn't hear him either."

"We need to go after him."

He nods slowly, his eyes on mine. "I don't know how long he has been gone."

My heart races, but my instincts roar at me. I keep my expression blank as I nod, turning away.

He's...lying.

I don't understand why. Does he think I would judge him for failing to keep Calysian from leaving?

Scooping up my clothes, I move into the forest, ducking behind a tree as I dress. The edges of my mind begin to itch once more, a sense of dread burrowing deep into my chest. It's a feeling that I've missed something, a certainty that something is very, very wrong.

"If we move quickly, we might be able to catch him," I say when I return. Haldrik is slowly lumbering around camp. He blinks blearily at me, in no hurry to move. Every other day, he has been the first up and ready to go, pacing impatiently while I eat and bathe.

A dark, ugly suspicion takes up residence in my gut.

Haldrik slowly gets to his feet. "Ah, Madinia. Those eyes just gave you away. They flashed with such hatred, it chilled me to my bones."

My heart leaps into my throat. He gives me a sad smile. He's less than ten footspans away, his knife already sheathed at his hip.

My sword is lying next to my sleeping mat, too far for me to reach without leaping towards it. But I go nowhere without my knife, and the hilt is a cool comfort in my hand.

I stare at the man who insisted on traveling with us. My heart wilts, and I can barely breathe, betrayal choking the air from my lungs.

I've been so, so stupid.

"I spent an entire month in that tower wondering how Kyldare found us that last time. Daharak constantly changed her plans. Only a few people knew the exact route we would take. You must have been one of them. You were the one who told Kyldare where to find us. You knew we were going to be attacked. That's why you disappeared in Ambrelis."

Haldrik hunches his shoulders, a deep line appearing between his brows. He looks old and frail and tired. "Kyldare promised he would only take you. He said the others would live."

"He lied. Carix died that day. He was your friend."

I remember that much. I remember Carix gently teasing Haldrik about how well he could hold his liquor, remember Haldrik grinning back at him as he agreed to a drinking game.

Haldrik flinches back, looking suddenly lost. I have no sympathy for him.

"They held a knife to Carosa's throat. Kyldare was going to kill her without a second thought. There was so much blood on the deck of that ship, my boots were painted with it, Haldrik."

"Then you should have gone with them!"

I let out a bitter laugh. "You know what Kyldare wants, don't you?" Daharak was so careful to only tell those in her trusted circle. I don't remember Haldrik being one of those people, but clearly he had been spying for some time. "Were you truly prepared for what would happen if that grimoire made its way into the wrong hands? You know what Regner did to us!"

"I was tired!" he roars. "I never wanted to fight in a war. I wanted to enjoy the freedom of the open seas!"

I curl my lip at him. "Daharak will kill you for this."

"Daharak's dead." His voice is flat, and I stumble backward. "What—"

"It's the only logical assumption."

My lungs unfreeze. "But you have no proof."

He sends me a pitying look, but I don't miss the guilt that flashes through his pale eyes. "Kyldare is a monster. We both know he never would have let them live."

My mind races. Haldrik is going to try to kill me. He has to. Within moments, I'll be fighting for my life. But I can't remember what power he has. Which means I need to buy time.

"You're still working for Vicana."

Haldrik nods, shoulders slumping. "One of her advisors is fae. The first time I met them was when we docked in Ambrelis. They made me take a blood vow. I was given a list of things I was to do if I ever saw Calpharos. The moment I saw you with him, I knew."

My head whirls. We were so, so careful not to tell Haldrik we're searching for the grimoire. And yet he's known who Calysian is this whole time.

"How?"

"I saw the darkness in his eyes." He shakes his head at me. "You were right that day. Calpharos will still be alive when all of us are dust."

Rage ripples through me. Since the moment we met Haldrik, he's been plotting and spying.

Panic replaces the rage, my stomach churning as a grim knowledge sinks in. Calysian is still weakened from pouring his power into Fox. The action that saved my life may now end his.

"What's your plan, Haldrik?"

Haldrik shakes his head at me. "You're trying to buy time. It's clever, Madinia, but Calysian isn't coming back." He reaches into his pocket and I tense. Something flashes silver in his hand and he drops an oval stone onto the ground between us. An otherworldly glow spills from it, as if it holds captured moonlight.

My breath catches. I want to cup the stone in my hand and ponder it. I want to crush it into a million pieces and bury it.

The impulses clash within me, until I'm frozen in indecision.

Haldrik lets out a hollow laugh, and it takes all of my willpower to rip my gaze from the stone.

"Even *you* are caught in it. I wasn't expecting that."

"What is it?"

He shrugs. "Vicana gave it to me. It's from Calpharos's world. I was told when I came across the dark god, I was to make sure this stone was near him at all times. Vicana must have been working with a seer. She knew we would meet."

My mouth is so dry, I can barely speak. "What—what does it do?"

Haldrik smiles. And it's still that familiar, kind smile. "The weaker Calpharos is, the more difficult it is for him to fight against his true self."

And he's been fighting against that *true self* since Haldrik joined us. Calysian was doing everything he could to stay human, while I was pushing him away, furious that the *grimoire* was stealing him from me.

But it wasn't the grimoire at all.

This is why Calysian seemed like he was back to his normal self two days ago at the river. And it explains why Haldrik was so furious that he'd gone to bathe without him.

I'd lashed out at him for ignoring me, accused him of only noticing me because I was naked. But it was because Calysian was no longer in the vicinity of that stone.

Haldrik stayed by his side the entire day, ensuring his stone was close. So close, something within Calysian snapped, and he left. Alone.

"I'm sorry, Madinia. But I'm at the mercy of the blood vow."

"Where is Calysian going?"

"Toward his grimoire. And Vicana."

Terror rips a hole in my chest. Calysian is still nowhere near full strength, and Vicana has witches and fae and regiments of soldiers.

I have to get to him.

Haldrik shakes his head at me. "You're too late." Sadness gleams in his eyes. "Sometimes, we just have to accept our mistakes."

"Accept this." Fire sweeps from my hands, and I shove my flames at him until I'm dizzy. The smoke clears, and Haldrik bares his teeth in a feral grin, his ward flashing between us.

Suddenly, I remember Carix teasing him for more than just his alcohol tolerance.

Haldrik is half fae.

No one would know by looking at his craggy face, his stooped shoulders, his short stature. He didn't get fae beauty or grace.

But he got a nice hit of power—a ward that would likely rival Calysian's.

245

A ward that will outlast my flames.

It gleams a dark blue, held in place by his will alone.

What other powers did he inherit from his fae father?

My heart thunders in my chest, but I force myself to think about Daharak and the others, betrayed by the man they considered family. And then I focus on Calysian, currently walking into a trap.

Fine. I'll kill Haldrik without magic.

Anticipation and terror war within me. I have to kill him fast. Before Calysian walks into the trap Vicana has set for him.

With a nod, Haldrik unsheathes his own dagger. The world narrows, until all I can see is him as he slowly walks toward me. His knife is long, thin, and I catch strange runes carved into the hilt.

My stomach churns. It has been a long, long time since those days on the ship, when Lonn bullied me into training with him. But if I die here, Calysian dies too. And I have no doubt Vicana will turn this continent to ruin.

Haldrik doesn't waste time. He launches himself at me, moving faster than I thought he could.

I dodge, sending him a smirk. "Looks like your father passed down a few gifts, Haldrik. And yet he never stayed to raise you, did he? Some part of him must have known you'd become a spineless coward who would turn on his own family the moment he had the chance."

His eyes widen, then narrow, and he slashes out, his knife slicing close to my throat. Too close.

I dance backward, but he's still coming, lips thinned, cheeks flushed. I'd known my best chance was to get under his skin, but even I hadn't anticipated his rage.

Rage that has likely been burning within him for years.

"Take your time. Study the feet and the chest. Don't get impatient." Lonn's voice echoes through my mind. *"Let them tire themselves out."*

THIS VICIOUS DREAM

Haldrik slashes out again, and I dodge, but he's too fast, his blade a blur as he swipes at me. I thrust my own knife up, and the clash of steel sets my teeth on edge. I twist, freeing my blade and thrust my knife at him, but he jolts back, out of my range.

With a curse, he barrels into me, his body careening into mine. My knife goes flying as we hit the ground and roll. I gape, breathless, momentarily winded. But I manage to strike out, slamming his knife from his hand.

I'm just so stupid. So slow. So unworthy. If I was a better person, maybe this wouldn't have happened. If there was anything in me worth loving, I wouldn't have spent so much of my life alone.

I deserve to die. I should just give up now.

My limbs weaken. Haldrik grunts, as if he's already tiring.

And I know what his true power is now.

Doubt.

Did he use that power to eat at Calysian too?

Cold spreads through my chest, and I choke on a sob.

I'm hurtful and vicious and mean. I've been that way since the day I was born. I'm always going to be alone. Calysian is better without me. *Everyone* is better without me.

Haldrik's eyes turn intent. "Just give in, Madinia. It will all be over soon." His gaze fixes on my throat, his eyes lighting with victory.

I let my hands relax from where they're slammed against his chest. Haldrik leans closer.

I slash out with my nails, raking a path down his face. He roars, rearing back, and I fight like a cat, desperate and ruthless. I wiggle my leg free from beneath him, slamming my boot into his groin.

Haldrik lets out a choked groan. I take the opportunity to roll to my stomach, clawing at the ground. If I can just make it to my knees—

Pain explodes through my scalp. The bastard has my hair

in his fist. He drags me to my knees, and blood rushes into my ears, terror searing my chest and exploding through my limbs.

The flash of a blade. I suck in a breath and aim my flames at the bare skin along his arms and face.

Haldrik screams, releasing me instantly. His ward reappears, and he slams his fist into my face. Stars spill across my vision and I slump forward.

Gods, it hurts.

"I thought I would regret this," Haldrik pants, shoving me onto my back. My head spins, my face on fire. Those huge fucking fists...he didn't just inherit that shiny ward, and his insidious power. He inherited fae strength too. A strength he must have kept carefully hidden on the ship, or I would have heard about it.

I kick out again, but Haldrik shoves my feet aside, straddling me as his hands wrap around my throat and squeeze. He leans close, avidly watching as I buck and claw at his hands.

No. Not like this.

I writhe, lungs screaming.

My hand grasps blindly at the ground for something...for anything. My fingers find cool stone.

The rock is heavy in my hand. But I smash it into his face. CRACK.

Blood spurts, and I rear up, as Haldrik cups his nose.

If he hadn't been leaning so close, it wouldn't have worked. But he was enjoying watching me fight for my life.

This man I trusted. This man I thought was a friend. This man who sold all of us out.

I slam the rock toward his head again, but his hand slashes out, knocking it from my grip. The move makes him unbalanced, and I kick out, knocking him off me.

Blood pours from his nose, and when he snarls, his teeth are painted with it. I twist, crawling toward my knife. This time, when Haldrik grabs my hair, I'm ready.

I shove my blade deep into his gut, watching as his eyes widen, realization sliding over his face.

"Die, you bastard."

I push the blade deeper, twisting. And then I pour my flames into him, the darkest part of me reveling in his screams.

I stumble to my feet, pulling my flames from his body. It was a quicker death than he deserved. And yet the scent of burned flesh crawls up my nostrils.

Turning, I retch, heaving. When I stumble toward my waterskin, I'm trembling. Sobbing.

The water is cool, and I pour it over my face, still unable to look at the corpse behind me.

"Madinia." The voice is feminine, shocked, and filled with compassion.

The world stops. My knees turn weak.

I know that voice.

Slowly, I turn.

Am I…dreaming?

No. That's Asinia walking toward me, her face freckled from the sun, her hair swept back in a braid. Demos is at her side, his amber eyes almost glowing against his tanned skin. Those eyes narrow, and he gives me that same familiar, vaguely impatient look.

Rythos steps through the trees behind them. His pointed ear is pierced, and the gold ring suits him. One eyebrow arches as he takes in Haldrik, his expression turing approving. "Somehow, I'm not surprised to find you in the aftermath of murder." He grins, his white teeth stark against his dark skin.

My knees straighten. My vision sharpens.

They're truly here.

Asinia wraps her arms around me. And I'm suddenly sobbing again, limbs weak, tears rolling down my face.

"Madinia?" Her arms tighten, but I can hear the shock in

her voice. I don't blame her. I've never fallen apart in front of her like this. I don't even recognize myself.

Rythos grins at me, holding out his arms. He seems surprised when I step into them.

"How...I don't understand."

"Your bird," Demos says wryly, and Eamonn flutters down to sit on his shoulder.

"You...how did you know?"

Eamonn angles his tiny head. "You talk in your sleep. And when you were fevered, you raved. I found it unlikely that they wouldn't have looked for you. We can talk about this later. First, you need to destroy that stone."

We all turn to look.

It's still sitting on the ground where Haldrik left it, the color of fog.

I test my flames, and the fire licks at the stone.

Nothing.

Demos steps forward. "Allow me."

His power shaped him to be Prisca's right hand—and to be a lethal threat on the battlefield. He's faster and stronger than even some of the fae. So I don't argue when he pulls a hammer from his saddlebag and slams it against the stone.

It shatters into tiny pieces. And the moment that silver glow disappears, something settles deep in my chest.

"How did you find me?" My voice is hoarse, and Asinia reaches for Demos's hand, the movement easy, natural. He presses a kiss to her knuckles, but his eyes remain on mine.

"When we didn't hear from you, Prisca began sending out groups of soldiers." He shakes his head. "But foreign kingdoms don't take too kindly to that. Eventually, we realized you must really be in trouble, which meant we needed to be more discreet with our search."

"Prisca went looking for you herself," Asinia says. "With Lorian. They left the kingdom in competent hands, but then..."

My hands shake, and the world turns blurry. "What happened?"

Asinia gives me a gentle smile. "No, nothing like that. Prisca's pregnant, Madinia. At first, we searched together. And then we took turns so Demos could keep an eye on things while she was gone." I stare at her, and her smile deepens. "Lorian finally put his foot down, and even Prisca was forced to admit she needed to stay in our kingdom to protect her heir."

Demos nods. "Eventually, one of our spies returned with a story about a red-haired witch who was killing men and displaying their corpses in a garden of thorns. We knew that couldn't be you, but we figured…"

He trails off, staring at me. Asinia's mouth drops open. Rythos lets out a booming laugh.

I wince. "It's not as bad as it sounds."

Rythos throws his arm around my shoulder. "I'm sure they had it coming."

I grin up at him, my throat suddenly too thick for me to speak.

I was so, so sure they'd abandoned me. I was certain that after I left, they'd never thought of me again.

Instead, they've been searching for me for three years. Prisca even left her kingdom to search personally.

"I don't know what to say."

Asinia leans against Demos, her eyes on mine. "How about you start with what happened to you?"

I take a deep, shaky breath, and Rythos tightens his arm. "That bad, huh?"

"You have no idea. I'll tell you everything. But first I need your help."

Demos raises one eyebrow. "With what?"

"We need to find the dark god."

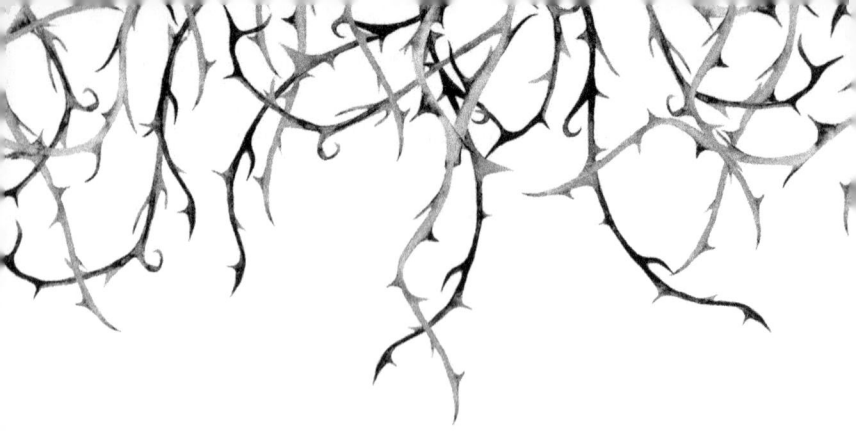

CHAPTER TWENTY-THREE

CALYSIAN

I NUDGE MY HORSE, URGING IT TO GO FASTER, TOWARD the call of the grimoire. The forest has become a blur, the wind snapping at me as we gallop east toward my memories. Toward my power.

"I always suspected you would be a power-hungry bastard. I ignored my instincts, but I won't do that again."

For some strange reason, the mortal's words continue to echo in my head.

I grind my teeth, pushing them away and urging my horse on.

I should not be in this world.

I should not have spent centuries wandering blindly.

I should not be almost powerless.

The strange interest I had for the mortal is now gone, and she will stay behind while I—

Stay behind. With the other mortal. The male.

I clench my teeth until my jaw aches. Irrelevant. Mortal lives mean nothing to me. The woman is little more than a speck of dust to one such as I.

Agony seizes me.

It erupts through my head, stealing my breath, my thoughts.

I'm forced to bury my hands in my horse's mane as I hunch, muscles seizing, my vision blurring at the edges.

I suck in a deep breath and the world seems to snap into place, my thoughts sharpening once more as the pain finally ends.

Easing Fox to a stop, I slowly lift my head.

I left her.

I left her *alone*.

Madinia, who has been abandoned by so many people.

Worse, I left her with Haldrik.

Haldrik, who has been a wedge between us since the moment we met.

Realization slams into me with startling clarity.

Haldrik.

Almost every time I attempted to talk to Madinia alone, he interrupted. Each time I attempted to cajole her into my bed, Haldrik reminded her of who and what I was. Each time we attempted to bridge the widening gap between us, he introduced some new distraction, some new calamity.

My mind is sharp. Clear.

Hot, lethal rage burns through me, until I can feel it in my bones, can taste it on my tongue.

"I'm sorry," I murmur to Fox. "But we have to go back."

I've pushed him hard. Too hard. But he gives me a gallop, legs stretching as he eats at the distance. I push my power into him, giving him everything I have left, well aware that I'll be weakened when I find Madinia.

Dread burrows into my stomach. Madinia Farrow is a survivor. But she likes Haldrik. And she won't see this betrayal coming.

My rage is endless, but it's the helplessness that burns hotter than even Madinia's fire.

Stay alive. Just stay alive.

It takes hours to retrace my path. Twice, I have to stop to let Fox rest, impatience burning through me. And then I hear it.

Hooves pounding against the ground. Multiple horses.

I mount, turning Fox toward the road.

Even in the dim light of the evening, it's Madinia who I see first. Her hair catches the last faltering rays of the sun, and my heart stops.

Mottled bruises cover one side of her face, and she's splattered with blood. Her mouth is set with grim determination, and her eyes are narrowed, filled with wrath.

She slows, as do the three others she rides with. But I only have eyes for her.

"Calysian?" Madinia's voice is quiet, more hesitant than I've ever heard.

"Who hurt you?"

Relief flashes across her face and she dismounts from her horse. She stumbles, and I launch myself from Fox, catching her.

She freezes. "I've never seen you move *that* fast."

My hand trembles as I tuck a strand of her hair behind her ear, taking in the blue and purple bruises. "It was Haldrik, wasn't it?"

"Yes," she murmurs. "He's dead."

The others dismount, and I pull her close, breathing in her scent. "I shouldn't have left you. I'm sorry." The words stick in my throat.

"It's not your fault. We'll talk about it later." She pulls away. "Calysian, this is Asinia, Demos, and Rythos." Her eyes shine in a way I've never seen before. "They've been looking for me."

I nod at them, ignoring the suspicious looks aimed my way.

Madinia glances at Fox. "He needs to rest."

Remorse flashes through me as I walk to him, taking in his lowered head and heaving sides. "I'm sorry, old friend." It will be at least two days before I can risk mounting him again.

Madinia approaches, stroking his nose, and Fox nuzzles her hand. "Let's make camp. And you can tell me about Haldrik."

Demos, Rythos, and Asinia have brought plenty of supplies. Within an hour, we're seated around a fire, and flames are flickering across Madinia's bruised face as she tells me about Haldrik's betrayal. She curls her arms around herself, and I want nothing more than to turn back time and kill him for her.

Eventually, Madinia tells the others about her capture and the three years she spent in Kyldare's tower. She keeps her voice light, glossing over the worst of the horror, but I catch the sorrow in Asinia's eyes, the way Demos's hand flexes on his knee.

"He's dead," Rythos vows, and I meet his eyes.

"That task belongs to me."

"No," Madinia says cooly. "It belongs to *me*."

The others are quiet, but Asinia begins talking about life in the hybrid kingdom, and eventually, Rythos teases Madinia about their time spent imprisoned together during the war.

As much as I would like to listen, to learn all I can about Madinia's past, there's something else I need to do.

I caught sight of Eamonn earlier, following Madinia in his leopard form. With a nod at the others, I get to my feet, heading in his direction.

I find him lounging on a flat rock near the stream, his tail flicking back and forth.

"You returned," I murmur.

He gets to his feet, stretching his large form. His eyes turn to the forest and I wince.

"Wait."

Slowly, Eamonn turns his head, his yellow eyes cold. I did damage with my words. Damage I somehow need to fix.

"Thank you," I say. "For finding Madinia's friends."

"I didn't do it for you."

"I know."

He turns again, and I clench my fists. "I'm sorry. I was…

enraged when we spoke last time. I understand—that you couldn't tell me. I know what it's like to be forced to act in ways you would never choose to."

Silence stretches between us. Finally, he inclines his head. "I forgive you."

Relief surges though me as he disappears into the forest. Watching Madinia with her friends has reinforced my own lack. Eamonn was right. He was the only one to consistently be there for me since I returned to this continent. Truthfully, he's the only one I have trusted since the moment I opened my eyes in that forest all those centuries ago.

At least until I met Madinia.

Madinia

I wake up wrapped in Calysian's arms. His hands are gentle as he plays with my hair, his eyes hard as he stares into the distance.

I attempt to move, and Calysian tightens his grip, his eyes meeting mine. "This is becoming familiar." He grins crookedly, and that grin is so normal, so *him*, that something in my heart twists.

We shared his sleeping mat last night, and at some point, I drifted from the edge of the mat. Now, I'm sprawled over Calysian's hard chest.

I'm not entirely sure that he's the one to blame.

I lift my head. "Where is everyone?"

Calysian shrugs. "They left us to sleep." His tone is disinterested, his eyes focused on my mouth.

I should get up. But I'm still so tired. He gently strokes my bruised cheek. "That looks painful."

"I'm fine."

Calysian nods, but a muscle ticks in his jaw. "I should have realized Haldrik was a traitor."

With a sigh, I lay my head back on Calysian's chest, listening to the comforting thud of his heart. "*I* should have. I knew him." Even now, it's difficult to reconcile the man who tried to kill me with the same man who sat with me those few nights in the galley. He'd been a silent support while I trembled from the remnants of my nightmares. "You were trying to fight the pull from that stone. What is it, anyway?"

"I don't know. I remember nothing of any other worlds." He hesitates, and then firms his jaw. "I know you left something out last night. What did Haldrik do to you?"

I tense, and he sweeps his hand down my back soothingly.

When I don't speak, he cups my chin, lifting my head.

I wriggle even closer to his warmth. "He was half fae. I'd always wondered what his power was, but he was so...ordinary. I guess I began to assume he didn't *get* any power. I'm sure Daharak thought the same. Now I wonder if he ever used that power on her."

"I wish you'd told me he was half fae."

I sigh. "Honestly, I'd forgotten until we were in that clearing. Haldrik worked hard to appear as normal and unthreatening as possible."

Calysian tenses at the reminder, and I shrug, letting my eyes drift closed again.

"You haven't told me."

I feel my lower lip stick out and valiantly pull it back where it belongs. "Maybe I don't want to talk about it." My tone is sullen, but Calysian merely waits me out.

"I thought his power was *doubt*," I say finally, opening my eyes. "But I'm not sure if that's exactly what it was. It was like my thoughts weren't my own any more. All I could think was that I wasn't good enough, wasn't lovable. I knew, in my bones that I was a bad person, that I deserved to be alone, and that the world would be better if I was gone."

My eyes sting, and Calysian pulls me up his body, until his face is inches from mine. "You know that's not true."

I shrug. "I'm not sure if he used his power on you. He had that stupid stone, after all, so he probably didn't need to."

"I'm sorry. For leaving you."

I attempt a smile. "You didn't have a choice. Besides, I can look after myself."

"You certainly proved that."

"And then Asinia and Demos and Rythos arrived."

He gives me a slow nod, but his eyes are cool. I can't help but reach down and run my nails across his scalp. His hair is so dark it seems to swallow the light. And yet it's so thick, the texture silky smooth. "What's wrong?"

Calysian arches his head like a cat, chasing my fingers. "I don't like how he looks at you."

I blink at him. "Who?"

His eyes narrow, as if he thinks I'm being intentionally dense. "Rythos."

"Rythos?" My voice is incredulous, and Calysian scowls.

"You have a history with him."

"We were briefly imprisoned together. Our history mostly consists of bickering and ignoring each other with the occasional moment of cooperation."

Calysian's scowl deepens, and my mouth twitches.

Yes, that sounds not unlike *our* relationship at times. But it's different. With Calysian, our arguments are heated, often dripping with subtext, and usually leading to fantasies about strangling him even as I press my lips to his.

"Rythos is a friend," I say carefully, and Calysian sneers at me. His expression is sullen, but his eyes flicker with what looks almost like…bewilderment.

My heart twists. Jealousy is clearly a new emotion for him,

and one he's obviously finding difficult to deal with. Something thrills within me at the knowledge that Calysian has no real experience wrestling with this kind of possessive need. Until now.

"You don't need to worry about Rythos," I murmur.

When Calysian continues to scowl, I run my finger across his forehead, attempting to stroke away his dark expression. He catches my hand in his, his eyes harden. "Tell me you don't want him."

My heart thuds. "I don't want him."

"Tell me you want me."

"I want you."

Our mouths meet, and he rolls until I'm on my back, his huge body caging mine as he seems to breathe me in. I'm aware of his strength and the frustration coiled within him at this moment. And yet all I can think about is how good his body feels against mine, and how solid and *real* he feels as I arch my hips, grinding against him.

"The others…" my words are muffled against his lips and he lifts his head with a frown, listening.

"They're seeing to the horses. Now tell me you want me again."

This man always wants so much of me. "Do you truly think this will soothe your jealousy?"

He buries his hand in my hair, holding me still for him. "It will help."

I have to fight the urge to give him what he wants. And all *I* want is to curl up against him and hear him say everything will be fine.

But he would be lying.

Because nothing will be fine.

In a few days, I might need to *kill* him.

I shove at his chest. "What exactly do you think will happen once you become a god, Calysian?"

"I *am* a god."

"You know what I mean. Say you don't destroy my world. What will happen once you have your precious grimoires?"

Calysian's gaze turns flat, and I shove again. He merely moves his hand from my hair, neatly capturing my wrists.

"You'll go on living," I snap. "Forever. And I won't pine for you. I refuse. I'll find someone, and I'll live a normal, mortal life." It will be a longer life than most—my hybrid blood is a gift that I can finally appreciate now that I'm free from that tower. But my life won't be endless.

I wouldn't want it to be.

There are only two possible outcomes if we continue this way: Calysian gets his grimoires and manages to temper his wrath, keeping our world safe even as he finds his vengeance. Or Calysian gets his grimoires and becomes a monster, and I'm forced to kill him.

Neither of these outcomes comes with a long, happy life for us.

I push against him with my hips and shoulder, until he releases my wrists and rolls off me, shoving one hand through his hair.

"What do you want from me, Madinia?"

I shake my head, wrapping a blanket around myself. "It doesn't matter. It's clear you'll never be able to give it to me."

His expression darkens as he gets to his feet. I leave him in the clearing, my chest tight, hands trembling as I dress.

When I return, the others are gathered around the fire. Asinia's eyes search my face and I shake my head.

Demos is speaking quietly with Calysian. "When do you think your stallion will be able to travel?"

"Tomorrow, perhaps."

Despite the bitterness flooding me, I can't help but smile. I know Calysian wants to be traveling, wants to make his way towards the second grimoire.

But he won't risk Fox.

That, more than anything gives me hope. Maybe, if he does manage to get the last two grimoires, he'll be able to remain just mortal enough to retain some compassion. Some kindness.

Demos throws another log into the fire before getting to his feet to pace. "What do you know about Vicana?"

The words are simple, but his tone is filled with carefully banked fury. This is a man who spent years in Regner's dungeon. A man who watched his friends and family die beneath the tyrannical rule of a power-hungry despot.

He won't allow such a thing to happen again.

"She has been looking for the grimoires for years. She learned that the first grimoire would be brought to this continent—and that I had it—and she's done everything she can to get her hands on it. Vicana has been stealing territory from Telanthris, and I have no doubt if she was to find a grimoire, she would create just as much pain and death and suffering as Regner—perhaps more."

"So we have to prevent that from happening," Rythos says.

"Yes," Demos nods. "And we need to make such an example of her that any who think to follow in her footsteps will think again."

My mind provides me with memories of that last battle—the screams, the stench, the *suffering*.

Calysian moves to my side, wrapping his arm around me. It's a possessive, proprietary move, and he ignores the dark look I send his way.

Hope feels foreign, and yet the fact that I'm currently talking to Demos, Asinia, and Rythos proves that I can maybe afford to let myself feel it more often.

My eyes meet Asinia's, and she jerks her head. I shrug off Calysian's arm and he gives me an indulgent look, leaning close to murmur in my ear. "Enjoy your *woman talk* with your friend. Be sure to tell her just how much I satisfy you in bed."

I know he's trying to pull me from the memories that are

clawing at me even now. "I'll be sure to tell her the only thing god-like about you is your ego," I hiss, and he smirks at me.

I follow Asinia toward the river, both of us quiet until we reach the shore. The water crashes against the rocks, thundering in my ears.

"I'm so glad we found you," she murmurs, sitting on a large, flat rock. Idly, she reaches for a twig, twirling it between her fingers. "Madinia…Demos wants us to travel with you to the next grimoire."

My stomach churns. "Because he thinks Calysian will need to die, and he doesn't think I can kill him."

Asinia winces, dropping her gaze to the twig and snapping it in two. "Do you really think you'd be able to be objective?"

I open my mouth to argue, but there's nothing I can say. "I didn't expect this."

She gives me a look filled with so much sympathy, I have to glance away. "None of us ever do. Prisca certainly wasn't expecting Lorian, and you know how I felt about Demos."

My lips twitch. I've never truly connected with Demos, and I know he's never fully trusted me. And yet he still left his kingdom when I disappeared. He still joined the search.

A flap of wings, and I glance up, expecting to see Eamonn. Instead, a pigeon lands on Asinia's shoulder, and she gives the bird a stroke, gently plucking the note tied to its leg.

I'm immediately filled with unwelcome memories of a hundred pigeons sent back and forth during the war.

"We already sent word to Prisca that you're alive. Now we'll be able to keep in touch," Asinia says. "Say hello."

With a sigh, I reach out and stroke the pigeon's tiny head.

"Thank you," I murmur when she's finished scrawling her reply. "For finding me."

Asinia gives me an impatient look. "Do you know what your problem is?"

I heave a sigh, and her eyes narrow. "You grew up in that

castle where you saw the worst in people. And still, despite all your attempts, you remained mostly good. You saved our lives time and time again, and yet you believed we wouldn't do the same for you. That hurts, Madinia. And it would kill something in Prisca if she ever learned of it."

"Three years, Asinia. Three years of Kyldare assuring me that I was completely alone. That no one was coming." And still, I can see her point. I sigh, glancing at the pigeon. "Don't tell Prisca."

"I won't. If you promise me something. When all this is done, you visit. And you stay awhile."

I close my eyes. When all of this is done, Calysian will be gone, and Kyldare and Vicana will be dead. What will I have left after that?

"Fine."

"Demos and I disagree," she mutters, throwing the broken remnants of her twig into the river and sending the pigeon away with her reply. When her eyes meet mine, they're dark and sad. "I believe you can kill Calysian if you don't make it to the grimoire before he does. Out of all of us, you're the best at doing the hard things. The things that need to be done. Oh, you suffer for it. And this would kill the little remaining softness you have. But you could do it."

My eyes burn, and I sit down next to Asinia, staring blindly at the water.

She shifts closer, taking my hand. "You're going to try to convince him not to take the grimoire. To choose you instead."

"And I'm going to fail." The certainty is heavy in my gut, the knowledge inescapable. "He's spent centuries wandering this world, Asinia, with no knowledge or memories of his past. How could he give up his chance to become whole?"

"There's another option."

I stare at her, my mind racing. "What do you—" It hits me. "Rythos."

"You've seen his power. You know what he can do."

Yes, I've seen it. And I've seen Rythos trembling and vomiting in the aftermath.

His power is terrible and frightening, and the thought of him using it on Calysian makes my palms burn.

Asinia yelps, ripping her hand from mine.

My chest wrenches and I snatch it back, searching for a burn. "Are you hurt?"

"No. The heat just startled me." She meets my eyes. "Rythos could be our only chance."

"I can't do it, Asinia. I can't."

"So *we'll* do it. Me and Demos and Rythos. It's just a test. To see if his power can even work on Calysian."

"And if it can?"

"Then we'll know that if all else fails and it looks like this world will fall, we can leash the dark god until we have a better plan."

The thought of Calysian being *leashed* makes bile burn up the back of my throat, and I turn my head, avoiding Asinia's gaze once more. I have a feeling she sees far too much.

And yet, what's the alternative? My own plans hinge around either convincing Calysian not to take the grimoire, or getting to it first and hiding it from both him and Vicana.

"Fine," I croak. "But tell Rythos he has one chance. I won't have him working on Calysian the way Haldrik did with that fucking stone."

Asinia sighs. "Of course you couldn't fall in love with an ordinary man. You couldn't choose a fae or a hybrid, or a prince. No, you had to go and fall in love with a *god*."

I bare my teeth. "I'm not in love with him. We've enjoyed each other's bodies. That's all."

She gives me a pitying look. "If you say so."

CHAPTER TWENTY-FOUR

Madinia

When I return, Calysian is holding Fox's lead rope as he takes him on a gentle walk down the trail. The horse nudges at him with his nose, and Calysian murmurs something too low for me to hear.

"How is he?"

Calysian turns, guiding Fox toward me. "Surprisingly fine. I've been monitoring him closely, and we should be able to travel tomorrow as long as we keep the pace slow."

"You're not worried about Kyldare finding the grimoire?"

"Of course I am. But when I explore the link, I can't yet sense our enemies approaching it."

Fox nuzzles Calysian again, and he reaches into his pocket, pulling out an apple and offering it. "I don't know why I worried about you."

"I don't, either," I say. "That horse is invincible."

Amusement flickers through his eyes, and he leads Fox back to the trees where we've tied the others' horses.

I take a brush, grooming Hope, although I can see someone else has already brushed her today. Still, the long, sweeping motions calm the worst of my anxiety.

Until Asinia walks past, sending me an intent look.

Panic flutters in my chest.

I should never have agreed to this. I want to take my agreement back, want to refuse even the thought of such a plan. But...

Rythos strides toward Calysian, a smile on his face. Even without his power, he's charismatic. Compelling.

It's too late.

Threads of his power drift towards us, and I stiffen, my hands warming. But Rythos aims that power away from me, spearing it directly at Calysian.

My stomach swims, my mouth turning watery. This is wrong. *Wrong.*

"Calysian," Rythos says, his eyes bright, his expression warm and inviting. "It has been a pleasure to get to know you. I hope we can be friends."

He takes a step closer, and I can see a hint of strain in his eyes. He's pouring every drop of his power into this.

I hold my breath, lungs burning.

For a moment, nothing happens.

Then Calysian lets out a lethal, inhuman snarl, whirling to face Rythos. The temperature around us plummets, until each of my breaths become clouds of fog. Calysian's eyes are cold and calculating, his expression feral. I clamp down on the urge to step between them.

Rythos continues to watch Calysian with that easy smile, but I know him well enough to catch the hint of disquiet in his eyes.

And then Calysian is moving, blazingly fast. Asinia sprints towards us. "Stop!"

But it's too late. Calysian wraps his hand around Rythos's throat, his teeth bared.

"Do you think I have no knowledge of your power? I've met many such as you through the centuries. Tell me," he lowers his voice conversationally, ignoring Rythos's struggles, "how many times have you used that power on Madinia? Is she truly your *friend*? Are any of them?"

Rythos jerks his hand, and a scream rips from my throat as he sinks his blade into Calysian's forearm.

I sweep my flames toward both men. I'm careful, aiming for their clothes and banishing the fire before it can do more than singe their skin. Still, it shocks them enough that Calysian loosens his hold, and Rythos jumps backward, staring at the ruins of his shirt.

He shakes his head. "I liked that shirt." His voice is hoarse, the bruising around his throat already beginning to heal. His eyes are grave as they meet mine. "He's a monster, Madinia. You deserve better."

Calysian flinches. Refusing to look at me, he turns and stalks into the forest. A hot ache spreads through my chest.

Asinia trembles, her breaths coming in sharp pants, and even Demos looks spooked as he pulls her into his arms. With a muttered curse, Rythos disappears in the other direction.

"Well," Demos says. "That didn't work."

I narrow my eyes at him, and surprisingly, he smiles back. "Powerful bastard. I'd almost be impressed if it didn't mean we were in big trouble."

Asinia shakes her head at him, and Demos grins down at her, dropping a kiss to her forehead. He's...different than he was three years ago. Quicker to smile.

He mutters something about hunting for dinner and leaves us alone in the clearing. I move back to the horses, and Fox snaps his teeth in my direction, as if even the stallion is judging me.

"Are you going to go after him?" Asinia steers clear of Fox as she strokes Hope's neck, her eyes on me.

I shake my head. "Not yet. He needs a little...time."

"You had to try," Asinia murmurs. "And now we know."

"Yes." My voice is bitter. "Now we know."

"That might have been the stupidest thing you've ever

done," Eamonn says conversationally, jumping down from the tree branch above our heads. He's in his panther form, his muscles bulging beneath sleek fur.

My heart jolts, and when his eyes meet mine, I'm engulfed with hot shame.

"I didn't hear you offering any brilliant plans," Asinia says, and Eamonn just stares at her. He doesn't bother looking at me again, just slowly prowls back into the forest.

I study Asinia. The last few years have been good to her. The thin, hunted look most of us had worn so well during the war is nowhere to be seen. Her arms are toned, her face no longer gaunt. Knowing Demos, he still insists on training her himself every day.

We've had no time to truly talk about everything that has happened since I left. And I'm suddenly desperately curious.

"You were going to be a seamstress," I say.

A hint of grief enters Asinia's eyes and she gives me a shaky smile. "We can talk about that later. For now, I need you to make a decision."

"What kind of decision?"

"I think Demos, Rythos and I should go look for Daharak. After what just happened, Calysian likely won't tolerate us traveling with you to find the grimoire. And if Vicana is as dangerous as you've said, we may need Daharak's fleet."

Grief threatens to swallow me whole. "They're gone, Asinia. It's the only explanation for the fact that no one has seen them."

Asinia frowns, tucking her hair behind her ear. "If by *gone* you mean they likely sailed north when they couldn't find you."

I stare at her. "North?"

"To the northern continent. We don't have proof," she cautions. "But most of Daharak's remaining fleet were seen in those waters. It makes sense that she would have met up with them after you disappeared. We have a ship. And I think we should look for them while you continue on with Calysian."

"Yes," I say, barely breathing. "I'd like that."

"It's settled then. We'll leave tomorrow."

Despite my newfound hope, my chest tightens. "I don't want you to go."

Surprise flashes through Asinia's eyes and she grins at me. "You're making progress. You never could have said those words in Eprotha."

I walk back toward the fire, the familiar warmth of the flames offering little comfort. "Everything I learned about friendship, I learned from you, Prisca, and Daharak. And then I was all alone. For three years. It did something to me, Asinia. The loneliness, combined with the grimoire I used…it made me a little…mad. I sunk power into the thorns surrounding my prison and grew them large and sharp enough to kill. And I *reveled* in their deaths."

"Do you think anyone could blame you for that? Do you think Prisca would? All of us have done things we're not proud of to stay alive."

"But have you *enjoyed* them the way I did?"

Asinia tuts. "You're so quick to paint yourself as a villain, Madinia."

I shrug, and we fall into silence as we begin to pack for tomorrow morning. Each time I close my eyes, all I see is the rage in Calysian's eyes, the cold wrath when he thought Rythos had used that power on me.

He would have killed Rythos if he'd learned he'd aimed his power my way. And yet I allowed Rythos to attempt such a thing with him.

Rythos returns, his gaze flying to mine as he strides across the clearing with the fae grace I used to loathe. "You can barely look at me."

"You did what we asked. I don't blame you." I, more than anyone, know what it cost him.

He sighs. "And yet you blame yourself. You once told me that if we were going to win, we had to use every weapon available to us."

"That's the problem. It doesn't feel like winning when Calysian is going to lose so much."

We eat, feed the horses, talk quietly to each other. But Calysian doesn't return. I'm distracted, unable to enjoy my last night with the others. It's only the knowledge that Calysian wouldn't leave Fox behind that prevents me from searching for him.

Clearly, he wants to be left alone.

I can't blame him.

The sleeping mat is narrow, and yet it feels empty without his large body curling around mine.

Annoyance flashes through me. I swore I wouldn't pine for Calysian, and yet here I am, already unable to sleep without him near me.

It's infuriating.

Night gives way to dawn, the cool breeze stirring tree branches above my head, casting flickering sunlight across my face.

Finally, I abandon any hope of sleep, sitting up and curling my arms around my knees. I'm not the only one with heavy-lidded eyes. On the other side of the fire, Demos leans into Asinia, murmuring something that makes her smile before kissing his way down her cheek to her mouth.

I look away, swallowing the ache.

Wishing won't change anything. Wanting is a waste of time.

I dress, eat, pack, attend to the horses. All while scanning the clearing for any sign of Calysian.

And then he returns.

His eyes are shadowed, his expression flat. He's bandaged

his arm, but I can see splotches of blood leaking through. He steers clear of Rythos, replying only to questions about our travels, and only with the occasional grunt.

Before I know it, before I'm truly ready, it's time to leave. And this time, I hug each of them—even Demos. Calysian tightens Fox's girth, nodding once at the others before turning to mount his horse.

"We'll write," Asinia promises.

And then they're gone.

My eyes burn as I mount Hope, following Calysian back to the road. We ride in silence for hours, reaching the southern tip of the Lacana mountains and the border between Dracmire and Evethia. Eamonn is nowhere to be seen, although I'm sure he's up to something. He was, after all, the one who found Asinia and the others.

When we stop to water the horses, Calysian finally speaks. "Did you know Rythos was going to attempt to snare me with his power?"

His words are a low rumble, and I have to force myself to meet his cold eyes.

"Yes."

He stares at me for a long moment, as if expecting me to snatch the word back.

I force myself to hold his gaze. "I'm sorry. You're a threat, Calysian. We had to know if you could be contained."

His eyes ice over, and suddenly, I'm speaking with Calpharos.

"Contained. I'd have thought your experience with such horrors would keep you from inflicting them on others."

I wince. "Calysian."

"It was a good plan. Pity it didn't work."

"I—"

He mounts his horse, and nudges Fox into a canter. A dull throb begins in my temples, rivaling the ache in my chest.

The ground turns pitted and rocky, and we're forced to slow our pace as we traverse the foothills. There are no signs of any temples here, but sharp ridges of stone lay across the earth, sparse patches of grass clinging to the rocky terrain, the blades yellowed and brittle.

Boulders—some larger than the horses—are scattered across the slopes, streaked with moss and lichen. The air still smells of pine and damp stone, although the trees have been replaced by twisted shrubs.

The path slopes unevenly with loose gravel. To our right, the valley sprawls into the distance, interrupted by rivers that glint like molten silver in the sunlight.

I catch Calysian's eyes on my face, intent on my bruised cheek. He seems obsessed with the evidence of Haldrik's duplicity, and I give him a tentative smile.

"It doesn't hurt."

A bitter smile curves his lips. "And still you lie to me."

"It...throbs occasionally. That's all."

A sharp nod. "I'm glad you got to see your friends."

It's a difficult subject—especially now. But at least he's speaking to me.

"You...you don't have many friends, do you?"

He glances away. "I have Eamonn. And I have...associates in various kingdoms. We've worked together over the years."

But they've always died. I can see it in the tightening of his lips, in the way his eyes glint with ancient sorrow when he turns his head.

My skin suddenly feels too tight, my stomach twisting viciously. I've seen how touch-starved Calysian is, how he struggles to relate to mortals, even after walking amongst us for centuries. I saw the occasional crooked smile he gave Asinia when she teased him about his true nature. The hunger in his eyes when Demos and Rythos ribbed each other good-naturedly.

THIS VICIOUS DREAM

I dangled my own friends in front of him. And then I let them betray him.

"Calysian. I'm sorry. I don't know if I would change what I did—we need *some* way to stop you if you become a true threat—but I never wanted to hurt you."

His eyes blaze, and he opens his mouth. I set my shoulders.

Just as the earth bucks and rolls beneath us.

CHAPTER TWENTY-FIVE

Calysian

MADINIA'S HORSE BOLTS, HOOVES SKIDDING AS THEY disappear into the fog of dust rising around us. Fox staggers beneath me, his ears flattened against his head, muscles bunching and trembling each time the ground shudders.

I lean low over his neck and dig my heals in, urging him on as loose rocks and clumps of dirt tumble down the hillside behind us. The sharp cracks of splitting stone echo through the air, and Fox leaps forward, hooves scattering gravel in every direction.

My gaze locks on Madinia's receding form as her mare gallops blindly ahead. Trees uproot, and a fissure splits the ground just footspans ahead.

Her horse rears, and Madinia buries her hands in Hope's mane.

Fox doesn't hesitate, giving me a burst of speed, his hooves barely finding purchase as the ground beneath us continues to fracture.

Ahead, Hope stumbles. Madinia hurtles through the air, thrown violently from the horse's back.

The world sharpens, time slowing, my pulse pounding in my ears.

Madinia hits the ground hard, a landslide of rocks pouring toward her like a wave. Her mare turns and bolts, leaping out of sight.

The slope behind Madinia groans, boulders the size of whisky barrels breaking free and tumbling toward her—as if directed by some dark force.

I launch myself from the saddle and slap Fox on the arse. "Go!" I sprint for Madinia.

She's trying to push herself to her feet, her ankle twisted beneath her. She hits the ground once more, her face a mask of pain. I reach her as the first of the smaller rocks slam into her body, pushing her toward the edge of the chasm. For once, she doesn't fight, allowing me to throw her over my shoulder as I strike out with my power, breaking the larger boulders into smaller pieces.

But they keep coming, and I can feel the malevolence within them.

"Faster," Madinia demands, and despite the danger, despite my irritation with her, I almost laugh.

"Quiet, harridan. Let me save us in peace."

She struggles, attempting to wiggle free, and I slap her arse. A feral snarl. "I'll kill you."

"That will need to wait until I've finished saving your life."

I'm still weakened after using so much of my power to push Fox just days ago, so I rely mostly on my physical strength, clenching my teeth as I sprint for safety.

We clear the edge of the slide, and I let out a single breath of relief. Close. That was too close.

A deafening crack splits the air, and the ground in front of us gives way. A jagged chasm yawns open, swallowing the path and everything on it.

I have no choice. I throw Madinia to the right, where the only stable ground remains.

She hits the ground and rolls. My boots skid in the loose dirt as I launch myself after her, but the earth shifts beneath me, bucking like a living thing. The chasm splits wider, chunks of rock splintering as the ledge crumbles beneath my feet.

I lunge sideways, landing hard on my shoulder, legs dangling over the hole.

Madinia crawls toward me, her face pale, streaked with dirt. Her hand finds my tunic and she pulls.

"I'm too heavy," I grunt, my entire body straining, until I finally manage to roll myself over the edge.

The ground settles, and Madinia coughs, waving at the dusty air between us. I wipe a smear of blood from her chin and she narrows her eyes. "Next time, give me a little warning before you hurl me into oblivion."

"Noted. You're welcome."

Her lips curve. And for some unknown reason, I have the strangest urge to chuckle.

Fox is nowhere to be seen, but his hoof prints lead toward the forest at our back. Madinia's mare bolted in the same direction, so hopefully he will corral her…if she hasn't snapped a leg in her desperate flight.

Madinia shifts, barely hiding a wince.

I lean close. "Can you move?"

"I'm fine."

This woman. "Be still. Let me look."

She allows me to gently shift her leather leggings, and this time I'm the one who winces.

"It's swelling. We'll leave your boot on for now, and I'll examine it once we're away from this place." More bruises are already appearing on her face, and I clench my teeth.

Madinia flicks her hand toward the ruin of the landscape. "That wasn't natural."

"No." I scan the ridge above us, where the landslide began. Rocks and debris are still shuffling, but no obvious culprit steps forward to claim responsibility. The air feels wrong. Heavy. Charged with something more than the aftermath of an earthquake.

Something that feels like my power. But not.

The sound of hooves fills the air, distant but unmistakable.

Madinia stiffens. "It's another regiment. Or worse—Kyldare and his witch. How much power do you have?"

"Enough to kill twenty or so. Most of my power still hasn't regenerated. You?"

She shakes her head. "Nothing from the grimoire. That link is…gone. Just my own power."

We both wait, attention turned toward the approaching regiment.

"They're coming from the east," she says.

The exact direction we're heading. I lift her into my arms as the sound of hooves grows louder. When a cloud of dust appears to our left, I sprint for cover, placing Madinia behind a cluster of jagged rocks and positioning myself behind her.

Her betrayal still lingers like a dull ache. And yet we've seamlessly fallen back into our own rhythm.

"If we kill the soldiers, we leave obvious signs that we were here," Madinia hisses.

I'm already pushing my power across the expanse, sweeping our hoof prints away, as the regiment crests the ridge. The soldier at the front slows to a careful trot as he surveys the ruined ground.

"Do you see them?" one of the soldiers calls.

"Them? I thought Kyldare killed the woman."

"Kyldare seems to think she would have survived. Do you see any evidence they were here?"

"No."

Dust clings to the air, thick and choking, but it will work

to our advantage, making it more difficult to spot us. I pull at my cloak, arranging the hood over Madinia's hair.

She leans heavily against me, her breath coming in shallow gasps. My teeth clench, the sight of her fear offensive on the deepest level.

Something dark stirs within me.

I've changed my mind.

I'll kill them all.

Madinia tenses. "Don't you dare," she mouths.

She's right. This is the best way to ensure Kyldare can't pinpoint our location.

And still.

The soldiers spread out, moving with unnerving precision, guiding their horses carefully through the uneven terrain, hooves striking loose gravel. They don't speak. They don't need to. It's clear this methodical hunt has become routine for them.

Madinia's fingers tighten on my sleeve. "They're going to find us. You need to move."

"I'm not leaving you."

She gives me a sneer that makes me want to crush my mouth to hers. When she elbows me, I drag my gaze from her lips, meeting her narrowed eyes.

"Don't baby me, Calysian."

"I'm not. If I stay with you, I can use you as a shield when my ward fails."

Her lips twitch. "I'm not saying you should abandon me. If you *did*, I would make you pay. But if you sneak around the other side of the chasm, you can cause a distraction."

The soldiers are approaching slowly, but they're spread out, at least ten footspans between them. My only option is to go up the hill behind us. But the ground has been loosened, rocks and dirt still trickling down in a steady stream.

The closest cover for Madinia is a patch of twisted tree roots—half exposed from the shifting ground. Even from here

I can see the space is cramped, but if we don't move now, the solider riding toward us will discover us within moments.

I point to it. "Can you get there?" My mouth is against her ear, and any other time I would smile at the feel of her shiver.

She cooly surveys the distance she needs to cross. Her mouth thins, and she gives a stiff nod. I don't press her. If Madinia Farrow says she'll do something, she will do it.

"I'll head to the left. When I do, you need to crawl." I pull the hood of my cloak up even further over her head. "Go."

"Dismount," one of the soldiers calls to the others. "The ground is too unsteady for the horses."

The distraction is all we need, and I duck low, sprinting for the hill. I catch one glimpse of Madinia's round arse, her foot held up in an effort to protect her ankle as she crawls toward the hole.

I find a sparse bush. It's not enough cover, and my jaw aches from clenching my teeth as the soldiers begin moving forward once more.

Kill them all.

The voice sounds like mine, if I was stripped of all life.

And yet I receive no flood of power from the grimoire I'm searching for.

Truthfully, the advice is sound. And I *crave* these soldiers' deaths.

I was not created to hide from threats as insignificant as these men.

But I'm forced to admit our plan stands. If the regiment goes missing, it will point to our exact location. But if these soldiers find no sign of us, they may assume we chose a different route, ensuring we have a clear path to the grimoire.

As long as our horses also stay out of sight.

A solider lingers near our first hiding spot, peering down at something. When he lifts a hand, a victorious smile on his face, I tremble with rage.

Even from here, I can see the long strand of red hair pinched between his finger and thumb as his head whips toward Madinia's hiding place.

My veins flood with power.

The earth begins to tremble once more, and screams cut through the air as soldiers scatter.

Distraction? I'll provide a distraction.

The earth begins to split, this time directly beneath the closest soldier's feet.

He screams, arms flailing, legs stumbling over unsteady ground. A gaping hole opens up, and moments later, I hear the pleasing crack of his neck.

Distantly, I wonder if he's still holding Madinia's hair.

The other soldiers are spooked as they approach, eyes wide as they glance in all directions.

"No sign of them. Perhaps this was just a natural phenomenon."

"And if they *were* here? Will you be the one to tell Kyldare his little obsession eluded us yet again?"

His little obsession.

Already, Kyldare was going to die screaming. This has added days of torture to his death.

The scars on Madinia's back flash through my mind, the sound of her choked breaths as she stared at the arrow lodged in her chest.

The earth rumbles once more, and the soldiers scatter, crying out.

My skin prickles, and I slowly turn my head, meeting blue eyes.

"What are you doing?" she mouths.

I give her a slow grin I know will incense her. Her eyes fire, and my power begins to drift out of reach.

I'm unsure how I accessed that power, unsure why I was

able to link to the grimoire *now*, and unsure why that access appears to be temporary.

"Kyldare is no longer our problem," the captain says, his voice tense. "The queen wants the dark god and the grimoire."

My attention sharpens. Now *that's* interesting.

"We'll leave sentries," he continues. Clearly the captain is also convinced the quake was natural, otherwise he wouldn't be loudly announcing the locations of those sentries as he points in each direction. "It doesn't matter if they're in the area. Vicana will have the grimoire within days."

Icy fury sweeps through me. Mine. They think to take what is mine.

Kill them all. Make them suffer.

The sleeve of my tunic catches fire. The flame is small, but it licks at my arm, and I'm forced to extinguish it before it draws attention.

My skin is reddened, and I stare down at it. The little witch burned me. Again.

Her expression is unrepentant. She gives me a smirk, and I roll my eyes at her. Her smirk widens.

Gods, she's beautiful.

Even with dirt on her face, her face bruised, her hair dusty where it has slipped free of the hood of her cloak. *My* cloak. Just as she sleeps in *my* shirt.

Keep protesting, sweetheart. But your actions tell me you want to belong to me.

Whatever she sees on my face makes her cheeks flame, and I wish she was next to me so I could wrap my hand around her long hair and hold her still while I ravaged her mouth.

Personally, I think a tumble would allow both of us to relieve some tension. A good distraction from both the danger stalking us, and her betrayal yesterday.

And still, her words echo in my head.

"I'm sorry. You're a threat, Calysian. We had to know if you could be contained."

Madinia had studied me as if I was an insect. A potentially dangerous insect. And the truth had revealed itself to me.

Whatever feelings she has—and despite her pretenses, I *know* she has such feelings—they are for the man who wandered alone for centuries. They're not for the dark god. And they never will be.

By finding my grimoires, I'm losing her. And each moment I spend with her will make that loss more painful.

But I can't end my search. To do so would leave me purposeless. Empty.

The soldiers have retreated, but I hold up a hand, gesturing for Madinia to stay put. She rolls her eyes, waving a hand at her ankle, which must be throbbing by now, and I turn my attention to the wide expanse of ruin in front of us.

My instincts were correct. Three soldiers return within ten minutes, scanning the area for any sign of movement.

I wait them out, and stay hidden, even as the action eats at the darkest part of me.

I do not hide. I am a god.

Clenching my teeth, I force myself to stay put, unsurprised when the soldiers return yet again, half an hour later, disappearing after a quick scan of the fractured earth.

I get to my feet, muscles cramped as I make my way to Madinia.

"Nice distraction," she says. "Subtle."

I shrug, and she angles her head, her eyes still on me.

I can't tell her that the choice wasn't entirely mine. That I saw the solider with that strand of her hair, saw him look to where she was hiding, and something dark was released within me. Something I could only access at that exact moment.

"Stay out of sight. I'll check the horses."

They're wandering the forest nearby—thankfully both

unharmed. Hope is clearly still spooked, but she allows me to catch her, while Fox snaps his teeth at me but complies when I lead both horses back toward Madinia.

I lift her into my arms, and she doesn't protest, which means she must be in pain. I should have killed the soldiers. And yet *they* weren't the ones responsible for this.

"Are you sure he's dead?" She points at the hole as we walk past.

I lean over, allowing her to see the crumpled body, the soldier's head lying at an unnatural angle. "If he wasn't, they wouldn't have left him behind."

Madinia nods, and I scan her face. She can be ruthless when necessary, but she also has a softer heart than she would like to admit.

Our eyes meet, and Madinia raises one eyebrow.

"Would you like me to wring my hands? Would you approve if I wallowed in guilt for the lives lost since this began?" Her beautiful face turns cold. "I heard what they said, and anyone who tries to return me to Kyldare deserves all this and more."

A strange kind of warmth seeps through my chest. "You're right. They do."

Our gazes hold for a long moment before she clears her throat and scans our surroundings. "Why did this happen? What does it mean?"

"It means I'm not the only god walking this continent. One of the others has decided to involve themselves, and they're attempting to stop me from finding my grimoires."

She clenches her teeth. "And how long have you had that suspicion?"

"From the moment I saw those bones sucked clean in the swamp. Some of the older gods used to enjoy their...sacrifices that way. Even I've heard of *that*."

"You didn't tell me." Her mouth tightens, and she glances away.

I place her on my horse. "Just as you didn't tell me Rythos would attempt to *befriend* me."

She winces, and I swing myself up behind her. "Stay quiet. The soldiers may have posted sentries."

Madinia

We spend the next few hours taking narrow trails, staying far from the main roads where Vicana's regiments are likely patrolling.

One of Calysian's strong arms encircles my waist, the other holding Fox's reins. His hard chest is pressed against my back, his warm breath feathering against my neck, his body surrounding mine…

I shift in the saddle, and he tightens his grip.

"Are you in pain?"

"No." I'm glad I'm facing forward, so he can't see the heat sweeping across my skin.

He leans even closer, clearly sensing my arousal. "Ah, beautiful woman. Even after your betrayal, I would never deny you *that*." His voice is a low croon, thick with amusement, and I tense. Fox tosses his head warningly, and Calysian chuckles.

My jaw aches, and I force myself to unclench it. "I apologized for what happened with Rythos."

He leans his chin on my shoulder. "Well, then, all is forgiven."

Lies. I know him, and I know how much he values vengeance. It's one of the few things we have in common. And even if he *does* forgive me, he will never forget.

THIS VICIOUS DREAM

Hissing, I shrug him off. "Tell me you wouldn't have done the same if you were me."

Calysian is quiet as he considers my words. "Perhaps I would have," he concedes. He leans close once more, burying his nose in my hair and inhaling.

"Are you sniffing me?"

"You smell good."

"I smell like dust."

"Hmmm. And woman."

"You know, your moods are beginning to become rather… unstable."

His teeth sink lightly into my neck and I shiver.

He smiles against my skin. "You have an annoying tendency towards near-death experiences. I find them unsettling."

Ah. So watching me hurtle towards that chasm had encouraged him to move past my betrayal. I'm not sure if I'm pleased or displeased by this.

"And then there's the other reason."

"The other reason?"

"When you've lived as long as I have, you notice patterns. You didn't like it when I forced you to admit you wanted me. When you realized you were *mine*. So you lashed out. Rythos's treachery was a convenient tool for you."

I scowl over my shoulder at him, and he shakes his head with mock disappointment. "So predictable."

"I will hurt you."

Calysian laughs. "For telling the truth? Besides," he continues. "You're a cold, calculating woman with a deep ruthless streak. I've always known that about you. And I like it."

"Oh, do you?" I grit out.

He ignores my sarcastic tone. "I do. Because despite your frigid exterior and your ice-cold heart, you still melt for me." He leans close again, nipping at my ear, and heat pools low in my belly.

Impulses war within me. I want to snap at him. I also want to turn my head, bury my hand in his hair, and guide his mouth to mine.

Thankfully, Calysian is already turning Fox off the trail, while Hope plods along behind us. "We'll camp here tonight."

He lifts me from Fox, placing me gently on the ground, where I balance on one foot. When I attempt to limp away, he catches my upper arm. "Wait here."

My ankle aches enough that I comply. He sees to the horses, then returns, carrying me to a spot he has picked near a small stream.

"We'll need to boil our drinking water," he murmurs. "Now let me take a look at that ankle."

He frowns over it, wrapping it in a cool, damp rag.

"This should help with the swelling. I'll wrap it properly when I return."

"Return?"

"Dinner. I'll hunt."

Calysian is a dedicated carnivore. And he stayed away from camp last night, missing dinner. My own stomach rumbles, and he smiles down at it.

"Don't fret," he says, his eyes meeting mine, "I'll see to *all* your needs."

My thighs clench. "I thought you were furious with me."

"I am. And I'm pleased to be the one to introduce you to angry sex." His eyes darken, and he gives me a look filled with so much dark lust, my breath catches in my throat.

I should deny him. Should deny that I want him. Calysian waits, and when I don't speak he brushes my hair tenderly back from my face.

"Stay here," he says, his gaze turning clinical as he sweeps his eyes over my weapons. He gives the knife at my side an approving nod. "Keep off that ankle."

He prowls into the forest, but I know he'll stay close.

I watch the horses as they lower their heads, nibbling at the scarce grass. Calysian will feed them properly when they've cooled down.

Angry sex.

My skin heats, as I watch water rippling in the stream. It has been days since we touched each other that way.

I should have known my commitment to "just one night" would weaken. And yet, that little voice whispers that I just need *one more*, and then I'll be able to calmly walk away from him.

That voice is a liar. I snort, shaking my head.

Maybe if I—

My instincts scream a warning, and I push from the tree stump, attempting to surge to my feet.

But it's too late.

A huge hand clamps over my mouth, strong, male arms dragging me across the camp. I sweep my flames toward my attacker.

Shielded.

An unnatural, reinforced ward.

One I've seen before. One I've *felt* before.

Thick, choking terror fills my lungs, turning my limbs to water.

Kyldare.

CHAPTER TWENTY-SIX

Madinia

Numbness sweeps through my body.
Time stops.
Confusion reigns.

The world snaps into place once more, and terror slices into me, as sharp and deadly as a blade.

I fight like a wild animal, clawing at the hand on my mouth. But my fear makes me clumsy, slow. I lash out with my fist, but I'm off-balance.

My pulse thunders in my ears. How did he find me? Where is Calysian? Did he give me up? Is this his form of revenge for my own betrayal?

No. He would never.

My mind sharpens, and I reach for my knife, my body acting on instinct as I attempt to twist, thrusting my blade at Kyldare. But the movement is awkward, and he slams his fist into the back of my hand. The knife falls to the ground.

"Madinia."

My vision turns white. This panic is achingly familiar. And that hateful voice is so close. Too close.

I kick out, bucking, and Kyldare releases my mouth. I suck

in one desperate breath, but before I can scream, his arm is around my throat, his lips at my ear.

"I don't need to hurt you, but I will if you don't calm down. I'm not here to kill you."

It takes several long moments for his words to sink in. Moments Kyldare uses to squeeze harder, until my limbs begin to weaken.

He lets out an impatient growl. "Tell me you'll listen to me, and I'll release you."

Listen to him? I'll *murder* him.

His arm tightens further, and my vision begins to dim. "We don't have time for this," he hisses. "If I wanted to kill you, you'd already be dead."

There are things worse than death.

He taught me that.

But the thought of Kyldare starving me of air long enough to send me into unconsciousness…

The thought of being entirely unaware and helpless…

Intolerable.

Gritting my teeth, I force my body to go still. Slowly, Kyldare begins to release his arm. "Will you listen?"

I nod. I've lost one knife, but I have another dagger at my ankle, my sword strapped to my back. I have no chance of getting the sword free with him this close, but I can get to the dagger.

He chuckles humorlessly. "You still think you're going to kill me, don't you?"

"Speak." My voice is hoarse, my throat aching. Kyldare removes his arm entirely and I whirl, pulling my sword. My breaths come in shallow pants, my lungs burning.

He holds up both hands, as if I'm a wild animal and *he's* the one in danger. "I truly mean you no harm."

I curl my lip at him, my heart still thundering in my chest. "Why didn't Calysian sense you? Why didn't I hear you approaching?"

"A temporary gift from my goddess."

"Your goddess?"

"It's a long story."

"Then you better start talking. Because the moment Calysian returns, he'll kill you."

Kyldare sneers, but his gaze flickers across the clearing, his eyes intent. When his attention returns to me, I have to fight the urge to swing my sword at his throat.

And yet...I *am* curious.

Kyldare's boots are dusty, his cloak torn. He desperately needs a shave, and a purple bruise has bloomed across his jaw, as if he recently took a punch.

I've never seen him look so...disheveled.

And the soldier's words from earlier run on a loop in my mind.

"Kyldare is no longer our problem."

"You betrayed Vicana," I breathe, and his expression tightens.

"Yes. And now I'm offering an alliance."

"An alliance?" My voice carries across the clearing, high and thready. *"You told me you killed my friends!"*

I keep my gaze planted on him, my hand tightening around the hilt of my sword. In a fight to the death, Kyldare will likely kill me. But I'll still make him bleed.

"I could have ended *you* at any time," Kyldare says, arching an eyebrow meaningfully. "And I didn't. Ask yourself why."

"You needed me to tell you where the grimoire was."

"And yet I left you alone and safe for months at a time."

"Trapped inside my own body!"

He idly waves one hand. "Do you truly think I couldn't have tortured that information out of you? I convinced both the witch *and* the queen that you were unbreakable. I convinced them that the only way to learn the location was to hold you prisoner until your mind gave out." He gives me a slow, knowing smile. "But we both know I could have broken you."

A cold, greasy sweat breaks out on the back of my neck, and I squeeze the hilt of my sword even tighter, my hand beginning to throb.

No. He doesn't get to do this.

I force my hand to relax, taking one deep breath. And then another.

I'd already given so much of my mind away in that tower, there was little left for Kyldare to break. And I won't let him watch me break now.

I force my expression into something grimly neutral. "So why didn't you?"

"My goddess didn't want you dead. She wanted you to meet Calpharos."

"Why?"

"Because years ago, she had a dream. And she knew that together, you and the dark god would find the grimoires."

"So you thought you'd allow us to get close to the grimoires and then what…take them for yourself?" Understanding flickers within my mind. "You were never planning to give the first grimoire to Vicana. You wanted to give it to your goddess instead."

"Vicana is arrogant. She used one of her fae underlings to bind me with a blood vow. I vowed to do everything I could to find the grimoires. But I never vowed to give them to her." He smiles. "A ludicrous oversight. And one that worked out for me since my goddess told me the best way for me to find the grimoire would be to wait until *you* met the dark god."

"You kept me trapped and alone in that fucking tower, hoping Calpharos would find me. So you could follow us."

"I didn't anticipate you being able to use the grimoire's power to break free. And I didn't know that the man who approached that day was the dark god. I can sense the power of the gods, and yet I sensed nothing from him."

"Because he hadn't yet found the grimoires."

Kyldare glances away, his shoulders hunching. "Yes, well

that was a mistake, and one I was punished for. I should have known the dark god might appear as a mortal."

"That's why you were hunting me? Why you tried to take me back? Because you thought I hadn't yet met the dark god?"

"Yes. It wasn't until that day by the lake that I realized the man you were traveling with *was* the dark god. But Vicana wanted you, and I couldn't risk Bridin growing suspicious." He frowns at me. "I really wish you had killed the witch."

"It's taking everything in me not to kill *you* right now."

A cold, dark presence spills across the clearing and goosebumps form across my skin.

"No need, sweetheart. I'll do it for you." Calysian's voice is low, filled with the promise of endless pain.

"Wait!" Kyldare takes a step back, and the terror in his eyes is delicious. "You don't want to kill me."

Calysian rakes his eyes over me, his gaze lingering at my throat. He prowls toward Kyldare. "Oh, yes I do."

"You're about to walk into a trap!" Kyldare's eyes widen as Calysian doesn't slow his pace.

With a sigh, I step between them. Calysian reaches out, hands clasping my upper arms, and I know he's about to move me aside. Something inhuman stares out at me from behind his eyes, and my throat tightens.

"Wait."

His gaze shifts behind me, and I reach out, burying my fingers in his shirt. "Believe me, I don't want to protect him. But we need to consider all our options."

"I see two options. Personally, I'd like to beat him to death, but I know you're partial to fire." Calysian's voice is flat, but the strange otherworldly light is draining from his eyes.

Slowly, he releases my arms, taking a step back. But his struggle for self-control is evident, and he keeps his gaze carefully away from Kyldare as he stalks to his saddlebag—as if even looking at Kyldare would be enough to make him rip out his throat.

THIS VICIOUS DREAM

Kyldare releases a long, shuddering breath behind me. "Thank you."

"Don't thank me. Tell us what you know. Now."

"First, you have to agree not to kill me."

"We don't need any information from him," Calysian says as he approaches, the heavy chains from my tower in his hand. "Now that we know there's a trap waiting for us, we know to be even more careful. Hold out your arms."

Kyldare bares his teeth, his ward jumping into place. "You're not chaining me."

Calysian shrugs. "I chain you, or you die."

"You only have one grimoire. I can still kill you." Kyldare meets my eyes. "And I can kill *you*."

Calysian steps in front of me. "Don't talk to her. Don't even look at her."

Perhaps it's because I'm still rattled from Kyldare's surprise appearance—and my own vulnerability when he had his arm around my throat—but something about Calysian's overprotectiveness makes warmth spread through my chest.

Thick, black fog begins to spread through the clearing. My heart races, and Kyldare jolts backward. "What are you doing?"

I shift so I can see Calysian. He's using the little remaining power he has left after the quake today. And it's enough to make the blood drain from Kyldare's face.

"What's wrong, Kyldare?" I muse. "Not so brave without a regiment standing in front of you?"

Calysian drops the chains at Kyldare's feet. "Do it. Now."

Kyldare's eyes dart between us, and a dark, vicious satisfaction spreads through me. Whatever he was anticipating when he came here, it wasn't this. He has always pretended to be braver than he is. But right now he's not standing behind a regiment. He's not standing next to a powerful witch.

"I do this, and you'll listen to me?"

"Yes," I say, mostly because I want to watch Kyldare snap

those manacles around his wrists. I want to see the horror in his eyes as he loses even the barest whisper of his power.

He takes a long time to think it through. Calysian merely waits him out. Finally, Kyldare complies, the heavy chain dangling between his hands. His limbs begin to tremble.

"Not particularly enjoyable, is it?" I smirk.

He ignores me, lifting his head. "I did what you want. Will you listen to my proposal now?"

Calysian frowns, taking a step closer to Kyldare. His eyes light with surprise.

My stomach churns. "What is it?"

"He's god-touched. I should have recognized it sooner. But perhaps I can only see it because I've taken the first grimoire."

"What does that mean?"

"It means he was blessed by his goddess. He'll live as long as she does. Unless someone kills him." The smile Calysian gives Kyldare is chilling. "Talk."

Kyldare swallows. "You're right. My goddess blessed me. She knew she would need someone in this kingdom when you arrived, and she also knew I would be the one to find her." He nods at me. "I was ordered to cooperate with Vicana and find the grimoire. Everything was going according to plan until the witch became suspicious." His mouth tightens. "She slipped one of her putrid tonics into my drink and made me confess my duplicity."

"And yet you managed to escape and come to us," Calysian says, planting his hands on his hips.

Kyldare lets out a bitter laugh. "You think I'm setting you up? I wish I was. I barely escaped with my life. My goddess told me to travel in this direction. She said I would know where to find you. When I felt the quake, learned where it was centered, I knew she was giving me a sign."

"Name your goddess," Calysian orders.

Kyldare just shakes his head. "I can't. She has stilled my

THIS VICIOUS DREAM

tongue so that I immediately forget her name if I attempt to say it to someone who does not already know it."

Realization flickers through Calysian's eyes. He knows who the goddess is.

"You put a bolt through Madinia's lung," he growls. "Did your goddess tell you to do *that* too?"

Kyldare drops his gaze. "I was...frustrated. I knew my goddess would be angry with me for losing the first grimoire. I wanted to punish Madinia for ruining my plans over and over again. And I knew you would not let her die."

I shake my head. He's lying. He wanted me dead in that moment. He may have regretted his actions after, but his words echo in my head even now.

"Think of me as you die choking on your own blood."

My lungs tighten at the memory of the agony. The terror. Shoving that memory away, I look down my nose at Kyldare. "So what you're saying is you're a puppet. And *two* women are holding your strings."

Kyldare's jaw clenches, and humor dances in Calysian's eyes. "She has a point." His eyes meet mine, and I jerk my head, gesturing for him to move out of Kyldare's earshot. Calysian takes a long length of rope, tying Kyldare's feet and looping the rope through the chains and around a wide tree trunk.

"This is unnecessary," Kyldare hisses. "I came here with the intention of cooperating."

Calysian ignores him, taking my hand and leading me away from the clearing. My ankle throbs, but I force myself not to limp.

Calysian's brows lower as he scans my face.

"Are you..."

"I'm fine."

"You're trembling."

I meet his eyes. "He snuck up on me, Calysian. If he'd wanted to kill me, he could have thrust a blade into my heart at that moment."

A muscle jumps in Calysian's jaw. "I should have been here."

I'm already shaking my head. It's not his job to protect me. It's mine. And I failed. It all could have been over, because I let down my guard.

I felt safe, and I shouldn't have.

"We need to decide what to do with him," I say. "Can you remove his...god-touch?"

The corner of Calysian's eyes crease, and he runs a hand over his mouth. "No, I can't remove it. Not when another god got there first. Besides, such a thing would require me to have found all three of my grimoires."

My mind races. Personally, I want Kyldare dead. I don't trust him, and I don't even want to breathe the same air as him.

A muscle ticks in Calysian's jaw, and he turns to pace. A strange sense of unease trickles into my gut.

"I know what I need to do," he says finally as he turns to face me. His shirt clings to his chest, his muscles rippling as he places his hands on his hips.

He gives me the kind of slow smile that tells me he knows exactly where my attention drifted. But his gaze flicks back towards Kyldare, and his expression hardens. "I need you to trust me."

The last time he asked me to trust him, he pulled my own power from me, ruthlessly using my link to his grimoire.

And yet, he has also saved my life. Many times.

My stomach tightens. "Calysian. That's not how this works."

Both of us know the unspoken rules. We can trust each other with our lives, but no more than that. Not for the first time, I wish things could be different.

"It's the way it needs to work."

I study his face. Darkness still lurks within his eyes, but I catch a glimpse of frustrated impatience.

"Are you going to tell me why?" I ask.

"No."

My nails dig into my palms as I wrestle with my instincts.

THIS VICIOUS DREAM

Calysian steps closer, his eyes glittering with sympathy. It helps, that he knows how difficult this is for me. Because giving anyone any measure of trust is just as difficult for him.

"Fine."

He gives me an approving look, his hands sweeping over my shoulders. His mouth brushes mine, and I breathe him in.

"We shouldn't leave him for long," he says against my lips, and I nod.

Kyldare is lounging against the tree trunk at his back, one leg stretched out in front of him. But he fails to hide the sullen set of his mouth, the rage glittering in his eyes.

Calysian angles his head. "Tell me about the trap."

"If we're truly allies, you have to remove these chains."

"We don't have to do anything," I snap.

"Then I won't tell you anything. Go ahead and kill me," he says. "It will be a mercy compared to what Vicana would do to me." For once, his voice rings with honesty.

With a shrug, Calysian pulls his sword. "Fine."

He strolls toward Kyldare, who jolts, holding up his hands. "Wait!"

"I'm losing patience." Calysian's voice is frigid. "Speak."

Kyldare's gaze finds mine, and I almost shiver at the hatred within his eyes. He's a coward who *knows* he's a coward. And he hates that the woman he tortured and victimized can see just how much of a coward he is. "Vicana wants you dead," he tells me.

Calysian's shoulders tense. "Why?"

"The queen has wanted the grimoires since she learned of them. The moment she heard you knew the location of the first one, she expected to have it in her hands within days. Madinia ensured that didn't happen."

"And the trap?" Calysian growls.

"Three regiments," Kyldare says. "Unchain me. You know I won't go anywhere. I have nowhere to go."

Calysian is still for a long moment. I stare at the back of his head, wishing I could see what he's thinking. Distantly, I wonder where Eamonn is. If he were here, Kyldare wouldn't have been able to take me by surprise. And Eamonn would be able to tell us where Vicana's regiments are.

When Calysian leans forward to loosen Kyldare's chains, every muscle in my body tightens.

"Wait. You seriously want to work with him?" Something in my chest hollows out, and Calysian gives me an impatient look. Kyldare just watches us avidly.

"He's telling the truth. I can sense it. Allying with him *temporarily* will allow us to get to the second grimoire."

The chasm in my chest widens, pushing against my lungs until I can barely breath. Kyldare shoots me a smug look.

The second grimoire. That's all that matters. *That's* why Calysian wants me to trust him. Even if it means traveling with the man who hunted me, whipped me, imprisoned me. The man who tried to *kill* me.

Calysian keeps his gaze carefully away from mine, but Kyldare gives me a wide grin, his expression victorious.

Something heavy settles in my chest, even as my blood heats with vengeance.

Calysian knows what he needs to do?

Well, so do I.

I sweep one final glance at both the dark god, and the man who stole three years of my life.

And then I turn and walk away.

CHAPTER TWENTY-SEVEN

Madinia

I spend the night as far from both Kyldare and Calysian as I can while still remaining within the clearing. Kyldare attempts to strike up a conversation with Calysian a few times, finally falling silent when Calysian continues to ignore him.

Now that he's got what he wanted, Calysian no longer needs to speak to Vicana's right hand.

Twice, Calysian attempts to look at my ankle. And twice, I make sure my expression communicates exactly what I think of him.

I wrap it myself. It's tender, but nothing is broken.

As soon as the sun rises, Kyldare spreads out a map and points out all of the regiments waiting for us. Calysian studies the map with a frown.

They certainly look cozy as they work together.

When it's time to leave, Calysian directs Kyldare toward my mare. Fury rushes through me in a wave. "Absolutely not."

Calysian gives me an impatient look. "He needs a horse."

"Then he can ride with you."

I'm slung over his shoulder and onto Fox before I can blink.

I strike out at Calysian, my elbow hitting his gut, and he merely wraps his huge arm around my waist with a put-upon sigh.

My blood burns. "I hate you."

"I'm not feeling particularly warm towards you this morning either," he mutters.

Calysian's arm tightens around my waist, as if he's reading my mind, and his lips brush my ear. "You agreed to trust me."

My chest is too tight to speak, so I just shake my head.

"We needed to get past this regiment." Calysian raises his voice just enough that I'm certain Kyldare can hear him. "In all truth, we're lucky Kyldare approached us. Vicana was clever, posting her regiments on three sides. We were trapped."

I ignore him some more. And I continue to ignore him as Kyldare travels with us for three days.

Three. Long. Days.

We stop once at a small town—too small and too far from the coast from anyone to have heard of Daharak or her ship. But Asinia's pigeon returns, and I watch Calysian for several long minutes before I write my reply.

I won't be caught unaware again.

On the third day, we finally reach the crossroad Kyldare warned us about. We hear the soldiers before we see them—the low murmur of voices blending with the faint clink of metal against metal.

Our own horses are tied next to me as we stand on a small incline, Kyldare and Calysian a few footspans above me. The incline is too low to be considered a hill, but it's forested enough that it allows us to see our enemies before they see us. At least a hundred men, most of them sitting idle, scattered across the crossroads in a loose formation. According to Kyldare, they've been waiting here for days, and even from here, I can smell sweat, oiled steel, and the musty scent of horses.

Helmets glint beneath the overcast sky, and a wide-shouldered general sits astride a dark mare at the center of the road, his ward already raised.

Kyldare narrows his eyes. "One of Vicana's generals. He would have enjoyed hearing the queen demand my head."

I ignore him. It's not the general I'm interested in. It's the witch at his side.

If Bridin were anyone else, I might feel pity when I look at her stooped shoulders, her thin bones, her gray hair. But my body reacts to her presence like an animal who has only known pain. The world seems to shrink, the trees surrounding us too close, tension vibrating through the air, pressing against my chest. My instincts scream at me to turn back, to run for my life. But something darker, deeper urges me to lash out. To make her *pay*.

As if he can hear my thoughts, Calysian slowly turns his head. His eyes are cool and calm as they meet mine, and my traitorous heart slows.

Kyldare gives Calysian a long look. "You said you have enough power for us to kill them all. I hope you're not overconfident about your abilities."

Calysian smiles, and Kyldare's shoulders relax. He turns back to face the regiment.

My heart thunders in my chest.

"If I can't have your life, I'll gladly take your death. Think of me as you die choking on your own blood."

Time turns slow and sluggish. Each heartbeat feels like an eternity. My pulse thunders in my ears.

But I don't hesitate.

I aim my power in a burst, and the tree next to Kyldare is suddenly engulfed in flames.

He stumbles back, but I'm already twisting, shoving my hand into Fox's saddlebag and lifting the chains.

Kyldare begins to move, and I direct my flames to his pants. He lets out a sharp yelp, dropping to his knees in an attempt to smother the fire.

I have one cuff around his hand before he understands.

"What—" Realization flickers in Kyldare's eyes and he strikes out, his blade flashing toward my face.

But Calysian is there.

In a blazingly fast movement, he knocks the knife from Kyldare's hand, shoves that hand behind Kyldare's back, and clamps the other chain around his wrist.

The click of the second cuff is loud and final. I extinguish my flames. Kyldare's legs are burned just enough to be painful, but not enough to cripple him.

I gape at Calysian.

The color drains from Kyldare's face, terror stark in his eyes. "You fucking traitor."

Calysian just gives me a wicked smile and turns, waving one hand at me. "By all means, continue."

There's no time to attempt to understand him now.

Ignoring Kyldare's curses, I walk down the other side of the incline and into view.

The entire regiment comes to attention.

"Ah, Madinia," Bridin says. "We were wondering when you would appear."

"I have a trade," I say, my voice carrying across empty expanse between us. I gesture behind me to Kyldare, and the witch angles her head.

"We have our orders," she says. "Why would we not just kill you all?"

Her eyes are cold, reptilian. Oh yes, she would enjoy watching me die.

"You tried that once," I say with a smirk, letting my gaze linger on the deep lines etched into her face. I glance back at Calysian. His stare burns into the witch, heavy with retribution. "Do you really want to try again? Let us pass now, and we'll become the next regiment's problem." I nod toward Kyldare. "And you will have your revenge."

THIS VICIOUS DREAM

"I will make you *suffer* if you do this," Kyldare hisses.

Bridin stares at us for several long moments. I know what she's thinking. She wants to kill us. Wants to make Calysian pay for what his power did to her face, her body.

And yet she's not sure she can. Even with fifty soldiers at her back.

The general at her side doesn't say a word. His presence is a formality. Everyone knows the witch will make this decision.

Bridin's eyes shift to Kyldare, and I'm willing to bet she's reliving every order he gave her in that tower, every snarled comment, every insult.

She smiles at me. "You are only delaying your fate," she says. "But as you said, you will become the next regiment's problem."

I almost snort. Bridin will go back on her word the moment she can. Which means we need to stay one step ahead of her.

Kyldare begins to tremble—just as *I* trembled each time he ordered his men to restrain me in that tower. "Please," he croaks, turning to face Calysian.

Cold rage fills Calysian's eyes. "You never should have touched her. And you *definitely* shouldn't have caged her. Remember that as you succumb to what is sure to be an agonizing death." His smile is dark and feral as he leans close to Kyldare, lowering his voice to a whisper. "As you die, your last thought will be this: Harming Madinia Farrow was the biggest mistake of your life."

My heart stops, and then starts again, beating irregularly in my chest. I take a deep, shuddering breath as Calysian takes Kyldare's arm and hauls him toward the witch.

I stay put, watching as Kyldare fights desperately for his life. But the chains have left him vulnerable. Powerless. Weak.

Perhaps I should show mercy. Perhaps I should at least feel some regret.

But I don't. I feel vindicated. I feel satisfied. I feel *content*.

I hold my breath, preparing for duplicity from Vicana's people, but they don't move. Calysian unchains Kyldare and shoves him toward the witch. She immediately strikes out with her power, and Kyldare slumps to the ground. Several soldiers lift him, hauling him away.

Calysian slings the chains over his shoulder and saunters back to my side. He shows no concern for the soldiers surrounding him, his gaze fixed on my face.

Bridin gives us a nod, and with a wave of her hand, the soldiers begin to march south, leaving the trail empty.

I follow Calysian up the incline. He unties Hope, leading her toward me. His hands shift to my waist, but I grab his wrists before he can lift me onto my horse.

"Wait." I press my hands to his chest. "I don't understand."

"I know you, and I knew what you were planning the moment you refused to sleep near me." His hands tighten on my waist.

"Why didn't you tell me you knew? Why did you agree to Kyldare's plan?"

"Kyldare wouldn't have believed instant cooperation from both of us. He saw my agreement as a victory, and your unhappiness as proof I would not betray him. No one could miss the hurt in your eyes over the past few days. The betrayal."

"And did you enjoy that? The hurt? The betrayal?"

He leans close. "I should have. Some part of me even thought I would. But no. I didn't. I wanted to shake you for your distrust. And yet I can't blame you for it."

My throat tightens. "You could have stopped me. It would have been easier for you to get the second grimoire."

His eyes are cool and clear as they meet mine. "I promised you I would make them pay for every second of life they stole from you. This is just the first. What I will do to that witch will be spoken about for centuries."

My heart jolts. "Calysian."

He cups my cheek. "Kyldare has made enemies amongst Vicana's people. Now he's a traitor. Vicana's witch will keep him alive. Nothing we could do to him could be worse than what that witch will do. And there's something particularly delicious about knowing the horror he turned on you will be turned on him."

Volatile emotions war within me. Shock, relief, fury, joy—all of them merge, until I'm unsure *what* I feel.

My eyes heat. "What are we doing, Calysian?"

He places one finger beneath my chin, using it to tilt my head back. "You know what this is. Even as you refuse to admit it."

I open my mouth, but I can't find the words. Calysian just shakes his head. "Stubborn woman."

His lips are warm and firm on mine, and he pulls away too soon, helping me mount Hope, before turning to swing himself onto Fox's back. His ward forms around us, glittering silver in the weak sunlight. Neither of us speak as we continue past the regiment. Calysian is tense, his eyes scanning for any sign of duplicity from the witch.

I hold my breath, skin prickling. Still, I don't speak until several long minutes have passed, and I'm certain we won't be overheard.

"They're going to come after us."

"And yet you have a plan for that too. Don't you?"

I can't help but grin. "I left a map near your sleeping mat last night. It shows our route to the grimoire. Kyldare memorized it when he thought I wasn't paying attention. He'll give them that route up under torture, and Bridin will tell Vicana where to position her regiments. We just have to make sure we don't go near that route."

Calysian matches my grin. "Brilliant woman."

My throat tightens. He hadn't known about this part of my plan. For all he knew, we would be in more danger than ever before. And yet he'd gone along with it anyway.

"You don't think Kyldare's goddess will save him?"

"He has failed her. She would punish him just as harshly as the witch will."

I think of the recognition in Calysian's eyes when Kyldare spoke of the quake. "You know who she is."

"Yes. She's my sister."

I stare at him. "Creas. The goddess of memory?"

He gives me a humorless smile before turning his attention back to the trail. "The ability to steal memories is just one of her powers, but *that* power is the reason she can make Kyldare forget her name. She is also known for her ability to shake the earth."

"She caused the quake. Was she trying to kill you?"

The trail splits, and Calysian guides Fox left, the stallion's hooves clopping against the hard-packed ground. This road is wider, scarred with deep ruts that twist and intersect—evidence of years of carts grinding their way through mud and dust. The trees are thinning out, but the scent of damp stone is still heavy in the air.

"No." Calysian finally says. "She knew she couldn't kill me from afar, even as weakened as I am now. She was trying to kill *you*."

"Why?"

"I don't know. To hurt me perhaps. To slow me down." His shoulders tense, and he avoids my eyes.

Perhaps I should change the subject. "Which direction are we traveling now?"

His wide shoulders relax and he flashes me a grin. "We're taking the main road straight to Aghalon. It's a rather charming coastal city. We'll rest the horses there. I'm assuming this wasn't part of the route you created for Kyldare."

"No. I doubted he would believe we would take a main road."

His grin widens. "And neither will anyone else."

"And the grimoire?"

"It's in a temple outside of the city. We will get to it tomorrow."

Tomorrow.

Calysian's being surprisingly forthcoming, although there's little I can do with that information.

"Are you still hoping to get to my grimoire before I can?" he asks.

I sniff. "Of course not. I'm just here to make sure you don't destroy my world, and to ensure none of your grimoires end up in Vicana's hands."

He shakes his head at my obvious lie but lets it go.

It hasn't escaped my notice that Calysian hasn't lost himself this close to the grimoire. The last time he neared one—as we approached the swamp—he became less human, distant, consumed, his mind fixated on his task.

Maybe...maybe as he gets closer to reclaiming his whole soul, he's able to retain control.

Or maybe I'm just grasping at any hope I can find.

We fall into silence for the rest of the afternoon. Twice, we stop to water the horses and stretch our legs. The sun begins to sink, streaks of gold radiating outward, the sky painted with deep purples and soft pinks. I take it in, watching the wisps of cloud catching the light.

Awareness flutters across my skin, and I find Calysian watching me. "I enjoy seeing this world through your eyes."

I shrug. "I never truly appreciated it until I was trapped in that tower. Each time my mind cleared and I was *me* again, I promised myself that when I finally managed to free myself, I would never take that freedom for granted again."

In the distance, stone towers thrust skyward. The city of Aghalon is an uneven sprawl of slate-gray stone and copper roofs that glimmer like molten metal beneath the setting sun. A thick haze clings to the air above the city, and within minutes I catch the scent of burning wood and charred meat. My stomach rumbles.

As we approach Aghalon, I can see the distant movement of figures atop the city walls. Massive wooden gates loom at the western entrance, and we come across more people—carts loaded with vegetables and grain, carriages filled with nobles hidden behind velvet curtains, the occasional solo traveler making their way home.

My eyes are heavy, and Calysian responds to the questions from the guards at the gate. He leads us past several inns, continuing past a series of taverns and a bustling night market.

The streets become broader, laid with smooth cobblestones that glint in the dim light, free from the thick crust of mud elsewhere in the city. The buildings are tall and elegant—painted in soft creams, pale blues, and the occasional sunny yellow. Wrought iron balconies curl outward from the upper floors, draped with vines that trail lazily toward the street below.

Calysian dismounts outside an inviting inn with walls of worn, honeyed stone. Warm light spills out, and even from here I can hear the faint hum of music, the low murmur of conversation.

"I stayed here once, several years ago," he murmurs, avoiding my gaze as I dismount. "I thought you might like it."

Calysian turns the horses over to a stablehand. "Stables are around the back," the stablehands says cheerfully. "We even have a grazing field."

It takes me a moment to understand—a moment Calysian uses to take my hand, leading me to the inn's entrance. He pauses before we walk inside, his mouth taking mine. His kiss is tinged with desperation, and he pulls me close, his arms wrapping tightly around my back.

And then it hits me.

Calysian chose this place as a gift. It's a place where we will make final memories together before he takes his grimoire.

A gift…and a goodbye.

CHAPTER TWENTY-EIGHT

Madinia

Calysian arranges for our room, sending me occasional concerned glances. The innkeeper leads us upstairs, chattering the entire time, and I nod at the right places, unable to focus on anything she's saying.

Finally, she beams at Calysian, thrusting out her chest so the candlelight plays across her impressive breasts. "Let me know if there's anything you need. Anything at all," she says.

"That will be all." My voice is cold, and Calysian gives me an amused look as the innkeeper disappears.

"I…I need a few minutes," I tell him.

He frowns. "Have I done something wrong?"

"No. I just…I need some air." It's a terrible excuse considering we've been traveling all day, and Calysian's eyes turn flat.

"Fine."

I leave him standing in the plush room and hurry downstairs, sucking in deep breaths. My chest is tight, my ears ringing, and I walk aimlessly, until a familiar neighing sound jolts me into awareness.

I've made my way behind the inn, near the stables. The grazing field is small but impressive considering we're in the middle of the city. And yet all of the horses are stabled. I lean on the fence and stare into the inky darkness of the field, my chest tight.

This is my own fault.

I made a conscious choice to work with Calysian. I chose to take him to bed, chose to wake up in his arms, chose to trust him with my life.

If anyone is to blame for the crack in my heart, it's me.

I tighten my hands on the wooden fence, forcing my breathing to slow. It's fine. I'm not in love with him. He's simply the first man to keep his promises, the first man to see beyond my face and *care* about who I am as a woman. Of course that would be a novelty for someone like me. Of course it would lead me to believe there was something deeper between us.

Besides, even if there *was* something deeper, it wouldn't matter. Calysian will always choose his grimoires.

And I will always choose to betray him.

As if my thought has conjured it, Asinia's pigeon lands on the fence in front of me. With a sigh, I gently ease the note free, reading Asinia's careful handwriting.

Even after all this time, it takes me only a few moments to break the code.

We are on the way. Everything is arranged. You know what to do.

My stomach swims, but I reply, sending the pigeon on its way.

"Madinia."

I jolt, whirl, and press my back against the fence. I know better than to be lost in my own thoughts out here alone.

I'm so busy berating myself, it takes me a moment to recognize the girl standing near the door of the stables.

"Fliora?" My mind spins. She's covered in mud and dust, her hair tangled, her lips chapped. She looks like she has been traveling since I left her with her aunt Yalanda weeks ago. "What are you doing here?"

Guilt stabs through my chest. I ruined this girl's life. And I've only thought of her a few times since.

"I had to find you. It took a long time. But Eamonn helped."

A gray dog darts into the stable and plants itself at Fliora's feet. Eamonn opens his mouth, letting his tongue loll.

And I'd been wondering if he was safe.

"When did you get here? Where are you staying? I'll get you a room."

"No. Wait." Even in this form, Eamonn is somehow able to level me with a hard stare. "This is important." He turns his head, listening. And then he trots around the field, Fliora shrugs at me and follows his footsteps.

With a sigh, I trail after them, until Eamonn is sure we're alone. He plants himself on the grass, staring solemnly up at me.

My skin suddenly feels too tight for my body, and there's a strange fluttering in my stomach.

Fliora sits cross-legged on the grass. "When you left me with my aunt, she was fine for a few days. And then something began to change. She kept leaving, disappearing for hours at a time. Eventually, I followed her." Fliora chews on her lower lip and plucks a handful of grass, absently running it through her fingers. "She walked into the forest until she came to an…altar. She knelt, bowing her head. And she began to pray aloud."

I resist the urge to shake her, to demand she gets to the point.

"She began to pray…" I say encouragingly.

Fliora meets my eyes. "I learned my aunt worships someone who wants to hurt you."

"Someone who—I don't understand."

Fliora holds out a flask. "I know. That's why I stole this. My aunt was planning to use it for one of her clients."

"Someone who wanted to remember their past life," I

guess, my mind showing me that kitchen, the blightflower petals, the vials.

Fliora smirks. "The woman is convinced she was once a queen. Why is it that no one ever thinks they might have been a maid in their past life?"

My lips twitch. "Why is it you think I need this? I don't have a past life."

She sends me an impatient look. "That's exactly what someone who can't remember their past life would say."

Eamonn stretches. "She has a point."

I give him a hard stare. "I'm responsible for her mother's death. Her aunt worships someone who wants to hurt me. And you want me to drink her tonic?"

Fliora grins at me. It's a surprisingly charming grin, and it reminds me of the brief smile her mother gave me. "It sounds bad when you describe it like *that*," she admits. Her expression turns serious. "I'm having visions too. Not as many as my mother…" her voice catches, and her eyes glisten.

"One of those visions told you I need to learn about a past life."

She nods, wiping at her eyes.

"Drink it." Eamonn's voice is low, insistent, and my skin prickles.

A strange sensation washes over me. A sensation that's not quite dread but close to it. It feels as if I'm at a turning point in my life. Choose one way, and I can go on as I have. Choose the other, and my life will fundamentally change.

I'm not sure I have the strength for another fundamental change.

And yet I can feel time ticking down.

"Will it help me stop Calysian?"

Fliora shrugs. "All I know is my aunt wouldn't want you to drink it."

Her face flashes in my mind, and I can see the cold fury in her eyes when she looked at Calysian.

I glance at Eamonn. "If this is poison, I expect you to avenge me."

Eamonn pads closer, angling his head as he gazes up at me. "Trust may not come easily to you, Madinia, but I'm asking for it with this."

"Calysian—"

"This could be the key to saving him. Drink."

Fear curls in my body, even as both of them stare at me expectantly. Taking the flask, I suck in a deep breath. The tonic is bitter, sour, and somehow...smoky. I gag once, and then I'm swept away.

We walk slowly, filing into the temple—ten women, all of whom have devoted our lives to our goddess. The marble floor is cool beneath my bare feet, the air thick with the scent of sacred oils—the faint tang of copper lingering beneath.

Fires shift and tremble in the braziers, making shadows dance across walls etched with the stories of Anarthys, goddess of fire and sacred sacrifice.

One by one, my sisters walk down the aisle toward our goddess. Even after so many years, I barely dare to breathe as I approach, bowing my head.

The goddess Anarthys may not be known for her mercy, but she is known for her power. All of us were plucked from our small mortal lives as children, purely because we were pleasing to her in some way. While we may not have been given a choice to serve, we were rewarded with the gift of reincarnation.

We will serve her in this life, along with all others.

Anarthys sits on her gold throne, her head canted as she watches us. Her long blonde hair tumbles down her back, her green eyes so vibrant, they seem to glow.

Someone snorts. The sound is so out of place in our goddess's temple, I stiffen—as do several of my sisters. Two men stand at the temple's entrance. Both are shockingly handsome, and both radiate the kind of power that makes my knees weak.

Gods.

They step into the temple, ignoring our gasps. The one on the left is blond, with pale blue eyes and a vaguely pleasant expression. It is as if the one next to him is his image in reverse, with dark hair and eyes, his expression indolent.

"Is all this really necessary, Anarthys?" The darker one asks, waving his hand to encompass the entire temple. His eyes meet mine briefly before moving on, and yet my cheeks flame, and I shift my feet as one of my sisters hisses a breath.

We are not supposed to gaze at men. Anarthys made that much clear when she took us.

"I am a goddess," Anarthys purrs. "I should be worshipped as such."

"You tried to convince the seer to tell you my foretelling," the dark-haired one says, and his voice echoes with a subtle threat.

Anarthys merely smiles. "Are you truly so weak that my visit to the seer would concern you?"

"Seers cannot share someone else's fate. Cease your games. Our time together is over."

"It is over when I say it is over. Men do not cast me aside, Calpharos."

Calpharos. I've heard of him and his twin. One truly is dark, the other light. Together, they represent balance. Apart, they create chaos.

My skin prickles, and I lift my gaze, finding the dark god staring unapologetically at me.

Anarthys hisses a warning, and I drop my eyes, but not before I narrow them at the god who dared upset my goddess.

A flicker of amusement crosses his face, and then all I can see is Anarthys's bare feet as she strides from her throne, her gauzy gown swirling around her ankles.

"If you wish to speak to me, we will converse elsewhere," she says.

And then all three of them are gone.

"Ugh," I clamp a hand to my temple, as pain slices into my mind, sharp as a blade. "What is this?"

Eamonn's eyes meet mine. "Memories."

"Impossible."

But I'm already bracing myself once more.

"Will you join us sister? We will go the river and bathe."

"Perhaps later. I'd like to take a walk."

Liona nods, linking her arm through Yalanda's. "We will join you later then."

They walk down the temple steps, and a strange sense of restlessness burns through me. Truthfully, I would like to wander the city, would like to watch the people gathered in the market, the children racing through the streets.

I would like to see my parents.

Such a thought is shocking, and I glance behind me, as if Anarthys will appear and punish me.

But I am being unnecessarily morbid. Anarthys may not be known for her benevolence, but she has never caused any of us harm.

And even she cannot read our minds.

"It is good to see you again." The low male voice comes from behind me, and I jolt, whirl, and stumble, all at once.

A strong hand catches my arm, ensuring I keep my feet. I look into familiar dark eyes and suck in a breath, lowering my head in a bow.

He catches my chin. "Look at me."

His brows lower, and my heart thrashes in my chest. The dark god. If he wanted, he could strike me down in a moment.

The rumors I've heard…

"You're trembling."

"You are the dark god."

Something I don't recognize flickers through those eyes, but I get the strange feeling my fear...disappoints him.

Impossible.

He releases me with a sigh, raking a hand through his hair and suddenly...he's not so terrifying. If anything, he looks bewildered by my reaction.

My heart twists. How often must he see such fear from others?

"I was going to go for a walk," I say. "Would you like to join me?"

His gaze...gentles. "I am afraid I cannot." He cuts his eyes to the temple behind me, and the sky darkens above us, thick clouds covering the sun.

"Oh." My cheeks flame, and I wish I could disappear. This man is a god. He is here to visit a goddess. "Of course you cannot." I force myself to bow my head once more. "Goodbye."

A warm hand cups my chin, and my heart skips a beat. "I cannot *today," he says. "But I will have to insist you walk with me another time."*

I'm suddenly speechless, my mouth dry. Calpharos gives me a look that seems almost... fond. And then he's prowling toward the temple.

The clouds burst, unleashing a torrent of rain.

I stumble dizzily, and Fliora takes my arm, helping me sit. "What are you remembering?"

"They're not memories. They can't be. This is some kind of trick."

But fog is creeping into my mind, and I'm swept up in them once more.

"Anarthys wants to see you."

Liona's eyes hold a deep concern, her hands shaking.

My heart leaps into my throat. "What is wrong?"

"I do not know. But I have a deep certainty that you are in grave danger, sister."

"You cannot believe Anarthys would harm me." Such a suggestion is blasphemy. And yet...

I have woken several times over the past few nights, my heart pounding at the memory of the poisonous look the goddess gave me last time I saw her.

I cannot understand what I have done to upset her so.

Either way, I cannot deny her my presence.

Liona throws her arms around me in an embrace that is deeply unusual for her. I squeeze her back. "I will be fine. We will eat together tonight."

"Finally," Anarthys says when I reach the temple. Yalanda stands beside our goddess, her gaze shifting to the ground.

"You're dismissed," Anarthys snaps, and Yalanda walks away, her eyes still carefully averted from mine. *"And you,"* Anarthys says, stepping close to me as I kneel at her feet. *"Cease your pretense at devotion."*

Hurt flashes through me and I dare to meet her eyes. My pretense? I have been devoted to my goddess since I was a small child. Since the moment she informed my parents she would be taking me.

"I do not understand."

"Do not lie to me. Tell me, how long have you been sneaking away to meet with Calpharos?"

The words are a shock, and I blink. "I have not."

The dark god. She's speaking of the dark god. But the one and only time I spoke to him was on the steps of this temple.

"I saw the way he looked at you!"

Hands grab my arms, and I'm dragged to my feet. Guards. In here? Never has the goddess allowed human males into this sacred space before.

A deep sense of dread sparks in my stomach, spreading throughout my body. Liona was right.

But I can't imagine why Anarthys would be so incensed with me.

She prowls toward me, her eyes frigid. When she holds out her hand, one of the guards at my side gives her a dagger.

Horror turns my lips numb, my knees weak. "Please—"

"One of my own acolytes, attempting to take from me. Such betrayal will be spoken of for centuries!"

"I would never betray you, Anarthys!"

"Oh, you would. You may not have betrayed me in all the ways that count, yet—but you would. Calpharos would seduce you as easily as blinking."

My mouth falls open at the mere suggestion, and this seems to incense her further.

BOOM

Doors slam wide, and Calpharos's twin stalks toward us. "Do not do this, Anarthys. It will not give you what you want."

"You come to warn me, Eamonn? You, who suggested Calpharos visit the seer who told him who she would be to him?"

"You cannot change fate. No matter how many seers you torture and kill."

Eamonn's eyes meet mine, and they're...kind. I've never spoken to him, but he's looking at me as if he knows me.

Anarthys moves her dagger close to my neck, her breath warm on my face. "Fate?" *She laughs, and it sounds like ringing bells.* "I will bend fate to *my* wishes."

Panic slides across Eamonn's face. "She is the other half of his soul. You do this, and he will take his revenge."

My heart jumps into my throat, my vision wavering. The other half of his soul?

Anarthys gives a hollow laugh. "Once this human is ended, he will return to my arms."

I tense, and the guards tighten their hold. My limbs begin to shake.

"Anarthys. He will kill you." *Truth saturates Eamonn's words.*

A hint of something that might be fear flashes across Anarthys's face, but her lush lips curve and she throws her head back with a vibrant laugh.

"Kill me? A goddess? He can try."

"You think you know what he is. But you don't. Calpharos will make you beg for death."

"Such pleading is beneath you, Eamonn. With each word, you reveal your weakness. Calpharos won't kill me. He is the dark god. This girl is a plaything, and one he will not miss."

"Please…" My voice trembles, and Anarthys grabs my face, squeezing my cheeks.

"Silence. If you are truly meant to be, he can find you in a future life." She smiles. "By then, I may be tired of him."

The temple begins to shake, throwing us off balance. The guards curse as they're forced to release me, their hands grabbing for me as my knees hit the ground. But I'm already crawling away, towards my only hope. Towards Eamonn.

He sprints for me, zig-zagging through slabs of stone and marble.

Pain lashes through my scalp. Someone has grabbed my hair, and they're pulling me to my knees.

"How dare you!" Anarthys roars behind me, positioning her knife at my throat.

I catch sight of the bejeweled blade. I've carried that blade to her altar every day for two decades. How ironic that it is now to be used to kill me.

"This is not my doing," Eamonn holds his hands up, although he's now walking towards us, his eyes wild. "It's Calpharos. He has learned of what you plan. His rage will destroy you."

Thick, dark fog sweeps through the temple. From the fog, a dark shadow steps forward. His eyes are black, and my heart jolts as they meet mine. They shift above my head, and I see the promise of a death filled with suffering.

"Release her." His voice echoes through the temple. Guards sprint towards him and he holds up a hand.

Thud. Thud. Thud.

Three bodies drop. The others go very still.

"Hello, lover." Anarthys's voice is steady, but her hand tightens in my hair, her breaths turning shallow.

"Release her *now*."

She lets out a humorless laugh. "You think you can take one of my acolytes? Would you breed with her, Calpharos? Would you watch as she grew fat and old and ugly and then would you cry as you buried her? Or would you choose a mortal life?" Her voice is filled with a deep disdain, and a strange sense of shame flickers in my chest.

Can I truly blame this goddess for being so enraged, when fate has tied the man she loves to a mortal?

It is difficult to believe such a thing could be true, but I can see the knowledge in Calpharos's eyes. And I felt that deep, familiar knowing when we spoke. Despite my fear, I wanted to see him again. Wanted to talk to him.

A strange longing slides through my veins. A longing for something intangible. Something that might have been.

"I am doing you a favor," Anarthys says. "Soulmates are not for ones such as us. And never mortal soulmates. She would make you weak. I am saving you from mourning later."

"You are lashing out because I no longer want you. Such an action is beneath you, Anarthys. Release her, and we will settle this ourselves."

"Would you kill me, Calpharos? For daring to touch your little mortal?"

He takes a single step closer, and Anarthys presses the blade to my skin. A sharp sting, and I feel the first drops of blood drip down my neck.

The dark god freezes. And his expression turns predatory. He focuses all that feral intent on Anarthys, and I feel her shudder.

"You would. You would kill me even now. I told you I wanted to be with you for eternity."

"I never said the same to you. I never gave you false promises."

"You are mine!"

The remaining guards slump to the floor. I can see one of them to my left, almost close enough to nudge with my foot. His eyes are open as he stares vacantly at nothing.

Dead.

"I should have known you would lash out like this," Anarthys says. *"I thought I would give you a chance to be reasonable, but I have other plans in place. And you will regret this for the rest of your days."*

Eamonn's eyes meet mine. They're haunted, shocked. He's looking at me as if I'm already dead.

Pain.

Vicious, all-encompassing pain that burns like a fire in my chest.

"No!" Calpharos's roar makes the temple shake, and he lunges toward us.

And then I'm floating high above my body, drifting toward the ceiling as Calpharos holds me.

No. He's holding my corpse.

I'm…dead.

"I will find you again," Calpharos whispers over and over. *"Come back, and I will find you again."*

When he looks up, his eyes are lifeless. Dark smoke pours from him once more, wrapping around Anarthys's neck.

Slowly, gently, he lays my body on the ground. "You dare take from me?"

Anarthys chokes, and he releases his smoke long enough for her to answer.

"You stole my future from me." Her words are a low taunt. "So I took yours from you. You didn't think I'd allow you to live in happiness, did you, lover?"

The temple begins to collapse. Columns near the altar crash to the ground, and fear flashes across her face.

This woman I worshipped has ended my life. She took any hint of happiness I might have found and ruined it.

Cold rage floods me. Oh, I will return. And I will make her pay.

Calpharos steps closer to her with a vicious, predatory smile.

Her eyes widen. "Your siblings are coming for you," she gasps out. "I'm warning you so you can fight."

Guards rush through the temple doors, and it's Eamonn who stalks toward them, his face gray. Eamonn who calls a sword to his hand and cuts the guards down himself. With a last glance at Calpharos, he steps out of the temple to face any who think to interfere.

"You didn't think I'd allow you to live *after taking her from me, did you lover?" Calpharos's laugh is cold, and I want to stay. Want to watch as he makes her hurt the way I hurt.*

But I'm already being pulled in another direction, towards a place of warmth and light.

I lean over and empty my stomach. Fliora lets out a gasp, and I feel cool fingers pulling strands of my hair away from my face.

"Madinia? What is it?"

Eamonn sighs. "She likely just relived her murder. Give her a moment to come to terms with it."

I retch again, and Fliora rubs my back, but her attention is still on Eamonn.

When I lift my head, he's sitting in front of me, his round eyes solemn.

"I don't understand." My voice is hoarse, and I sit, the world spinning around me as I manage to focus on Fliora. "Your aunt is the one who told Anarthys I had been with Calpharos. But in…this life…she also told me to find the grimoires before Calpharos could. She made it sound like I would be protecting the world. She insisted I find them and keep them safe."

"I don't know what you saw," Fliora says apologetically. "My aunt was in your memories?"

"She was one of the goddess's acolytes. She betrayed me."

Eamonn places one paw on my thigh. "Of course they would want you to take the grimoire. If you get to the grimoire first, someone can still take it from you. If Calysian gets to it first, they can't."

"Because once Calpharos takes the grimoires, they disappear."

"Yes. They meld back into his soul."

"Fliora," I get out. "Can you give us a moment?"

She nods, getting to her feet and passing me a water skin. When she wanders toward the stable, I feel Eamonn keeping one eye on her.

"You tried to save me," I murmur.

He lowers his head. "I failed. I failed you, and I failed Calpharos. I was too late."

"I'm...reincarnated."

"Yes. Anarthys was unable to take that gift back. I have no doubt she would have stolen it from you if it was possible."

"Have I...had other lives?"

"I do not know. It is likely."

"And you were cursed too. By your siblings?"

"Yes. Calpharos went to a seer who told him that one of Anarthys's acolytes would be his soulmate. Meanwhile, Anarthys received a vision of her own—one that made her desperate to learn what it was that Calpharos's seer had seen. Anarthys knew the seer's vision would make Calpharos break from her for eternity."

"And Calpharos learned what she had done."

"Yes. That was the day he insisted on going directly to her temple—the first time he saw you."

"And then Anarthys learned who I was."

"Yes. She tortured the seer until she told the goddess of

Calpharos's prophecy. The seer gave Anarthys enough information to lead her to believe you were his soulmate. And then one of the other acolytes told the goddess you had been seen with Calpharos, confirming her suspicions."

Yalanda.

"Anarthys had been plotting, working with our siblings. If my brother didn't choose her, she would have her revenge," Eamonn says. "Our other siblings learned I had tried to save you. They knew my loyalty would always be to Calpharos, so they bound my powers, took my true form from me, and banished me to this world. It took centuries for me to find my twin. And that's when I learned they had also found a way to prevent me from telling him who he was."

"I just…I don't understand. I've heard about how powerful the dark god is so many times. How were they able to…"

"You." There's no blame in Eamonn's voice, but I flinch anyway. When he looks up at me, I don't see his canine form at all. I see the man who attempted to save my life. His eyes may be different, but they still hold that same kindness.

"Me?"

"Calpharos used so much of his power attempting to kill Anarthys to avenge your death, he was weakened. You were the one chink in his armor. The one weakness he had never before shown. You were his undoing."

"And his enemies struck at the first sign of that weakness. No wonder he wants his revenge."

But there's one thing I don't understand. The Calpharos from my memories—and I'm still attempting to accept those memories—was kinder. Gentler. Oh, he'd terrified the sheltered, innocent woman I'd been. But he'd intrigued her too.

The glimpses I've seen of Calpharos so far have been of a man so entirely *other* that he sends a chill down my spine. The Calpharos I saw in the swamp when he took the grimoire…there was nothing redeeming about him. Nothing soft. He radiated a predatory cruelty, an all-encompassing rage that warned that any who attempted to stop him would die.

"What are you thinking?" Eamonn asks.

Idly, I stroke his head, scratching him behind the ear, and his eyes turn heavy lidded.

I fill him in, and he sighs. "You have to understand. His last memories of his true self were directly after you were taken from him. Losing you before he ever truly knew you…watching you die in front of him… he will never be the man he was again."

"And he wants revenge."

"Yes. Our siblings didn't have enough power to kill him—or they would have removed him as a threat for good. Instead, they merely bought themselves time. With every grimoire, he will remember more, will be able to access more of his power. And when he is unleashed…"

I shake my head. "Do you understand why I need to stop him?"

"I understand that this world has been terrible to you." His voice turns hard. "You have suffered great losses. And still, you would protect it."

"You've walked in this world for centuries. Can you truly tell me the innocents here deserve to die?"

A long pause. "No. Our only hope is that Calpharos remembers who you are to him."

If I told him, would he believe me? What would I say? *Hello Calpharos, it turns out I'm your…soulmate. And I need you to give up your revenge for me.*

I know exactly how hot the flames of vengeance burn. They flicker within me even now. For Vicana. For her witch. And for that bitch goddess who stabbed me in the heart.

Because I am not the innocent, sheltered acolyte who knelt at Anarthys's feet and allowed herself to be killed. Not in *this* life.

All the suffering and pain has hardened me. It shaped me into a survivor.

What if I tell Calysian, and he goes for the grimoire anyway? Telling him he lost his soulmate could make him even more eager to get to his grimoire and take back his power. He'd be one step closer to getting his revenge—a revenge that could ruin this world.

"Why didn't you tell me who I am earlier? Why did you lie for so long?"

Eamonn sighs. "I didn't lie. I just chose the right time to tell you. What would you have done if you'd learned this information earlier, before you truly began to feel something for him?"

I would have run.

Slowly, I get to my feet. "Fliora?"

"I'll take care of her."

My head is spinning, my knees weak. "What am I supposed to do tomorrow when he goes after the grimoire?"

"You're the other half of Calysian's soul. That means you can access his power too. Forget trying to get to the grimoire before him. You need to go *with* him. When he takes the second grimoire, he'll be distracted. You can take his link to the third grimoire, ensuring he won't be able to locate it."

I grit my teeth. Eamonn isn't giving me any advice to help me take and hide the second grimoire. He's willing to let Calysian become even more powerful.

Fine. I have my own plans in place.

"And tonight? Do I tell him who he is to me?"

Eamonn's eyes glitter with sympathy. "Only you can make that decision."

CHAPTER TWENTY-NINE

CALYSIAN

MADINIA IS BONE-WHITE WHEN SHE RETURNS, AND despite the dark clouds roiling within my mind, I can't help but go to her, clasping her shoulders. "What happened?"

"I don't want to talk about it."

"Madinia."

"Later." Her eyes hold mine pleadingly, and I sigh. When she offers me a crooked smile, I pull her further into the room.

I've wandered this world for centuries, and yet my chest still puffs out when her eyes glitter with appreciation.

This woman was raised in a castle, and since she met me, she has spent her nights in tiny, ill-equipped inns, and on sleeping mats on the hard ground. She's never complained. But I have a need to ensure her comfort tonight.

The bath I ordered for her is still steaming—I had the water refreshed after washing away the dust of our travels while she was getting her *fresh air*. Madinia wanders to the paneled dressing screen in the corner, peering around it to the tub beyond.

She glances over her shoulder at me with a wicked smirk, and my body heats. Stepping behind the screen, she drops her shirt, purposefully leaving it on the floor next to the screen, in my full view.

Her leather leggings are next, and it takes her a little longer to remove them. I harden as I picture her easing them down those long, smooth legs. My muscles twitch with the urge to stalk behind that screen and bend her over the tub.

She's toying with me.

But I like the games we play.

She throws her leggings over the screen, and I angle my head, watching hungrily as the candlelight flickers, providing me with a silhouette of her incredible body. She bends, one hand trailing low to check the temperature of the water, and steps into the bath, sinking down with a throaty moan.

I nearly groan in response.

"Need me to wash your back?" My voice is rough, and Madinia lets out a low laugh.

"I think I can manage."

The air is humid, steam drifting through the room, and I yank at the neckline of my shirt.

The fabric tears, and I curse, stripping it off and dropping it to the floor.

I know exactly what Madinia looks like when she's relaxing in a tub of warm water. Her eyelids grow heavy, her cheeks flush pink, her expression turns slumberous.

I pace, unable to ignore each of her soft sighs, the sound of water, the memories of our last bath flashing through my mind.

Finally, Madinia stands, and my mouth goes dry as I imagine the water streaming from her body. She steps out of the bath, her body little more than a shadow, but my mind provides all of the missing details.

More rustling as she dries herself. She didn't take clean clothes with her, so I wait, tense. Will she wrap a towel around her and walk into view, digging through her satchel?

Or will she—

THIS VICIOUS DREAM

Madinia saunters out from behind the screen, and my mouth drops open.

She's naked, the warm candlelight flickering lovingly over her skin. I almost trip over my feet, and amusement flashes through her eyes.

She knows what she does to me. She enjoys it.

"You've had your fun." I barely recognize the rough growl that spills from my throat. "Now come here."

One eyebrow shoots up, and she reaches up a hand, releasing her hair from its clip. Miles of wine-colored hair fall over her shoulders, reaching to her lower back.

I drink her in. "Are you enjoying teasing me?"

She bites her tongue and gives me a wide smile. "Are you enjoying being teased?"

I am.

But only to a point.

Her eyes widen as I lunge toward her, lifting her into my arms. She clutches my shoulders at the sudden movement, a laugh spilling from her lips, and I bask in the sound as I stride to the bed, dropping her onto the soft sheets.

Red lips curve and she stares up at me. "I'm surprised you lasted as long as you did. I half expected you to haul me out of the water."

"Baths relax you," I mutter, my voice gruff. "I was *trying* to control myself."

Those incredible eyes soften, and she sinks her teeth into her lower lip. "You don't need to control yourself now."

"You'd like that wouldn't you? You'd like for me to lose control." I lower my head, pressing a gentle kiss to those lush lips. My body is tense, muscles trembling with the need to take her, to make her mine. And yet…

Her eyes narrow. "You have something else in mind?"

"Oh, sweetheart, you have no idea."

She tenses, and I brush my lips against hers. She chases my mouth as I pull away and shake my head. "Do you trust me?"

"No." The word is belligerent. Sulky. And I can't help the laugh that spills from me.

I strip off my pants, enjoying the way her eyes darken as her gaze drifts over my body.

"I don't trust you either. You're a deceptive, haughty little liar. And yet I've never wanted anyone the way I want you."

Her brow furrows. I could spend hours studying Madinia's face. She often hides her thoughts behind her cool, blank expressions, and yet I know her well enough now to recognize her tells. I've spent an embarrassing amount of time watching the way her eyes widen minutely when she's surprised, the way they turn to slits when she's infuriated. I've memorized the arch of her eyebrow, the darkening of her eyes, the way she tucks her hair behind her ear when she's uncomfortable.

Like she does now. "It must be difficult for you," she murmurs. "Wanting someone you don't particularly like." There's a strange knowledge in her eyes, and I get the sudden sense she's hiding something from me.

"I never said I didn't like you."

She sniffs, attempting to push against my chest. I merely capture her wrists with one of my hands. Her jaw tightens, but she stares over my shoulder.

"You said I have an ice-cold heart."

And she's been holding onto *that*? I can't help but smile. "You do. It's the only way you could have survived. But your soul? Your soul is pure fire."

Her eyes meet mine, and this time when I kiss her, she wraps her legs around my waist, holding me prisoner the only way she can.

She grinds against me, hot and wet and warm. I let out a hiss as all of my blood surges south. "You won't rush me."

"You're not in charge here."

THIS VICIOUS DREAM

"Bigger than you, sweetheart. Stronger than you too. You'll take what I give you."

I'm prepared for her fire, and I raise my ward just in time to prevent the singe of skin. My laugh catches in my throat as she shifts beneath me, attempting to flip me to my back.

"Cute," I tell her, and flames dance in her eyes. I scrape my teeth gently against her neck, enjoying her shiver. My lips replace my teeth, and her breath catches as she tilts her head, silently ordering me to continue.

I shift to her mouth instead, moving my hand to her throat as I claim her lips. I can feel her life beneath my hand, her breaths coming in short pants. Her tongue tangles with mine, and I get lost in her, until I'm not sure where she ends and I begin.

I sink into her, feast on her, *revel* in her. She lets out a broken moan and I come back to myself, slowly lifting my head.

Her eyes are molten blue, her lips puffy and wet. She looks dazed, needy, and most importantly... *mine*.

I brush my thumb over her nipple and she hisses, arching her back.

"Hmm. You like that?"

She stays stubbornly silent until I switch from my fingers to my mouth. And then she lets out one of those breathless groans that make me tense in response.

"If anyone else ever hears you make that sound, I'll kill them." The words are out before I'm aware I've spoken, and Madinia freezes.

"Calysian."

Silence stretches between us. She's waiting for me to take the words back.

Strangely, I don't.

Instead, I push inside her, watching her eyes widen, darken, drift shut.

"No," I murmur. "Look at me."

Somehow, I find the self-control to wait until those long

lashes flutter and her eyes open. And then I thrust once more, watching as her eyes turn glazed.

"You feel so fucking good." I push deeper, withdraw, angle my hips, and I'm rewarded when her nails sink into my shoulders and she sucks in a shaky breath.

"Don't stop."

The words are both command and plea, and I sink into her again and again, losing myself in her body. She writhes beneath me, sweat slicking her skin, her nipples hard against my chest. I take her mouth, swallowing her breaths as she groans out another plea for more.

Her legs begin to tremble and I grit my teeth, focusing on anything but the feel of her inner muscles clamping around me.

She comes with a throaty moan. Our eyes meet, and for a moment it's as if we're somewhere else, in another time and place. I thrust once, twice, and then I'm curling my body around hers as I shudder, pleasure lashing through me.

I slip out of her with a hiss, watching my release trickle out of her. When I push it back where it belongs, Madinia shivers, and I'm immediately hard once more.

Flipping her onto her knees, I sink inside her again.

And again.

MADINIA

My body aches in places that make me blush as I languidly stretch, reaching for Calysian.

But when I sweep my hand over his side of the bed, I find only cool sheets.

My stomach falls, my eyes pop open and I sit up, scanning the room. Empty. His things? Gone.

The knowledge is a brutal blow, but one I should have seen coming.

He out-maneuvered me.

If not for the fact that such machinations could mean the end of this world, I'd be impressed.

Instead, panic spreads wings in my chest and I roll from the bed, darting around the room to find my clothes.

My aching muscles make themselves known as I dress, and my cheeks flame. The bastard slid inside me over and over last night, until I was limp and sated and exhausted.

Too exhausted to even stir when he slipped from this bed.

Oh, he will pay.

I was going to tell him who I am to him. Not last night—he successfully drove all thought from my mind. But this morning. I was going to tell him…

I reach for my tunic and freeze. The long mirror on the wall reveals more than just the patchwork of scars slicing across my back. And yet it's not the scars that catch my attention.

It's the strange black marks positioned along my spine.

Dark as ink, they've been etched with unsettling precision—curves and lines interwoven into a pattern that makes no sense and yet feels deliberate…almost sacred. They wind down my spine from the base of my neck, following the grooves of my bones and ending between the dimples of my lower back.

My fingers tremble as I brush them over my skin. My scars feel rough, the raised edges making me flinch as memories of the pain and helplessness flash though me. But…the strange marks are somehow beneath my skin. They feel wrong. And yet…not.

A sick dread coils in my stomach as I lean closer, twisting my head as much as I can. The black marks ripple with my movement, and my heart thrums in my throat.

My hands shake, and the room does one slow spin.

But I have no time to investigate this new crisis. Not if I'm going to catch up to Calysian.

I yank on my tunic, then sweep clothes and weapons into my satchel. Minutes later, I'm striding out the door.

Only to find Hope's stall empty.

"Where is my horse?"

The stablehand grins at me, his gaze sweeping from my feet to my tousled hair. "Your husband took the mare earlier this morning. He said he was leaving you to sleep."

"Cease. Speaking."

Surprisingly, he does. I turn and leave him standing by the open stall door.

Nausea ripples through me. This isn't the same as abandoning me in our bed. Taking Hope…Calysian truly doesn't want me to follow.

The symbolism isn't lost on me. I named my horse Hope, and Calysian snatched her away from me the moment I needed her the most.

He left me.

He. Left. Me.

I blow out a breath. I don't have time to wallow in this deep, crushing sense of loss. I'll need to borrow or rent a horse, which will take me time. As Calysian knew it would.

I'm not surprised when Asinia's pigeon swoops into the stable. I read her note, my hands shaking.

We are ready.

I let the pigeon return without a message. The rest is up to me.

"What's wrong?"

I jump, yelp, and spin, all at once.

Fliora lets out a giggle. It's the first time she's truly seemed like a child, and despite my current situation, I attempt a smile. "You need to learn to make some noise."

She grins at me. "Eamonn has been teaching me to spy."

I search for any sign of him. "Is he here?"

"Nope."

"Then I need you to listen to me."

Fliora's grin disappears at my intent tone, and I lean close, lowering my voice to a whisper. "I need you to make your way to the dock." I press a few coins into her hand. "Get yourself something to eat. You'll see a small bench next to a tailor's shop. Sit on that bench and stay there."

Her lower lip trembles. "Why?"

"I need you to trust me."

Slowly, she nods. "You trusted me enough to take that tonic. So I'll trust you too. But Madinia...you should know something. It was Eamonn who found me and encouraged me to follow my aunt. He was the one who told me to steal the tonic."

I file this information away. It's not unexpected.

"I'll see you soon."

Fliora darts out of the stable, and I make my way toward the front of the inn. Hopefully, the innkeeper will know someone who will let me borrow a horse for a few hours.

Eamonn trots toward me in his dog form. "Calysian took your horse?"

"Yes. I won't be able to catch him now."

"Yes you will." Eamonn backs away, and within a blink, he's a huge, white stallion.

I stare. "I thought larger forms were more difficult for you to hold."

"They are. But I can hold it long enough for you to get to Calysian. Now let's go." He sidesteps until he's next to the fence, and I climb onto his back.

"I should have told Calysian who I am to him."

"You did more for him by merely being with him last night."

A strange sense of awareness slides through me, and suddenly I can sense Calysian in my mind. My heart leaps into my throat. "What is happening?"

Eamonn turns, making his way toward the road. "You

opened yourself to your soulmate last night. There's a link between you now. You must have seen the symbols on your back."

Fury burns through me. "You told me to be with him. Did you know this would happen?"

"I watched when you arrived yesterday. I saw the way Calysian looked at you. The way he touched you."

"That sounds like a yes," I hiss. "Who gave you the right to play with my life? To manipulate me like this?"

"Would you like to argue about it or find him?"

I grind my teeth. "We will talk about this later."

Eamonn sighs. "Think of Calysian's face. Picture him in your mind. Think about the way he stands, the way he moves, the sound of his voice."

And there he is.

I can see him in my mind's eye, riding towards the ruins of another temple.

"South," I choke out as Eamonn trots down the road. "He's moving south."

We make it to the dock, and I keep my gaze deliberately averted from the ships looming just beyond my periphery, the ropes twisted around masts, sails hanging slack, patched and stained.

But one ship draws my attention despite my best efforts, and I snap my gaze away as Eamonn immediately breaks into a canter, and then a gallop. I hold tight to his mane, squeezing with my thighs as I relive every moment with Calysian over and over again, searching for some way this could have ended differently.

Memories flash through me—the stark look in his eyes last night in front of the inn. The way his hands shook when he cupped my face so tenderly the last time he sank inside me. The feel of his arms around me, holding me close.

Eamonn takes a right, and the waves crash against the shore as we leave through the southern gates and onto the main road leading south.

THIS VICIOUS DREAM

I duck my head, leaning low over Eamonn.

"Despite Calysian's loss of memories, I've seen the way his instincts have whispered to him that you are his," Eamonn says. "The grimoire must have tightened its hold on him—he would never have left you otherwise."

"We're going to lose him." The words are out before I'm aware I've said them, and Eamonn tosses his head. His gallop is relentless, the ground rushing beneath us in a blur of roots and mud.

"No, we're not." Eamonn's voice is grim. "If he does manage to take the second grimoire, you know what to do."

Steal the link to the third grimoire.

"It will never work."

"It will. Did you never wonder just how you were able to wield Calysian's power so easily? It's because it's *your* power too. You're the other half of his soul."

"But...I couldn't feel this grimoire."

"And why do you think that is?" His voice is breathless from his gallop, a sheen of sweat forming across his neck.

"I'm sure you have a theory." My words are icy and Eamonn lets out a nicker that sounds suspiciously like a laugh.

"I think you became *frightened*." He says the word as if fear is somehow beneath me, his voice dripping with disdain. "You saw how the grimoire overtook him, and subconsciously rejected any ties to Calysian's power. By doing that, you rejected Calysian the man."

"You say that like you're disappointed," I snap. "You don't even like me."

Eamonn veers to the right, galloping just close enough to a tree for the leaves of a low-hanging branch hit me in the face.

I spit a leaf from my mouth with a low growl. "Seriously?"

"Can you imagine what it was like, Madinia? For me to know who you were to my brother? To know that because I was too late, too *slow*, he lost you?"

"Yes, I'm sure that experience was really painful for *you*," I mutter, my memory presenting me with the feeling of cold steel sliding into my heart.

And yet I *do* remember the horror in Eamonn's eyes. The self-loathing.

"You want to save your precious world?" Eamonn snarls. "Open yourself fully to your soulmate."

"I thought I did that last night."

"You cracked open a window. You need to throw open the door."

"That sounds very…permanent."

"I wasn't aware you had so many other men lining up, ready to love and protect you for the rest of your days."

"You don't know me at all if you think that's what I want."

"*Now* who's lying?"

We're silent for the remainder of the journey and I focus on holding tight to Eamonn, my muscles aching from the strain. I direct him toward Calysian, and we move from the main road onto a winding trail where our fastest speed is a jolting trot.

Finally, the trees clear, and the temple comes into view. Ancient pillars stand crooked and fractured, worn smooth by centuries of wind and rain. Marble is streaked with moss and creeping ivy, while the stones closest to the entrance have been blackened by fire. The air feels heavy and oppressive, charged with a faint hum that sets my teeth on edge.

Rustling sounds to my right, and I catch sight of Fox tied to a tree at the edge of the clearing. Hope is nowhere to be seen, and I force myself to turn back to the temple.

Shattered statues lie across the ground like corpses, their faces weathered and featureless. Words and symbols have been carved into the temple's facade—too faint for me to read…even if I could understand the language.

Even if I'd managed to sneak away from Calysian days ago, I wouldn't have found this grimoire. I'd been so convinced it was hidden in the forest somewhere before Calysian admitted it was in a temple.

Now I know exactly why Calpharos would have left it in such a place.

Calysian stands in the center of the temple, hands on his hips as he ponders the altar, his head angled strangely. Eamonn slows, his hooves striking cracked stone.

"This is it." His voice is heavy with weariness. This form has cost him. "You know what to do."

My heart kicks in my chest but I dismount, stumbling toward the temple entrance on unsteady legs.

"Calysian."

He ignores me, and my body breaks out in a cold sweat. "Calysian, please."

His gaze remains on the altar. "This was always the plan, Madinia."

"Your plan was to leave me alone in bed and come here without me?"

I thought I wanted him to look at me, but when he does, dread coils in my stomach. There's nothing human left in his eyes.

"Last night I dreamed," he says. "Strange dreams about another life. *My* life. You were in them."

My throat tightens, but he shakes his head, already dismissing me as he returns his gaze to the altar. "Soon I will know the truth." A wave of his hand, and the huge slab of marble laying across the altar goes flying, crashing into the cracked remnants of a pillar.

"Calysian. You don't want to do this."

My pleas are useless—just as Eamonn warned they would be. And yet something in my chest wrenches as Calysian ignores me.

The ground shudders beneath our feet, and I drop to my knees. Even Calysian stumbles.

"Creas!" He roars, "show yourself!"

A low, female laugh. Huge cracks appear in the stone floor and I stumble to my feet.

Calysian's sister. Once again, she's attempting to prevent him from taking his grimoire.

Eamonn lands on my shoulder, now in the form of a small bird.

"Are you ready?"

I dodge a chunk of marble as it falls from somewhere above my head. "No!"

Calysian reaches down, into the space below the altar. He pulls the grimoire free, and the cover flies open, the pages a blur. Dark power fills the temple, and my knees turn weak.

"Now, Madinia!" Eamonn's voice is incessant, and I close my eyes. His low voice urges me on. "Reach *past* this power. Do you feel its link to the third grimoire?"

"Yes."

"You need to break the link and grasp it for it yourself."

It's a wild, audacious risk. But it's my only chance to stop Calpharos.

"How do I break it?"

"Use your fire."

I don't have time to argue. I can sense the link, visible only when I close my eyes and reach for it. My flames may be invisible, but they're filled with my power. And they leap toward the link with a whoosh, engulfing it in seconds. But it burns slowly. Too slowly.

"More," Eamonn urges.

I throw more flames at the link, power pouring from me in a dizzying rush. Just as the link is almost completely burned, I reach for it, cupping it in invisible hands, and guiding it to *me*.

Instantly, I can feel the third grimoire, on another continent far from this place. Large, male hands are wrapped around it, and my gaze drifts up muscular arms, to a brutally handsome face. It's the face of a warrior.

Dark, green eyes scan my body, and they hold a glint of appreciation when they meet mine. "And, who," he murmurs across time and space, "are you?"

He can see me?

I gasp, and the link between us snaps closed.

"You did it," Eamonn breathes.

The second grimoire is already fading in Calpharos's hands, his eyes completely black as he reunites with this part of his soul.

And still, the ground trembles.

Calpharos's eyes meet mine, and I stumble back. Because he's looking out at the world as if it has wronged him on such a deep level, it *should* burn.

"You," Calpharos says. "You took from me." A hint of confusion flickers across his face, replacing some of the wrath. "Woman. *My* woman."

CHAPTER THIRTY

Madinia

Eamonn takes off, flying up towards one of the few marble pillars still standing.

Calpharos prowls towards me and I stumble backwards, tripping on a loose piece of marble. I wince as I hit the ground, and Calpharos is suddenly there, hauling me to my feet.

He nuzzles at my throat, and I tremble. "I can scent my power within you," he whispers. "Calling us both."

My lungs turn to stone. He knows I took his link to the third grimoire. Which means he knows he needs *me* to find it.

I don't hesitate. Twisting out of Calpharos's hold, I lunge left, rolling free.

Creas chooses that moment to shake the earth again, and Calpharos lets out another roar. I stay low, crawling across the cool marble.

This time, I don't need a tonic to remember crawling through another temple in an attempt to save my own life.

I half expect to feel Anarthys's hand in my hair at any moment.

THIS VICIOUS DREAM

The ground continues to shift and buck, thick, choking dust rising as stone and marble crumbles.

"Madinia!"

I roll just in time to avoid a huge stone column as it slams into the floor, directly where I was crawling.

Eamonn flutters around my head, but I grit my teeth, ignoring him.

Reaching for my link to the third grimoire, I use it to pour power into my flames. They burn as high as Calpharos's head, a fiery wall between us.

I launch myself to my feet.

And run.

"What are you doing!" Eamonn slams a wing into my face and I duck, still too furious to speak to him.

Calpharos hasn't yet made it through my flames, but he will. My breaths are sharp sobs, the world spinning around me.

But I make it to Fox, yanking his lead rope free.

Shockingly, the stallion allows me to pull him away from the temple.

"Don't do this, Madinia." Desperation coats Eamonn's voice, and I have no doubt that if he could shift into a larger animal, he would be attempting to prevent my escape.

"Calpharos," a feminine voice calls, and I go still.

That voice.

"Get down," Eamonn hisses, and I drop to the ground, Fox carelessly munching on the grass next to me.

Several soldiers march from behind the temple. One of them carries Vicana's flag.

My mouth goes dry. We're sheltered behind a few trees, but it wouldn't take much for someone to see us.

The soldiers part, and I catch sight of the witch first. Despite her rounded shoulders and stooped posture, Bridin walks with a spring in her step.

Behind her, the queen glides toward the temple. She's

wearing a long, crimson gown, a ruby-studded crown encircling her head.

My body turns hot and then ice cold.

I know that face.

"Eamonn." My voice trembles as my mind attempts to understand what I'm seeing. He lands on my shoulder. "Why didn't you tell me Vicana was the goddess who killed me?" I stare at Anarthys, bile burning up my throat.

Eamonn's voice is a shocked whisper. "I didn't know. I've never seen her face before. This should be impossible."

It makes sense now. Calpharos's sister is still working with Anarthys. She attempted to slow him down, buying time for the goddess to reach this temple.

I'm not sure how Anarthys ended up in this world, but I'm not surprised that she made herself a queen. She always loved being worshiped.

Something dark and possessive spills through me at the thought of the bitch-goddess touching Calysian. I can't forget her black poison from the bolt at the lake, or the way a mere graze with that poisoned bolt sent Calysian into unconsciousness.

But he's not Calysian now.

He's Calpharos.

It takes everything in me to watch as Vicana and the witch step into the temple. But I do it.

And then I swing myself into the saddle, nudging Fox into motion.

"What are you doing? You're truly leaving him?" Panic coats Eamonn's voice, but I block him out. I half expect the demon horse to throw me from his back. Instead, he breaks into a trot.

"Madinia." Eamonn flaps his wings, creating a tiny breeze around my head. "Talk to me."

I can't even speak. All I can do is hold on to Fox as he

moves into a smooth gallop and I attempt to block out the sight of Vicana and Bridin walking into that temple.

I trapped Calpharos with my flames. I practically handed him to them.

The city gates loom in the distance, and relief shudders through my body. It's enough to help me talk around the lump in my throat.

"Last night, you told me I could take the link to the third grimoire. You didn't have a plan to get to the second grimoire, because you wanted your brother to take it. And this morning… you could have woken me when Calysian left. But you needed to ensure he had enough of a head start to take the second grimoire. And yet you also needed me to make it here in time to steal his link to the last grimoire." My voice cracks. "That's some impressive timing."

Silence.

I blink back hot tears. "You need Calpharos to have all three grimoires. It's the only way you'll be able to get your true form back. You need a *god* to fix you. Would that mark on my back have appeared if you hadn't given me my memories back yesterday?"

"I don't know."

"I suppose you couldn't risk it not working. You needed me to at least open that *window*, didn't you?"

Eamonn may have helped me steal Calysian's connection to the third grimoire, but it wasn't supposed to be a permanent solution. It was supposed to be temporary. Calysian would recognize who I was, I would lead him to the third grimoire, Eamonn would get his true form back, and Calysian would kill Anarthys.

Everyone would be happy.

Except those who lived in this world, when a war between gods inevitably began to tear our world at the seams.

Eamonn lands on my shoulder. I don't bother shaking him off.

"And what was your plan, Madinia? What's your plan now?"

A choked laugh is wrenched from my chest. My plan? I didn't want to take the link to the *third* grimoire. I wanted to steal the second grimoire and meet Asinia. She would take the grimoire, hide it, and I would find a way to convince Calysian he didn't need it.

It was a thin plan, but it was all I had.

Now, Calpharos is even more powerful, even as he's likely fighting for his life.

We make it through the city gates. Eamonn is silent as I ride toward the dock. I dismount, leading Fox toward the bench outside the tailor. But I don't see Fliora.

My pulse stutters.

"Madinia!"

I scan the dock. A group of fishermen walk past me toward a tavern, jostling and laughing. And that's when I see her.

Asinia.

Fliora stands by her side, a wide grin on her face as they approach. "She said I could trust her, and that you would be here soon. Why didn't you tell me you were friends with pirates?"

I let my gaze drift past them, and my breath shudders from my lungs.

Daharak smirks at me. The pirate queen's umber skin is a little darker, the tiny lines at the corners of her eyes a little more pronounced. Her sleeves are rolled up, one arm still covered in scars from various fae blood vows.

She swaggers toward me, and her smirk widens. "I told you I'd find you."

Asinia gives her a look. "*We* found *you*."

I launch myself at Daharak and feel her jolt as her arms wrap around me.

"We need to go," Asinia says. "Since I don't see any sign of the grimoire, we need to go *now*."

"I'm taking Fox. I can't just leave him here."

Asinia sighs. "That horse is going to kill someone."

Shockingly, the stallion cooperates, allowing me to lead him down the dock toward the ship I so carefully ignored just a couple of hours ago. Eamonn swoops around my head.

"You planned this." His voice is empty. "You never planned to stay with him. You were always going to leave."

"No," I grit out. "I would have given Asinia the second grimoire if I'd gotten to it first. And I would have stayed. For him. Calysian made a choice. And now I'm making one."

"The only thing you're *making* is the biggest mistake of your life."

Wiping my damp face, I take one last look in the direction of the temple.

Last night changed everything for me. I thought it had changed everything for Calysian too. And still, he left me in that bed. He still chose the grimoire.

He did exactly what I expected him to do. And still, I'll never forgive him.

"What if they killed him?" Eamonn snaps.

"They didn't." I know, because if I close my eyes and focus, I can sense Calpharos. I can feel him sprinting toward the city even now. He's likely using the same power he funneled into the horses the day I almost died. And yet this time, he'll be the one to kill me if he reaches me.

But it's not just Calpharos I can feel. I can also feel the third grimoire, my link to it gossamer thin but surprisingly strong.

"I know where the last grimoire is," I murmur, and Asinia throws her arm around my shoulders. "I stole Calysian's link to it."

A low whistle sounds, Demos holds out his hand in an

attempt to take Fox's lead rope from me. Fox snaps his teeth at him.

Demos shakes his head at the horse and leaves him to me. "At least that's something," he says. "So the dark god can't find that grimoire without you?"

"No."

"Unless he kills her," Eamonn snarls. "By running from him, she's made herself a threat."

"Madinia!" Calpharos's roar echoes across the dock.

Daharak whips her head to our left, her eyes widening. Demos grabs my arm with one hand, Asinia's with the other.

"Move!"

Pushy bastard. I yank my arm from him and drop Fox's lead rope. The four of us take off down the dock toward the ship.

I glance over my shoulder. Anyone stupid enough to get in Calpharos's way goes flying, and our eyes meet for one brief moment.

My breath catches, and I force myself to run as he roars my name again.

"Do not run from me!"

The dark god is racing after us. Even from here I can see his bared teeth, his murderous expression.

Daharak gives an order, and the ship must have been ready, because the moment we're up the gangplank, pirates scramble across the deck. The anchor creaks and groans as it's wrenched from the depths—someone using their power to haul it up faster than I've ever seen before.

The gangplank is yanked aboard, and the ship lurches.

Someone hands Asinia her crossbow and she aims at Calpharos.

My heart jumps. "Wait!"

She fires, and Calpharos *catches* the bolt. He throws it into the water, and Daharak shouts something else I don't catch.

As one, every pirate who can shield raises their wards.

Calpharos comes to a stop at the edge of the dock. We're far enough away that not even he can make the jump. But he considers it.

The ship lurches, and I clutch at the railing. Fox trots over to Calysian, and the dark god gently strokes his nose, as if he's not currently planning my murder.

"Maybe it's a good thing Prisca is on her way," Asinia says softly.

Denial flashes through me. "No. Write to her. Tell her to stay in her kingdom."

"It's too late for that. If Lorian couldn't convince her to stay put, we don't have a chance. I informed her of your plans and she insisted on helping."

Demos sighs. "Honestly, after what I just saw, I think we need both her, *and* the bloodthirsty prince."

"Don't call him that," Asinia and I say in unison, and Demos lets out a faint laugh.

Calpharos's eyes meet mine once more, and I shiver at the dark promise in their depths.

I don't need to hear his words. I can read his lips.

"I will find you."

The end.

AUTHOR NOTE

Thank you for reading This Vicious Dream. Madinia's story continues (and ends) with the final book in this duology *This Ancient Feud.*

If you haven't yet read my Kingdom of Lies series, you can find it here at www.amazon.com/dp/B0BWX1LY33

I also have a new release coming in January 2026! *We Who Will Die* is a high-stakes romantasy pitched as Vampire Diaries meets Gladiator in a world of power-hungry royals and vengeful gods. I can't wait for you to read it!

ACKNOWLEDGMENTS

Thank you to my family, who put up with me editing this book while I was in New Zealand—when I was *supposed* to be on vacation. I promise next time I'll actually take time off.

And yes, I know you've heard that before.

To my amazing agent Kim Whalen—thank you for everything you do to get my books into readers' hands around the world.

Cristina, thank you for keeping everything afloat during the most chaotic, intense, deadline-filled period of my career. I couldn't have done it without you!

Sav, your optimism and easygoing attitude are a constant gift. You're a ray of sunshine and I love working with you.

To Sarah Waites, thank you for another incredible map!

Becca Mysoor, thank you for your support and for always being willing to jump on last-minute plot-fixing calls with me!

Thank you to Kelly Helmick for your editing, and to Kristen Aitkin for proofreading.

And last—but never least—thank you to my incredible readers. While I left *Kingdom of Lies* open for me to continue Madinia's story, it was your ~~hounding~~ polite requests that made this happen so soon after the release of *A Queen this Fierce and Deadly*. I truly believe I have the most amazing readers in the world.

www.ingramcontent.com/pod-product-compliance
Ingram Content Group UK Ltd.
Pitfield, Milton Keynes, MK11 3LW, UK
UKHW040328140525
5898UKWH00002B/202

9 781959 293286